GRAY STOOD BEHIND MAGGIE,
HIS GAZE CATCHING HERS IN THE MIRROR.

The candles on the dressing table cast her reflection in a luminescent glow that made her eyes sparkle like sapphires. Her neck was now bare but for the cascade of mahogany curls tumbling across her creamy shoulders. In the mirror, Maggie's eyes darkened and her lips parted. He barely stifled a groan. His hand was almost trembling with the desire coursing through him as he lifted the hair-brush and gently drew it through her hair. Inside he felt like tinder awaiting a spark to burst into flames. Dropping the brush, Gray buried both hands in her thick tresses.

She rose and swayed against him. His eyes flew open and he grabbed her arm to steady her. His vision filled with her, so close, so soft in his arms. She ran her hand down the front of his shirt and up again to settle against the bare skin exposed by the gap at his collar.

"Oh, Gray." She gave a long sigh. "Does this mean you will share this bed with me?"

Please turn to the back of this book for a preview of Diane Perkins's new novel, *The Marriage Bargain*.

The IMPROPER WIFE

DIANE PERKINS

WARNER FOREVER

NEW YORK   BOSTON

Copyright © 2004 by Diane Perkins
Excerpt from *The Marriage Bargain* copyright © 2004 by Diane Perkins

Cover design by Diane Luger
Cover illustration by Franco Accornero
Book design by Giorgetta Bell McRee

Warner Books

Time Warner Book Group
1271 Avenue of the Americas
New York, NY 10020
Visit our Web site at www.twbookmark.com

Printed in the United States of America

First Paperback Printing: November 2004

10 9 8 7 6 5 4 3 2 1

To Darlene Gardner, Karen Anders,
and Lisa Dyson, my *Sisters of the Moon*.
For your friendship and support.
And for helping me reach for the stars.

Acknowledgments

My most special thanks go to my husband, son, and daughter for all their patience and support during the years it took to finally achieve my dream of publication. Thanks also to my sisters, Marilyn and Judy, who continued to be excited about this latest scheme of mine, even when it was not bearing much fruit. I only wish my mother, father, and aunt could have lived to see this book in print, but I thank them as well. From my mother I learned to love (and to love reading Romance), from my father I learned to always do my best, and from my aunt I learned to never give up, no matter what. This book is a part of all of them.

Sincere gratitude as well to:

My writing friends, who were there from the inception to the final "The End" of *The Improper Wife*—Darlene Gardner, Karen Anders, Lisa Dyson, Julie Halperson, Helen Hester-Ossa, and Virginia Vitucci. And other writing friends who helped along the way, including all the ladies from my e-mail group "All of Us," especially Australian author Melissa James. Also Regency authors Amanda McCabe and Mary Blayney, and the members of

The Beau Monde, who generously shared their expertise of Regency history.

Washington Romance Writers, my home chapter, and Romance Writers of America, the national chapter, for bringing me a multitude of cherished friendships, as well as helping me hone my skills and learn the mysteries of publication.

Beth de Guzman, Editorial Director at Warner Books, who first gave me encouragement that I might have a future at Warner, and Melanie Murray, my editor, who believed in this story even before it was finished. To all the Warner Forever team with whom it has been my pleasure to work. And my agent Richard Curtis, who took on this new writer with little more than a leap of faith.

And finally, Mary Blayney again for providing me with my motto, *Never, Never, Never Give Up*—(Winston Churchill).

Chapter ONE

May, 1814

The pounding of French cannon thudded in John Grayson's brain. Acrid smoke stung his nostrils while his horse's hooves dug into the dry Spanish earth. Screams of dying soldiers assaulted his ears. The battle raged around him, and Gray lost his bearings. He swung his horse toward a clearing. From the mist a figure ran toward him, a woman clad in a gown as yellow as the sunshine, raven hair billowing behind her. Rosa? What was she doing in this ungodly place? He spurred his horse toward her. The fool. He'd told her not to follow him.

"*¡Vete!*" he yelled. "Go back!"

Oblivious of the carnage around her, she stretched her arms toward him. Her bright-colored dress fluttered behind her like butterfly wings, molding against her rounded belly as she ran.

Canister continued to shower from the incessant guns, its shot spattering the ground around him. He opened his mouth to bid her take heed, but an explosion of cannonade drowned his words. In the sky where threads of blue still peeked through the smoke, the canister arced and headed directly toward her.

As the canister tore her apart, sending pieces of her skittering through the dirt and flying into the trees, Gray heard amused laughter.

Leonard Lansing's face loomed before him, grinning as Lansing so often did when scorning the rules. "What luck! Free of the leg-shackle, old fellow."

Gray woke in a sweat, half sprawled on his bed, panting as if the French cannon had been pelting his dingy London rooms. It had not been real. It had merely been *The Dream*. The only battles he waged these days were with his own demons.

The pounding continued, more urgent and coming from his door. The sound echoed in his skull like ricocheting musket balls. Gray clutched his head and forced his body into an upright position. A sharp pain in his side made his breath catch. He'd moved too quickly for his still-healing wound.

"Stubble it!" he growled. "I'm coming."

Ah, his head! How many bottles of brandy had he consumed? He could not precisely recall. In fact, he barely recalled staggering back to his rooms.

Something caught around his feet and he stumbled, grabbing the back of a chair to keep from falling. His coat, thrown in a heap on the floor. At least he'd not slept in it, though he still wore the clothing he'd put on the previous day. His waistcoat flapped open and his shirt hung out of his trousers. Both reeked of stale alcohol and cheap tobacco.

More pounding. Who the devil would call at this ungodly hour?

Gray flung the door wide.

The bright midday sun poured in from the hallway, blinding him and throwing the figure standing in the doorway into silhouette. For a brief second he thought it was Rosa returning to haunt him. He clamped his eyes closed, rubbed them with his fingers, and cautiously opened them again.

"Are these Captain Grayson's rooms?" The woman's voice was tight and her breath rapid.

Gray's heart pounded so hard he could not speak. But this was not Rosa. Too tall. Too English. Skin too pale, like French porcelain.

He forced his mouth to move. "One might say."

She stepped forward, grabbing the doorjamb and leaning against it. "Please. May I enter?"

Gray stepped back. Her face was taut. She nearly fell into the room.

"Have . . . have I made your acquaintance?" He did not recall her, though she looked the sort a man would not likely forget. Her fair skin was framed by hair the color of polished mahogany. Her large eyes were the blue of a clear spring sky, but they were rimmed with red. Her rosebud-pink lips were compressed into a thin line.

She wrapped her arms around her waist, a gasp escaped her perfectly formed mouth. It was then Gray noticed the swelling of her belly.

By God, she was with child.

Gray drew his hand through his hair. What hellish retribution was this? The only fathomable reason for a pregnant woman to seek him out was . . . *unfathomable*. A nightmare of a new sort.

"Oh," she moaned, squeezing her waist. "The baby is coming! It is too soon. Too soon."

Gray pressed his fingers against his throbbing temple. Let it not be so. She could not possibly give birth to a baby in front of him. It was too cruel a joke for God to play.

She reached out, as if trying to grab hold of something. Gray obliged her by stepping forward, and bloodless fingers wrapped around his arm like a vise.

"Please get help. The baby. I can feel the baby." Her voice trailed into a wail and her knees buckled.

Silently cursing, he helped her to the threadbare rug on the floor. The dust tramped into its nap by countless boots wafted into his nostrils. Who was this woman? He considered running out the door. If he ran far enough perhaps the nightmare would cease, or perhaps he could find help. Some woman. *Any* woman.

She rolled to her side, grabbing her knees and rocking. The skirt of her dress was wet. That meant something, but Gray was uncertain what—except that there was no time to seek help.

Gray wheeled around wildly, considering what to do. At the same time he tried to mentally compute the months. Where had he been nine months ago?

After Vitoria, after that ill-fated night of lovemaking with Rosa, he'd accompanied Lansing to Gloucestershire. Lansing had traded his commission in the 13th Light Dragoons for a militia post, and Gray had thought to have one last lark with his friend. That was before Lansing's antics turned sour on Gray's tongue, however. Gray shook the memory out of his still-throbbing head and opened the cabinet where the maid-of-all-work stored blankets, towels, and linens. He grabbed them all.

The woman's breath was coming in rapid bursts. Her eyes were wide and bulging. He'd seen a foaling mare with that same expression.

Terror.

It inexplicably registered with him that this woman had the appearance and speech of a well-brought-up young lady. He would not have dallied with a respectable miss, would he?

Could he have repeated the dishonorable behavior that still plagued his conscience? Truth was, he and Lansing had remained quite permanently drunk in Gloucestershire, and Gray could not recall everything he had done there.

He dropped the linens at her feet.

"Will my baby die?" she managed between breaths.

He gaped at her. Now she'd given him another even worse anxiety. His conscience could bear only so much. She clutched her abdomen, grimacing in pain.

"Do not fret." He attempted a reassuring smile, although he could barely reassure himself. "I know precisely what to do. I grew up on a farm and have witnessed calving and lambing and . . . what might you call it? . . . kittening?"

"Get me a proper midwife!" She rose up off the floor, grabbing the cloth of his shirt in her fists. Daggers shot from her blue eyes. She was like one of the Furies. Tisi-phone, the avenger of murder.

That was fitting.

Good God! Citing the classics. He was turning damned bookish.

No time to dwell on that. He had bigger problems to ponder. Like a baby about to be born on his floor.

Gray eased the Fury back to the floor and fell to his knees. The woman convulsed in pain. Trembling himself, Gray pushed the blankets underneath her, pulled off her shoes and stockings, and pushed her skirt above her waist. Hesitating only a moment, he worked at removing her undergarments, fumbling like a lad taking his first tumble. He needn't have worried. Her eyes no longer focused, the liquid blue hardening like glass. She stared past him, concentration inward.

"The child is coming." Her voice turned eerily calm. Gray felt a line of sweat trickle down his back.

From between her legs, something round and full of dark hair appeared. "The baby's head!" he said, his voice cracking.

This could not be happening. Gray thought longingly of the bottle of brandy on his bureau. Would that he could pour the warming liquid down his throat until sweet oblivion was his.

Instead he grabbed a towel and held it ready.

Half sitting, she strained, face red. She made a low moan that gradually rose in pitch. Gray watched in fascination as the dark-haired head pushed out of its confines. She collapsed and the head disappeared again.

"You've lost it," Gray said.

"What do you mean, I've lost it?" she gasped, her eyes looking a bit wild.

"It went back . . . inside."

"Don't you think I know that?" she rasped. "It's inside *me*." Her face was red now, and her muscles tensed. Suddenly she wailed. The intensity of the sound pierced deep into his gut.

"It is coming!" He dropped the towel.

The head moved out slowly as she strained. With one final feral cry, she pushed. The baby shot out, landing in Gray's bare hands.

The woman sat up, grasping for the baby. "Is my baby alive? Is my baby alive?" Her fury was gone, replaced by fear.

Gray turned away from her. The infant made no sound, no movement. It was deep purple. *Oh, God.* That could not be a good sign. He hurriedly wiped off the child, jostling it as he did so. It was a boy, but so small, much smaller than he'd expected. Would such a tiny baby creature have had any chance to survive?

"Give me my baby!" She grabbed his arm, nearly knocking him off balance. How the devil could he tell this woman her baby was dead?

At that precise second, a cry burst from the miniature mouth. Tiny arms fluttered and shook. Gray laughed with relief.

"Oh!" the woman cried. She released Gray's arm and held out her hands for the infant.

He unwrapped the cord from around the newborn's abdomen and placed him into her hands. Deuce. He'd have to cut the damned thing. But before he figured out that unpleasant task, she groaned again. As she clutched the baby to her chest, her body convulsed once more.

The afterbirth. "Bloody hell."

Unmindful of his difficulties, the woman cradled the baby in her arms. "Dear, dear baby." Tears rolled down her cheeks, but her face was radiant with joy. She fingered each tiny hand, counted every tiny toe, examined every inch of him. "You are a boy! A lovely boy."

Gray stared at the infant. He'd never seen a newborn, except for his nephew, and that had been only a glimpse after the boy was swathed in blankets. "He's well equipped."

She glanced at him. "Well equipped?"

He gestured with his fingers. "You know, his . . . male parts."

Lifting one eyebrow, she regarded him with reproach.

He cleared his throat and jumped up to rummage through a box on the bureau, searching for a piece of string. He grabbed his razor. Not wishing to think too much on the task he would put the razor to, he tied off the cord and cut it, wincing at the same time. That odious job done, he pulled the blankets out from under her and folded them into a bundle containing all the unpleasantries of the birth.

Turning back, he caught sight of her gazing down at her baby. Her face was aglow as if lit from within. Her dark hair had come loose of its pins and tumbled around her shoulders in disordered curls. She put Gray in mind of a statue of the Madonna he'd seen in a Barcelona church. As he watched, she placed her lips on the soft down of the baby's head.

His throat went dry.

An overwhelming wave of regret washed over him, leaving an incredible void inside. He continued to stare at the mother and child, but all he saw were the blackest recesses of his soul. Had he been a better man, he might have held another infant the way she held this babe. Would that child have been as wrinkled as this little one? Would it have turned the same healthy shade of pink? Would its cries have been as angry? This little creature ought to be angry. Gray had delivered him into an abominable world.

The woman then lifted her eyes to Gray. Tears clung to her dark lashes like tiny jewels. She smiled at him, a look of wonder on her face. Gray's breath caught in his throat. She was a living, breathing Madonna, sharing with him an intimate moment he did not deserve. He thrust his own misery aside.

"Let me help you to the bed," he said. "Hold the baby tight."

He lifted her in his arms and carried them to the bed. Straightening the rumpled linens, he realized there were more tasks to perform. He lifted her skirt and, with a shaking hand, gently wiped her off. He fashioned padding from another towel and placed it between her legs to stanch the flow of blood.

She did not attend to this strange intimacy. For her, nothing existed but the infant, who now rooted against her chest. He cleared his throat. "We must remove that dress of yours. It is wet."

She cooperated with his undressing her as if she were a child herself, keeping hold of her baby, lifting her arms one by one as he slipped her dress and shift over her head. He watched transfixed as she guided the nipple of her breast to the baby's eager mouth. When the baby found it at last, she shot Gray another awed glance.

He quickly averted his eyes. "I'll find something for you to wear."

"And something I may wrap my baby in?" She smiled sweetly.

"Of course." Trying to still the heart thumping in his chest, he returned to the spot on the floor where the baby had been born. Something jabbed through the stocking on his heel. Hopping on the other foot, he pulled out a hairpin. Stifling an oath he grabbed a towel that had somehow escaped the untidiness of the birth. He limped back to hand it to her. She gently eased it around the tiny baby.

Now he had a sore foot, a naked woman in his bed, and a newborn baby he still didn't know for sure wasn't his. To top it all off, his head ached. She was oblivious to it all.

He limped over to his chest and pulled out a clean shirt. "Let's put this on you."

He slipped the cambric shirt over her head. Her skin was smooth beneath his hands. The infant lost his hold when she put first one and then the other arm through the sleeves. The small creature let out a shrill cry that felt like a bludgeon in Gray's head. She brought the baby to her breast again and the infant sucked, emitting a small, sweet, contented sound.

"You are kind," she said, an apparent afterthought.

He did not feel kind. He felt as if he'd landed in Bedlam, where he'd surely end up if this trial lasted much longer.

Gray grabbed a glass and his bottle of brandy from the bureau and sank into a chair. He poured the brandy to the brim, his shaking hands clinking the bottle against the glass. The familiar woody fragrance filled his nostrils as he swished the burning amber liquid around in his mouth, letting it slide slowly down his throat to heat his chest. He regarded her through slitted lids.

Why could he not recall meeting her? A man must be mad not to remember such a woman. True, he had drunk himself insensible those days with Lansing.

No. No. *No!*

Gray sat up like a bolt. Now that he thought of it, she

had not known him when he answered the door. Surely if they had met in *that* fashion, she would have recalled.

She did not know him!

Every muscle in his body relaxed. He was not the man responsible this time.

"Sir?"

"Yes?" She didn't even know his name. He almost grinned.

"May I have a drink of water?"

Gray shot out of the chair, his body back on alert. This inclination to help her seemed totally reflexive. He'd damned well lost any will of his own. "Certainly." He walked over to the pitcher of water on the bureau. After using his sleeve to wipe the glass out of which he had just drunk, he poured her the water and walked over to her side. "I fear I am a poor host."

She stared at him with a blank expression, completely missing the irony in his voice.

He shrugged and handed her the glass.

"Thank you." She sipped the water as if trying to keep from drinking it too fast. When she finished, she placed the glass on the table next to the bed and immediately checked her little son, as if something might have gone amiss with him during her infinitesimal moment of inattention.

Gray retrieved the glass and went back to his chair, pouring himself another drink. He let his eyes rest on his two unwished-for charges. Who the deuce was she?

He was about to speak when her eyes fluttered shut. She turned her head so that her forehead nearly touched the infant's.

Another pretty picture. Much more of this and he'd

have to secure himself another bottle of brandy. Gray drained his glass and held it against his forehead.

What might his life be like right now, if Rosa had obeyed his orders and remained with her father?

Foolish girl. She'd fled her father's house and followed Gray into battle, arriving in Orthes in the thick of an artillery assault, not having the sense to seek a place of safety.

Instead, God saw fit to throw another woman and baby in his path. Hell, straight into his hands. Irony, again.

He'd drink to irony. Gray poured himself another full glass of brandy, drained it, and wearily rose to his feet. He pulled on his boots and shrugged into his jacket. Grabbing the bundle of soiled blankets, he walked out the door, almost tripping on the threshold.

Maggie woke with a jolt, heart pounding. Where was she? Her eyes quickly focused on the baby, and she remembered. She stroked the infant's cheek with her finger, tenderness welling inside her. How was it possible to feel so acutely? This much love was almost painful.

She raised herself on one elbow and sank back, exhausted. The man was not here.

Maggie had been shocked when he first opened the door. Not only was he not who she expected, he looked like the blackest pirate ever to grace a Minerva Press novel. He was tall with the widest shoulders she'd ever seen. His clothes were wrinkled and his open shirtfront revealed a chest peppered with dark hair. The hair on his head was equally dark, hanging in curls nearly to his shoulders, in sad need of tying in a queue. His chin and cheeks were covered with stubble. Not the genteel appearance of the man she'd come to find. Most jarring, however, was the etching of pain in the corners of his eyes. If she had encountered this man on an empty street, she would have crossed to the other side, for fear he would murder her.

Instead, he'd removed her clothes, wiped her off. He'd seen and touched the most private parts of her body . . . no, she would not think of that. He delivered her baby safely, and she would be forever grateful to him.

Even though something about him made her tremble.

She glanced around the room again, peeking into corners, spying small drifts of dust skittering at the floor's edge.

Where was her husband? Why had that man opened his door?

Maggie had been near despair in the shabby Chelsea inn where she'd been staying. Down to her last shilling. No place to go. No family to take her in. Then she'd picked up a discarded London newspaper and read John's name. He was soon to leave for the Continent to rejoin his regiment, the paper said.

John? Alive? She still could barely believe it. The last she'd seen of him—God knows she could not wipe that scene from her mind—was his shocked expression as he slid off the river's edge and tumbled into the gray, rain-fed water.

All these months she'd thought she killed him, but he was alive, here in London. He would have to help her.

Maggie gazed at her baby, his miniature face like a miracle, one piece of beauty and joy rising from the debacle of her life. She'd do anything to make sure he survived.

The door opened and Maggie braced herself to face John.

Instead, the man who delivered her baby walked into the room.

"You are awake." There was no friendliness in his tone, and the room filled with his presence. It also filled with the scent of food, and Maggie momentarily forgot everything but the emptiness of her belly.

"Meat pasties." He placed the food on the table. "Would you like one?"

Maggie struggled to get up. "Please."

"Stay where you are." He lifted the table and brought it to the side of her bed. "There's some light ale, too."

Before his hands released the table, Maggie grabbed for the meat pasty, not even able to utter thanks. It was still warm from baking and fragrant of cooked beef and buttery crust. She held it in both hands and took bite after bite after bite.

His huge hand fastened on her wrist, stopping her. "Go slowly," he ordered. His grip was firm and his skin rough, from soldiering, she imagined. "Chew carefully. You want to keep the food down."

He did not release her, so she did as he commanded, looking into his face and forcing her jaws to rise and fall at the pace of a snail.

He gave her a curt nod when she swallowed, and released her wrist. She attempted a smaller bite, licking a crumb from her lip. She glanced at him again.

His brow furrowed. She took another bite.

"Drink some ale." He handed her the tankard.

She dutifully took a sip, but quickly bit into the meat

pasty again, chewing slowly and deliberately, conscious that he watched her every move.

The bit of food only whetted her appetite. She remained ravenous. He handed her the tankard again, and the ale cooled her throat.

"Forgive me," she said after gulping the ale. "I must seem wholly without breeding."

He frowned. "When did you last eat?"

She shrugged, having no wish for this man to know the extent of her miserable circumstances. "Two or three days. Maybe four, I cannot recollect."

He stared at her with eyes the color of cold steel.

He reached for the remaining meat pasty and brought it halfway to his mouth. Unable to help herself, Maggie's eyes traced its progress.

"Deuce." He scowled, but handed it over to her.

She ought to refuse, but . . . She took it and forced herself not to gobble it down this time.

"Finish the ale," he said.

Maggie obeyed, though she hardly required him to tell her to fill her stomach. By the time she placed the tankard down on the table, she felt pleasantly full. She lay back down next to her baby. Dear baby! She touched his soft little cheek. His mouth made sucking movements as he slept. She smiled.

The man cleared his throat. Maggie looked up.

He sat in the chair with his legs crossed. "Madam," he said. "I regret there is not the means to be properly introduced, but might I know who the deuce you are and why you knocked on my door?"

"Your door?" She blinked in confusion, resting her

cheek against the baby's head. "My husband's door, you mean."

"No." His voice was patient. "*My* door."

She struggled to sit up again. "Sir, are you in my husband's employ?"

He barked out a laugh. "I dare say not."

She released an exasperated breath, but attempted to sound polite. "I do not perfectly understand why you are in my husband's rooms."

He raised an eyebrow. His eyes remained flinty. "I do not perfectly understand why you should think these your husband's rooms."

"His regimental offices gave me this direction."

His face relaxed, and his mouth turned up at one corner. "Ah, regimental inefficiency. That does explain it." He rose and crossed the room, picking up a bottle and raising it to the light to check its contents. He paused, ready to pour the liquid into a glass. "Who is your husband, by the way? Perhaps I know him." He glanced back at her.

"John Grayson."

He started, spilling the brandy. "The devil he is." His voice deepened with anger.

Maggie regarded him with alarm. "I assure you, sir, my husband is Captain John Grayson."

He strode to the side of the bed, his gray eyes glinting. "Madam." He spoke in even and measured tones, as if humoring a lunatic. "*I* am Captain John Grayson."

Chapter TWO

Maggie's blood felt as if it had turned to ice. "This is a cruel jest, sir."

"Jest? I assure you, madam, this is no jest. I am John Grayson." His eyes flashed.

She straightened her posture. "John Grayson is my husband. You most certainly are not."

He laughed, the sound malevolent. "Indeed I am not."

Maggie wrapped the shirt he'd given her more tightly around her body. "Tell me where my husband is."

"Tell me *who* he is and perhaps I may do so." In a mimicking gesture, he folded his arms across his wide chest.

"I told you who he is. Who are you?" She met his insolent gaze. He stood at the foot of the bed, each hand gripping a bedpost. His bulk loomed over her.

He let go of the posts and snapped to attention, a sneer on his lips. "John Grayson, Captain, 13th Light Dragoons."

The 13th Light Dragoons was John's regiment. How could this man mock her so? Had John discovered her presence in London? Was this his ploy to prevent her finding him? Surely, he would not be that cruel. "You lie."

His eyes threw sparks. "If one of us is a liar, it is you, madam."

Maggie clamped her mouth shut. He was too deftly throwing her words back into her face, and she must not let him see the panic deep within her belly. She would proceed more cautiously. This imposter could be anyone, a gambler, thief—a murderer, like she'd thought herself until reading John's name.

"Do you know what I think?" he asked.

She turned her face away and gazed upon the spare furnishings of the room, the bureau cluttered with his belongings. A cracked mirror. Clothing strewn about.

He leaned down close to her face. "I think you are playing a rum game, madam. You knock on my door. Drop your baby into my hands, then blink those big blue eyes at me and expect me to believe you are searching for a husband who has my name." His eyes flashed. "Cut line."

Maggie rose to her knees on the bed, bending toward him, forcing herself to stare directly into his flinty eyes, no matter how piratical they appeared. "I did not choose to have my baby in this place. With you."

Their gazes held.

He drew back abruptly. Tapping his fingers to his lips, he paced to and fro, stopping again in front of her. "Madam, why were you required to search for your husband? Should he not have been by your side at this . . . delicate time?"

Maggie made a pretense of checking the sleeping

baby, remembering precisely why she must search for her husband.

"Did he know of the child?"

She shook her head, and mentally kicked herself for revealing so much.

She'd been so foolish to marry John. As green as grass. All too ready to believe the first pretty words spoken to her. At the time a secret marriage had sounded so romantic.

She'd grown wiser since.

She lay back and ran her finger over the baby's downy head. One thing she did not regret was this baby. She would never regret him. He was her family, her only family.

Gray stood with hands on his hips, watching her. A street hawker's song, "White turnips and fine carrots ho! White turnips and fine carrots ho!" sounded in his ears. What he would not give to walk straight out his door and lose himself in the throngs of peddlers, beggars, merchants, and thieves filling the nearby streets, to put distance between him and this woman who tempted him with her eyes and connived to cause him to assume responsibility for her.

There was no husband, of that he was certain, though there obviously was a man who fathered the child. She was too clever by half, with this story of searching for a husband. How the devil she came upon his name was the mystery. And why the devil did she think she could twist him in her coil? Her trick was worse than any Lansing had masterminded during their days in the Peninsula.

He trod over to the table, picked up the bottle of brandy, and shook it. No use. "Deuce," he muttered.

He glanced back at his unwelcome guest. She sat up and wrapped her arms around her bended knees, staring into the distance. With her dark curls tumbling about her shoulders she looked like a man's fantasy. Her skin was smooth and pale as cream, but her cheeks were warm with color that reflected the array of her emotions. Her lips had the definite bow-shape a portrait artist would yearn to paint, their pink tint a nearly irresistible temptation. Her hands were graceful and delicate, a lady's hands.

Perhaps she'd been some gentleman's discarded mistress. A credible idea. The man might have known Gray and spoken of him. But who would do so? He'd hardly mixed in society since he'd been sent back to England three months ago, ostensibly to recuperate from the wound he suffered at Orthes. After witnessing Rosa's death, he hadn't cared a fig where he went, but General Fane thought it prudent to get him out of the path of her vengeful, grieving father.

Damned if Gray had not managed to create a political incident after all, along with all his other sins. He thought he'd averted political scandal by marrying Rosa when he'd returned from Gloucestershire. But all that had been yesterday's debacle. Today he must worry about this new woman in his bed.

Suddenly she scrambled from beneath the covers and swung her exquisitely shaped legs over the side of the bed. She stood, holding on to the bedpost to get her balance.

"What the devil are you doing?" he snapped.

"I am looking for my dress." She took two shaky steps forward.

That soiled rag? "What the devil for?"

She answered him with a hostile look.

Gray snatched the dress from the floor. "Why do you want this wretched thing?"

The dress was a drab garment, now a damp mess. Hardly a dress belonging to a gentleman's mistress, come to think of it.

"I wish to leave." She grabbed for the dress and stumbled.

Tossing the garment aside, he caught her as she fell. She slammed against his healing wound, causing a stab of pain that nearly knocked him off his feet.

She swooned against his chest, and the pain receded to be replaced by a stirring in his groin. Through the thin linen of the shirt she wore, he felt the fullness of her breasts. Her stomach, all soft and round, pressed against him.

She was so very vulnerable. So in need of comfort.

He wrapped his arms around her, holding her close like he would a hurt child. She clung to him.

After a moment, she pushed away with a strangled cry and almost fell again. Gray swept her into his arms, her weak struggles in vain as he carried her to the bed and set her down, careful not to disturb the infant.

"Hold fast," he commanded, covering her with the bed linens and tucking the blankets around her. "Do not get up again."

Her eyes glistened with tears, like liquid jewels.

Damn her. How much did she think he could bear?

"You wish to leave?" He valiantly resisted the pull of her tears. "Believe me, madam, I would be delighted."

Her chin lifted and her lips pursed, though the tears still shone in her eyes.

"I assure you I have made arrangements to be rid of you," he went on, his voice harsh to his ears. "I have sent for my cousin's wife to convey you to your home. I can hardly be seen accompanying you, can I? I expect her presently, but you must remain in bed until she arrives."

"Why should I put myself in her care? Why do you not simply put me in the street?" Her tone was defiant, but her voice trembled.

He stared down at her. She looked like an abandoned kitten, small and weak. "I have been asking myself that very question." He forced a smile.

A lone tear trickled down her cheek and she swiped at it with the back of her hand. "Simply tell me of my husband and he will see to my care. I need not trouble you further."

He raised his eyebrows. "Ah, this fictional husband, again. If Grayson is your husband and I am Grayson, then you must obey me, I believe. I am consigning you to the care of my cousin's wife. She will convey you and the baby back from where you came. That will conclude my husbandly duties."

The baby wailed. His tiny body shuddered and his arms and legs trembled. She instantly sat up and gathered him in her arms. She jiggled him and patted his back. He continued to cry. A look of panic flickered in her eyes.

"Put him to your breast."

She pulled the shirt away from her breast and again guided the nipple into the baby's mouth. The baby quieted instantly. He stared at her, riveted again. She glanced up, the hint of a smile on her lips. Quickly he turned his head.

He strolled to the window, not daring to look back at her. To watch the baby nurse at her breast touched off something warm and tender inside him, a feeling he did not wish to examine too closely. The sooner Tess came, the better.

In spite of his resolve, Gray glanced back at her, now looking beatific. The Madonna of the Barcelona church.

He swung back to the window, rapping his fingers distractedly on the sash, keeping time with the horses' hooves on cobblestones. Outside a carriage pulled up, his cousin's crest painted on the side.

"She has arrived," he said.

He hurried out the door and reached the street just as his cousin's wife, the Baroness Caufield, was being assisted from the carriage by her footman. When she saw him, she gasped in alarm and rushed forward with a flounce of lilac skirts and bobbing blond ringlets. "Gray, I came as soon as I—oh, my, you are ill! Is it your injury? It has turned putrid, I know it has—"

He took her arm. "I am perfectly well, I assure you."

"No, you are not! You look a fright. You must come with me to Curzon Street this instant!" She put a gloved hand to his cheek. "Indeed, you ought to have done so when you arrived. Harry ought to have insisted you allow us to care for you."

Gray removed her hand and gave it an affectionate squeeze. "I am recovered, Tess." He steered her out of the earshot of her footman, who was making a poor attempt at looking blandly disinterested. "But I am in the devil of a fix."

Gray paused at the doorway. "There is a lady inside—"

"You have a . . . a female in your rooms?" Her eyes widened, kindled with interest.

"Not that," he snapped. Gray took a deep breath. "I opened my door to a woman and she gave birth on my carpet. I need your help to rid me of her."

Tess gave a small shriek. "Do not say so! She gave birth? But why should such a creature come to your rooms? It is nonsensical."

"I agree. Very nonsensical."

Gray launched into a more detailed explanation of the day's events. He considered telling Tess about the woman's claim to be Mrs. John Grayson, but decided not to do so. Who could predict what Tess would make of that information? No, he'd let the beauty tell Tess whatever story now suited her.

He must have captured Tess's complete attention, because she listened to him without once interrupting. When he finished, she adjusted the paisley shawl around her shoulders. "Well, let us go in. I will promise nothing, however."

"I merely need you to convey her home. I certainly cannot."

With a swish of her skirts, Tess passed through the door he held open for her and entered his rooms. The woman held the baby in her arms. She was no longer nursing him.

"Here she is, Tess," he said, bringing his cousin forward. "Madam, may I present Baroness Caufield."

The woman had turned very pale. "Ma'am," she said, barely audible.

"Oh, my dear." Tess rushed to her side. "I am Lady Caufield, but you must call me Tess. Is this your dear little baby? What a love he is. I say 'he,' but I don't know, do I? Silly. I suppose we always hope for a boy. Is he a boy? So tiny, poor thing. Are you in any distress? I cannot imagine what you have been through with only Gray, of all people."

"I have not fared ill," the mother said, darting a glance toward Gray.

Tess continued. "I am astonished, as one might expect, but we must convey you to your home at once. We will concoct a story that you happened upon my house. We cannot allow it to be known that an unmarried gentleman assisted you. Think of the scandal! Simply give Gray the direction of your home and he may tell Coachman. What a dear little baby you have. Has he a name? No, it is too soon, I am sure. My husband's given name is Harry, which is a lovely name, do you not agree? You may certainly use it if you like." She finally took a breath. "Oh, he is so sweet. May I hold him for you? The dear thing."

The mother looked as if a cannon had exploded next to her ear, but Tess often had that effect on people. She handed the child over to the cooing and ahhing Lady Caufield.

Gray congratulated himself for the scheme of sending for Tess. His cousin's wife had no children of her own and, as a result, thought it her duty to bestow her maternal proclivities upon everyone else.

Tess would sweep mother and child away, and in a few moments, Gray's solitude would be restored.

"I must find my dress," Maggie said, struggling to get out of the bed.

Gray picked up the garment and addressed Tess. "She cannot wear this," he said. He ought to have thrown it away with the rest of the towels and blankets. Some rag picker would be in for a surprise when he came across that bundle in the alley.

"Oh, my!" exclaimed Tess, wrinkling her nose at the crumpled, damp garment.

"Wrap her in my greatcoat," Gray said, tossing the dress aside and walking over to where it hung on a peg.

Tess rocked the infant back and forth in her arms. "A man's greatcoat will never do. Why did you not ask me to bring some clothes?"

Because if he had asked such a thing, Tess would not have come, Gray thought, but did not speak out loud.

It perturbed him that the young woman should have to wear the ruined dress, but why the devil he should care escaped comprehension. He shrugged his shoulders and handed her the garment, turning his back as she struggled to put it on.

"She needs help, Gray," Tess said. She thrust the infant into his hands and rushed over to assist.

Gray thought to protest, but the baby stared at him with the same wide eyes as the mother. Gray felt a stab in the vicinity of his heart. "Hello, little fellow," he whispered. "Remember me?"

The baby opened his mouth and yawned, looking exactly like a tiny little person. Gray grinned in spite of himself.

"For God's sake, turn away, Gray," Tess demanded. "I am dressing her."

Gray obeyed, but gave the infant a conspiratorial wink. "I suppose she thinks I delivered you with my eyes closed."

The baby stared.

Tess soon snatched the baby back, ridding him of his burden. Gray told himself he was grateful.

"Come, dear." Tess headed for the door. She stopped abruptly. "My goodness! I do not even know your name!"

Gray glanced at her. What would she tell Tess?

"It is Maggie," she said. "Maggie . . . Smith."

"Maggie, then." Tess tossed Gray a knowing look. "Gray will assist you. Tell him where we must take you, and we will be off. I cannot like you in that dress. We must get you home posthaste." Tess hurried out the door, wrapping the baby in her shawl as she went.

Maggie stood frozen in place. She raised a hand to her temple and pressed hard. Her head felt light and she dared not move or she might faint dead away onto the carpet where her baby had been born.

The baroness knew this gentleman. She *knew* him! She'd addressed him as Gray several times now and she seemed too genuine, too kind, to aid and abet the man in deception.

He came to her side and offered his arm.

She shrugged it away and whirled on him. "Are you truly Captain John Grayson of the 13th?" She could barely make her voice work.

He looked puzzled. "I thought we had settled that."

She grabbed the lapel of his coat, swaying as she did so. "Truly?"

He grasped her arm, steadying her. "Yes."

He urged her toward the door. Maggie did not resist. Her mind raced.

If he was John Grayson, then who was her husband?

Had her husband given a false name? There did not seem any other explanation. There could not be two John Graysons in the 13th regiment, otherwise, surely this man would have known.

"Where shall we deliver you, Miss . . . ah . . . Smith," he asked.

She tried to pull away from him. "Nowhere." Her voice broke. "I have nowhere to go." All hope that she'd not killed her husband had now been dashed.

Dear God, what would happen to her now? To her son?

"You have nowhere to go?" the real Captain Grayson repeated.

His words jolted her back. "I . . . I was unable to pay my charges at the inn. I cannot return there. Not even for my portmanteau."

She'd fled the inn that morning, running on slippery cobbles while the innkeeper's wife bellowed curses at her fleeing back. Her flight had most likely brought on her labor.

"Surely you have family."

She shook her head. "There is no one." She'd always been an unwanted encumbrance to her uncle, not welcome in his house even when a child. How many holidays and summers had she spent at school when the other girls had gone home? Could she throw herself upon the mercy of the headmistress of her boarding school? Not after the relentless lectures of the shame of fallen women.

"Bloody hell." The captain's grip tightened on her arm.

Lady Caufield's head popped through the doorway. "Gray, really. Do not speak so. It is not fitting. Hurry, please. The coachman waits."

"She bloody well has no place to go," he snapped.

Lady Caufield gave the captain a disapproving glare, but turned on Maggie a melting look of sympathy. "Oh, you poor darling! Well, there is nothing else for it. You and the child must come home with me."

Maggie's lips trembled at the unexpected kindness.

Captain Grayson propelled her out of the apartments to the street below. His arm felt secure around her. And determined.

They reached the pavement. "Tell me the name of the inn," he said, his breath warm against her ear as he spoke.

"The inn?"

"Where you stayed."

She blinked into his face, which looked no less pirate-like. "The Wanderer in Chelsea, but—"

He ignored her.

Lady Caufield waved them on to the coach. She thrust the baby into the captain's hands so the footman could assist her into the coach. The footman wrinkled his nose as he assisted Maggie next. Lady Caufield reached for the infant. The captain hesitated a moment before lifting the baby into her arms.

"Call upon us soon, Gray," Lady Caufield said.

Maggie looked out the window as the coach pulled away. Captain Grayson stood on the pavement, hands on his hips. He remained there until the coach turned the corner and she could no longer see him.

*   *   *

That evening, Gray sat at the back table of the dark, musty tavern around the corner from his lodgings. The smell of smoke mixed with the sour stench of unwashed bodies, hops, and roasting meat, but the brandy was tolerable and the oyster stew quite tasty. Besides, the rumble of voices and laughter softened into a hum that shut out his thoughts. Gray poured another glass, downed the liquid, and stared into the haze.

A gentleman entered, his immaculate evening dress a contrast to the soot-stained, brown-coated men who were there to drink their gin and ale. The gentleman looked about the room and hesitantly wound his way through the crowd, skipping aside to avoid collision with the unwashed bodies.

He spied Gray and hurried to his table, a grin spreading over his face.

"Thank God, Gray. I've been searching for you in every establishment on the street."

"Harry."

Gray's cousin, a kind-eyed, fair-haired man in his early thirties, eyed the chair across from Gray with dismay. He pulled a handkerchief from his coat pocket and spread it on the seat before sitting down.

"Do you want a drink?" Gray signaled to the serving girl.

Harry's eyebrows rose. "Is it safe?"

Gray gave a dry laugh. "Hasn't killed me yet."

The serving girl leaned over and favored him with a glimpse of her ample bosom, giving him the bizarre thought that the last breast he'd seen had had a baby attached to it. He suspected that was not the image she'd intended to invoke.

The girl brought a bottle and a second glass. Gray nodded his thanks to her. He poured for his cousin.

Harry held the glass up to what scanty light was available and cautiously peered at its contents.

"So what brings you here?" Gray asked.

"Well you know, Gray"—Harry took a wary sip, raised his brows in surprised approval, and followed it with another bolder one—"I have in my care a young lady and an infant, and I came to inquire what you intend to do about them."

Gray gazed lazily at his cousin, the twitch in the corner of his mouth betraying an amused irony. "Do about them? I thought myself rather clever to fob them off on your good-hearted wife."

"Just so," Harry muttered.

"They are not my responsibility."

"You cannot mean that." Harry placed his glass on the table. "Surely you have not sunk so low."

He shrugged and took a long swig of his drink.

Harry's eyes kindled. "What are you about, Gray? Are you still ill? Has your injury troubled you? I wish you would have accepted my invitation to stay with us at Curzon Street. You've been a recluse. No one sees you in town. Are you certain you are well?"

"I have never been better," Gray lied. "The wound is a mere nothing. I am in no need of a nursemaid."

"Are you not?" Harry raised his eyebrows. "You look the very devil."

He took a gulp of his brandy. He had no wish to spar with his genial cousin.

Harry went on, "And now this Miss Smith, as she calls herself. I declare, Gray, it astonishes me that you would dishonor a female, let alone abandon her to her fate. I cannot believe it."

A vision of Rosa flashed through Gray's mind, that vision he could never escape. What would Harry think of him if he knew about Rosa?

But he'd be damned if he'd be leg-shackled to another such female. "Miss Smith is not my responsibility. Her presence in my rooms was a lamentable accident."

Harry shot him a very skeptical look.

Gray sighed. There was no point in arguing. "I will call in two or three days." It appeared God would not be so kind as to rid him of this annoyance quite yet.

His cousin smiled. "Very good." Harry raised his glass and regarded him with a friendly gaze. "Gray, perhaps you might clean yourself up a little before calling? Where is your valet?"

Gray laughed. "I have little need of a valet. I grew used to taking care of myself while in the Peninsula."

Harry raised his quizzing glass to his eye. "Yes, I can see you care for yourself very well. All the same, I could send my valet to assist you, if you like."

"Spare me that. I will contrive to look presentable, do not fear."

"Excellent." Harry reached in his pocket and pulled out his timepiece. "And I must leave presently. I have promised to escort Tess to the Harrington rout, though I believe she'd rather stay home and play nurse."

Harry stood up and retrieved his handkerchief, folding it with precision and returning it to his pocket. "We will expect you soon." He offered Gray his hand and Gray accepted without further comment. Harry then took a deep breath and resolutely picked his way back through the untidy throng.

Gray sat twirling his glass with his fingers.

His cousin would like to play Gray's conscience, it seemed. If Harry only knew he needed no auxiliary in that department. His own conscience was quite skillful at tormenting him.

Let Harry take responsibility this time. Gray refused to consider this woman any charge of his merely because she'd found her way to his door with a story of being his wife. He needed no wife and certainly did not need family to dictate his duty. He'd joined the army and traveled to the Peninsula to avoid family demands, and well Harry knew it.

He took another long sip of his brandy.

He'd certainly made a mull of things all the same.

After the heady victory at Vitoria, he'd been primed for celebration. His friend Lansing assured him he'd found two fresh Spanish girls eager to entertain the two English officers. They'd all spent a rollicking night together, the Madeira flowing in abundance.

Gray had been too full of drink to precisely recall bedding Rosa, but Lansing assured him he'd had a splendid night. When Gray returned from his leave in Gloucestershire three months later, Rosa identified him as the man who sired the baby she carried in her womb. Her father insisted Gray do the honorable thing by her.

So he had married her. What else could he have done? He'd strictly forbidden her to accompany him on the campaign, but she followed him to Orthes. Perhaps she feared he would desert her, as Lansing deserted her cousin by returning to England.

Gray would be damned if he'd allow himself to be embroiled in another female's troubles, especially when those troubles were not of his making. He delivered her baby and paid her charges at the inn. Her belongings were bound for Curzon Street. It was enough.

Gray drained his glass and placed the cork back in the bottle. He threw some coins on the table and stuck the bottle into his pocket.

No bloody way he would call on his cousin. Let good-hearted Harry solve the woman's problems. Gray washed his hands of her.

Chapter THREE

Three days later Gray stepped up to the door of the comfortably elegant townhouse on Curzon Street. He wore his new regimentals, the blue coat more presentable than the worn uniform that earned the 13th the nickname Ragged Brigade.

He'd found a man to cut his hair and he'd shaved his cheeks smooth, using the same razor that cut the baby's cord, but Gray disliked thinking of that.

Why the devil was he standing upon this doorstep at all? The sky was almost blue this fine May afternoon. He could be walking through Hyde Park, pretending to be in the country.

More likely he'd be searching for some dark room in which to gamble or drink. Perhaps it was just as well he was doing precisely what his cousin wished. Gray sighed. He disliked following family dictates on a manner of principle. God knew he'd defied plenty of them.

No, his reasons for making this call were selfish, no other way about it. The past two nights had brought nightmares, more horrific than he'd experienced before. The repeat of Rosa's death was no surprise, but this time

Maggie Smith and her child took Rosa's place, over and over, a kaleidoscope of destruction. Brandy no longer guaranteed oblivion. The images returned whenever he closed his eyes.

Gray drew the line at witnessing babies blown to smithereens, even in a dream, so he entered into a bargain with God. If God would stop the nightmares, Gray would atone for his sins.

God invited him to go first.

Gray sounded the gleaming brass knocker. The door was promptly answered by a footman who bowed as he entered. The butler appeared in the foyer.

"Is the baron in?" Gray asked, handing the footman his shako and gloves.

"Lord Caufield is not at home, sir," the butler answered, eyeing him with one brow slightly raised.

It was testimony to Gray's rare appearance in the house that the servants did not know him. "Lady Caufield, then." He handed the man his card.

The butler glanced at it and apparently recognized his connection. "If the captain would be so good as to wait in the parlor."

Gray followed the man above stairs to a sun-filled room with glass doors opening onto a stone balcony. A breeze stirred the curtains and sent cool air through the room and into the hallway. Gray wandered onto the balcony and gazed out. Even the tiniest London garden gave pleasure in the spring.

He would leave England within the week. Perhaps in these next few days, he'd catch his last glimpse of the country's verdant beauty. Country hills awash with wildflowers. Fragrant, plowed fields awaiting spring planting.

Trees fluttering canopies of new green leaves. He ought to have scheduled time to wander the countryside on horseback, savoring its beauty, instead of passing hours in dingy taverns. A soldier had no guarantee of seeing another spring.

Summerton Hall had always been at its most beautiful in the spring. Gray used to love watching his father's land come to life after the bleakness of winter, his mother's gardens a riot of color. He wondered if someone tended to her gardens now she'd been gone nearly fifteen years. It had been six years since he'd been to Summerton to see.

"John?" A feminine voice came from behind him.

He turned, expecting to see Tess.

Maggie Smith stood framed in the doorway.

Dash it. He'd not planned to encounter her. Weren't women supposed to closet themselves in their rooms after childbirth? His plan had been to conduct his business with his cousin and be on his way.

For a moment she looked as if she'd seen a ghost. Her face flushed pink as he walked over to greet her.

"I beg your pardon, sir," she murmured, casting her eyes down. "I thought you were . . . someone else." She turned to leave.

"Wait," he said.

She paused.

He regarded her. "How do you fare, madam? I trust you are well?"

Miss Smith looked up at him, her delicately arched brows knit. "Do I know you, sir?"

Amusing. She did not recognize him. He must have appeared as big a fright as his cousin had indicated.

"Am I so altered?" He stepped closer and leaned down so his face was inches from hers.

Recognition dawned. She took a step back. "Oh, it is you."

Gray laughed. "How do you fare, madam?"

Her eyes narrowed. "I am well."

"And the child?" he asked politely.

"He is also well."

Apparently she overcame the rigors of childbirth quite swiftly. She was in remarkable good looks. Her luxuriant hair was nearly tamed into a knot on her head. Wild tendrils escaped, curling around her face and down the long nape of her neck. Her blue eyes shone as vivid as sapphires, enhanced by the pale blue morning dress she wore, her generous breasts straining against the bodice. Gray remembered his glimpses of her breasts, how white and round they'd appeared when the baby suckled in her arms, how drawn to her he'd felt in those moments.

God help him.

As if reading his thoughts, or perhaps following the direction of his eyes, she covered herself with the shawl draped over her shoulders.

"Oh, my goodness!" Tess hurried down the staircase from an upper floor. "Maggie, what are you doing up? You must rest."

The young mother's cheeks flushed pink again. "I needed to . . . to pick a rose."

Gray smiled. It had been a long time since he'd heard a female use that euphemism for the privy.

"That may be," Tess interrupted. "But I have told you to let the servants empty the—" She finally took notice of him. "Oh, Gray, dear, did I say hello?"

He opened his mouth to respond, but to no avail.

Tess continued in her breathless way. "No, I expect I did not. Hello, Gray, it is good to see you. I almost gave you up." She presented her cheek for him to kiss. "You look very handsome, I declare. Nothing like a man in regimentals to turn ladies' heads. But what am I to do with Maggie?"

She took the new mother by the arm and walked her into the room, breezing past Gray. "She insists on waiting upon herself, and heaven knows I must not hire a wet nurse for the baby—she will not hear of it. I am sure it is everything admirable, but it cannot be good for her to have the baby at her breast all the time. She is too delicate, I fear. I do wish you would speak to her, Gray. Convince her."

Damn Tess's runaway mouth for reminding him again of that strange connection he felt to the mother nursing her infant. He glanced at Miss Smith whose cheeks flushed an even deeper red.

"It is not my place to convince her, Tess," he said as blandly as he could manage.

Tess gave him an exasperated look. "Well, I believe it is your place, but never mind. Do you stay for dinner, Gray? You simply must. You depart soon, do you not?"

"Depart?" asked Miss Smith.

"For the Peninsula. He goes back to war, although I do wish he would sell out. He has already been wounded once, and I expect he is not as well healed as he pretends."

Miss Smith's brows rose, widening her crystalline blue eyes. "You were injured, sir?"

"Yes, he was." Tess turned to Gray. "You ought to

have allowed Harry's doctor to make a visit. I told Harry—"

Gray raised his hands. "Enough, Tess. It was a scratch."

She shook her finger at him. "Don't speak fustian to me, sir. The army does not send its officers home for a scratch."

No, but they send them home to avoid the wrath of influential Spanish fathers, although Gray could not very well explain that to Tess.

He backtracked. "I fear I am engaged for dinner," he lied. Unless one supposed that hanging about the city's gaming hells for a final night was an engagement that could not be broken.

"Tomorrow, then," Tess said, taking a seat on a sofa and pulling on her companion's arm so that Maggie was dragged down beside her.

Resigned at having to remain in the Madonna's company for a polite interval, Gray settled in a nearby chair. "Tomorrow I depart for the coast."

"No!" exclaimed Tess. "I won't have it. You have not once dined with us. It is too bad of you, Gray."

"Indeed, I do apologize," he said.

The deep rose brocade sofa was so near the chair that Maggie's knees almost touched the captain's. She kept her eyes downcast and her hands clasped in her lap, only half listening to his repartee with Lady Caufield. She fervently hoped their voices drowned out the loud beating of her heart.

She'd thought he was her John when she'd caught sight of him from the back, in uniform, silhouetted in the patio doors. She glanced at him now.

For the hundredth time she wondered why John had used this man's name. Her John must have known him. She yearned to ask this Captain Grayson, who sat chatting with her generous hostess, but she was afraid. What if he figured out who her husband really was? Would he not know the man was dead?

And, then, would it not be a very short time before she was questioned about the death and accused of it? Heaven knew what would happen to her baby then.

She watched the captain through her lashes. Only a hint of the pirate remained in his granite-gray eyes. His hair gleamed as black as before, but it no longer brushed his shoulders. His clean-shaven face revealed a strong square jawline. His lips were full and expressive.

He lifted his hand to those lips, a large, strong hand, the hand that had caught her baby at birth, that had undressed her, wiped her clean. Maggie felt herself flush again. In a way, he'd been more intimate with her than her husband ever had. Having no more than a few hours together, she and her husband had never even fully undressed.

To think she'd believed that furtive act had been love. No, her husband had deceived her, tricked her, *lied* to her.

She'd believed him when he told her they must keep their marriage secret. His family aspired for him to marry high, he'd said. A lady's companion would never do in their eyes. He had no money now, he said. As if that had mattered to her. He would inherit a competence when his grandmother died, he said. She was ill. It would not be long.

Maggie had believed it all. She'd believed him when he said he could not wait, he loved her so. When she lay with him, she'd thought her future complete. No longer would she be alone.

Maggie blinked. Lady Caufield's sewing lay casually on one of the side tables, the baron's book open next to it. She could picture the baron and baroness sitting here on cozy evenings, comfortable together. Chatting about the day's events.

She envied them.

Her gaze wandered to the window where a tree half obscuring the rooftops of the surrounding houses fluttered in the breeze. She was lucky to be in this lovely place instead of on the streets. Indeed, what would have happened to her had Captain Grayson slammed his door in her face and forced her to give birth in some alleyway? She was convinced her baby would be dead.

As dead as the lying, deceitful man who had fathered him.

"Maggie, dear." Lady Caufield's voice came as if from the bottom of an empty barrel. "Maggie."

Startled, Maggie glanced up. The captain stared at her, his steely eyes somehow reproachful. She blinked rapidly and turned to Lady Caufield. "I am sorry, I was not attending."

"Gray asked if your belongings were returned to you. I told him your portmanteau arrived yesterday. I declare, there was not much in it by the looks of it. Did you find it in order?"

She'd almost forgotten. This was another debt she owed him. "I confess I did not examine it."

She'd had so little to take with her. A change of clothes. A brush, a comb. An oval gold locket her father had given to her on her ninth birthday. A miniature of her mother, vibrantly young. Her brother's painted wooden toy horse. These meager treasures were all she had left of them.

The baroness patted her hand. "You have been busy with the baby, that is true, and it is just days since your confinement."

Maggie gave the captain a direct look, and her heart raced inexplicably. "I ought to have expressed my gratitude to you, sir. Indeed, I do not know how I can repay you for discharging my debts and returning my belongings."

His granite-gray eyes revealed nothing of what he might be thinking, but held her gaze captive. Would he expose her as a conniver and a liar? The baron's generosity would be short-lived in that event. The captain held her future in his large, strong hands just as he'd held the baby fresh from her womb.

The corner of his expressive mouth turned up in a rakish half smile, reminding her too much of how like a pirate he'd once appeared. "And my midwifery? I gather that does not deserve such merit?"

Maggie's cheeks grew hot. She adjusted her shawl, bringing it nearly to her chin.

Lady Caufield rapped him on the wrist. "Do not be ill-bred, Gray. I declare you should not mention that . . . well . . . that indelicate matter. I do not see how you can be so ill-mannered." She turned to Maggie with an apologetic smile. "You must not even think of repayment, Maggie. Gray is comfortably situated, thanks to his grandmother, no matter that he chooses to live in a . . . a sty."

The captain adopted an affronted look. "You are free with my blunt, Lady Caufield."

Maggie twirled the fringe of her shawl. He had a grandmother's inheritance? Her fictional husband had promised a grandmother's inheritance. Another lie borrowed from this man's life, no doubt. "I shall pay you back when I'm able, Captain."

His eyes widened momentarily. His mouth pursed.

"Nonsense!" exclaimed Lady Caufield. "He will not hear of it, will you, Gray? Such a sum would be of no consequence, is that not right?"

That possibly mocking, possibly serious look returned to his face. "Of no consequence at all, Tess."

From the upper floor an urgent wail sounded, becoming louder with each breath. Maggie stood, heart thudding in her chest. She tightened her grip on the shawl. "The baby. If you will excuse me, sir."

The captain rose.

Lady Caufield pulled Maggie back to the sofa as she stood up herself. "I will see to him. Stay here and entertain Gray."

Before Maggie could protest, Lady Caufield was out of the room with a swish of skirts. The baby's cry echoed throughout Maggie's body. Her breasts grew hard. She glanced at the captain, who remained standing. He sauntered back to the open balcony doors, throwing his tall form back into the silhouette she'd seen when she first stepped into the room. He gazed out into the garden for a long time.

The baby cried again, gasping wails that made Maggie's breasts ache and her stomach clench. She did not wish to be trapped in this room with the captain while her son needed her. She yearned for the quiet pleasure of his tiny mouth sucking her milk, the peacefulness of a world consisting of just her and him. She stood and moved about the room, restlessly straightening the items on the tables.

His voice came from behind her. "How much have you told Tess?"

The candlestick she held in her hand clattered as she placed it back on the side table and faced him. "Nothing more. She has asked nothing."

He folded his arms across his rather expansive chest and leaned against the doorjamb, in a seemingly relaxed stance.

She lifted her chin. "Do you tell her, then?"

As easily as his posture relaxed, it changed to taut readiness. "Tell her that faradiddle you fed me? I would not. But it is time you tell me who you are, madam."

"I have done so. Mrs. John Grayson." Her bravado faltered and she glanced down to the floor. "Or so I had thought."

He stepped closer to her. "I checked at regimental headquarters, thinking perhaps there might be another John Grayson and the names confused." He stood inches from her, lifting her chin with his finger so that she must look into his stormy eyes. "There was no other."

Maggie tried to hold his gaze, but her traitorous eyes focused somewhere to the left of his head.

"Tell me who you are and how you came to knock upon my door."

The baby's cries came closer, more insistent. Maggie winced from the pressure of her milk and her child's need. She placed her hand upon her breast. The fabric of her dress was soaked. The captain's gaze lowered, and she knew he saw the circle of moisture staining the pale blue dress. She covered herself with her hand. He stepped back, cheeks burnished.

A distressed Lady Caufield swept into the room with the squalling infant in her arms. "Maggie, I cannot quiet him."

"I'll take him," Maggie said, simultaneously relieved at being reunited with her baby and escaping Captain Grayson. She scooped him away and rushed from the room without another word.

"Well!" Tess said.

Gray took a breath, attempting to regain his composure. He shook his head and looked over to find Tess regarding him quizzically.

"Did you and Maggie have a chance to talk, then?" She gave him a smile that revealed her coquettish dimple.

He frowned. "What are you driving at, Tess?"

"I thought perhaps you might settle things." Her smile faded and a small crease appeared on her brow.

"There is nothing to settle, Tess."

The baron walked into the room, and Gray was spared further protestations.

"Gray, good to see you." The baron offered Gray a firm handshake before turning to his wife and giving her a kiss. "Tess, you look ravishing as usual."

She giggled with pleasure.

"Might I have a few moments of your time, Harry?" Gray was eager to leave this house and the disturbance of seeing Miss Smith again.

"I believe I shall check on Maggie." Tess swished out of the room.

Gray and Harry removed themselves to the library.

"I have some fine claret, Gray," said Harry. "Are you interested?"

Might as well start drinking now as later, Gray thought. "Certainly."

Harry picked up a crystal decanter from the side table, poured a glass, and handed it to Gray.

"Now, what is this about, Gray? You have matters to discuss?"

Gray swirled the ruby liquid in his glass before taking a sip. How was he to explain to his cousin?

"I leave for the Peninsula tomorrow, Harry."

"I see you are prepared." His cousin gestured to his uniform. "Will you not be visiting Summerton Hall before you sail?"

"Summerton?" Gray nearly choked on his claret. "What the devil makes you think I'd even consider it?"

Harry peered at him, looking like every self-righteous schoolboy who'd ever ratted on him at school. "Because you ought to make the visit, Gray. How long has it been?"

Gray straightened. "Since the day my father told me to never again darken his door."

"Oh, fiddle," Harry said. "You must know your father spoke in anger. I am sure he misses you very much."

Gray gulped his drink. "Has he said so to you?"

Harry tapped on the stem of his glass. "No, not exactly, but dash it, Gray, he is your father."

Gray stood and walked to the shelves, running his finger along the leather bindings of the books. Thucydides. Ovid. Sophocles.

"I defied him, Harry. You must know my father has no intention of forgiving such a transgression. I purchased my colors against his wishes, and he banished me from his lands and his life. It was a fair trade."

Harry sighed. "I confess I do not understand either of you, but never mind. I will not tease you further." He rose to pour Gray more claret. "What did you wish to discuss?"

"Your houseguest."

Harry's brows twitched, and he smiled. "I see."

"Damn it, Harry. You do not see at all." Gray walked over to the window. "I will not try to convince you that there is no obligation on my part regarding Maggie Smith, as she calls herself, but there is not."

"What is her name, then?" Harry said ingenuously.

"How the devil should I know?" Gray said. "It is no business of mine what game she plays. She can go to perdition for all I care."

Harry's eyes widened. "Do you mean that, Gray?"

Gray rubbed his brow. "No, I suppose not, because I have decided to assist her. For reasons of my own, I assure you. It has nothing to do with her." This was his pact with God. He would assist Maggie Smith in order to atone for Rosa. But he could not explain that to Harry.

"Very well. Whatever you wish, Gray." Harry raised his palms.

Gray walked over to his cousin and pulled a leather envelope from his jacket. "Here is some money to help her get settled, to find the baby's father. I must leave arrangements to you, Harry. I hope you will agree to assist her."

"Find the father. Of course," said Harry with some sarcasm. He examined the contents of the envelope through his quizzing glass. "This is dashed generous of you, Gray."

Gray glared at him. "I'll not starve."

Harry carefully replaced the bank draft into the envelope and tucked it into his pocket. "I'll take care of it."

"One more thing, Harry," Gray said.

"Yes?"

"I do not wish her to know about this."

Harry's eyes narrowed. "How am I to explain, then?"

"I do not care what you say." Gray walked back to the table and finished the glass of claret. "Tell her the money is from you. It matters not to me. But give me your word on it."

Harry stood. "Of course, it shall be as you wish, but—"

"I must leave." Gray extended his hand to his cousin.

Harry caught him in a hug instead. Patting Gray's back, Harry said, "Take care, Gray. Take care."

Gray extricated himself, touched by his cousin's genuine concern. He stretched his mouth into a grin. "I always do."

A moment later, when Gray reached the pavement outside his cousin's house, he paused to breathe in the cool air. God ought to agree he'd done well. Perhaps it would take only one bottle of brandy to sleep this night.

Almost lighthearted, as if a bag of cannonballs had been lifted off his shoulder, he placed his shako on his head, and turned back toward the house. His eye caught a figure in the upper-floor window. The mother held the baby and rocked it slowly in her arms. When she turned to the window, she stilled, and he had the sense she'd seen him.

He could not move, until she turned and disappeared

from his sight. He took a breath and strode purposefully toward St. James Street.

After his cousin left, Baron Caufield pulled the leather envelope from his pocket and examined the contents once more.

By God, Gray had given this woman a nice piece of change. If she were very frugal she could live for a year on this sum. What foxed Harry was why Gray did all this for a woman with whom he vowed he had no connection. It was not to be believed.

He stared into his claret, musing on when and where Gray might have met the girl. She did not look the sort who would have visited the Peninsula. He must have met her some other place. Gray had visited England in the last year, had he not? The trip had been brief, so brief he'd not managed more than a short note to Harry at the time.

Harry counted the months on his fingers. Yes, it was very likely Gray had met her on that trip. He'd have sailed back to Spain without knowing he'd gotten her with child. It fit very well.

The door swung open and Tess dashed into the room. "Harry, thank goodness you are here."

"Of course I am here, my dear. Where else might I be?"

She skipped back to the door and peered into the hallway before shutting it. "I have something to show you!" she exclaimed. "I must hurry, because she does not know I have found it. Indeed, I was merely trying to help her unpack her portmanteau. She does accept so little help, I believe—"

Harry waved his hand at her. "What is it, Tess?"

She handed him a rolled up paper. "Marriage papers. She is married to him!"

Harry unrolled the paper and read carefully. "My God." He released its end so that it curled again. "This I did not expect."

"Nor I," admitted his wife. "Although, one could tell there was a past between them. If you could see how they look at each other. I declare, I was suspicious from the first. I mean, why would she come to him, and so close to her time? Why allow any man near you, except—well, you do see what I mean."

"Indeed," agreed Harry. "Gray gave me no inkling of this turn of events. It makes some sense now, I believe."

Tess unraveled the papers again. "This is his signature, is it not?"

Harry pulled out the bank draft from the envelope in his pocket and compared the signatures. "It appears to be."

"I would wager this is her real name. *Margaret Delaney.*" Tess pointed to it. "Maggie Smith is a false name, I think."

Harry gave her a fond smile. "Do you?"

"I do." She nodded seriously. "What are we to do?"

"This does change things, does it not, Tess?" Harry pondered.

"It does," his wife agreed. She stared at the paper again. "She is married to him."

Harry stood up and began pacing. Tess rolled up the papers again. The marriage papers. Harry had not conceived that Gray had actually married the girl. He did not seem so generous now. He ought to have acknowledged her as his wife and settled her comfortably.

That was badly done of him. Dishonorable. If Gray were still present he would give him a well-deserved tongue-lashing.

Harry tapped his lips with his fingers as he paced.

"Say something, Harry," his wife cried. "What must we do? I think I should tell Maggie we know her secret, but if I do, she will know I've rummaged through her possessions. She would not like it, would she?" She began pacing as well.

The two of them crisscrossed the room like skaters on a pond.

Harry stopped. "I have it, Tess!"

"Have what, dear? I thought we were seeking a solution to this dilemma." Tess looked puzzled.

"But I have the solution!" Harry marched over to her and grabbed her hands, bringing them to his lips.

Tess smiled and blushed as prettily as if she were still the ingénue he'd fallen in love with years ago.

"I believe that we must undo the wrong Gray has done," Harry began. "It is our obligation."

"I am sure it is," Tess said, adoration in her eyes. "But how?"

Harry was certain he looked as wise as he felt. "Where should a soldier's wife reside while she waits for his return?"

"Well, my former schoolmate, Horatia Bromley—do you recall her, Harry? She had a large nose, but otherwise was perfectly amiable—she married a military man, who is now a colonel, I believe." She placed a finger on her cheek and tilted her head. "Or is it a general? I cannot recall. Anyway, when he went to the colonies, she remained at the family estate, his father and mother still lived, you see, and she stayed with them, even though her husband was the younger son, not the heir at all. He was a shocking man. Spent most of his time in those gambling places, I think. What do you call them, dear?"

"Gaming hells." Harry smiled at her. "And you have the right of it, my love. We shall take Maggie and the child to where they belong. When Gray returns, he will have to seek her there and that will bring him back to where he belongs as well."

Tess blinked up at him. "Where, dearest?"

Harry squeezed her hands. "We will take Gray's wife and child to the place and people Gray has neglected these many years. To Summerton Hall. To his father."

Chapter FOUR

The traveling carriage, in spite of its well-sprung design, weaved and bumped its way down roads roughened by recent rains. Maggie braced herself against the red velvet upholstery, arms weary from tightly clutching the baby to keep him from lurching out of her grasp. At one month of age he was still so tiny, much too young and fragile for such a journey.

When the baron and baroness desired to quit London for the summer, Maggie had no choice but to accompany them. She had no other place to go. Indeed, she was fortunate they cared enough to invite her. Both had been so kind. What would she and her baby have done without their help?

She shivered, though the bright sunshine of the countryside kept the interior of the carriage comfortably warm. Lady Caufield dozed. Her mouth opened slightly as she snuggled herself in the opposite corner of the carriage, crushing the willow-green satin ribbons and violet silk flowers of her straw bonnet. The sun filtering through the window bathed her face with a soft light, making her appear as peaceful and innocent as the sleeping baby. Maggie smiled in spite of her discomfort. There was nothing peaceful about Lady Caufield, whose incessant chatter, good-natured as it was, fatigued Maggie almost more than the bouncing and swaying of the carriage.

Maggie gave her knuckles a mental rap, all she could manage at present with arms full. Such unkind thoughts, however fleeting, were undeserved. All these dear people had done was help. In fact, yesterday and today, the baroness had held the baby nearly as long as she. Thank goodness he was asleep as well. If not for the aching of her arms, Maggie might have savored the momentary calm.

Instead, her nose wrinkled. Wafting up from the basket at her feet came the sour scent of soiled nappies. No wonder Lord Caufield had chosen to ride, rather than share the dubious comforts of the carriage. After two days cooped up in it, Maggie envied him.

She leaned toward the window, trying to fill her lungs with fresh country air. It was glorious to be in the country again, with its clover-filled hills all white and pink with flower.

Maggie was grateful that the baron's lands were in the east country, far from Gloucestershire, where she would always fear encountering someone she knew. It was much safer to be Maggie Smith, rather than the pregnant Maggie Delaney, sent away at the same time the young officer was drowned. At least that was how she imagined it. After she left, his body would have been found all white and bloated as . . . as . . .

Tears suddenly blurred the green hills and their dottings of flowers.

The swollen, disfigured bodies of her mother, father,

and seven-year-old brother, their dear, familiar features made grotesque by the ravages of the Severn River, swam before her eyes.

Her father, the impoverished third son of an Irish landowner, had struggled to provide for his wife and children. He'd been enthusiastic about his new post as schoolmaster. Maggie's high-born mother, banished from her family when she married Sean Delaney, had joyfully accepted the role of a schoolmaster's wife. Maggie, at nine years old, had merely been grateful for the house provided for them. On that fateful day she'd chosen to remain in the tiny house rather than join her father, mother, and brother on an excursion to Gloucester Cathedral.

A sudden storm capsized their boat and swept them under the cold gray water of the Severn River, the same river that had taken the man she'd thought was her husband.

The carriage jerked and tilted, jolting Maggie back to the present. She blinked her tears away and sniffed as quietly as she could. The baby wiggled in her tired arms, and she feared for a moment she'd awakened him. His little face puckered and reddened, but with a reflexive movement of his mouth, he settled back into sleep.

She'd named him Sean, after her father. Lord and Lady Caufield had raised their eyebrows in unison when she'd announced her choice of a name. Maggie supposed the Irishness of it gave them pause. She could always say the baby's father had been Irish. She could say anything she liked about the baby's father. Anything would be preferable to the truth.

She stared into little Sean's tiny face, eyelids fringed with feathery black lashes, a nose no bigger than a button, but lips as perfectly shaped as an adult's. He was her family now, and through him flowed the blood of her mother, father, and brother. His father's blood also flowed through him. Perhaps that would make up for his father's loss of life, too.

Maggie could not precisely remember what her false husband looked like. His image was fading from her memory. She could easily recall the dark hair, full lips, and steely gray eyes of Captain Grayson, however.

Lord Caufield rode up to her window. "We'll be changing horses soon. There's a posting inn up the road. Is Tess sleeping?"

"Yes," answered Maggie. "Both she and the babe."

His face softened. "She always sleeps in the carriage. I suppose you'd better wake her." He trotted off.

By the time they'd reached the inn, Maggie had woken Lady Caufield and helped her straighten her bonnet. Little Sean was in full wail, and their descent from the carriage was accompanied by Lady Caufield calling orders to whoever would listen. The innkeeper hurried them into a private parlor, no doubt to protect the other patrons from the assault of a baby crying with a lung power truly remarkable in such a tiny body. Lord Caufield quickly excused himself, ostensibly to procure them some refreshment, but Maggie suspected it was to avoid the noise and allow her the privacy to nurse. As she'd learned that day in the parlor with Captain Grayson, her breasts ached when the baby cried. She could never tell when the milk might flow unbidden, embarrassing her once more.

Putting the baby to her breast, she remembered the stunned look on the captain's face when he saw her dress stained with milk. It was the last she'd seen of him.

No, not the last. He'd stood outside the townhouse when she came to the window, holding the baby. He'd stood a long time.

Little Sean was more fussy than hungry, but his little stomach won the war with his need for protest. Maggie held him against her shoulder after nursing him until he emitted a satisfying burp, another sound unexpectedly loud for such a little creature. Maggie placed him in the small cradle Lady Caufield had bought for him. She held her breath lest he wake, and tried to quiet the queasiness in her stomach left over from the constant motion of the carriage.

Soon a serving girl carried in food and drink. Lord Caufield peered in cautiously. Seeing the baby was no longer at her breast, he entered.

"Harry, darling." His wife raised her hand to her husband as if she'd not seen him in an age. "I declare, I must have slept the whole morning. Did I miss much of the countryside?"

He leaned down and kissed her hand soundly. "No sights you've not slept through before, love," he replied, regarding her fondly. He turned to Maggie. "How have you fared, my dear?"

"Not too ill when the baby slept." Maggie's voice came out sharper than she'd intended and she bit her lip. She did not wish him to think she complained.

"He's a lusty little lad, that is sure." Lord Caufield sank into a chair next to his wife. "This is the last leg of our journey. We shall arrive in less than two hours."

The serving girl placed the dishes on the table and, with a curtsy, left the room. Maggie's companions, always loquacious beyond measure, lapsed into a tense silence.

"I am curious to see Caufield House," Maggie said with a try at polite conversation. "I imagine it is a lovely place."

"Oh, it is," exclaimed Lady Caufield a little too brightly. "It is indeed lovely."

The silence descended again, and Lord Caufield busied himself buttering a biscuit. His expression was uncharacteristically stern. Lady Caufield quickly dipped her head and poured a pitcher of cream over a dish of raspberries. Maggie gaped at them from across the table.

Lord Caufield lifted his knife, butter still clinging to it. He pointed it toward Maggie and opened his mouth as if to speak. He shut it again, sighed heavily, and placed the knife crosswise on his plate.

"We are not arriving at Caufield House today." He spoke with slow deliberation, as if imparting important news to a very slow child. "Caufield House is another day's journey."

"I see," said Maggie, though she did not at all see why this information should be accompanied by so serious a face. "Where is it we are bound, then?"

Lady Caufield choked on a sip of lemonade. She sputtered and coughed. Her husband patted her back, fussing and cooing over her. Maggie grasped her hands tightly in her lap, waiting somewhat impatiently for his solicitude to run its course.

His wife restored, Lord Caufield folded his hands and rested them on the table's edge. He turned his attention back to Maggie. "We are bound for Summerton Hall."

This meant nothing to her. "Summerton Hall?"

"Summerton Hall," echoed Lady Caufield.

Maggie stared at them without comprehension.

"Gray's home," Lady Caufield said.

The captain? It might prove embarrassing to visit his home, that was sure. Had he family there? she wondered. A wife, perhaps? That thought unexpectedly disturbed her.

Lord and Lady Caufield both regarded her expectantly. She looked from one to the other.

Finally Lord Caufield leaned toward her. "We realize it was not well done of us to conceal this from you, my dear, but we thought it for the best."

Maggie still failed to comprehend their concern. "I assure you, sir, I would not protest wherever you wish to visit. I am too indebted to you for your kindness. Whatever would I do if you had not invited me into your home?"

Lady Caufield made a high-pitched sound.

Her husband clasped and unclasped his hands. "That is just the thing, my dear. We are not taking you to Caufield House. We are taking you to Summerton Hall."

"But, why?" Maggie blinked in confusion.

Lady Caufield moaned.

Lord Caufield cleared his throat. "Tess and I decided that it would be best if you stayed at Summerton. It is the logical thing, you see."

Maggie spoke carefully. "I fear, sir, that I am unable to comprehend the logic."

Lady Caufield wailed, "It is my doing. I should not have looked in your portmanteau." She reached across the table and grasped Maggie's wrist. "I assure you, I had no idea what I would find and I was only trying to help—"

"She was only trying to help—" interjected her husband.

"What else could we do? We are so fond of Gray and, indeed, have come to love you as well—" she went on.

"—for your own good and his, you see," he added.

"Wait!" Maggie threw up her hands.

The Lord and Lady Caufield went wide-eyed simultaneously.

"Stop." Maggie made her voice less harsh. "Please explain yourselves. What did you find, and why does it matter?"

"Why, the paper saying you are married to Gray," Lady Caufield said.

Maggie felt the blood drain from her face. "But I am not—" she began, but clamped her mouth shut. To disavow marriage to Captain Grayson would require explaining about the man who had used his name. The baron was just the sort who would insist on making inquiries. She suspected Lord Caufield could discover the mystery of her husband's identity, but if he did, no doubt the knowledge would send Maggie straight to the gallows.

Lord Caufield looked at her with a kind expression. "Now you need not tell us why the secrecy, or what the difficulty is between you and Gray. That is none of our concern."

"Unless you'd care to—" began his wife. He put a stilling hand on her arm.

"But," he continued with an indulgent glance toward Tess, "we do believe it best that you live with Gray's family. Of course, if they will not have you, you must come to Caufield House with us, but we think Lord Summerton will thaw when he sees the child, no matter his present feelings toward Gray."

"Which are perfectly conciliatory by now, I am sure," added his wife helpfully.

What kind of coil would encircle her now? Maggie's heart sank so low she was certain she would be unable to stand. "I shall yield to your judgment, of course," she managed.

The baroness smiled happily, and the baron's shoulders visibly relaxed. Baby Sean wailed and Maggie was glad for the distraction. His nappy was soaked, as was his dress and the bedding in the cradle. She grabbed the small cloth bag that contained the baby's things and busied herself changing the linens and the infant.

If going to Summerton Hall was what she must do to care for her son, then that was what she would do.

Four hours later, Maggie stood in the foyer at Summerton Hall, near one of the wooden pillars painted to look like white marble. She'd come down the elegant curved stairway past the mural of classical scenes that gave the illusion of wandering about ancient Greece. She paused, unsure of where to find the parlor, or more accurately, afraid it might be the room from which she heard voices raised in anger.

"Whose maggot-brained idea was it to bring them here?" one man shouted. "Was it his? I'll be damned if he can just send any doxy he fancies to be housed and fed at my expense."

That voice belonged to the Earl of Summerton, Captain Grayson's father. Upon their arrival, she'd met him briefly, before the earl closeted himself with Lord Caufield. The earl might have once been nearly as tall as his son, but now he was stoop-shouldered, with one lame leg.

She heard his walking stick pound sharply on polished wood floors. "I won't have it, I tell you!!"

Lord Caufield's milder voice responded, "Now, Uncle, I told you, *I* am asking this of you. Not Gray. I thought it best."

"You thought it best!" came the older man's retort. "This is my house and I decide what is best. She's no wife, and that baby's naught but a bastard."

"No," Lord Caufield said. "She's his wife, all right. I don't know why . . ."

The voices became muffled. Maggie took a step closer to the door, but still could not hear. Or perhaps she had heard enough. She closed her eyes and leaned her cheek against the column, which was almost as cool as if it had been marble. She hoped the baby would be all right. She'd insisted he be put in the same bedroom as she, not sent down one of the cavernous hallways where an old nursery would have been located. A round-faced, cheerful-looking maid was dispatched to look after him while Maggie attended dinner. She'd made the maid promise to send for her immediately if the baby should cry.

"He has a frightful temper," someone whispered. Maggie's eyes flew open. The earl's daughter-in-law, the young Lady Palmely, stood a foot from her. Had this wraith of a woman been wearing white, Maggie would have thought she was a spirit, but she wore a shapeless gray gown that hung on her thin body.

Maggie glanced at the doorway from which the angry voices persisted. "I shall not stay."

Lady Palmely did not change expression. "You will stay. He will not pass up the opportunity."

"Opportunity?"

The wraith almost smiled. "To punish him through you." Lady Palmely drifted away, almost floating as if she were indeed a spirit. She hovered by a door near the room from where Lord Summerton's and Lord Caufield's voices could be heard. She turned to Maggie. "Come into the parlor. The earl will soon be ready for dinner."

Maggie followed her into the room.

A gentleman with thinning blond hair and dressed in riding boots and wool jacket stood to greet Lady Palmely. Who was he? He'd been among the seeming multitude of people who'd materialized when they first arrived. Most had been servants who quickly scattered in the wake of baby Sean's ill-timed display of temper and the earl's confused orders. She and Lady Caufield had been whisked above stairs by the housekeeper where a battle soon broke out regarding the nursery. Bless Lady Caufield for taking her side, unfashionable though it was. Maggie could barely endure this present separation, let alone the distance a nursery would entail.

The gentleman walked over to her. "Mrs. Grayson, please sit down and be comfortable. I suspect the earl will be along directly."

As if on cue, the earl's voice, raised in a furious roar, carried in through the open windows. Maggie flinched, though she did not know if it was from the earl's anger or the enormity of realizing she was truly parading as Mrs. Grayson.

The gentleman inclined his head toward the sound, taking Maggie's hand. "Pay him no heed, my dear."

This man was like the eye of a storm, a calm place around which wind, rain, and thunder raged. Part of the storm was inside her as well. She raised her gaze to his calm eyes. "I have no wish to upset the earl. I must not stay."

"Nonsense!" the man said, escorting her to a chair next to Lady Palmely, who sat staring absently at hands folded in her lap. "This house has seen a lot of sadness. Perhaps you and your son will cheer it up." He glanced at Lady Palmely briefly before smiling toward Maggie again.

It was a kind thing for him to say. In truth, she'd met with more kindness than trouble since Captain Grayson had opened his door and delivered Sean safely into her arms.

Maggie smiled. "Forgive me, sir. I have forgotten our introduction."

He gave a little laugh. "Well you should. I'm afraid your entrance was a bit more hectic than grand. I am Sir Francis Betton and my place here is in the capacity of old family friend. My property borders Summerton, you see."

Maggie extended her hand and he clasped it. "I am pleased to meet you. I'm sorry if I gave you any slight at first."

"You had your hands full," he added, helpfully. He turned to Lady Palmely, his smile becoming wistful. "Were you formally introduced to Viscountess Palmely?"

The lady in question raised her head at the mention of her name and said, "We met."

"It will be nice for you to have some female company at Summerton, won't it, Olivia?" His voice became even more gentle than before.

"Yes," she said without inflection. "It will."

Maggie longed to ask Sir Francis about this family. He, at least, appeared to be a comfortable companion. The earl had been near apoplexy since she'd been introduced as his son's wife, and the Lady Palmely looked haunted. Maggie regarded her. She had a fragile beauty, blond hair pulled up into a severe knot on top of her head. She was too pale and too thin, and the gray dress did nothing to enhance her appearance.

Maggie attempted conversation. "I seem to remember a little boy when we arrived." A pale-faced lad of six or seven, she'd guessed, pulling at the arm of a nanny. "Is that your son?"

"It is," the wraith responded.

Usually mothers loved to talk about their children, but Lady Palmely said no more. Maggie tried again to engage her.

"Will . . . will your husband be joining us for dinner?" she asked.

Lady Palmely's eyes filled with tears, and she turned her head, hiding her face with one hand.

"The viscount died of the fever," Sir Francis said in a quiet voice. "You didn't know?"

Maggie felt stricken. It explained Lady Palmely's gray dress. Half-mourning. "No, I am so sorry, madam. I did not know."

"Gray did not mention it?" Sir Francis's eyebrows lifted.

Maggie felt her cheeks flush. "No."

How would she know anything of Captain Grayson's family? It was folly to suppose she could succeed at this masquerade. Already her ignorance had caused poor Lady Palmely distress.

Sir Francis bestowed a sympathetic look on Lady Palmely, who dabbed at her eyes with a lace-edged handkerchief. "It happened a little over six years ago, before Gray left for Spain."

Six years ago? And his wife still wore gray and looked as if she were mourning a loss of a few days? What sort of people were these?

Lady Caufield entered at that moment. "Ah, here you all are. Well, not all of you. Harry and the earl are not here yet. I suppose they will be coming along soon. I hope anyway. They say women talk too much, but, I declare, men do go on and on."

Again the earl's voice penetrated into the room. The phrase "that damned fool" was clearly audible.

Lady Caufield remained undaunted. "See? What nonsense. I'm sure dinner is waiting." She fluttered over to the window as if that would somehow make her husband and his uncle cease their argument and restore enough harmony for the meal to commence.

"I'm sure Lord Summerton will be about soon," said Sir Francis. "He likes a prompt meal."

Sure enough, the earl stalked into the parlor a few minutes later, followed by his nephew. Once in the room, he stood with one fisted hand pressed against his hip and the other clasping his ebony cane so tightly his knuckles were white. He glared at Maggie. She'd done nothing to deserve this man's wrath. Or, at least, nothing he knew about. Nevertheless, she refused to cower. She lifted her chin and met his eyes, not gray like his son's, but an unfriendly pale brown.

"Parker knows we are ready for dinner. No need for him to announce it."

Lady Palmely rose and took the old man's arm, the baron and baroness came next, then Maggie escorted by Sir Francis.

The dining room was dominated by a long mahogany table with chairs enough to seat twelve. The six place settings were all at one end. The party slowed as the earl hobbled to the head of the table past the long sideboard of the same dark wood.

When he reached his chair he pointed a bony finger at Maggie. "You girl, you sit here." He pounded the place next to him.

Maggie did as she was told. Harry Caufield took the chair opposite her, avoiding her eye.

The food was placed on the table, *à la français.* Lord Summerton gestured to Maggie to serve the soup from the tureen sitting in front of him.

Before she'd had time to pass bowls to the others, the earl dipped his spoon into his soup. After one noisy slurp he banged the spoon against his bowl. "Parker, this soup is too hot."

The butler stood in the corner of the room, his face expressionless. "My apologies, your lordship."

"Well, don't stand there, man," the earl barked at the butler. "Leave us."

Parker bowed and left the room.

Lord Summerton ate with single-minded absorption. Lady Palmely picked at her food. Lord Caufield's thoughts seemed miles away. Only Sir Francis and Lady Caufield made stabs at conversation. Maggie felt a searing anger. Irrational, because she was certainly not blameless in this charade, but Lord Summerton's patent rejection of her and her son enraged her. Why should he dislike her so? He could not know her, except as his son's wife. Was that enough to despise her?

His lordship cleaned his plate, wiped his fingers on the tablecloth, and leaned back in his chair. He peered at Maggie through slitted eyes.

"Were you increasing? Was that it? Was that why that scapegrace son of mine married you?"

Maggie felt her cheeks grow hot. Educated with society's daughters and living on its fringe as a ladies companion, she'd never heard such a question addressed during a meal. Lewd remarks were confined to hallways and gardens when one was unaccompanied and unfortunate enough to encounter a man looking for sport. Her birth was respectable, though her station in life was not, and she refused to think herself as undeserving of good manners. Indeed, no woman, no matter what her birth, should suffer such treatment.

She lifted her chin. "You insult me, sir. And your son."

The earl glared at her. "You do not deny it, I see."

Maggie took a breath and held it. She ought to remain silent. Meekness and passivity were demanded of her as a companion. She'd thought those traits worthy of a wife as well, but where had they gotten her? Had she not waited so long for her husband to come see her, had she informed his superior officer, his duplicity might have been exposed and he'd have been forced to marry her legitimately.

Somehow that did not seem any more desirable an outcome than this.

"Ha, ha!" Lord Summerton added triumphantly.

She could not leave the impression that his son had misused her. Surely Captain Grayson did not deserve that. Her knowledge of him was limited to their two strange encounters. The first time, he'd looked like a man who could do more than deflower a maiden, but that was also the day he'd safely delivered her baby. She owed the captain everything.

"I do deny it." Let meekness fly, she figured. "You, sir, owe me and your son an apology for your uncivil words."

"Hmmph!" The older man tapped his fingers on the edge of the table, a gesture oddly reminiscent of his son. "I'll not apologize to that rascal, that disgraceful reprobate."

"I will thank you not to speak of him in that manner, my lord." Maggie kept her voice even. She'd defend the captain in his absence. It was the least she could do.

The elderly man's eyes bulged and his lips, wrinkled and thin, twitched into something resembling a smile. "I will say whatever I wish about him. He is a dishonor to his family. The worst of men."

Lord Caufield said, "See here, sir—"

The earl silenced his nephew with a flick of his hand. Maggie glanced at the others at the table. Lady Caufield was pale. Lady Palmely, abstracted as if she'd heard nothing. She could not see Sir Francis at her elbow, but felt his body stiffen.

The earl whipped back to Maggie. "My son thinks of nothing but his own pleasure." His lips pursed. "Why is he not here with you? Did he abandon you, too?"

Maggie gaped at him. She would never stay in this house, with this appalling man. She had no idea what transpired between father and son for him to speak this way, but it was unthinkable to do so in front of the woman who was supposed to be his wife.

"Sir." Her voice remained low and barely above a whisper. "Your son left because he was ordered back to war. He put me in the care of his cousin; therefore, it cannot be said he abandoned me."

Gracious, she was sounding like a wife, though she'd been careful not to say anything that was not strictly true. It was what she avoided speaking of that was reprehensible. The captain, however, was blameless in all of this. He knew nothing of her shameful misuse of him.

"Bah," the earl went on. "The fool will probably get himself killed, but that would be no great loss to me."

Maggie's jaw dropped. To lose a member of one's family was the worst pain in creation. How could this man say such a thing? She was prepared to do anything for her son. Lie. Cheat. Steal, if it came to that. Anything to keep him alive. She was willing to dupe this family and make use of their home, food, and status to keep her baby safe until she could contrive a more honest life. She would not lose Sean like she'd lost everyone else.

She stood. "I am appalled at you, sir. He is your *son*." Her voice rose. "I would risk all for my son. I would bleed if he bled. If I lost him I would lose all. Do you have so many sons that you can afford to lose this one?"

She heard a collective gasp from the others and saw that tears rolled down Lady Palmely's face. Oh, dear, she ought not to have referred to losing sons. She'd not meant to hurt that poor woman. Lord Summerton's lips became even thinner. He stared at his empty plate.

The tableau was reflected in a gilt-edged mirror that hung on the far wall. As Maggie walked out of the room the reflection resembled a somber family portrait, one that she was leaving. She hurried to the curved stairway, and ran past the Grecian temples and gardens to seek solace in holding her son. As she neared the room she heard him cry, calling her to his side.

As evening descended Maggie held her baby, rocking slowly to and fro in the rocking chair someone had been thoughtful enough to provide. She gazed out the window onto the gardens below, where the waning rose-colored sunset made the blossoms glow.

The grounds of Summerton were as beautiful as the house, as grand a residence as she'd ever seen. Still, all seemed in repose, lacking whatever spark brought a place to life. Had Lord Summerton sucked all the life out of the house and grounds, even out of his daughter-in-law? Maggie had no wish to suffer the same fate.

She let her gaze wander over the pathways of the garden, let herself imagine strolling there, pulling a stray weed, cutting flowers for the hall table. Flowers were absent in the rooms of Summerton Hall, perhaps one of the reasons it seemed a dead place. Beautiful, but unloved.

The door to the room swung open and closed as swiftly. The little boy Maggie had seen when she arrived, Lady Palmely's son, rushed in, skidding to a halt when he saw her sitting by the window. From the hallway, a high-pitched voice called, "Master Rodney? Master Rodney?"

The boy stood stock-still, staring at Maggie with wide, wary eyes.

"Are you hiding?" She gave him a friendly smile.

He nodded, but did not return her smile.

"Why?" she asked.

"I do not want to go to bed," he replied, his expression still solemn. Do not any of these Graysons smile?

A memory of the captain's smile struck her, rakish, ironic, but like the others of his family, not happy.

Someone knocked on her door. The little boy clapped his hand over his mouth. Before Maggie could speak, he bolted to the door that connected the room with another bedchamber, opened it, and disappeared.

There was another knock. Expecting the nanny, Maggie said, "Come in."

Lord Summerton entered, shuffling with his cane.

Maggie's arms tensed and the baby stirred in response. Her heart accelerated.

"I found you." He leaned on his cane with both his hands. His tone was nearly as hostile as at dinner.

Maggie did not answer him, but raised one eyebrow.

"You will stay here," he growled.

Was that a demand, or a question? She could not tell.

Maggie rocked and the baby settled against her chest again. "I cannot ascertain, sir, if you wish me to stay or to leave."

He blinked in surprise, almost losing his grip on the cane. "Didn't you hear me, girl? I said you will stay."

She did not expect this. "You wish me to stay?"

"Of course. Stay. I don't know what ramshackle game my son plays." His voice rose and he pointed the cane at the baby. "Is that his son?"

Maggie glanced down at Sean, sleeping so innocently against her chest. Pretending this was the earl's grandson was a terrible deceit, but if Lord Summerton wanted her here, most likely she'd no longer be welcome in Lord and Lady Caufield's home.

It would be inexcusable to masquerade as the wife of this man's son, wouldn't it? Perhaps she could assist them in some way. If she tried very hard to help them, would that make amends for her deceit?

Very slowly, hardly breathing, she nodded.

Lord Summerton weaved precariously before regaining his balance. "So, you will stay?"

Maggie regarded the elderly man closely. His lips were pursed, but she thought she saw a childlike pleading in those eyes.

With a wave of sympathy for the old gentleman and a pang of conscience all her own, Maggie forced a smile.

"I will stay, sir."

Chapter FIVE

May, 1816

Gray leaned over the railing of the ship and watched the inky blue water rise in peaks, one after the other, like a never-ending parade of ghostly soldiers.

The salt spray of the sea tingled in his nostrils and cooled his cheeks. The sky was cloudless at last. He'd had enough of being cooped up below, puking his guts out while three days of storms buffeted the ship.

Today they finally weighed anchor. The wind filled the sails and the ship sped its way toward England.

This roll of the sea was manageable, and he would keep his last meal down while contemplating his return to England after nearly two years.

Should he not feel joyous? Other men on the ship were at this moment hoisting cups of rum, toasting their imminent return. They would have wives, children, fathers, mothers, brothers, and sisters waiting to welcome them home.

Home.

Home, where Summerton's fields would be fragrant with spring planting. A breeze would rustle through the trees lining the lane winding through the estate. Around a bend in the lane, the house would rise majestically, its white stone glistening in the sunlight.

Gray rubbed his face and made his eyes focus on the white caps formed by the ship cutting through the waves. There would be no family homecoming for him. He would not be welcome at Summerton Hall. His father had made that very clear eight years ago. Eight long, life-altering years.

Gray was no longer the same young man who had first set foot on the shores of Portugal, his head filled with the adventure and glory of the cavalry. He'd had enough of war. Waterloo destroyed any lingering illusions Gray had of glory, its victory spoiled by the memory of waves of dead soldiers, one body after the other, covering the Belgian farmland.

Gray blinked rapidly against the sea air. The army in peacetime was not a prospect to gladly anticipate either. During the brief peace before Napoleon escaped from Elba, Gray had been posted in Ireland, policing the same Irishmen with whom he'd fought side by side in the Peninsula, an abhorrent task. Where else might he be posted? The West Indies? Few escaped death in that fever-ridden place.

No, he had made his decision. He would sell out. He would purchase a small property somewhere and try to build something solid and enduring. Someplace he might call home.

"There you are," a voice said behind him.

Gray turned to see Leonard Lansing advancing upon

him, a crooked smile on his face. Damn the man. The last person he wished to see.

"Lansing," he responded in his most uninviting voice.

Lansing had rejoined the regiment for the glories of Napoleon's final defeat. In the eleven months since that battle, Gray had made a practice of avoiding him. It was difficult to believe Lansing had once been his constant companion and fast friend.

"I had hoped for a chance to speak with you, Gray."

Gray made a noncommittal grunt.

Lansing took a place next to him, resting his forearms on the rail, bending one leg, mimicking Gray's position. If it were not for Lansing's fair hair, they might appear as bookends. He gave Lansing the briefest of glances, and saw the man's boyishly handsome features schooled into an affable expression.

"It will be pleasant to see England again, will it not?" Lansing asked.

It seemed a statement not requiring an answer, which suited Gray very well. He continued to stare out at sea.

"Ah, yes," Lansing went on. "It is time we returned home. The peace is secure. Napoleon won't be escaping from St. Helena."

Lansing spoke as if he had personally vanquished the emperor. Truth to tell, when the 13th charged the French Imperial Guard at Waterloo, Lansing had not been in the fray. Gray learned later he'd suffered a minor injury before the attack and had retreated to the safety of a surgeon's tent, unfit to ride the rest of the day.

When they served together in the Peninsula more than two years ago, Gray had defended Lansing when their fellow officers mumbled about how he always managed to avoid the thick of battle. Gray had chalked it up to his friend's ill luck. That is, until his eyes were opened to Lansing's true character.

"Are you bound for Summerton Hall, then?" Lansing continued, as if his conversation had been welcome.

Gray gave him a sideways glance. "Why do you ask?"

Lansing shrugged. "No reason. I merely supposed you would be visiting your father."

Many a night over the warmth of a campfire, with a bottle passed back and forth between them, Gray had filled Lansing's ear with talk of his difficult relationship with his father, the Earl of Summerton. Lansing well knew of their estrangement.

"You might recall I am banished from there," Gray responded.

Lansing turned, and Gray felt the man's eyes fixed upon him. He suspected they were kindled with interest, an interest he now knew was feigned.

"Still?" Lansing's brows rose. "I would have supposed you reconciled with your father before this."

Gray pushed himself away from the ship's railing. "I fail to see why any of this is your concern."

Lansing let out a low whistle. "I say. I perceive some animosity, old fellow. How disappointing when we have been such friends. Have I done something to deserve this? You have avoided my company these past months—"

"And I wish to avoid you still," Gray shot back.

Lansing gave him a crooked smile, the kind that was supposed to charm any potential adversary or any available female. "Why, Gray. You astonish me. Whatever have I done to deserve such anger?"

Gray felt his face grow hot. "What have you done?

What have you not done? I need not mention all the scrapes in which you embroiled me when we were in Portugal and Spain. Those pale in comparison. Think, if you please, of those two Spanish girls you found for us, right before you left for the militia."

Lansing grinned lasciviously. "With great pleasure."

Gray glared at him. "You knew who they were. You knew they were respectable daughters, with an equally respectable aristocratic father. How could you have used them so ill?"

"I'd hardly call them respectable. They were mad for English officers. I merely obliged them." Lansing chuckled. "But what of it? We had a gay night, did we not?"

Gray dug his fingers into the ship's rail. "You failed to inform me of who they were."

Lansing's eyes momentarily flickered with malice. "Well, you failed to ask, old fellow."

The barb stung. Gray had not sought any information about the pretty girls, though he'd recognized their youth and seen their fine clothes. No, he'd not been blameless in that escapade and he—and Lansing—knew it.

Gray spoke through gritted teeth. "Do you wish to know what happened to the unfortunate girl you paired me with?"

Lansing sighed. "I suppose I cannot avoid you telling me."

Gray gave Lansing a piercing stare. "When I returned to Spain, she was with child. There was nothing for it but to marry her." He paused. "She followed me to Orthes and was killed."

Lansing laughed. "What a sorry jest! Well, of course, *you* would assume if she named you the father, it must be so and you must marry her." He smiled patronizingly. "But regard the situation in this manner, old fellow. You slipped the leg-shackle in the end and no harm done. Your luck holds."

Lansing's words were so near to the words spoken in Gray's dream, it was as if the old nightmare had returned to plague him.

Gray grabbed the lapel of Lansing's jacket and brought his face within an inch of Lansing's. "If I spend a moment longer in your presence, I might kill you. Do not approach me again."

Gray released him suddenly, slamming Lansing against the rail with such force the man landed in a heap on the deck. Gray spun away and strode off, eager to put as much distance between him and Lansing as the small ship would allow.

Lansing pulled himself back to his feet, straightened his jacket, and watched Gray round the corner, disappearing behind some barrels lashed to the deck.

He shrugged and leaned against the railing again, gazing out to sea, in much the same position as he'd found Gray.

Well, that had gone badly.

Who could have guessed one night with those Spanish girls would cause so much fuss? They'd been a mere diversion, a refreshing change from seasoned prostitutes or well-used widows. A fitting adieu to that horrid peasant-filled country.

Gray's misguided sense of honor created his problems. There was no reason Gray should have accepted responsibility for the the Spanish girl when the tryst had been her idea at the outset. It was foolish of Gray to assume he'd gotten the girl with child, when she'd probably gone on to bed plenty of other men.

Lansing sighed. That one escapade had thoroughly dashed any hope of renewing Gray's friendship. As an earl's son, Gray would have been useful in giving Lansing an entrée into polite society and its money and influence.

Lansing glanced over his shoulder in the direction Gray had disappeared. He scowled, swallowing the sour taste that rose in his mouth. As an earl's son, Gray was welcomed everywhere, trusted, respected. In the regiment, Gray's men regarded him with respect, obeying him without delay. When women met him, their eyes widened and their smiles grew brighter. All because Gray was a member of the *ton*, the son of a peer.

Lansing had as much aristocratic blood flowing through his veins, though he was not precisely sure which of his mother's titled gentlemen had fathered him. Dorothea Lansing, famed courtesan, would never say. Possibly she did not know. For countless years she'd been all the rage, and several men vied for her favors, paying huge sums for the privilege of sharing her bed.

Ironically, Lansing once fancied it had been the Earl of Summerton, Gray's father, who sired him. He remembered the tall, distinguished earl visiting his mother and condescending to be friendly to her young son. But then his mother explained that she'd not met the earl until after Lansing was born, so he'd been forced to give up that illusion.

Imagine Lansing's surprise when John Grayson, the Earl of Summerton's younger son, turned up in the 13th

Light Dragoons, the same regiment as he. Lansing's mother had twisted some influential arms to get him into the prestigious cavalry regiment, but the earl's son had not met with such difficulty. His commission had been easily procured.

In the officers' mess, all the men immediately took to Gray, while Lansing's presence had been politely tolerated. Until he courted and won Gray's friendship, that is. That had been a stroke of genius on Lansing's part, even if it meant pretending to celebrate while Gray rose easily in esteem and rank.

It had been foolish of Lansing to transfer to the militia, a move designed mainly to preserve his life—a man could be killed in battle, after all. If he'd stayed in the Peninsula with Gray, he might have extricated Gray from the difficulty with the Spanish chit, and then he would not have lost the borrowed esteem of being Gray's friend. Rejoining the regiment for that last ghastly battle had also not worked. Until this day, Gray had pointedly avoided conversation with him.

Well, the devil with Gray. Lansing would find some other way to insinuate himself into society. He'd decided a rich, aristocratic wife would suit him very well.

Lansing laughed into the sea air. Thinking of wives, somewhere in Gloucestershire lived a lady's companion who thought herself married to Captain John Grayson. Was that not a lark?

That trick had afforded Lansing much entertainment. Until she pushed him into the river, the little shrew. Why, he nearly drowned.

His luck had held, as it nearly always did, and he'd

had a nice long recovery at a distant vicarage with a very obliging vicar's daughter to tend to his every need.

He laughed again, the wind blowing the sound back to his ears. His luck would hold this time, as well. He did not need Gray to secure his future. Lansing would triumph, and no trifling earl's son would keep him from it.

After the ship docked at Dover, Gray recovered his horse and rode to London, putting Lansing completely out of his mind. He found a place to stable the horse and took a room at Stephen's Hotel on Bond Street, a cut above the dingy rooms that had satisfied him two years previous.

His first order of business was to visit the regimental offices to take the initial steps to sell out. His next was to go to Scott's to be fitted for proper civilian clothes. He must adapt to being Mr. John Grayson, rather than Captain John Grayson of the 13th Light Dragoons. The loss of that rank and regiment would cause some pangs of regret.

Amazed at how quickly Scott could outfit him, not even a fortnight had passed before Gray approached his cousin's townhouse door, both dreading the obligatory visit and eager to see the familiar faces of Harry and Tess. They would be delighted to see him, he knew. It gratified him that someone would welcome his return to English soil.

He adjusted the cuffs of his new morning coat made of the best blue superfine. The buff pantaloons and salmon waistcoat completing his outfit were, he was assured, the very height of fashion. He might as well be wearing a domino in a masquerade for how foreign the clothes felt.

Would they ever feel a part of him, like his uniform had felt?

His presence was announced to Lord and Lady Caufield. As he stepped into their parlor, his cousin rushed forward.

"Welcome home, Gray." Harry gripped his hand in an enthusiastic handshake.

Tess skipped to his side and hugged him, presenting her cheek for him to kiss. "We are so glad to see you! When did you arrive? Look at you! My how fine you look! So very handsome, is he not, Harry?"

"Indeed, you look splendid, Gray. Come sit. Tell us how you go on. Do your fine clothes signify some change for you?"

Gray smiled at his cousin's attempt to be diplomatic.

"Oh, he's sold out, Harry! That must be it! It is, isn't it, Gray? You have sold out." Tess had no qualms about direct speaking.

"You almost have the right of it, Tess." Gray laughed. "I have set the wheels in motion to sell out. Do I not look like a gentleman farmer? For that is what I aspire to be."

Tess regarded him again, her hands resting on her hips. "No," she said with a serious expression. "You look very much like a town gentleman."

"You must sit, Gray." Harry put an arm around his shoulders and led him to a chair. "Tess, ring for refreshments, if you please. I believe I have some port here somewhere."

Tess summoned the butler standing outside the room. Harry poured two glasses of port, handing one of them to Gray, who took a sip and let the liquid warm his throat the way his cousin's welcome had warmed his heart.

"But, Gray"—Tess perched on the settee near him—"how long have you been in London? You ought to have come to us earlier, you know. Where are you staying? You ought to stay with us. Is that not so, Harry?"

"I'm very comfortable at Stephen's Hotel," Gray protested. "No need to put yourselves out. I'm not in town for long, just until I can line up some property to look at."

Harry swallowed his sip of port. "Shall I have my man of business put out some feelers for you? Land prices have escalated since the end of the war, but then all prices are high at the moment."

"I'd be grateful for that." Gray took a sip of his drink, touched at his cousin's ready offer to help. "I should warn you that my trunk may show up here in a day or so. I directed it here, not knowing precisely where I might be. I hope you do not mind."

"Not at all," his cousin said.

"You will stay to dinner, won't you, Gray?" Tess insisted. "We dine alone tonight and we are quite without plans for the evening."

Their warmth and familiarity were more gratifying than Gray could have believed. What else had the evening to offer him? A card game somewhere? The Demimonde? Neither held more appeal than a comfortable meal shared with members of his family.

"I would be delighted, Tess."

She beamed with pleasure. "I'll just step out to tell Trimble."

Dinner was a comfortable affair, the fowl succulent and the company pleasant. Afterward when Tess left the men to their brandy, Harry and Gray talked at length about farming, the price controls on grain, and the hardship created by the rising cost of bread and abundance of out-of-work soldiers. Gray shared his hopes of finding a small farm, and they debated the advantages of various localities. They carried their conversation into the parlor, where Tess awaited them with tea.

Gray settled into a comfortable chair. With a cheerful fire in the fireplace, the room was spared the evening chill. Tess sat near a branch of candles, attending to some sewing. The lethargy of a full stomach and a surfeit of brandy settled peacefully on Gray. He tried to recall if he'd ever before found such an evening of domesticity anything more than a dead bore. Perhaps he was ready to be settled. Perhaps he ought to stay in London. The Season was in progress, and he could look over the current crop of eligible misses, make a selection of a wife.

His dinner suddenly congealed in his stomach, and his brow became damp with sweat. It was too soon to consider marriage again, he told himself. Much too soon. He'd find land first, a place to call home.

Tess's chatter washed over him, as calming as the drone of bees around a hive, as sweet as the cup of hot tea in his hands. She enthusiastically chronicled events of people whose names he barely recalled, speaking as though they'd been his bosom beaus. She progressed to distant relatives, and boredom descended after all.

"By the way," he interrupted when she took a rare breath, "whatever happened to the young woman with the baby?" Her fate held more interest to him than anyone Tess had mentioned thus far. He hoped to hear her comfortably settled, to know his attempt at recompense had not been in vain. Perhaps Harry would tell him where she resided. It might be polite to call upon the dark-haired beauty himself.

No. He rattled that idea out of his brain with great swiftness. Was he a fool? She'd tried to trap him with her own scheme once, hadn't she? What would stop her from doing so again, if it suited her needs?

It took him a moment to realize neither Harry nor Tess had answered him. He asked, "Did she find the child's father?"

Harry grimaced, and Tess glanced at him in alarm.

Panic rose in his chest. "Good God, Harry, did something happen to her . . . and the child? Did some harm come to them?" His heart pounded against his rib cage. He was loathe to bear another mother and child added to his tally of bitter regrets.

Harry and Tess stared at him.

Ready to propel himself from the chair, he raised his voice. "What the devil happened to them?"

Harry placed a placating hand on his arm. "Calm yourself. We will tell you directly."

Tess bit her lower lip and twisted the cloth she'd been working on in her hands.

"Tell me now," Gray insisted, drumming his fingers, anything but calm.

"She and the child are well," Harry reassured him.

Tess took in a big breath and held it. As panic receded, Gray had the impression he would not much fancy whatever his cousin was about to say.

"We took her to where she rightfully belonged, you see."

"It was for the best," Tess added.

"And where did you take her?" he asked in a strained voice.

Harry rubbed the back of his neck. "To Summerton Hall."

Gray's chin dropped. "Summerton Hall?"

"It was for the best," repeated Tess, vigorously nodding.

"Why the devil—?" He looked from one to the other, trying to make some sense of this.

"I can explain, Gray," Harry said. "The connection between you and Maggie meant—"

"There is no connection." A feeling of dread slowly oozed through him. "Did she tell you there was a connection?"

Tess sprang from her chair and restlessly paced in front of him. "She did not tell us anything. It was my doing." She threw up her hands. "I did not mean to look. Indeed, I meant merely to help her unpack, but once I saw it, what else could I do? Harry agreed I'd done right—"

"Enough roundaboutation." Gray's fingers gripped the mahogany arms of his chair. "*Tell* me."

Harry favored him with an intent expression. "We saw marriage papers."

"Marriage papers?"

"With your name on them," Harry added. "Your signature, too."

Gray shot to his feet, cold fury tensing every limb. "She is passing herself off as my wife?"

"But she is your wife, isn't she?" Tess said in a tiny voice.

"The deuce she is," Gray spat. Marriage papers? Forgeries for certain. That minx had more up her sleeve than he'd thought. What the devil were marriage papers? He thought married people merely signed a parish register.

"No need for foul language." Harry gave him a stern look.

Gray shot back with a lethal glance.

Harry met his eye, lifting his chin. "We do not need to know precisely what happened between the two of you—"

"Unless you wish to tell us," interjected Tess hopefully.

"But now that you are back in England, it is imperative you attend to your wife and your child."

"They are not—" Gray started, but both Harry's and Tess's faces were set. He would never convince them. He rubbed his brow. "Why the devil did you take her to Summerton?"

Harry adopted the self-righteous schoolboy attitude that could always be counted upon to drive Gray mad. "She belonged with family, Gray. Your family. The boy is third in line for the title, after Vincent's son and you. What if you had died in battle? The child would be second in line."

An appalling thought. A bastard child inheriting his father's title. "But he's not—"

Harry held up a hand to silence his protest. "Even more important, it is past time you took care of the matter with your father, you know. He's not getting any younger. You must go to Summerton to settle things with your wife, and while there you may settle things with your father as well. It is the only honorable thing to do."

"Honorable? How much honor is there in meddling in my life? By damn, you've been busy." Gray stood before his cousin, looming over him. "Who the devil gave you the right?"

Harry met his angry gaze calmly. "You charged me with your wife's care, and I did as I saw fit."

Gray's hands clenched into fists. "Your interference is the outside of enough, Cousin. Give me one good reason why I should not beat you to a bloody pulp."

Eyes wide with alarm, Harry's hand flew to his heart. Tess flung her arms around her husband and burst into tears.

He glared at them both, his temper so volatile a single movement from his cousin would touch it off. There was only one way to keep from pounding his fist into his cousin's nose. Gray turned on his heel and strode from the room.

"Mama! Mama! Ball. Ball." The tousle-headed toddler flung his arms wide and jumped up and down in excitement. Maggie picked up the ball and threw it to him, but his chubby arms came together a second too late, and the ball rolled past him on the green grass. His fat legs pumped hard as he ran after it.

"You almost caught it!" Maggie called encouragingly.

Nine-year-old Rodney, Viscount Palmely, sprinted after the little boy and the ball, kicking it away as soon as the boy reached it.

"No. No," protested the child. Rodney scooped up the ball and threw it carefully so that the toddler caught it and squealed with delight.

"Good catch, Sean," Rodney said. He pretended to miss the ball when the boy flung it in his direction, making an exaggerated lunge and sprawling dramatically on the grass.

"Oh, do be careful, Rodney," his mother said, adjusting her bonnet against the bright May sunlight of early afternoon.

Maggie laughed. "Olivia, he is merely pretending."

"I know," Lady Palmely replied in wounded tones. "But he might injure himself all the same."

"Nonsense," said Maggie. "Little boys are the sturdiest of creatures."

She walked over to Lady Palmely and stood watching her tiny two-year-old son as he valiantly tried to keep up with the lively older Rodney. The nine-year-old reminded Maggie of her brother, who'd been a scant two years younger when he died. Rodney was constantly on the move, such a contrast to the withdrawn little boy she'd first spied when arriving at Summerton.

At the moment, the two mothers were giving Rodney's tutor and Sean's governess a much needed respite. The pale, thin young man had, Maggie believed, accompanied the rosy-cheeked young woman on a stroll into town. Maggie smelled romance brewing in that quarter. She smiled inwardly. It had been her idea to relieve the two young people of their duties at the same time, and to insist Olivia come outside in the fresh air of early summer to watch the antics of their two sons.

Olivia clapped her hands in delight when Rodney jumped and caught the ball crazily thrown by little Sean. Though Olivia had carefully shielded her complexion from the sun, her cheeks were flushed pink from the brisk breeze. She looked the picture of health and happiness. Maggie grinned. Olivia had blossomed into a stunningly beautiful young woman, so altered from the hand-wringing wraith she'd been when Maggie first saw her.

Maggie turned in a circle to see all around her, the white stones of the house shimmering in the sunlight, the green park with its curved roadway lined with trees glorious with leaves. Summerton was the most beautiful place in the world, she thought. She soaked up the moment, the clear blue sky, the laughter of the boys, the majesty of the house, and sighed in contentment.

"Oh, look," said Olivia, pointing to the end of the roadway leading up to the house. "There is a rider coming."

Rodney dropped the ball and looked to where his mother pointed. Little Sean did exactly as Rodney did, then ran over to Maggie, jumping up and down. "Horfe! Mama. Horfe!"

"Yes I see," she responded, mildly curious as to who visited. It was probably Sir Francis, who had an uncanny ability to show up whenever Olivia was at loose ends and needed entertaining. But Sir Francis usually drove his curricle, leaving room for a passenger should Olivia fancy an outing.

This man approached alone on horseback, riding at a leisurely pace. He sat well in the saddle, as if he were part of the horse. Someone come to see Lord Summerton? She wondered if she could contrive to be present when the gentleman met with the earl. Lord Summerton would make a mull out of any complicated business, that was for certain. Perhaps she should send for Mr. Murray? Perhaps as estate manager he could discover the man's business and intervene before the old lord embarrassed himself.

"Oh, my," gasped Olivia. "Could it be?" She shaded her eyes with her hand, though the lip of her bonnet did the job more efficiently. "I believe it is! Oh, my. Maggie."

"Who is it?" Maggie asked.

"It's . . . it's . . ." she stammered, then turned to her son. "Rodney! Quick! Run inside and tell your grandfather . . . Oh, and tell Parker, too. Run and tell them your uncle is come."

Rodney squinted at her, cocking his head.

"Hurry," she cried, and he sprinted up the front steps and disappeared behind the big door.

"Who is it?" Maggie asked again.

Sean pulled on her skirts, pointing to the rider. "Horfe, Mama! Horfe!"

Olivia grabbed her shoulders. "Maggie, it is Gray. I'm sure it is Gray." Skirts flying, Olivia ran toward the road to greet him.

Maggie froze. Sean tried to pull her hand to run after Olivia, but she felt turned to stone. She picked him up and held him tightly as the rider came closer and closer. She'd deluded herself into thinking this day would never come. She was supposed to have found employment, a way to support Sean so she could leave here, but life had been so pleasant at Summerton and Sean was still so small.

Sean struggled to free himself from her grasp. He pulled at her bonnet and it fell off, hanging around her neck by its ribbons. Her hair came loose and curly strands blew into her face. She watched as the gentleman dismounted in one fluid motion. He greeted Lady Palmely with a peck on the cheek. A groom ran from the direction of the stables, hurrying to grab the horse's bridle. The man gave the groom directions and spoke a few more words to Olivia.

Maggie clutched her son tighter. Perhaps sensing her tension, Sean ceased his squirming, instead clamping his chubby arms around her neck. The man turned to her, staring for a long tense moment. He left Lady Palmely without a backward glance and advanced toward her. Maggie's heart thundered in her chest.

Never taking his eyes off her, his tall figure advanced, coming so close she could smell the scent of horse about him. Her mouth went dry.

"Madam," he said. His handsome face was as piratical as it had first appeared to her. A beard shadowed his face. His brown riding coat was covered with dust, and his black boots, splattered with mud.

"Captain," she managed in no more than a whisper.

His gray eyes pierced her like steel-bladed knives. "I've come to settle things."

Chapter SIX

Maggie moved as if in a dream, blindly climbing the steps with Captain Grayson and Olivia. She passed through the huge doorway, and heard rather touching greetings from Parker and Mrs. Thomas, the housekeeper. Their pleasure at the exiled son's return was evident, but Maggie remained a silent, detached witness of this important family event.

Her idyll had passed. She was an outsider, an intruder, deceiving them all so that her son might have food to eat and a roof over his head. Her head pounded while the family scene played out in front of her.

"I've already got the maids working on your room, Master John," Mrs. Thomas was saying. "You'll be in the west wing."

"Do you have a man with you?" added Parker, happiness illuminating his normally expressionless face. "Shall I have his lordship's man attend you?"

"I am alone," Grayson said. His eyes glistened with just a touch of moisture, and his mouth quivered almost imperceptibly. "I merely need to wash off the dirt of the road, thank you."

Parker signaled a grinning footman. "Summon Wrigley."

Maggie remained at the foot of the stairs, Sean still wrapped around her neck, while Mrs. Thomas escorted Grayson to his room. Mrs. Thomas would put him in the room adjoining hers. The certainty of that left Maggie with a sick knot in her stomach. He paused on the landing. Over his shoulder, he gave her an icy stare before proceeding up the stairs.

"Who zat, Mama?" Sean asked, his tiny fingers twirling strands of her hair.

She could not reply.

Olivia, who had been standing at her elbow, hugged her tightly and gave Sean's cheek an affectionate pinch. "Why, Sean, sweetest, that is your papa!"

"Papa?" Sean parroted.

Sean knew nothing of papas. Papas were in short supply at Summerton, and Maggie knew how false it would be for Sean to repeat the word. Her head felt light. The colors of the Grecian scene blurred before her eyes.

"Maggie, are you not happy? He has come back to you." Olivia clapped her hands.

Maggie forced herself to breathe, trying to smile reassuringly to Olivia. Olivia was glad for her, misguided though that was. "I hardly know what to think," she managed to reply. *Or what to do. What am I to do?*

She glanced at the now-empty stairway, half tempted to run after him, babbling her explanations, but that cold look of his had frozen her blood. Maggie forced herself to breathe, to calm herself enough to gather her wits before speaking to him.

Miss Miles and Mr. Hendrick entered the hall. "What

is this we hear, Mrs. Grayson? Your husband is come home?"

"The captain has arrived, yes," she said, putting Sean down. At least she'd managed not to lie. Yet.

Sean ran to his governess. "Papa!" He pointed excitedly in the direction of the staircase.

Miss Miles took Sean by the hand. "Yes, your papa has come home. It is exciting. Now, Master Sean, Cook says she has a treat for you in the kitchen."

Mr. Hendrick's gaze followed Miss Miles from the room and only after she and Sean had disappeared did he turn to Maggie and Olivia. "I am in search of our young lord. For his lessons."

At that moment, the tutor's charge emerged from his grandfather's study. "I am here, sir," Rodney said, hurrying to Mr. Hendrick's side. "Aunt Maggie, Grandpapa wishes to see you."

Oh, dear.

Maggie squared her shoulders. "Thank you, Rodney." She pulled off her bonnet and made a vain attempt to smooth her hair before acceding to Lord Summerton's request.

Gray sat on the wooden chair watching Wrigley attack his new riding coat with a brush. When had Wrigley grown so old? Gray remembered him as a tall, stern figure from whom he and Vincent used to hide. Now he looked shrunken, gaunt, and bony. Gray had to resist the impulse to take the brush from his hand and insist he sit in the chair instead.

"It is quite nice to have you back, Master John."

Wrigley's voice was now the thin rasp of an old man. "Shall I unpack your valise for you?"

"Not necessary, Wrigley. I can attend to it. Just make me fit to see my father." If the earl would see him, that is. Lord Summerton might as easily consign his son to the devil.

But it was not really his father he'd come to see.

The woman—he did not feel on sufficient terms with her to use her given name, the only name he knew—had obviously been shaken to see him. Good.

By God, she'd looked like she belonged in this place, playing in the park with the boy, as his mother had played with him. Could the boy be the baby who had dropped into his hands . . . what . . . two years ago? Of course he must be. A beautiful child still.

The mother was beautiful, too, with her skirts molding to her body in the breeze and her dark hair fluttering around her face. Her cheek so smooth he'd had an urge to touch it with his finger to see if it was real.

Such nonsense. Of course, she'd possess an allure of some sort. She'd need some means to fool everyone into believing her. He recalled her blue eyes, wide with alarm, the dark lashes framed by delicately arched brows.

Yes indeed. She had plenty of allure.

Gray pulled at his boot, causing Wrigley to limp over and grab at it himself.

"Thank you, Wrigley," he said, bracing himself for when the boot came loose, convinced the man would fall backward and do himself a serious injury.

Wrigley was made of sterner stuff, however. He removed both boots with ease.

Gray glanced about the room as Wrigley picked up the

boots, ready to magically remove their dust and polish the leather to a mirrored finish. The room was familiar enough, though not etched in his memory. Not like his brother's room, smelling of the hunt after a long day on horseback. Or his mother's, softly hued and filled with satins, like a padded case designed to protect a precious jewel. Not his father's . . . The memories of his father's room were vivid, but not happy. Boot black and baize and his father's narrowed eyes and thinned lips.

He frowned. "Tell me, Wrigley, how do things go on here?"

The old servant paused, the boot brush poised in the air. Was there so much to tell, then? Or, rather, so much to conceal?

He looked at Gray with a surprisingly clear and steady eye. "Your father is not the man he used to be."

The statement was cryptic, but alarming. Wrigley would not have revealed even that much if he'd had no reason for concern.

Gray rose from the chair and paced to the window from which he glimpsed a corner of the gardens and the stables. The stables were as unchanged as the day he'd left. A feeling of nostalgia hit him, but he waved it away.

"And . . . and how does Mrs. Grayson go on?" He could not refer to her as his wife, but "Mrs. Grayson" felt quite as bad.

Wrigley broke into a smile, his teeth looking too big for his mouth. "Oh, famously, Master John. Famously. Don't know what we would do without her."

Before Gray could even formulate a thought regarding this surprising reply, there was a tap on the door.

"Come in," Gray said.

Parker entered. "Your father requests your presence, Master John."

Gray glanced from Parker to Wrigley, who had paused again in his attack on the boot. Both retainers wore carefully bland expressions—with identical lines of concern etched into the corners of their mouths.

He took a breath. "Well. Very good, Parker." He stood, buttoning his waistcoat. "Well."

Gray resisted the urge to rush down the stairs, like the recalcitrant boy he'd once been, in a pucker about keeping Papa waiting. He kept to a deliberate casual pace, though the sound of his newly polished boots on the marble floor beat as loud as an infantry's drum. Perhaps a battle analogy would be more apt than a childhood one.

As he neared his father's study, he heard voices, one distinctly feminine.

"You must be civil, Lord Summerton," the voice insisted. "Do not say anything in haste you may later regret."

His father's booming tenor replied, "I never regret what I say."

Gray stopped outside of the doorway. He'd not seen his father in eight years and had not a moment's regret at his decision to walk out this very door all those years ago. He'd asked his cousin for no news of his father in those years, though, in typical fashion, Harry had communicated what he wished Gray to know. That his father'd had an attack of apoplexy a while back. That he never traveled off the estate and had driven away any old friends who might have visited. Apparently, Francis Betton still called, but Gray suspected that might be in regard to neighborhood business.

What had life been like at Summerton these last years?

Feeling a pang of conscience for having left his sister-in-law and nephew in the oppressive atmosphere he'd escaped, Gray opened the door.

His father sat at the far end of the room, behind the big desk that had not changed a whit since his boyhood. Next to him stood . . . her.

He simply must figure out what to call her. Maggie? Too intimate. But "my wife" or "Mrs. Grayson" fairly burned his tongue.

She distracted him, standing with a hand proprietarily on the back of his father's chair. He forced himself to look upon his father.

He'd shrunk! Surely he'd shrunk, or a larger leather chair had been substituted for the one that had always been there. His father's hair had turned white and so thin Gray could see pink scalp through it, even from this distance. Bony fingers grasped a silver-hilted cane, as if the stick were needed to prop him up even in a chair. Familiar black eyes glared defiantly at his son, but what had happened to his shoulders? They were narrow and curved inward and his neck seemed to jut forth from them rather than hold the once-proud head ramrod-straight.

"Sir." He moved closer without realizing it, standing as if at attention.

"Hmmph," his father sniffed.

Gray kept his eyes slightly averted and waited. Thank God for military training. His vacant gaze unfortunately landed in *her* direction. She bit her lush bottom lip and clutched the back of the chair. She need not worry. He'd fight his battle with her all in good time. First he would reconnoiter. Discover the enemy's strengths and weaknesses, then plan his attack.

"What have you to say for yourself, boy?" His father's voice, while still as angry as ever, had become a pale echo of what it once had been.

Gray let one eyebrow rise as he met his father's gaze. "Sir?"

His father pointed a bony finger at him. "I told you never again to darken my door."

She gasped, hand flying to her mouth.

With effort, Gray maintained military bearing, the kind that allowed an officer to stand tall while an enemy line took aim and fired. Had he expected his father to kill the fatted calf for him? No, that was Harry's fiction.

"Lord Summerton . . ." *Her* voice sounded a warning, like his old nanny might have done catching him in some mischief.

To his surprise, the earl darted a contrite glance her way. "What I meant was," he said, blinking with the effort of forming his words, "to what do we owe the pleasure of your visit?"

The earl looked back at her as if for approval, and she nodded as if granting it. What the devil? Had the woman bamboozled his father as well as Harry?

He pointedly let his gaze rest on her. "I have some business to settle here, sir."

"Business?" His father reverted back to his more familiar character. "Ha! What business have you here? You forfeited all business here when you marched away to play soldier."

"Lord Summerton . . ." she warned again, but this time the old man did not heed her.

"Quiet, girl," he ordered, glaring at Gray. "Another matter, boy. What are you about, going off and leaving your wife?" Gray had the sense his father was more at home with this hostility than his effort at politeness.

The hostility was actually more comfortable for Gray as well. He regarded his father calmly. "What has happened or will happen between this lady and me will certainly be of a private nature, sir."

Gray did not miss the flash of alarm that crossed the lady's face.

His father slapped his palm on the desk. "Everything that happens in this house is my business! I insist you tell me your plans. Tell me this instant!"

"I will not air my private affairs with you, sir," Gray said, keeping his voice steady.

"Ha!" His father half rose in his chair, leaning on his cane to do so. "You foisted her off on me easy enough, didn't you? That makes it my business."

Gray's face grew hot. "Did I foist her off on you, Father? Did I?" He glared at the old man every bit as fiercely as his father glared at him. "By God, I only learned she and the boy were here four days ago."

His father looked bewildered a moment. "Four days ago? She's been here longer . . ." He staggered against the desk, covering his unsteadiness by shooting Gray an angry glance. "What kind of husband are you?" he roared.

"No kind of husband at all," Gray shot back. "No husband at all."

Her jaw dropped, and her hand seemed to experience a slight convulsion. She recovered quickly, however. "Enough of this," she commanded. "Lord Summerton, your son deserves a better welcome. I know you do not mean to be so uncivil."

The old man sank back in his chair and seemed to shrink even smaller. "You know no such thing," he muttered.

Gray regarded her with contempt. He could almost admire the control she wielded over his father, more than Gray had ever managed to have. She'd effectively deflected the earl's rising tirade and blocked Gray's attempt to discuss her presence. He would not underestimate her again.

Lord Summerton waved a dismissive hand. "Leave me now. You tire me."

Gray turned, not quite a military about-face, and walked out of the room. Not until he reached the hallway did he realize she'd followed him.

"Forgive his words, sir," she said in a quiet voice. "He cannot mean what he says."

Gray narrowed his eyes. "I know my father's character, ma'am. Perhaps better than you."

She had the grace to blush. "Yes, but I have known him lately."

He stepped close to her, so close he could inhale the lavender fragrance in her hair. She blinked rapidly and tilted her face to meet his gaze. He leaned closer. A pulse in her neck beat rapidly. Tendrils of her hair tickled his nose as he placed his lips near to her ear. "We have business, you and I, madam."

He felt her shudder. "I await you, sir."

"Later," he whispered. She moved slightly and his lips grazed the tender skin of her ear.

He stepped away from her. Her fingers went to her ear and her pupils were so wide they looked almost black.

She spun on her heel as if to run, but instead straightened her spine and lifted her head and walked away from him as if she were the lady of the manor.

The evening continued with no ease of tension, though Sir Francis had shown up in time for an invitation to dinner. Maggie picked at her food, her appetite lost in the strain of keeping the conversation pleasant and Lord Summerton civil, while trying desperately to figure out how she should go on when Captain Grayson finally confronted her.

His smoke-colored eyes upon her throughout the meal gave no assistance either. She rubbed her finger over the place on her ear his lips had touched, remembering how soft his lips had been and how the scent of him brought back the memory of the day two years ago when he'd placed Sean into her arms.

She had no intention, no intention at all, of ever falling under another man's spell. What a shock to learn that she was vulnerable to the sensation of this man's touch, his scent, his . . . aura. She'd thought she'd been cured of all that when John slipped away into oblivion.

Not John. Her husband, she meant. Her *false* husband.

After the meal, Maggie excused herself to tuck Sean into bed and sing him to sleep with lullabies. His little room had once been a dressing room attached to Maggie's bedchamber. All this time, she'd kept him close to her. Lord Summerton might send his flesh and blood away, but Maggie would move heaven and earth to keep hers by her side where she could protect him.

But how could she protect him now?

Sean was full of chatter, including something about "Papa." Maggie winced when he said the word.

Finally Sean allowed himself to be still for a moment and fell right to sleep. Maggie tiptoed from his room.

The earl, Grayson, and Sir Francis had been left to their brandies. She supposed she could trust Sir Francis to keep the discussion pleasant. Lord Summerton usually behaved himself when Sir Francis was around. She could not help but feel compassion for Captain Grayson whose face stiffened with pain whenever he looked upon his father. Surely Lord Summerton had enough sense left to understand the precious gift of family, no matter what the past had been between him and his son?

She paused on the stairs, anxiety at her situation making her heart pound painfully. The gentlemen emerged from the dining room. Lord Summerton walked next to Sir Francis, his hand on Sir Francis's shoulder, deep in conversation. Grayson lingered behind, walking alone.

"Captain," she said in greeting as he reached the stairway. Not even aware of her presence, Lord Summerton and Sir Francis continued toward the parlor.

Grayson gave her a sardonic smile and waited for her to descend. "I'll soon not be a captain, but it does afford you something to call me, does it not? The difficulty is, what do I call you? Wife?"

She felt herself flush. "No, of course you should not."

He did not offer his arm, but she fell in beside him.

"What shall I call you?" he demanded.

His anger was palpable. Well, tonight she would seek him out, speak to him, demand to know what he planned to do about her deception. Then she would figure out what she must do to provide for her son. No matter what, she would make sure her son was safe.

"Maggie will do," she said finally.

He laughed dryly. "Ah, permission to use your given name. I am honored. And I believe the expectation is that I tell you to call me Gray. Everyone does."

She did not respond, instead quickening her step and entering the parlor ahead of him, her heart beating fast in anticipation of what would eventually transpire between them.

Gray remained in the parlor after the others said their good nights. He ought to have immediately rushed up to Maggie's bedchamber to confront her, but his jumble of emotions caused him to hesitate. She had, after all, been in residence at Summerton for two years, while he had only arrived. He was not quite certain what her place was in this household, though he knew his own to be precarious.

Parker brought him another decanter of brandy, and he tried to contemplate what to say to her. The familiar taste of the brandy assisted in calming the disorder inside him. As he poured yet another glass from the now almost empty bottle, he gazed up at the painting that had hung there nearly his whole life.

It was a family portrait, painted by Romney, one of the most fashionable artists of his time, Gray's father often boasted. Gray had to admit the painter captured the essence of his family.

Gray, two years old, sat upon his mother's lap straining to be released from her grip. He peered at his youthful image. By God, with his dark curls he looked remarkably like Maggie's son. That wouldn't help him convince anyone he wasn't the boy's father.

He took another sip of his drink and regarded the portrait. He and his mother gazed into the distance, while his father and Vincent, the Viscount Palmely, aged ten at the time, stared directly at the artist, as if they were staring right at Gray now, an eerie sensation. His father wore his typically grim expression. Vincent's features, so like his father's, were touched even then with indelible goodness.

Vincent had been the kindest person Gray had ever known. Without effort, he'd had the knack of pleasing their father, while it had been very apparent to Gray, from the time he was out of leading strings, that nothing he would ever do could meet his father's approval. Gray had long ceased even trying.

Gray raised his glass in a toast to his brother, gone almost nine years now. "Father was correct, Vincent," he whispered. "It should have been me, not you."

He drained his glass and pulled himself out of the chair. Staggering slightly, he made his way slowly to the bedchamber. Not the room of his childhood, however, but the one next to his counterfeit wife.

His wife.

He'd watched her throughout the evening, sitting primly on the chair, vigilant of his father, tossing surreptitious glances his way with her liquid blue eyes. At least he'd unnerved her, judging from the rise and fall of her chest. But he ought not to muse upon her chest.

She was a beauty, all right, with her lush figure, pale complexion, and dark tresses. A man could lose himself in the pleasure of her. Gray paused at the doorway of her bedchamber, placing a hand on the wall to steady himself.

He laughed softly, stumbling toward his own door. What a pity she was not a proper wife.

Maggie heard voices and jumped from the bed, rushing to listen at the door. The hour was late, and she'd almost fallen asleep.

She heard Gray's voice. "Go to bed, Wrigley. I'll take care of myself. Been doing it for years."

"Very good, sir," the old retainer said. Poor Wrigley. He must be dead on his feet at this hour. "Good to have you home, sir."

She could not make out what Gray mumbled in reply. The door closed, and Wrigley's arthritic step sounded in the hall. She tiptoed to the door adjoining her room and Gray's, putting her ear to it.

She heard him bump into something, muttering unintelligibly. Squaring her shoulders, she inhaled deeply, tapped on the door, and opened it without waiting to see if he'd tell her to go away.

He stood leaning against the bed, in the process of pulling off his white linen shirt. His coat was on the floor, his waistcoat, flung over a chair. His shoes were halfway between him and the door to the hall.

"What the devil—?" He peered at her through the opening of his shirt, then with a devilish gleam in his eye, pulled it off, revealing a very muscular bare chest.

"I am sorry to intrude," Maggie began, determined not to allow even his dishabille to deter her. "May we speak now?"

He folded his arms across his chest, which only enhanced how wide it was, and crossed his legs at the ankle. The branch of candles nearby cast a glow, making him appear every bit the pirate she'd once thought him. His gaze raked over each part of her, all the parts of her he'd once seen free of clothing. Fully dressed though she was, her hand fluttered to where the low neckline of her gown exposed bare skin.

"Speak," he said.

She took a few more steps into the room. "I waited for us to be alone."

He raised an eyebrow, and she flushed—the room felt very warm to her. Perhaps this fireplace was more efficient than in the other rooms, or maybe the servants had indulged him with a great deal of wood for it.

She forced herself to stand tall and to look him directly in the eye. "Before you take any action about my presence at Summerton, I beg you will let me explain it."

"I shall be all ears." He raked his eyes over her again, making her realize how much more there was to him than ears.

She placed her hands on the back of a chair to steady herself. But also, it felt more secure to have a piece of furniture between her and Gray, who remained on the bed.

"I had little choice." She kept her gaze steady. "After the baby was born there was nowhere else for me to go. Your cousin made the assumption I was your wife and he brought me here. I had no recourse but to stay." She tried to keep her voice strong through to the last word.

He propelled himself away from the bed and sauntered toward her. "And what happened to the money I left with my cousin?"

"Money? I knew of no money." If she'd had money, perhaps she could have found a better way to care for Sean besides engaging in this masquerade.

He shot her a skeptical look. "So you chose instead to pass yourself off as my wife. To deceive my father and everyone else."

She lifted her chin. "No other choice was given to me."

He raised an eyebrow. "Oh? You might have told my father you were not my wife."

"And risk him asking me to leave? What would I have done then? I had an infant son to consider."

He approached the chair, placing his hands on its back next to hers and leaning over its seat so that his face was very close.

"Maggie." He spoke her name so softly the low timbre of his voice sent a shiver up her spine. His eyes were warm on her now. "And did you for one moment . . . consider me?"

She made a small noise in the back of her throat and started to pull away before his hands covered hers, stopping her.

She darted a glance at his face. "You were bound for the war, and it was not long before I learned you had been forbidden to return. Your family was quite reclusive. It seemed safe for me to remain here."

He gave her a half smile. "Perhaps you hoped some French lancer would put a period to my existence." He brought his lips next to her ear as he had done earlier that day. "Wouldn't that have been handy, eh?"

She smelled the brandy on his breath. Was the smoothness of his speech due to drink? Perhaps her visit was very ill-timed.

She tugged her hands from his grasp. "You are mistaken, sir. I never wished you ill." She took a step backward. "My actions have been deceitful, that is true, but everything I have done I have done for my son. You must give me time to devise some other means of seeing to his care."

He advanced on her, slowly, like a cat pursuing a mouse. "Maggie," he murmured. "You think I wish to end our marriage? It has hardly begun."

She continued to retreat. "Do not jest, sir."

He gave her a wounded look. She did not believe it was sincere.

"But I do not jest." He smiled, only one corner of his mouth lifting. "I thought perhaps you came to my room to fulfill your marital duty. You are my wife, are you not?"

Her heels hit the baseboard of the wall. He placed his arms on either side of her, his palms flat against the plaster, trapping her with his body. A frisson of alarm raced up her spine, as well as a throbbing excitement.

"You have not addressed my request." She lifted her chin in an effort of bravado.

A mistake. It put her lips within an inch of his. His lips would taste of brandy, she thought. Smooth and warming.

"I'll make a bargain," he continued in a low, seductive voice. "A trade. Allow me a husband's right, and I will allow you all the time you desire."

Her eyes widened. "You cannot mean this."

She vowed she would to do anything to keep Sean safe, but she could not do this, could she? Bed a man for such a reason?

She'd once bedded a man, thinking herself in love with him, thinking herself bound to him for life. That had all been illusion. At least with Grayson there would be no pretense. It might be a desperate act, but was she not desperate?

Gray's eyes were smoldering in the dimly lit room, and her heart skipped a beat. A wicked smile flashed across his face, and he bent down, touching his lips to hers.

His lips were warm, the taste of brandy on them as heady as the drink itself. His arms encircled her as he deepened the kiss, his tongue plundering the soft interior of her mouth. She felt herself melt against him, felt her body come to life under his skillful hands. Would it be so difficult to grant him his request?

"No." She pushed against his chest. "I cannot. It is not as if I am a proper wife. You know I am not."

"I do not wish for you to be proper." He laughed softly, twisting her words. He bent down to kiss her again.

The door between their rooms opened, revealing a tiny figure.

"Mama?" Sean rubbed his eyes with his fists. He blinked and burst into a big smile.

"Papa!" he cried.

Chapter SEVEN

"P apa?" Gray released her abruptly. "You told this child I was his father?" His head whirled, fogged by brandy.

"No, I wouldn't—" She stepped away from him, her expression a mixture of entreaty and confusion. "Olivia called you his papa, but he does not understand what it means."

The child toddled into the room, pointing. "Papa! Papa!"

"Sean, no." She scooped him into her arms.

"John?" Gray snapped. "By God, do not tell me you named him John?" There would not be a person alive who would believe he had not sired this child.

The boy struggled in her arms. "Not John. *Sean.* After my . . . ." She clamped her mouth shut.

The child quit squirming and popped his thumb in his mouth. He laid his curly head on her shoulder. With one last liquid-eyed look in Gray's direction, she fled the room.

Gray sank down onto the bed. What the devil was he about?

He'd almost taken her to his bed, almost bullied her into it, in fact. Some gentleman he was.

Too damned foxed, that's what he was, and more the

fool for succumbing to long-lashed eyes, rose-colored lips, and curves that begged for a man's hands to explore. What a colossal attack of idiocy. If he did not desire to be a husband, he ought not demand the rights of one. Which is what he had done. He'd damned near made her his wife.

He rubbed his face. Would she have stopped him? Would he have allowed her to stop him? Thank God the child interrupted. He'd be eternally grateful for that twist of luck.

If only his loins didn't still burn for her.

The next day the sun was high in the sky when Gray trod carefully down the stairs. Trying not to jar his aching head any more than necessary, he slunk toward the breakfast room. Even so, each step sounded like a French drum beating the *pas de charges*.

The scent of coffee quickened his pace.

The breakfast sideboard was laid out with rolls and toast, kippers and ham. Olivia sat at the table, along with the young man introduced to him at dinner as his nephew's tutor.

"Good morning, Gray," Olivia said brightly.

He winced, "Morning," he mumbled, nodding politely to the tutor. Mr. Hendrick was it? He filled a plate from the sideboard. The aroma of the kippers nearly made him retch.

"There is coffee, sir," Hendrick said.

"Or chocolate," added Olivia.

Damned if Olivia didn't have a loud voice.

"Good morning, Uncle," a smaller voice said.

Gray turned around and almost dropped his plate. "My God," he breathed. He'd not noticed the boy when entering the room, but there was no mistaking who he was.

"I'm Palmely," the boy said politely. "Rodney. You know, your nephew."

Tears stung Gray's eyes. It was like the parlor painting had come to life. "Yes, yes, I do know you," he said, his headache forgotten for the moment. "You are so like him."

The boy smiled, obviously pleased. "My father, do you mean?"

Gray nodded. "So very like him." He sat opposite his brother's son, still unable to take his eyes from him.

"Do not tax your uncle," Olivia broke in, and Gray's head resumed its cannonade.

"We have lessons, Lord Palmely," Hendrick added.

Gray started at the use of his brother's title. How much more disconcerting could this become? It was already like seeing Vincent return to life.

"Might I not stay a little?" Rodney asked. "I hoped to ask my uncle about the war."

A footman appeared at Gray's elbow with the coffee. He nodded gratefully for the man to pour.

"Do not be tedious, dear one," Olivia said. "I am sure your uncle has no wish to speak of war."

She had the right of it. There was too much horror in the remembering, too much he could not speak of. On the other hand, his nephew was the only one so far who had made more than a polite reference to his soldiering, the cause of his exile so long ago.

He took a sip of his coffee, not bothering to add milk or sugar. He'd done without in Spain and now preferred it plain. "I do not mind," he said. "What might you wish to know?"

Rodney beamed. "Well, I know you were in the 13th. What battle was your finest?"

"Waterloo," Gray responded.

Don't ask more, he silently begged. *I've no wish to speak of all that battle cost. It was the finest merely because it bloody ended the whole affair.*

Rodney nodded, a serious look on his face. "Did you kill many Frogs?"

"Really, Rodney. What kind of question is that?" Olivia broke in, raising her voice to the level of rocket fire. "Why on earth would your uncle wish to kill frogs?"

His nephew shot Gray an amused glance, looking so much like his brother that Gray laughed out loud. Either laugh or cry, not much of a choice, though both would make his head pound. The boy laughed too. The tutor covered his mouth with a handkerchief.

"I fail to see what is so amusing," Olivia sniffed.

"My lady," Hendrick said. " 'Frogs' are Frenchmen."

She colored. "Well, I don't see how I should know that."

"No reason at all." Gray cast her a fond look, before turning his attention to his nephew. "There is no glory in the killing, you know. Surviving the battle is the only thing."

Rodney gave another knowing nod, but he persisted, "Did you kill many, Uncle?"

"My share, Rodney." Gray twisted his napkin into a tight rope. "I killed my share."

Mr. Hendrick then insisted Rodney hurry off to his lessons. Gray poured himself another cup of coffee and forced himself to take a bite of an unbuttered roll. Not from appetite. His appetite fled with memories of war. Or was it being reminded of what he'd left behind to go to war? In any event, food would settle his stomach.

Olivia remained in the room, though she seemed to

have finished eating. Gray suspected she felt obliged to keep him company.

He could still vividly recall the day he'd first seen her, fair and golden-haired, as delicate as a bisque figurine. Vincent had brought her to visit Summerton after their betrothal. Gray had been home from school for the summer, a very impressionable fourteen-year-old. She must have been only a few years older than he, and he'd thought her the most beautiful creature who'd ever graced the earth. He was wildly jealous of his brother, who constantly was in her company, taking her arm, leaning over to share some words with her.

Olivia was still beautiful, Gray thought, observing her over his coffee cup. Not quite the newly bloomed rosebud of her youth, but far from the withering flower she'd been after his brother died. And he had left.

She must have caught him staring, because her hand fluttered nervously to her face.

"Olivia, I am sorry."

She flushed a becoming shade of pink. "For what?"

"For leaving you and Rodney after Vincent died. I thought of myself, I confess, not you."

"Oh," she said with a shy smile. "But it was important for you to fight Napoleon."

He could almost hear himself arguing with his father. It was his duty to his country, he'd claimed. His honor depended upon it. Their arguments had never been quiet ones, and Olivia must have heard many of them. He wondered now if all his lofty words were not merely excuses to escape his father.

"How did you fare after I left?"

Her expression changed, giving him a glimpse of the toll

his brother's loss and his abandonment took on her. "I was, I fear, in the dismals for a long time." She sighed. "I could not shake them off. Vincent was my whole world, you know, and all I had left was Rodney. I daresay I might have done something foolish if it had not been for him."

He'd failed another young mother and hadn't even thought to add her to his tally.

She went on, "I suppose it was Maggie who truly helped."

"Maggie?" He raised his brows.

She smiled. "Oh, yes. I am not certain how she accomplished it, but she raised my spirits." She gave him a pointed look. "I do not know how I would go on without her. She is an exceptional person, Gray."

He could not meet her eye. "Indeed. Exceptional."

Maggie.

Her name was like a splash of cold water dumped over his head. So Olivia was another of the woman's allies? He still had difficulty even thinking her name. "Maggie" caught in his throat, much too intimate for what he felt about her.

Liar, he told himself. *You whispered her name in the dark readily enough last night.*

"Where is the exceptional Maggie this morning?" he asked, eager to change the direction of his thoughts.

"With Lord Summerton, I believe," Olivia replied. "She usually spends time with him at this hour."

Consolidating her forces. Who knew what stories she poured in his father's ear? His lordship would be predisposed to think the worst of his son, of that he could be certain.

By God, he'd confront her sober this very day, before

she finished her work on his father and sister-in-law. He'd be damned if he would wait in line for her, though, cooling his heels outside his father's door until she was at liberty to grant him an interview. He knew very well when he could get her alone.

He stuffed a couple of rolls into his pocket and stood up. "I believe I'll take a look around the estate today, Olivia. Maybe ride into the village."

Olivia's brow furrowed. "I could fetch Maggie for you, if you wish."

"No. I've no need of her."

"Gray?" Olivia asked. "Might . . . might I ask what happened between you and Maggie? To estrange you from each other? I mean, if you do not mind telling me."

He gave her an intent look. "What does *she* say?"

Olivia rolled her eyes in exasperation. "Nothing."

"Perhaps she tells the truth."

Olivia's brow wrinkled at his remark.

"I'll be back in time for dinner," he added before leaving the room.

Maggie strolled behind Sean, who was giddy with the freedom of running and jumping without a hand to hold him fast. Never straying far, he ran back to her often lest the distance between them become too great.

They sang a song as they walked, or to be more accurate, Maggie sang and Sean added the words he knew, unless something more interesting, like a butterfly or a flower or a pebble, caught his interest.

> *"Abroad as I was walking*
> *Down by the river side,*

> *I gazed all around me,*
> *An Irish girl I spied . . ."*

As Maggie sang she swung her basket back and forth in time to the tune. It was heavy with the bread, jam, cheese, and two plucked fowl she was carrying to one of the tenants. The day was fine, with the peacefulness one could only find in the country. Sean was happy, and she could let go of her troubles for a time. It would do no good to worry about her next confrontation with Gray, not when there was such a glorious day to be savored. There might be precious few days left at Summerton.

> *"I wish my love was a red rose,*
> *And in the garden grew,*
> *And I to be the gardener;*
> *To her I would be true . . ."*

"Look, Mama." Sean stopped, his little finger pointing toward the field to their right. "Horfe."

Sure enough a horse and rider approached, cantering toward them. Maggie stopped singing, her hand steadying her bonnet.

Captain Grayson. She recognized him even at this distance. It had taken only one glimpse of his image on horseback to indelibly embed it in her mind. He headed straight for them.

She considered seizing Sean and running as if the devil pursued them, but much good that would do. She could not hope to outrun a horse, especially one ridden by a cavalry officer. Sean hopped up and down.

"Papa's horfe!" He suddenly took off like a shot straight toward the horse.

Maggie dropped her basket and ran after him, her skirts catching in the long grass. She grabbed him just as the rider reined in.

"I would not have run him over, you know." The captain's tone was unfriendly.

"Horfe, Mama. *Horfe.*" Sean struggled so in her arms that it took all her strength to contain him. She could not think about the man who sat so erect on his beautiful black horse.

"Bring him here." Grayson urged his mount closer.

Maggie hesitated, but Sean immediately caught on to what he offered. His little hands reached for Gray.

"I don't eat children, Maggie." Her name rolled off his tongue like sour-tasting berries. "Let him ride with me."

Against all her maternal inclinations and any good sense God had given her, she lifted Sean up into Gray's strong hands. He sat the boy in front of him on the saddle, one arm holding him in place.

"Mama! Mama!" Sean cried with joy. "Horfe."

Grayson nudged the horse into a walk, and Maggie followed them to the path where she'd left her basket. He waited for her while she picked it up.

"Where are you bound?" His gaze bore down at her.

She shaded her face with her hand as she looked up at him on the tall horse. "One of the tenants is near her time. Her husband broke his leg, so they are in some difficulty. I am bringing them food."

"Who is it?"

"Caleb Adams and his wife, Mary."

"Caleb, you say?" The veriest hint of emotion crept in.

"We were boys together. Are they in the old Adams cottage down this lane?"

"Yes."

"I will accompany you. I should like to see Caleb."

She nodded. What else could she do but agree?

He followed a pace or two behind her, which only made her more uneasy. She could not see Sean. Worse, she could feel Gray's eyes upon her.

She had expected to encounter him in the house before she left for her outing, had braced herself for his entrance in the breakfast room, had anticipated him pulling her into some room alone and renewing his shocking proposition.

There was no doubt in her mind that she was as susceptible as ever to a man's seduction. Why, she could even now still feel the heat of Gray's kiss, the reawakening of sensations she'd carefully buried . . . after her false husband's accident.

During the last two years, she had gone over in her mind every moment that had led to the folly of marrying him. Oh, at the time she had told herself theirs was a grand love match, romantic in its haste and secrecy, but in truth she had wanted the marital bed as much as he had. Now she realized the marital bed was *all* he had wanted. She had thought herself so virtuous to insist upon a wedding first, but he had utterly fooled her. He had been false from the start, pretending to be a person he was not. Pretending to be Captain John Grayson.

She glanced back at the real Captain Grayson. His eyes met hers and even from this distance she could feel the wrath in his gaze. She quickly turned away. His anger was more than justified. He had been ill-used indeed, first by her false husband . . . and now by her.

She ought to have anticipated his return. Sir Francis had long ago explained that Lord Summerton had banished the captain from the estate when he had joined the army. The earl favored the eldest son and had no use for the younger, Sir Francis said. The reason had something to do with Gray's mother.

It was no surprise to Maggie the earl had been a difficult father. Even now, after his strokes, he was capable of great cruelty, as he had demonstrated when speaking to his only remaining son the previous day. Perhaps she ought to be grateful the earl had banished Gray. It had given her two years of security for Sean.

She glanced back again at the man riding behind her. Now he had returned. What would happen to her?

Gray kept his eyes on the woman walking so determinedly in front of him. The child's body was warm and soft to hold, but why the devil had he exerted himself for the boy? Why invite himself on her errand? He told himself it was merely to discomfit her. He had not planned to see anyone or in any way involve himself in Summerton life. He was not planning to stay.

A small thatched cottage came into view. It had been Caleb's father's hut, Gray remembered. He urged his horse into a trot, passing Maggie. The small boy playing in the front yard might have been Caleb, if two decades had not passed. The child threw a stick for his mongrel dog to chase, but the dog, pricking up his ears at their approach, ran toward them barking loudly. A man hobbled from behind the house, a crude wooden crutch under his arm. It must be Caleb, no longer the boy he'd played with so long ago, but a grown man waiting for them with a wary stance.

Gray rode up to him, the mongrel running circles around his horse's nervous legs.

"Get the dog, boy!" the man cried.

"Good day to you, Caleb," Gray cried.

Caleb removed his battered straw hat, then broke out in a gap-toothed grin. "Do my eyes deceive me? Is that you, sir?"

Still holding Sean, Gray dismounted. The child wrapped his chubby arms tightly around Gray's neck as Gray approached Caleb.

"You are home?" Caleb exclaimed.

"I arrived yesterday." Gray thrust his hand forward to grasp Caleb's.

"Down!" commanded Sean, and suddenly Maggie appeared at his elbow. He handed the child to her.

"Good day to you, Mrs. Grayson." Caleb nodded to her.

Gray frowned. Of course the tenants would call her Mrs. Grayson. Everyone thought her his wife.

"I've brought you some food, Caleb," Maggie said. "I hope you can use it. I fear we've had a surplus at the house."

Gray glanced at her, grudgingly recognizing the deft way she preserved the dignity of even this lowly tenant.

"Doggie!" cried Sean, trying to pull from his mother's grasp to run after the dog.

"Bob can look after him, ma'am," Caleb said to Maggie. He turned to Gray with a proud expression on his face. "That is my son, Bob." He yelled to his son, "Come here and make a bow to Captain Grayson."

The boy did as his father told him and took Sean's hand, leading him off to pet the dog.

"He's a fine boy, Caleb," Gray said. "The image of you at that age."

Caleb tied Gray's horse to a nearby bush. A woman appeared at the doorway of the cottage, wiping her hands on an apron. She was heavy with child, larger than Maggie had been the day of Sean's birth. In spite of himself he remembered the pain and fear in Maggie's face when he'd opened his door that day and her look of wonder when the baby suckled at her breast.

"Gray—I mean, Captain Grayson, sir. Allow me to present my wife. She used to be Mary Collett. The Colletts worked over on the Bettons' land—"

Gray stepped forward, giving her a big smile. "No, Mary Collett was a skinny little thing in long braids."

Mary blushed and curtsied and seemed hardly to know where to look. "Good day, sir, and . . . and welcome."

Maggie came to her side, showing her the basket. "Look, Mary, we have brought you some food." The two women walked into the house, and Gray heard Maggie asking question after question about Mary's health.

Gray remembered accompanying his mother to this cottage and playing with Caleb in the yard while his mother carried a basket inside. It was like time had not passed.

"Would you like to come in, Captain?" Caleb asked in a sheepish tone. "I'd like to drink to your return."

Gray shook himself back to the present. "Thank you, Caleb. Nothing could please me more."

He crossed the threshold of Caleb's cottage, knowing the interior would look as it had when Caleb's parents had lived in it and their son had been a mere boy.

At Caleb's request, Mary poured both men a tankard of ale. She and Maggie then busied themselves with the contents of the basket. Caleb told Gray of the passing of his parents, the marriages of his sisters, and events in the lives of other Summerton families whom he had not even thought of for almost a decade. While Caleb talked, Gray watched Maggie help Mary stow away the food she had brought, as if they were old friends. It was difficult to reconcile the deceitful woman passing herself off as his wife with this warm, generous one.

After about a half hour, he and Maggie rose to leave. They found Sean outside with Caleb's son, still throwing the stick for the dog. Sean clapped his hands when the dog ran after it and brought it back in his mouth.

Maggie walked over to Sean and reached for his hand. "Come now. Time to go."

Sean snatched his hand away. "Noooooo!" He ran from her. The dog danced around her skirts, barking happily, acting as if it were part of the game to keep her from fetching the child.

"Sean," Gray shouted over the noise. "You may ride with me."

Sean came to an instant halt. He ran happily to where the horse stood nibbling on grass.

Gray picked him up and prepared to mount. Young Bob had extricated Maggie from the dog's enthusiasm. She hurried over.

Gray addressed her with exaggerated politeness. "With your permission, ma'am."

She gave him a gratifyingly exasperated look. "You must not inconvenience yourself, Captain." Her tone was equally as false.

"It is no inconvenience," he responded, still in kind. "Perhaps you would wish to ride as well? I can put you in front of me and you can hold the child." He gave her a wicked grin. "If you mount with me and we squeeze together very tightly, we shall have a jolly ride."

Her expression darkened, and he knew she had caught his bawdy reference. No green girl, this false wife of his.

"I shall walk, thank you," she said haughtily. She glanced over at Caleb and Mary Adams, waiting in the doorway to say good-bye. "Send word to Summerton Hall if you need anything."

As if she were the lady of the manor, Gray thought.

She did not wait but started off on the path at a very brisk walk, the now-empty basket swinging on her arm. With Sean clinging to his neck, Gray mounted. He urged the horse into motion a little too forcefully and the animal jumped ahead, ready to gallop. Gray had to pull him back. The horse turned a full circle until they were at rights again. Sean laughed.

Gray rode close to where Caleb and his wife stood. He extended his hand to Caleb once again. "It was very good to see you," he said. "Good day to you."

Maggie had nearly made it to the turn in the path, but he caught up to her easily.

"Are you sure I cannot convince you to ride?"

She tossed her answer over her shoulder. "I wish to walk."

"Indeed? And do you always get what you want?"

She stopped and put her hands on her hips. When the horse drew alongside of her, she looked up at Gray, her blue eyes suddenly sharp.

"I want nothing but a home for my son." Her voice was low and trembling.

The little boy in his lap cried, "Ride! Ride!"

Gray urged the horse back into a slow sedate walk. Maggie could keep up with him if she wished or she could go to the devil, for all he cared. He had taken a different route when he'd ridden out earlier in the day, but he well knew the path back to the house. Soon Sean's head began to bob with each step of the horse. Finally his little chin hit his chest.

Gray reached the crest of a hill, and he stopped to arrange his little passenger into a more secure position. He glanced out over the sprawling countryside, with the house and the other estate buildings shining in the sunlight, the grounds green and lush.

Maggie caught up to him. "It is beautiful," she said, surveying the scene.

"I had forgotten," he replied in a hushed voice.

They stood in silence as a bird soared and flew circles over the sight as if it too was awed by the beauty of it.

Maggie turned to him. "Do you want me to take Sean now?"

She stood between him and the scene below, making her appear as if she were a part of it. He finally made himself answer her. "He's sleeping."

"I know. I can carry him now."

But Gray realized he did not mind holding the boy who nestled so trustingly against him. He liked what he'd seen of the lad, so quick and bright and full of spirit.

"I will not drop him," Gray said, urging the horse back onto the path.

They walked the rest of the way in silence.

Chapter EIGHT

That night Maggie listened at her bedchamber door for Gray's footsteps in the hall, hoping he was not below stairs consuming as many glasses of brandy as he had the previous night. She had about given up when finally she could hear him walking toward his room. She hurried over to the adjoining door and pressed her ear to the wood.

"Good evening, sir."

That would be Decker, the footman selected to serve Gray. It was a splendid opportunity for the young man to elevate his status in life. Mr. Parker and Wrigley had chosen well, Maggie thought. Decker was industrious and capable of so much more than mere footman duties.

The voices were inaudible, but she could not mistake which was Gray's. She had resolved to confront him, to learn what he planned to do about her, to plead again on her son's behalf.

"Thank you, Decker. That will be all," she heard Gray say, after a very short time.

The fledgling valet replied, "Very good, sir."

The door opened and closed as Decker left. Maggie's

heart quickened its pace as she knocked on the connecting door.

"Come in, Maggie," came the reply.

Gray was seated at the small table where a crystal decanter and two glasses sparkled in the lamplight. He had removed his coat and waistcoat and his white shirt seemed to gleam in the darkened room.

He gestured to the glasses. "See? I expected you."

They had kept a distance from each other the whole evening. When made to address each other, they spoke with exaggerated politeness. There were plenty of barbs underneath, though Maggie suspected Olivia and the earl had missed them. Gray scowled at Maggie when she attended his father, but she could not blame him for resenting his father's attachment to her. Not when his father spoke only uncivil words to him.

As she walked over to the table, Gray poured from the decanter.

"Sit." He gestured to a chair adjacent to his. "Shall I pour you a drink? It is brandy. Not a lady's drink, but a fine taste to acquire."

She hesitated a moment, remembering how the brandy had tasted on his lips, then strode over to the chair. He handed her the glass before she sat, forcing her to take it.

She was none too pleased to take the drink, but dared not show him. Looking directly into his eyes, she lifted the glass to her lips and sipped. The heat of the brandy warmed her chest as she swallowed. She felt her heart settle to its normal speed. She took another sip, perhaps too quickly, leaving a drop of the liquid on her lip. She licked it off.

The captain shifted slightly and squeezed the stem of his glass. His eyes seemed as dark as the night.

"Have you come to fulfill your marital duties?" he asked using the same ironic tone of voice with which he'd addressed her all evening.

She deliberately took another sip of the brandy before she replied, "Do not be vulgar."

He lifted an eyebrow. "I confess, I do not know if that is a refusal or . . ." He leaned over to her. "Or an invitation."

She felt a nervous sound escape her. She fought to recover. "Are you foxed again? Because if you are, I will take my leave. I have no wish to be addressed in such an improper manner."

He gave her a wicked grin. "But I thought we agreed you were an improper wife."

She leveled him a severe look. "May I expect you to be civil? I desire a sensible conversation, with you behaving as a gentleman ought."

She saw his eyes flicker. "I would prefer another sort of intercourse, but it shall be as you wish."

Maggie's cheeks burned. She was losing patience with him. She put the glass to her lips again.

"Let me see." He tapped his fingers on the table. "Shall we start with why you've seen fit to pass yourself off as my wife? Why you came to *my* door in London? Why you have my name on marriage papers?"

"You know of the marriage papers?" Her hand flew to her throat. Yes, of course. Lord and Lady Caufield would have told him.

"Answer my questions, Maggie." He gave a disgusted laugh. "I do not even know if that is your true name."

"It is," she admitted vaguely, trying to think of how to proceed, what to tell him without revealing too much.

She rose and wandered over to the window. The moon was bright, nearly full, casting the landscape below in soft hues. Wind rustled the curtain and she touched it to keep it still.

She turned to face him. "There is not much more I can tell you. I came looking for my husband and I found you instead." Her voice wavered. "Please believe me. I have good reasons why I cannot tell you more."

He stood and advanced toward her. It had been a mistake to leave the table, Maggie realized. There would be no barrier between them. She straightened her spine.

"Yes, the missing husband." He came close. "I had charged my cousin to help you find this missing husband, or should I say the missing father of your child? The money I left for you was to pay for that search as well as see to your care. Do you know what Lord Caufield told me when I called upon him a week ago?"

"How could I know?" she countered bravely.

He glared at her. "He informed me the papers in your possession were signed with my signature. What game are you playing, ma'am?"

She felt the air leave her lungs.

"Answer me," he demanded.

She stared at him, light-headed. "*Your* signature?"

He backed her against the wall like the previous night and put one hand near her throat. "Do not play the innocent with me."

She slid away from his grasp, her heart racing in alarm. "Keep your hands off me!" she cried. "I do not know why it was your signature on the papers. It was none of my doing."

"I do not believe you," he growled.

She faced him again. "I know nothing of your signature on those papers. Or of money you say you gave me. I have no money. I have no position, no family, no friends. I have nothing of my own, but one thing I do know. There is a life that is totally innocent of any of these machinations of which you accuse me. My son's. It is he who will bear the consequences of whatever you do to me."

He flinched almost imperceptibly. "You should have thought of your son before this."

"I did," she cried, glaring at him. "He is the only reason I—" She stopped herself, feeling it was useless to repeat that Sean's welfare had motivated her to engage in this terrible deception. She put her head in her hands.

When she lifted her head again, she stared directly into his face. "Never mind me or my son. If nothing else there is your family to consider—"

His eyes continued to bore into her.

"They will certainly suffer, will they not?" she went on. "What will it be like for them if you send me away?"

"Perhaps my family can weather the scandal." He tried not to sound ineffectual.

Her brow wrinkled. "The scandal?"

She had been thinking of how much they had come to depend upon her, how hard she tried to make their lives easier and happier, her way of paying for a place to pretend to belong.

"I never considered the scandal," she whispered, almost forgetting his presence. "Foolish of me, is it not? Perhaps I did not wish to think of it."

He advanced on her, anger still evident on his face. "What is your solution to this coil, Maggie?"

For the first time, his voice softened on her name, almost as if he were not speaking a curse. Even that tiny scrap of sympathy nearly undid her. She felt the sting of tears in her eyes. She quickly blinked them away.

He returned to the chair, fingering the glass in front of him. "If I expose you as a fraud, you have but to produce those damned papers. Because I know I did not marry you, I am convinced I could eventually prove it, but not before it would become the latest *cause célèbre* and my family's good name would have been raked through the mud."

The earl would not be touched by such a thing, but Olivia, who considered Maggie her friend? Would such exposure send Olivia back to the gloom from which she so recently emerged? Maggie would never forgive herself.

He downed the contents of his glass in one swallow. "Where does that leave us?" he went on. "Do you continue to play my wife?"

Maggie felt a tear slide down her cheek. "I do not know what to do."

She stood there, by the window, feeling the breeze cool her back, feeling her own hopelessness but also his. It gave her a strange sense of connection with him.

He stared at her, and even though she could not see him with the clarity of daylight, she felt the intensity of his gaze. It grabbed her and held her as intimately as he'd held her the previous night, when his kiss aroused such passions inside her. She was aware of each breath he took, of his finger rubbing the edge of his glass, of each beat of his heart.

If she crossed the room to him, would he kiss her again? Would he place his hands upon her body and stroke her until she felt she might go mad with wanting him? If she led him to the bed, would he undress her, lie atop her, drive into her? Would he give her, for one brief moment, that blissful forgetfulness?

With his eyes still upon her, she took one step toward him.

His gaze slipped to the floor, and she stopped.

"I think you had better leave now, Maggie," he said, in an entirely different tone, one low and deep and desolate.

In the silence she heard only the swish of her skirt as she turned and hurried out the door.

The next morning Gray rose early, having twisted the bed linens into knots with his tossing and turning. His all-too-brief interview with Maggie had yielded no solutions, but right before he'd sent her away, he'd been on the verge of more ungentlemanly behavior.

She had been so beautiful, standing in front of the window, with the breeze stirring her skirt and stray locks of her hair. She'd looked vulnerable, as if the breeze would carry her away. He had the strange impulse to fold her in his arms and make love to her. Not seduce her. Make love to her.

He made himself sit up.

She was a temptress unlike any he'd ever seen. Worthy of a Greek myth. No wonder she'd made a conquest of his father and Olivia. She had the power to charm and to make a man forget everything but wanting her.

He yawned and stretched his muscles and looked around him. Bountiful sunshine poured through the same window that had, the night before, cast a moonlit halo around her. Such a day was too good to be wasted. If only he could avoid a possible encounter with his father at breakfast. Or an encounter with Maggie. He had no desire to see anyone, not even the new valet.

No sooner had his feet hit the floor, however, than Decker appeared looking eager to assume his morning duties.

"Riding clothes, Decker," Gray said with a sigh.

Decker would help him on with his clothes, then Gray would escape for a while, like he'd done countless times as a child, like he'd tried to do the previous day. He'd mount his horse and ride wherever his fancy directed him. Maybe if he escaped for a while, he would be able to decide what to do about Maggie.

Decker proceeded with amazing efficiency for his second day at being a valet. Gray was clean-shaven and fully attired in less time than it would have taken him on his own. He was soon striding across the park in the directions of the stable.

He heard someone running after him.

"Uncle! Uncle! Wait!" Rodney, still fastening his jacket, ran to catch up with him.

Gray stopped and waited for the boy to approach.

It was like watching his brother. He could almost hear Vincent's voice calling, instead of Rodney's. He saw the same eager face, the same wind-tossed brown hair. Gray's eyes moistened.

Vincent. The person he'd loved most in the world.

"Are . . . are you . . . riding?" Rodney slid to a halt, nearly careening into him. The boy was out of breath, but obviously dressed for horseback.

It looked like there would be no solitary escape this day.

"Thought I might."

He could have told his nephew he had business to transact, places to go where a boy could not come with him, but Rodney looked up at him with such an earnest and hopeful expression. So very much like Vincent.

Gray gave a melancholy smile. "Would you care to ride with me?"

"Would I!" The boy's face lit up like one of Congreve's rockets.

Gray could not help but laugh. "Perhaps you'd like to see some of the places your father and I used to explore when we were boys."

"Would I!" Rodney repeated.

Gray put his hand on the boy's shoulder and together they headed toward the stables.

The thicket near the pond was now literally abuzz with activity as Maggie walked from its shade back into the sunshine. Ted Murray, the estate manager, was at her side.

"A swarm of bees in June . . . Is worth a silver spoon," the estate manager recited, a grin on his face.

"And why is that, Mr. Murray?"

"They take better to the hive, and bring more honey and make more beeswax. Soon you will have money enough to buy yourself a pretty silver spoon."

She smiled at him.

They could still hear one of the workers banging on a tin tray to keep the bees from escaping the tree branch where they'd settled, an undulating, buzzing, black mass. Three men remained in the thicket to cut away leaves from the branch so they could trap the swarm and carry it to the estate's hives.

Maggie glanced back to all the activity. "I do not believe I have ever seen such a swarm."

"It is good luck," Ted admitted.

From not too far away two figures left the stables, looking very companionable. Maggie's heart skittered. Gray and Rodney.

Early that morning one of the grooms had delivered the message that Rodney accompanied Gray on a morning ride. Now it was nearly midday and they were just returning? They could have gone all the way to Faversham and back. Not many gentlemen would choose to spend so much time in the company of a nine-year-old boy. She tucked that thought away with the ones having to do with him holding Sean on the horse and being so kind to the Adamses.

"Is that Captain Grayson?" Mr. Murray asked. "I've not seen him since his return. This is fine indeed."

Before she was forced to agree that it was indeed fine Gray had returned, Mr. Murray strode quickly toward him.

Maggie watched Gray break into a smile and extend his hand to the manager, clasping the man's arm fondly with his other hand. She could not hear all that was said, but the breeze brought her some of the words.

"By God it is good to see you," she heard Gray say.

Rodney ran up to her. "Mr. Murray said there is a swarm of bees!"

Glad to have the boy to distract her, she pointed. "In the trees over there. Hear the banging?"

Rodney nodded.

"That is to keep the bees from fleeing." As she wished she might do.

His nine-year-old eyes filled with excitement. "May I go watch them, Aunt Maggie? I should like to see the bees."

It was the sort of request Olivia would have refused, terrified her precious son might be stung, but Maggie could never forget how forlorn the child had been when she first arrived at Summerton. Anything that kindled his enthusiasm for life was permissible in her way of thinking.

"Go, but mind what the men say, and do not get too close."

Already on the run, he turned his head and called back, "I will be careful."

Grayson and Mr. Murray walked up to her. The warmth and good tidings with which Gray greeted the estate manager were not her due.

He merely nodded to her. "Do you involve yourself in the beekeeping, Maggie?" he asked in a sarcastic tone.

"Only watching the others work," she replied, determined to sound cheerful.

Mr. Murray spoke up. "Mrs. Grayson and I were going over the books, sir, when young William came running with news of the bees."

Gray's eyebrows rose. "The books, you say?"

Murray nodded. "The estate accounts."

Gray gave Maggie a very suspicious glance.

"She is a great help to me," Mr. Murray assured him. "Checks my tallying."

"I do not recall my father ever allowing anyone but himself and your father to see the books," Gray said.

Maggie did not miss the suspicion in his voice. "It is mere addition and subtraction." She nearly gritted her teeth. "Nothing to signify."

Mr. Murray glanced uneasily from Maggie to Gray. Poor man! What could he know of what really stood between them. "The earl—your father—he . . . he . . . relies upon Mrs. Grayson to help." He rubbed his chin. "Mayhaps you should give the books a look, too, Captain."

Gray gave a dry laugh. "I am the last person my father would trust."

"But—"

Maggie interrupted him. "I am sure the earl would welcome your help now."

Gray glared at her. "*You* are sure." His tone was contemptuous. "I thank you for that, Maggie."

A shout came from the thicket. One of the workers stepped into the clearing and called for Mr. Murray.

"I beg your leave." He bowed his head slightly.

Gray gave a wry smile. "So formal, Ted? Of course. Be off. Perhaps later we may catch up on old times."

Mr. Murray grinned. "I'll lift a tankard or two for your safe return."

Gray again extended his hand for Murray to shake, and with a tip of his hat to Maggie, the man was off.

Gray turned to her with a stormy expression. "You seem to have your fingers in many pies, Maggie."

She felt her temper strained. "And you, sir, reveal too

much in front of your father's employees. It served to make Mr. Murray uncomfortable." She marched off toward the house, not looking back to see if he followed.

She detoured through the formal gardens to give herself a little time to calm down.

If he gave her one snatch of opportunity, she might explain to him how things were at Summerton, why it was she had "fingers in every pie." But he was too ready to believe all evil rested in her.

She heard a feminine giggle.

Through the thick flora she glimpsed Miss Miles sitting quite close to Mr. Hendrick on the wrought-iron bench. They saw her and jumped apart. Mr. Hendrick stood.

Sean came flying down the path, his small legs pumping hard. "Mama! Mama!" he cried, flinging his chubby arms around her legs.

"We . . . we were giving him some sun and exercise," Miss Miles stammered, her cheeks tinged with pink. Hendrick extended his hand to the governess to help her stand.

The sweet gesture made Maggie smile. If these two thought their romance a secret they were sadly out of tune. "It is a lovely day. Too good to be missed," she agreed.

Hendrick gave her a thankful look. "Have you seen any sign of Lord Palmely? I confess, I did not think him to be gone so long."

"He has returned, but is now with Mr. Murray," Maggie replied. "There is a swarm of bees, you see, and he was keen to see them gathered for a hive."

"Ah." He nodded. "A lesson in apiary. That may be the

only lesson we contrive for him this day. I am certain he does not complain."

Sean suddenly freed her legs, nearly causing her a loss of balance. "Papa!" he cried.

Gray hesitated when he saw the little boy advancing on him.

"Sean, stop!" Maggie called to no effect, wincing at Sean calling Gray "Papa." How she wished Sean had never learned the word.

To her surprise, Gray leaned down to welcome Sean's leap into his arms. He swung the boy onto his shoulders and Sean giggled, grabbing on to Gray's hair as to the reins of a horse.

Gray gave Maggie an unfriendly look.

"Good day, Captain," Hendrick said. Miss Miles curtsied.

"Good day." His tone was affable toward them.

Sean leaned down from his perch as best he could to get Gray's attention. "Horfe?" he asked hopefully.

Gray smiled, reminding Maggie how his countenance could sometimes quite take one's breath away.

"Not today, soldier," he said with gentleness.

"Today," Sean demanded.

"Not today," Gray repeated.

"Nooo," cried Sean, and Gray's glance to her was now somewhat beseeching.

"I will take him," Maggie said, reaching for him.

"No, ma'am, I will take him." Miss Miles stepped in front of her. "I shall get him cleaned up for luncheon."

"Nooooo," cried Sean, but he laughed again as Gray made him turn a flip to get down.

Miss Miles took Sean's hand and hurried him off to the kitchens.

Hendrick gazed after her, watching until she disappeared. He turned back to Gray. "It was kind of you to take Lord Palmely for a ride, sir. I am certain it gave him great pleasure."

Gray shrugged. "My nephew is pleasant company. If you are due any credit for that, I commend you."

The young man looked quite pleased with this compliment. It pleased Maggie as well. Convincing Olivia to hire Hendrick, so fresh from university and so thin of experience, had worked out splendidly. Hendrick had quickly proven to be a fine tutor for a fatherless boy, and a fine example as well.

The earl, the only male family member available, barely noticed the children. Besides, the earl was not the sort of man a boy should emulate. Gray, however, would be a different matter. Maggie had seen strength of character in Gray, though she was not currently the recipient of his best behavior.

"Cook will be setting out a cold luncheon soon, Captain," Maggie said.

"Indeed?" He gave a scornful lift of his eyebrow. "Cook has not changed her routine, you inform me."

She felt her cheeks grow hot. She responded with false sweetness. "My apologies, sir. I was never cognizant of Summerton's routines before my arrival."

"Your arrival—" began Gray in a heated tone.

Hendrick broke in, "Well, I suppose I must go see these bees." The tutor smiled. "I wonder if our young lord will wish to leave this nature lesson and recite Latin instead? *That which is not good for the beehive cannot be good for the bees.*" His eyes twinkled. "Marcus Aurelius." He bowed to Maggie and Gray. "We shall not miss luncheon, I promise you."

The tutor walked away, and she was alone with Gray again.

"Are you certain *you* can be spared from capturing the bees?" the captain asked, irony dripping from his words.

He was forming an impression that she meddled in Summerton's affairs. Well, she did involve herself wherever she was needed, but she doubted he could ever be persuaded that she genuinely loved his family and would do anything for them.

She felt her temper bristle. "Sir, perhaps rather than engaging in uncivil comments, you and I should speak plainly to each other."

"Yes." His eyes flashed. "We have not finished, you and I. I await answers to my previous questions and to some new ones."

Answers she dare not give him.

She bit her lip. "Luncheon is approaching. Speaking now will not suit."

He rubbed his face, looking every bit as frustrated as she herself felt. "After luncheon? I am sure you can inform me which room is likely to give us privacy."

A bedchamber, she thought, but dared not give him any reminder of his request for "husbandly rights." Or herself.

"The gallery?" The servants were unlikely to even pass near its door.

"As you wish," he said curtly.

They walked stiffly side by side and entered the house through the door opening to the ballroom, the largest of the rooms on the main floor. Huge allegorical paintings hung on the walls and classical Roman statues stood like sentinels in the alcoves. Royal red velvet chairs lined the walls, separated at symmetrical intervals by gilt and marble tables. The painted ceiling reflected the design on the specially crafted carpet, completing the symmetrical effect so prized by the previous generation. Vases of fresh flowers from the garden gave the room its final polish.

Gray had not had occasion to visit this room since his arrival. His mother might have just stepped out of it, so much was it like when she was alive. He could almost see her, powdered hair piled high on her head, hand held by some gentleman in clothing more colorful than her own. They would be performing the intricate steps of a country dance with other couples, equally as festive, moving from one end of the room to the other.

No one had bothered to fill this room with flowers after his mother died, and no one danced here. Gray glanced back through the glass panes of the doors. No one had so lovingly tended the garden either, come to think of it, but that too had been restored to its former glory.

"This room looks splendid," he said more to himself than to the woman who had stepped in the room before him. Dressed in her pale yellow gown, she looked like another of the room's ornaments.

An awed look came over her face, as if she too had imagined the dancers. "Yes, it is so beautiful. It should always have flowers, I think."

He ignored her dreamy smile or the graceful way she turned around to capture the whole room in her blue eyes.

"*You* think?" he snapped. "Do you tend to the flowers

as well as to the estate books and bees and the devil knows what else?"

Her expression hardened. "Yes, Captain. I do."

Her candor effectively stilled his tongue. For the moment.

They entered the hall, and Gray noticed several vases of flowers adorning the tables there as well. When he'd left Summerton eight years ago, the house had been plunged in grief over his brother's death, but even before Vincent died, even after Olivia came to be the house's mistress, the house had not sparkled with life like it did now. Like it had when his mother lived.

The earl emerged from his study, breaking into a wide smile when he saw Maggie. "Maggie girl!"

He then noticed Gray, standing behind her. His smile vanished. The earl pointed to him. "You," he spat. "Be gone from my house."

Chapter NINE

It should not matter. Gray had long ceased caring about his father's animosity toward him. *It should not matter.*

But his body stiffened and he knew his face filled with color.

Maggie rushed to the earl's side, putting her arm around the old man's back. Making clear her alliances, Gray figured.

"Lord Summerton," she said in soothing tones. "What an unkind thing to say! Cease being so inhospitable toward your son. It is wrong of you."

"I do not want him here," his father replied in his most disagreeable voice. "If he has come to take you away, I will not stand for it."

She gave Gray an agonized glance before turning back to the earl. Forcing a little laugh, she said, "Nonsense!" The earl smiled back at her. "You are not to worry on that score."

Maggie turned to Parker who had been hovering nearby. "Parker, my lord wishes his luncheon, I believe. Is it ready yet?"

Parker gave her an understanding look before addressing the earl. "Not quite, my lord. Shall I pour you a glass of claret while you wait? It shall be ready directly."

"Very good, Parker," the earl said, as if he had ordered the claret himself.

Seeming to forget all about banishing his son for a second time, he followed the butler back into the study, his cane tapping loudly on the marble floor.

Gray watched Maggie release a breath. She glanced at him apologetically. "Perhaps I had better see luncheon hurried along."

Gray watched her rush out of the hall. He remained caught where he was, unable to move. It was not his father's pointed demand that he leave that froze him in place. He expected no more from the earl. No, it was Maggie's behavior that foxed him.

A word from her, whispered in his father's ear, could send Gray packing before the sun hit its high point in the sky. But rather than play upon his father's animosity, she had defended him. She'd mollified his father so he could remain at Summerton.

Gray shook his head and put his hand on the banister. It made no sense.

He went to his bedchamber to change out of his riding clothes. His new valet was there, ready to assist him.

Gray had not wished for a valet. He had not wanted to accept any more of his father's grudging hospitality than was absolutely necessary, but he realized Wrigley would attempt to attend to him and his father's ancient man looked as if he could barely attend to his father.

"Good morning, sir," his new valet said. He had already laid out fresh clothes for Gray.

The young man was pleasant and efficient at least.

Gray asked, "How long have you been in the earl's employ, Decker?" He surmised him to be not more than five years younger than himself.

"About six years, sir. Since I was seventeen." Decker placed the coat upon a chair and reached back to help with Gray's waistcoat. "My uncle arranged it. You might remember him, sir. He was a footman here at Summerton. Timms."

Gray pulled off his shirt himself. "Timms? Of course I remember him! I fear I tried his patience a time or two as a boy. I have not seen him. Is he pensioned off?"

Decker handed him a clean linen shirt. "Passed away, sir. Almost a year ago now." The valet conveyed somewhat more emotion than a gentleman's gentleman ought.

"I am sorry to hear of it. I was fond of him."

The young man shrugged and turned to hang up Gray's riding coat. "I'm grateful to your wife, sir. She made sure his last days were comfortable."

His wife.

Another involvement in Summerton affairs, but Gray could hardly condemn her for this one. It must have been a great kindness. He could all too readily imagine her sitting at the bedside, bathing the footman's face with cool water, speaking to him in the soothing tones with which she had just addressed Gray's father.

"Indeed," Gray managed to respond. "How good of her."

Decker nodded. "I'll not forget it."

Gray delayed his appearance at luncheon until he was certain his father had finished. When he entered the dining room, Maggie was also gone.

Rodney sat with Mr. Hendrick and gave Gray an exuberant greeting. As soon as Gray filled his plate, Rodney began a diverting moment-by-moment description of the capture of the bee swarm and its delivery to the hive.

Rodney completed his story, and Olivia came in, accompanied by Sir Francis, who had taken her for a morning ride in his curricle. Her cheeks were still pink from the fresh air and sunshine. She looked as if she had not a care in the world, almost like the young girl his brother had brought to visit all those years ago.

Rodney greeted his mother warmly, but he did not repeat the tale of the bees, and Mr. Hendrick soon rushed the boy out for some lessons.

After idle conversation with Sir Francis about the running of his estate and neighborhood matters, Gray turned to his sister-in-law. "How do you fare at running this household, Olivia? Is it burdensome for you?"

She darted a look toward Sir Francis and twisted the tablecloth with her fingers. "I confess I was never good at such things. Maggie helps me. Indeed, she does the most of it, though she is kind enough to often ask for my approval."

Sir Francis gave her a fond smile, which she returned gratefully, before glancing back at Gray.

"I see." Maggie, not Olivia, ran the household.

Gray excused himself as soon as was comfortable, and made his way to the gallery. Would she keep him cooling his heels there?

She did not. She was in the gallery cooling her heels for him.

The gallery was a long, narrow room used to display the portraits of Summerton ancestors, huge dark paintings that were too unfashionable to reside in the family living quarters. It also contained the Summerton armory, centuries of swords, shields, axes, and bows, as well as two full suits of armor, standing guard over all the weaponry.

Once when Gray was ten, unknown to his father, he set about trying on one set of armor. Vincent had helped him get into the contraption, but they'd had to summon Parker to help him out of it and return it to its appointed place. Luckily the earl never knew.

Maggie stood at the far end of the room, staring up at the portrait of the first Earl of Summerton resplendent in that same full armor that had almost trapped young Gray.

She turned at his approach, facing him with hands clasped casually in front of her, as if trying to treat this as a companionable visit rather than a skirmish that might ultimately decide the whole contest.

As he neared, she turned back to the portrait. "There is a beehive in this portrait," she said with a tiny laugh in her voice. "Is that not a coincidence on this day? It is in the background. You can barely see it."

"I believe bees signify industry," he replied blandly. "Our ancestor was an industrious fellow, according to family lore."

She gave a wan smile. "I have often gazed upon this painting. Is it not odd that only today, so full of bees, I should take notice of the hive?"

"I find it odd you take such an interest in old paintings."

Maggie frowned. "They are family portraits. I like family portraits."

She stared at him for a moment, then turned away and walked down the gallery away from the painting.

He followed her. "No more delay, Maggie. I want the truth from you. I will hear now why you have embroiled my family in this deception of yours."

She gave him an exasperated look. "I have told you! Your cousin—"

He put up his hand. "Enough of my cousin. There is more to this than you are telling me. I demand to know the whole of it."

She met his eye. "I have told you all I am able to tell."

"Your unwillingness to be candid helps nothing."

"I cannot be more candid."

He stepped closer to her, close enough to touch. "Why?"

Her face filled with color and she stared down at the carpet. When she looked back at him, her eyes were steady and seemed to bore into him. "I cannot tell you."

His breath caught and it took a moment for him to go on. "Your deceit causes the problems between us." He looked at her pointedly. "And the problems for Summerton. Do not deny it."

She did not waver. "I do not deny it. I will not repeat my reason for pretending to be your wife. You know it already."

Her son, she meant.

Gray wished to ignore the thought of that curly-headed, big-eyed child, who so much resembled Maggie. He wished also to ignore her clear blue eyes and the soft dark tendrils caressing her brow and neck. Even as he battled with her, Maggie was a compelling sight.

His senses heightened alarmingly. He felt the blood

rushing through his veins and heard the air filling and leaving his lungs. His vision became so acute he could see the tiny lines of stress around her eyes, the soft vulnerability of her mouth. His hands yearned to stroke her flushed cheek. His loins ached for her.

He snapped his eyes closed and held his breath to break this spell. Several seconds passed before he succeeded. He opened his eyes and glared at her. "You have not only deceived. But you have also insinuated yourself into every matter, event, and personal affair in Summerton. In my view it appears you have quite taken over everything, including my father's business."

Her eyes seemed to blaze. "Can you not guess why I have done so?"

He gave a huff. "I need not guess. I *know*. If you are indispensable to Summerton, you cannot be dislodged from it, not without it falling to pieces around everyone's ears." He gestured toward his ancestor's portrait. "You are like the queen bee, managing everything."

She stepped back. "The worker bee, don't you mean?" She shot him an angry look. "The one who does whatever the others cannot or will not do. And you think I do this so I will not be tossed out?"

He gave a harsh laugh. "Of course I do."

"You are mistaken, Captain." She lifted her chin. "I do not deny that I wish to remain at Summerton. I wish to raise my son here and stay among the people I have come to love—" Her voice cracked at that last word, and it took her a moment to recover. "Summerton is more home to me than anywhere else I have ever been, but none of that is of any consequence."

Was this dramatic recital intended to play on his sympathies? He crossed his arms over his chest. She need not trouble herself.

"Let me tell you why I have been so *industrious* at Summerton—" she continued.

"Please do," he drawled. "I have been waiting this age."

Her eyes flashed. "Your family needed help, and I helped them. It is how I have paid for my shelter and my food and my son's keep. Yes, I have deceived them about who I am. But you were not here to see the people I met two years ago. I have worked diligently to make Summerton a happy place, to bring your sister-in-law out of grief, to give her son some of the attention he so desperately needed, to take care of your father—" She broke off again. "You were not here to see how it was!" she cried, shooting daggers with her eyes.

The daggers found their mark. She nearly drew his blood.

He had not been at Summerton. He left his family when they needed him. *She* had cared for them in his place.

Gray took a step away from the burst of pain inside him. He walked slowly back to the first Earl of Summerton's portrait.

"You wish to stay at Summerton?" he asked, gazing at the beehive in the painting's background.

"I know I cannot." Her voice became very grim. "But I need a way to care for my son, and you are the only person I can ask to help me. Our lives are in your hands."

He turned back to her.

She wore an aching smile. "Our lives are in your hands once again. As they were before."

When she had knocked upon his door. When the baby had been born. What might have happened to them if he had not been there that day? Would she have had her baby in the street? Would either of them have lived?

He shook his head, not wanting to think of this.

She must have mistook the gesture. She walked back to him with defiance in her step. "What is it to be, Gray?"

His head snapped up. She'd called him by name. She'd not done that before.

He put his hands up as a warning not to come closer. He backed away from her and walked the length of the room and back.

There really was only one choice open to him, only one honorable recourse. She knew it as well as he.

"You may remain at Summerton," he said at last, feeling a great weariness come down upon him. "You may remain my wife. I will arrange an allowance for you and for your son, as a husband might do. No one, save you and I, will know you are not truly my wife."

For his family there would be no exposure, no scandal, no disruption of lives. For her and her son there would be safety.

He continued. "I will send a notice to the *Morning Post* announcing that we are married. No one will question it. You will be free to do as you wish, as if you were my wife."

Her face had gone pale.

"I will leave Summerton." Gray put more force into his voice. "I will leave for London on the morrow and I will *never* return."

If he had expected her to show triumph, he was disappointed. She gazed at him with sadness, almost as if she recognized the pain this decision caused him. No marriage of his own. No sons and daughters. No family.

He swung away from her, feeling her sympathy upon him like unwanted fingers. He walked the long length of the gallery and crossed over its threshold. He passed through the hallway with increased speed. By the time he exited the house and passed through the garden he was in a full run toward the stables.

But not even a hell-for-leather ride on horseback would change the course he had chosen.

The porcelain clock in Maggie's bedchamber chimed twice. Two o'clock in the morning, and he had not returned.

He had not returned for dinner. Nor when darkness fell. Nor when all the household retired to bed.

She sat in a chair by the window, looking out.

She feared he would not return at all. She feared he would ride straight on to London.

That would solve all her problems, it was true. But how miserable it was of her to forever deprive him of Summerton, of his family. Or the chance to create one of his own.

She well knew the pain of having no family. What gave her the right to cause such pain?

She had no right. She had only Sean, and he was the sole reason she would allow herself to forever alter a man's life.

She tucked her feet underneath her and wrapped her shawl more tightly around her shoulders, to guard against the chilly air seeping through the windowpane.

What if he had been thrown from that huge horse of his? Perhaps he had been so overwrought that he'd taken careless chances. What if he was lying by the side of the road at this moment, or in a field, or . . . or in a river?

She could not bear this thought.

She scanned the view outside. Nothing stirred but the leaves of the trees rustling when the breeze played with them. In daylight or at night, she loved this view, showing a bit of the garden to her left, the long sloping lawn of the park, the stable and outbuildings in the distance. On a clear day she could even glimpse the thatched roofs of some of the tenants' cottages.

Tears filled her eyes. She would never have to leave Summerton. And all it cost was the happiness of one honorable man.

She swiped at an escaped tear that rolled down her cheek. Blinking rapidly, she tried to rid herself of the others.

Something caught her eye. She leaned forward. A glow in one of the outbuildings, too bright to be a lantern. She stared at it a long time. The glow spread.

Fire!

Maggie vaulted from her chair and ran into the hall. "Parker! Someone! Come quick! Come quick!"

Decker emerged from Gray's room, and she grabbed him. "There is fire in one of the buildings. We must sound the alarm."

Decker sprang into action and rushed down the stairs, shouting for the other servants.

Olivia ran up to her. "What is it, Maggie? What has happened?"

"A fire in one of the buildings!"

Mr. Hendrick and Miss Miles appeared, Rodney behind them. Luckily, Sean had not awoken, and she hoped the earl slept as well.

"What is to be done?" cried Olivia, wringing her hands.

"You see to the earl," Maggie told her. "Keep him calm if he wakes." She turned to Miss Miles. "You stay with Sean in case he wakes and is frightened. The rest of us must help."

"Not Rodney!" Olivia gasped.

"I must, Mother," Rodney asserted himself. "It is my duty. Summerton will be mine someday."

"Let him go," Maggie insisted. "No one will allow him to be put in danger. We must hurry!"

Maggie dressed as quickly as she could, Miss Miles helping her with her laces. She ran down the stairs and out of the house. Lifting her skirts so she could run faster, she crossed the park and hurried toward the burning building—it was one used to store farm equipment. The area was already teeming with people. Tenants, groomsmen, laborers, house servants, all sprang into action. Mr. Murray was shouting instructions to all of them. Several bucket brigades had already formed to save the nearby stables and byre. Men led horses to safer ground. Others drove the livestock away. Flames roared from the windows of the building. Some men ran into the building, pulling out what equipment they could.

Maggie joined one of the lines of women passing empty buckets back to be refilled. In the distance a horse and rider galloped toward them.

Gray! He had returned! But to such a sight.

He dismounted before the horse had even come to a halt, close enough for her to hear him shout for one of the grooms to take the animal. Mr. Murray came up to him, gesturing wildly with his arms, pointing toward the fire.

He and Murray hurried toward the building. Fire raged through the structure, but Gray ran inside.

"No!" Maggie cried, dropping her bucket. He would be engulfed by flames. Overcome by smoke.

She clutched at her chest. The other women did not heed her but filled the gap and kept the buckets moving. A loud crack filled the air and the roof of the building began to collapse. Without thinking Maggie ran toward the fire.

Gray and two other men emerged from the doors of the building pulling out one of the plows. Her legs went weak in relief.

"Get away!" someone yelled. "It's about to go."

With a crack and a roar of flame, the entire roof caved in and the walls tumbled into the fire. Gray staggered backward, like the others, unable to keep his eyes from the sight.

He backed into Maggie, turning in time to grab her and keep them both from falling.

"Gray," she cried, clinging to his coat. "You might have been killed!"

His face captured all the horror of the scene, and it took a moment before she felt he actually saw her. His expression turned fierce. "What are you doing here? Get back to the house. This is no place for you."

A shower of glowing cinders rained down upon them. He dragged her away and frantically brushed the cinders from her hair.

"Go back to the house."

"No. I can help." She pulled away and ran back to the bucket brigade, looking over her shoulder to see him striding back to where Mr. Murray stood directing men to dampen down the nearby stables and coach house. This building was lost, and now all they could do was attempt to save the others.

Gray did not let himself think about Maggie while he worked to save the Summerton buildings. When he had grabbed her, her face had been lit by the raging flames. Cinder had rained on her hair. Where was her hat, for God's sake?

He climbed up one of the ladders to the roof of the stable where he took the buckets passed up to him to keep the roof damp. He stomped out places where burning embers fell—they were flying everywhere while the fire consumed the collapsed building.

The night became a series of buckets grabbed and dumped and passed back. When the horizon showed a glimmer of light through the thinning smoke, Gray was only dimly aware that the shower of embers had ceased. The air still smelled of charred wood. He stopped and stretched his aching back. From the height of the roof, he could see Maggie, her face smudged with ash and her skirts caked with mud, still passing the empty buckets to the woman behind her. He also saw his nephew. And Hendrick. And Decker. And countless other familiar faces, faces he'd all but forgotten while he had been off fighting Napoleon's army.

By God, he was proud of all of them.

"Come down," called an exhausted-looking Murray. "It is over. The job's done."

A cheer went up and the men on the roof clapped each other on the shoulders and shook Gray's hand. The women hugged, but the jubilation was tempered by sheer exhaustion. Like the rivulets of water that came from the buckets, the people began to stagger back to their homes and beds.

Gray slid down the ladder.

Murray waited for him at the bottom. "I believe all is secured, sir. I'll have a few men remain to make certain."

Gray glanced around him, surveying the damage from this vantage point. "I can stay."

Murray shook his head. "Not necessary, sir. You've done enough."

Gray put his hand on the man's shoulder. "You've done the most, Ted. I thank you."

Murray looked over to the burning ruin. "I lost the building."

"Don't be daft. You saved the coach house and the stables. And no one was hurt."

Murray gave a skeptical smile, his gaze going back to the now-destroyed building. One of the workers called to him, and with a quick nod to Gray, he was off.

Gray surveyed the damage once more. If he stayed to help the few tired men who remained, he would only be in their way. Now that the emergency was over, they would never allow the earl's son to do such menial, dirty work.

He started to walk back toward the house. Maggie was ahead of him, holding up her sodden skirts and moving with the exhaustion of a soldier who had marched twenty miles. Halfway to the house, she turned and gazed back at the charred ruins. She saw him following and waited for him.

When he reached her, she looked at him sadly. "It is lost."

He stood next to her and they both surveyed the scene. The sun had risen high enough to show groomsmen leading the horses back to the stables. Other men were herding the livestock.

"It could have been far worse." Gray gave silent

thanks to these people who had toiled through the night to save the other buildings.

She swiped her forehead with a grimy hand. "They made such a pretty picture, the stable and coach house and outbuildings all matching the white stone of the great house. They must have been designed that way." She sighed wearily. "It is all black now, like some horrible scar."

Gray had never thought much about the architecture of buildings he'd looked at every day growing up. They had been merely places for him to escape his father's temper, where men worked hard and spoke kindly to him. He saw the scene with fresh eyes, realizing anew how beautiful Summerton was, even with its scar.

"We'll rebuild," he said absently.

He glanced back at her, and she gave him a wan smile. She looked as if a mere feather would topple her over, and more by reflex than anything else, he put a steadying arm around her. She leaned against him and before he knew it, his other arm had encircled her. She buried her face into his chest, her fingers clinging to his coat. He held her close, rubbing his cheek against her silken hair, hair that smelled of smoke and soot, hair that might have gone up in flames when the cinders fell upon her.

They broke apart. He was not certain if it were he or she who moved away first, but her vivid blue eyes shone all the more brilliant in the early dawn light. With what expression?

Longing? Regret?

Or were those his emotions?

She turned and, pulling her skirts away from where they clung to her legs, nearly ran back to the house.

Chapter TEN

All Maggie wanted was to strip off her wet dress and wash the dirt from her body. She refused to think of how it had felt when Gray held her, when her cheek rested against his hard chest, when his strength seeped into her.

She longed for a bath, but how could she ask any of the servants to carry water for her? Even her maid had been at the fire, passing buckets all night long. Kitt, looking like a wrung-out washrag, came to Maggie's bedchamber to help her undress, but Maggie sent the girl to bed. She would make do with the water in the pitcher and would get herself ready for bed on her own.

She stood naked on a towel and scrubbed off the mud and soot as best she could. The water was cool, raising gooseflesh on her skin. She quickly dried herself and put on her nightdress. Sitting at her dressing table, she brushed the soot from her hair, wishing she hadn't forgotten to put on a hat. She dampened her hair with lavender water and brushed it some more, to free it of the fire's scent. By the time she had finished, Sean woke up, blessedly unaware of the frightening drama. Lovely Miss

Miles returned to fetch him, dressing him and packing him off for breakfast in the nursery.

Maggie lay upon the bed and tried to sleep, but when she closed her eyes all she could see was the terrifying sight of Gray running into the burning building. Her heart still raced with fright.

She heard him moving about in the next room. Had he pulled off his clothes as she had done to wash off the soot and grime? She remembered his bare chest from his first night at Summerton. The Roman statues in the ballroom displayed muscles like that, all rippling with strength.

She groaned and covered her head with her pillow. What folly to think of how he would look undressed. He was not a true husband to her, and she was not his proper wife.

And he was leaving.

She rolled onto her back and stared at the ceiling. He might be packing at this very moment. He might be preparing to leave Summerton, never to return, and it would be all her fault. For the rest of her life, she must live with what she had done to him. Her only wish now was to try to tell him how grateful she was to him.

Flinging aside the bed linens, she jumped out of bed and walked over to the door that joined her room to his. She pressed her ear against the cool wood.

His room was quiet. He could not have left already, could he? *Please let him merely be sleeping.*

She put her hand on the knob and turned it, but quickly let go and backed away from the door.

If he was sleeping, she did not wish to wake him, not after he had worked so ceaselessly battling the fire. She would have heard the door to his bedchamber open and close if he'd left. She would have heard his footsteps pass her door.

Her clock chimed nine o'clock. Lord Summerton's breakfast hour. Had the earl been roused by the commotion of the fire? He would only be more cross if his sleep had been disturbed.

She sat on the bed but could not make herself lie down again. Perhaps she ought to give Lord Summerton company, as he was accustomed to her doing.

If only she could reason with the earl. Tell him how hard his son worked at the fire. Convince him he ought to welcome this fine man into his heart, as a father ought his son.

It was no use. As long as she resided at Summerton, Gray's family would not be restored to him.

She crossed the room and pulled a morning dress from the wardrobe. Managing to fasten the dress herself and pin her hair up, she walked down to the breakfast room.

The earl was in his usual seat as she entered, his plate piled high with more food than he would be able to eat.

He lifted his fork, barely looking up at her. "Hmmmph. You are late." A bit of egg clung to the corner of his lower lip.

"Good morning to you, too, sir." She put her hands on his shoulders and gave him a kiss on the cheek.

The smell of the ham, eggs, and bread made her suddenly ravenous. Passing buckets all night did wonders for the appetite. She spooned two eggs from the warming dish, instead of one, adding a large slice of ham she would otherwise have forgone.

One of the footmen, dark circles under his eyes, appeared at her elbow to pour her tea. The poor man ought to be in his bed. "I think we can manage without you," she said to him.

He gave her a grateful bow and left. The earl noisily chewed his piece of toast.

"Were you awakened last night, my lord?" she asked tentatively.

"I sleep like the dead. I've told you that, girl. If one works hard, it is nothing to fall asleep at night." He jabbed at the air with his knife. "Mark my words."

"Wisely said, sir." Maggie leaned over and wiped the egg from his mouth with her handkerchief.

He waved her away. "Stop fussing. You treat me like an old man."

"Never, my lord." She smiled.

He shoveled more food into his mouth.

Maggie regarded him carefully between bites of her own. Cutting her ham, she asked somewhat tentatively, "Did anyone tell you of the fire last night?"

"What fire?" He twisted his head looking around the room. "I know of no fire."

"One of the outbuildings. The building was destroyed, I'm afraid, but no one was seriously hurt." She kept her voice calm.

The earl's cheek twitched, a sure sign of trouble to come.

The door opened, and Gray entered. Maggie's heart leapt at seeing him.

He gave her the briefest of glances. "Good morning."

"Hmmph," Lord Summerton responded. "Not sleeping the day away like usual, eh? Taking a page from my book for once. Rise early and prepare for the day . . ."

Gray seemed to not attend to this pontification. He

fixed his plate, and picked the seat across from Maggie, who poured some coffee for him.

". . . Never knew such a scapegrace for sleeping the day away." Lord Summerton pointed his knife at his son. "That boy kept town hours. No use at all. Now, Vincent rose early. Why, many was the time he rose before me. Out riding the property with Murray while I was still snoring in my bed . . ."

Maggie felt her face flush. Gray had probably not slept at all and this rant of his father's was so unfair. She would have attempted to stop it, but did not dare risk setting off the earl's temper.

Gray lifted his head with a shrug and said to Maggie in a low voice completely devoid of sarcasm, "My brother was a fine man."

He was a fine man as well, she wanted to protest! A man who'd labored all night to save his father's property. A man who would give up his home and family and future because of her.

"What did he say?" the earl asked her. "What did he say?"

"I said my brother was a fine man, Father," Gray answered in a flat tone.

"Yes, indeed," muttered the earl.

Gray turned his attention back to Maggie, but the sadness in his eyes nearly broke her heart. "Did you manage some sleep, then?"

"No." It was too painful to meet his gaze. "I could not settle."

"You don't sleep the day away, Maggie girl," Lord Summerton interjected.

"I referred to the fire last night, Father," Gray said.

His father dropped his fork with a clatter. "There was no fire."

"One of the outbuildings caught fire. I thought it might have woken you."

"I'm sure if there had been a fire, I would have woken, boy." Lord Summerton's face grew red. "There was no fire."

Do not argue with him, Maggie pleaded silently.

Gray gave his father a puzzled look. "I assure you there was a fire. You can still smell it—"

"Do not be insolent with me, young man!" Summerton's voice rose. "This is *my* property, and I'll brook no disrespect on my own land. Thought I sent you packing ages ago—"

The son stiffened.

Maggie quickly placed a calm hand on Lord Summerton's arm. "Of course, you demand respect," she said, soothing him but wanting more to soothe his son. "He meant no disrespect, my lord. Remember? I just told you about the fire."

"Hmmph," his lordship said. "He should not be here. I want him gone."

"You will get your wish soon enough," Gray shot back.

Maggie broke in. "Lord Summerton, you are being very unkind to your son." She kept her voice calm but firm. Sometimes the earl responded well when she spoke to him as if he were Sean's age. "I am very ashamed of you. I thought you a better man than that. Now let us have a civil breakfast."

"I have finished eating." His lordship glared at Gray and struggled to his feet.

Maggie jumped out of her chair to assist him. After he steadied himself with his cane, he shook her off and hobbled out of the room. Parker met him outside the door, and Maggie sat down again.

Gray, face red, shoved food into his mouth. His fork jabbed at the ham as if it were an enemy.

"He does not mean what he says."

His eyes flashed. "Indeed?"

"You don't understand . . ."

He put his cutlery down and gave her a level stare. "Do not explain my father to me, *Maggie girl.*" Venom might as well be pouring from his mouth. "You are welcome to him. I plan to put as much distance between my father and myself as I am able."

She extended her hand to him, but he waved it aside, attacking his food instead.

"I wished to speak to you of this." She took a bracing breath. "To tell you how sorry I am you must give up Summerton. It is your home."

He laughed. "My father banished me from this place. He said long ago that it was no longer my home." He glared at her. "Your apology would better address having forced my return. That I find difficult to forgive."

He could pretend to himself that his father and Summerton meant nothing to him, but she had seen his face when his father attacked him. And she'd seen him toil for Summerton.

She gave him an earnest look. "I realize the enormity of your sacrifice for me."

"Enough!" he shouted, standing abruptly and shoving the chair away with such force it fell over. Without another look at her, he strode out of the room.

Gray left the house and walked toward the stables. With any luck his horse would be fit for a long day's ride, and he could leave this place and return to London. The night had been a long one for animals as well as people, however. His horse was an old steed, one Gray purchased in Belgium after his horse had been shot from under him at Waterloo. He'd given this old animal quite a working the previous day, all morning riding with Rodney, all afternoon and evening in the village.

Of course, the horse had had plenty of time to rest in the village while Gray sat drinking in the inn. Old friends and neighbors soon heard he was there and came to chat, telling him how glad they were he'd come home from the war. Well, his homecoming would be very brief.

The acrid stench of burnt wood spoiled cool morning air. As he walked to the stables, Gray could see men still working around the charred building. A short detour would not hurt. He thought he might take stock of the damage now that the sun was out.

The building barely resembled its former self. Its stone walls had crumbled in places and were covered with soot and ash, every bit like the blackened scar Maggie had described. Wisps of smoke rose here and there, ghostly reminders of the inferno that had raged within the walls the night before. Men raked through the debris, salvaging any useful items that survived, stamping out any embers that still burned.

Murray was there, walking from one man to another, still in the scorched and soot-smeared clothes he'd worn the night before.

Gray approached him. "Good God, Ted, have you taken no rest?"

Murray shook his head. "Fine rest I'd have if we had a flare-up and another building caught fire." He gestured to Gray. "Come examine the damage with me."

Murray led Gray through the building's charred remains.

"Do you know how the fire started?" Gray asked.

Murray grimaced. "One of the lads had been entertaining a maid. They knocked over a lantern."

"You cannot mean it. Who was it?"

Murray gave him a worried look. "Are you going to dismiss them?"

Gray laughed. "Me? I have no authority here. You know that."

Murray regarded him quizzically, then poked at a pile of charred wood. "Well, since you were back, I assumed—"

Gray held up his hand. "I am merely visiting."

The estate manager's brow creased in worry, reminding Gray of the serious boy Ted had been, as serious as his father before him.

"I have not said how sorry I was to hear your father died, Ted. He was a good man."

Murray nodded, hands on his hips, his eyes still sweeping over the ruins. "It was a while back."

It seemed as if all the deaths were a while back. Caleb's parents. Decker's uncle. Ted's father. After the earl banished him from Summerton, he'd had no means of knowing who lived or died here.

"I am glad you took over for him," Gray said.

Murray laughed. "Your father thinks I *am* him half the time."

Gray responded with a smile, though Ted's words puzzled him.

Murray did another sweep of the damaged structure. "We ought to rebuild, but . . . I don't know."

"Of course rebuild." Gray nodded. "Nothing else for it."

"It's not that simple." Murray kicked at a half-burned piece of timber. "It will take capital."

"Surely my father can afford it." Summerton had always been prosperous. His father's iron-willed control over the estate had guaranteed it.

"That's not the point. It is how to get the earl to agree." A puff of black ash rose from where he'd kicked.

"You think my father won't agree?" His father might be a nip-farthing about most things, but Summerton always came first with him. Even before family. Especially before his youngest son.

Murray shrugged. "Perhaps you would talk to him."

Gray shook his head. "He will not listen to me."

"Mrs. Grayson, then. She has been a help in the past."

Gray frowned. Tallying sums in the estate books was one thing, but making decisions of such importance as this was quite another. Gray could not believe his father would listen to a woman advise him on estate matters. Not unless he'd gone daft. The earl had not even allowed Vincent to do that.

Gray opened his mouth to ask Murray if Maggie had mixed in other estate matters of this import, but gave it up. What did any of this matter to him if he was leaving?

One of the men called to Murray.

"Your permission, sir?" his boyhood friend asked.

"Go," said Gray, and Murray hurried off.

Gray crossed his arms over his chest. He glanced toward the stables, but instead of heading in that direction, he hesitated, kicking up clouds of ashes.

When the ash covered his boots, he tried to shake it off, with the thought he'd just made unnecessary work for Decker. But he need not be concerned about Decker either. Not if he was leaving.

On the other hand, what harm would it do to give his horse one full day of rest? Tomorrow would be time enough to leave Summerton.

He headed back to where Ted stood giving more instructions to his men. Maybe he could help determine if Summerton could afford to rebuild the outbuilding. If Ted shared the estate books with Maggie, surely he would not mind if Gray had a peek at them.

"I'll not sign anything!" Lord Summerton pounded the floor of his study with his cane.

It was late afternoon, not the earl's best time of day, especially when he had not taken a nap.

Maggie winced. Lord Summerton was not the only one suffering from lack of sleep. She was feeling lightheaded and her mind was a complete fog.

"My lord, please. I am sure it is right to sign this paper," she begged.

"We need to rebuild, sir," Mr. Murray added, standing at a respectful distance.

Murray ought not to have chosen today to address the issue of drawing upon the estate's capital. Maggie would have preferred to ease into the matter slowly, to make Lord Summerton used to the idea first. Murray was adamant, however. Lack of sleep must have addled his thinking, too.

Lord Summerton's face had turned an alarming shade of red. "Summerton has enough buildings! You'd fritter away my money with nonsense. Greek temples and such. I'll not have it!"

Maggie knelt next to his chair. She put her hand on his arm, stroking it gently. "Not Greek temples. No worry of that." She used the same voice she used to soothe Sean when he awakened from a bad dream. "But there was a fire, and it damaged one of the farm buildings, and it must be rebuilt."

"There was no fire!" the earl shouted. "I'm busy. I have work to do. I have papers . . ."

He began to move and stack papers around his desk, including the one to be signed. The door to the study opened quietly, and Gray stepped in.

Her heart danced at seeing him. Her first thought was that he'd not left Summerton after all. Her second was that he could not have picked a worse time to enter this room.

Luckily, the earl seemed not to notice him, and he remained in the room's shadows. At least Mr. Murray seemed relieved to see him.

"Lord Summerton," Maggie began again. "Please listen . . ."

He rearranged the papers into different piles. She'd lost track of the one he was to sign.

She took a breath to calm herself. "There was a fire and one of the buildings burned down. It needs to be rebuilt." It must be the tenth time she had explained. At least this time the earl had quit fussing with the papers.

"Mr. Murray needs permission to draw capital for the repairs. It is a necessary expense."

Lord Summerton drew circles on his desk with one bony finger, apparently thinking. She glanced up hopefully at Mr. Murray. Unfortunately Gray left the shadows and stood at Murray's side.

"Never dip into the capital," Lord Summerton repeated, also for the tenth time. "That's what my father told me, and I've always lived by that rule. Never dip into the capital."

Maggie felt a wave of desperation. "But you must sign, sir. You must."

"I'll not sign anything." He pounded the desk with his fist. "I'm no fool."

She stood again and pressed her fingers to her temple.

Gray stepped forward. His father put both palms on the desk and shouted, "You!"

"Good afternoon, Father." He smiled in what Maggie feared was a sarcastic way. If he set off one more temper outburst in his father, she would surely get a headache.

Gray strolled up to his father's desk. While Lord Summerton glared at him, Gray went through the stack of papers, finding the one under discussion. He read it.

"Give that back this instant!" his father demanded.

Gray handed it back. "I must say, I agree with you, Father."

Maggie thought she might sink to the floor right in front of all of them.

"You agree?" said the earl, a surprised expression on his face. "What the deuce do you know about it?"

"Oh, I have had a look at the estate books," Gray said in mild tones. "And I conclude this is precisely the decision I would make. You must not sign that paper, Father. In fact, I forbid you to sign it."

Lord Summerton nearly rose from his chair. "You *forbid* me? You? How dare you?" The earl snatched a pen and dipped it in the pot of ink as if stabbing it. "I'll thank you not to tell me my business. Give me the paper."

Gray had, in fact, placed the paper right in front of him. Maggie pointed to the proper spot. "This is where you sign, sir."

Lord Summerton signed with a flourish and, glaring at his son the whole time, handed the paper to Mr. Murray. Gray maintained a bland expression.

"Now, leave me," ordered his lordship. "I have work to do."

Mr. Murray hurriedly bowed himself out. Maggie and Gray followed him.

When they'd all gained the hallway, Murray said, "Did you find something amiss with the books, Captain?"

Gray shook his head. "Not at all. And I have no objection to using capital to pay for the repairs."

"Thank you, sir," said Murray. He rushed off, precious paper in hand.

Maggie looked at Gray, who was staring back at the door of the study. "You contrived his compliance."

He barely glanced at her. "Yes. I knew he would oppose me."

He looked so absorbed in thought she was loathe to disturb him, even though she longed to ask him if he still planned to leave this day.

She cleared her throat. "There is a problem in the kitchen I must attend to, but I beg you to give me a few moments of your time before . . . before you leave."

As she started to step away, he grabbed her arm. "I would speak with you now." He pulled her into the parlor.

She had seen him angry. Had seen him kind. Had seen him wounded to the core by his father, but she had not before seen him with such a look of despair. "What is it?" she whispered.

He grabbed both her upper arms, forcing her to look at him. "Tell me what is wrong with my father."

Chapter ELEVEN

M aggie searched his ashen face, his red-rimmed eyes. All the pain she saw there seemed to seep into her skin and cause her legs to weaken underneath her.

"I will tell you," she said, using the same soothing voice she'd used on the father. "But let us sit down."

He pulled her over to the settee. When they sat, he still had not released her from his firm grip.

"It is his apoplexy," she began. "The fits have . . . altered him."

"Stand to point, Maggie. Altered him how?"

She gave a heavy sigh. "They have affected his mind." She paused, searching for the right words. "He cannot think clearly. He often seems fine, really, but the least little problem upsets him. I . . . I gather from what others have told me that he was a decisive man, but now he can decide nothing. It becomes worse as time passes."

A muscle in his cheek flexed.

She wished she could spare him. "Your father cannot reason. He becomes confused and agitated when asked the simplest thing."

Gray released her, leaned back on the settee, and

rubbed his brow. "Murray has taken it upon himself to run the estate?"

"There was no one else to do it."

Gray flinched in pain as if he had been run through with a very blunt sword. "I was not here to do it, you mean." His throat constricted. "I was not here."

It had not been so long ago his father had towered over him, voice booming like the wrath of God, damning him for some prank or another. Like the time he'd decided to see how fast his father's new stallion could gallop. Or when he'd first stolen from the house to drink all night at the village inn. Gray once cowered under the ferocity of his father's temper, though pride prevented him from ever showing that fear to his father. He sank his head into his hands.

God help him, was this shell the same man?

His father had needed him, and he had not been here. His eyes burned. He should have been here.

A soft hand touched his back, warm and comforting. "We try to keep him comfortable." Maggie stroked him soothingly as if petting a child. "I assure you, he believes all is the same—at least most of the time."

She spoke with a timbre that seemed to reach deep inside him, a loving sound. It had been so very long since he'd felt loved, since he had been young enough for his mother to hold him in her arms. Since Vincent had been alive to wrap him in a brotherly hug. Without thinking, he turned to her, and she enfolded him in her arms. Holding his head against her breast, she rocked him gently back and forth. The comfort loosed his tears and threatened to loosen any semblance of control he still had over his emotions.

"It will be all right," she murmured. "I promise you."

It was so easy to fall into her comfort, to allow her to soothe him. Her intoxicating fragrance filled his nostrils. Lavender. She drew him to her as strongly as if she sang a Siren's song.

He abruptly pulled away from her. He did not deserve to be comforted.

"You promise?" he snapped, taking his self-hatred out on her. "What the devil has this to do with you?"

She merely returned another comforting look.

He leaned back and peered at her with still-stinging eyes. "I'll have you know, madam, that nothing has ever been all right between my father and me."

She gently brushed the hair off his forehead. "Why is that, Gray?"

His name so softly coming from her lips nearly shredded the last tattered bits of his control. He traced the line of those lips with his fingers and twisted his mouth into a poor excuse for a smile.

"I was born." His voice rasped with a pain he could no longer conceal.

Her eyes filled with tears, an acknowledgment of the aching wounds inside him. That she would weep for him snapped his control. He lowered his head and stilled her trembling lips with a kiss. She uttered a small cry, but her mouth became pliant against his.

By God, he wanted to bed her, no matter how she had played him for a fool. He wanted to lose himself in her, bury himself inside her, make love to her until they both collapsed in exhaustion and forgetfulness.

He urged her mouth open and plundered the soft inside with his tongue. She held her fingers against his cheek with a touch as light as gossamer, a touch both innocent and loving.

It would be so easy to take advantage of her, so easy to accept this new means of comfort.

He eased her away. She blinked up at him, dazed.

His attempt at a smile was no more successful than before. "That was not well done of me, madam. I beg your pardon."

"No—" she began.

He held up his hand.

"Please, Gray." She reached for him, but he turned away.

After a gentle squeeze of his fingers, she rose and walked across the room.

He slumped back on the settee, shading his eyes with his hand, trying not to feel like a cad for kissing her. What was the use? It only added to his many transgressions. He let his gaze wander around the room anywhere but where she stood. It landed on the family portrait.

Romney's genius had captured his grim-faced father as true as life. His father's image conveyed strength and intelligence. A light shone in his father's eyes, a light Gray realized was no longer there. His father was as lost to him as were Vincent and his mother. All his family gone.

The loneliness washed over him, as intense as the day he'd walked out of this house to join the regiment. Another emotion threatened, every bit as eager to engulf him.

Obligation.

He could not leave Summerton now. He owed it to Vincent to stand in his place and maintain the property for his son, who would inherit one day. He owed it to Olivia to give her a brother's protection, since his father's was mere illusion. He owed it to Rodney, too, who needed a man's guidance, a guardian's decision-making on important matters like school, university.

Most of all, he owed it to his father, who could no longer care for the estate that had meant more to him than his own sons. Gray could not desert his father again, no matter how much his father despised him.

Gray glanced away from the painting. Maggie still stood, quietly watching him.

Like it or not, Maggie and her son were his responsibility as well. By God, he'd gotten himself trapped into marriage again. He bit down on a maniacal laugh.

Turning to Maggie, he said, "Madam, do you realize what this account of my father's health signifies?"

She did not respond, merely looked at him.

"I must remain at Summerton."

He stayed drunk three days. He holed up in his bedchamber with only Decker to attend him and kept himself as foxed as he was able. The pleasant fog of intoxication was second only to total unconsciousness. Anything but the sober reality.

His behavior did him no credit at all in anyone's eyes, but he refused to care. He had a lifetime to be responsible to Summerton. What were three days of inebriation to that?

Even the weather cooperated with his mood. Three days of rain: bone-chilling, relentless rain, as dismal as the depths of his depression.

Decker hovered about like a mother hen, but refrained

from criticism, which was good, because in this mood Gray would not have hesitated to give him the sack. The fledgling valet dared, however, to skirt the boundaries of Gray's goodwill by insisting he eat, bringing trays of warm bread, rich cheeses, the sorts of food as easy to consume as they were to digest.

The young man worried about him, as well. Gray heard Decker's voice outside the room asking, "What should I do, ma'am? Should I send for the physician?"

Fool, Decker. A physician did not have the means to heal a disease of the spirit.

It was Maggie's voice who answered. "He will come around. I am sure of it. Keep him comfortable and give him as little drink as you can contrive."

Limiting his drink. Managing even his own dissipation. The devil with her! He wanted to forget her as well. Forget the sympathy in her eyes. Forget the comfort of her hand upon his back, the taste of her lips against his.

He drank port, the dark red wine of Portugal, and sometimes its haze made him think himself back on the Peninsula. Campo Mayor, Los Santos, Membrillo.

Orthes, where Rosa died.

He liked it better when the port made him forget.

He wallowed in his misery, indulging himself in every moment of total self-pity, but after three days he was sick of it, as disgusted with himself as would be everyone else. The family. The servants. Tenants. Village. Some war hero, he was. Some prodigal son.

He forced himself to sit up in bed, rubbing the three days' growth of beard on his chin and scratching his head. His mouth felt like it had been stuffed with cotton, cotton fouled with cow manure, that is. He slid himself off the bed and stumbled across the room to the pitcher of fresh water Decker provided every day.

Gray rinsed his mouth and splashed the cool water on his face. That felt better.

The room had no air. He wove his way to the window and opened it wide, breathing in the cool fresh air of dawn. He gazed out and saw clouds threaded through the sky, but in between there was a promise of blue as clear as . . . as clear as Maggie's eyes.

He groaned.

Maggie. His wife who was not a wife. She might be some sort of temptress, though. Teasing him by popping up throughout his reverie, fading in and out of the mist, interrupting gory scenes of battle, the horror of Rosa's death, and memories of his father ringing a peal over his head.

The pounding in his head made him nauseous. He took another big gulp of air, but lost his balance and banged his head against the wall.

It was a good thing he had not fallen out the open window. Or perhaps that was a bad thing. One long plummet to the shrubbery below and his broken body would bring eternal oblivion.

No, he was not quite ready for that level of forgetfulness.

A wave of nausea hit him again, and he nearly lost his balance once more, grasping the windowpane in time. He practically crawled back to his bed. Collapsing on the rumpled linens, he closed his eyes and waited for the room to stop spinning.

"Bang!" A cannon fired next to his ear.

No . . . no . . . it was a door slamming against the wall.

It merely felt like a cannon. Small feet pounded across the room and something propelled itself on top of him.

He opened one eye a tiny slit.

"Papa!"

A little boy bearing the weight of about ten grown men bounced on his chest. Sean.

"Papa, wake up!" Sean squealed, the sound ricocheting in his cranium.

Pain! His head had never hurt so much.

Yes, it had. The last time it hurt like this, a baby had been born. *This* baby.

Sean grabbed hold of Gray's hair and tried to pull him up.

"Ahhh," Gray cried. Words were still a bit beyond him.

Sean giggled and tugged some more.

Maggie rushed into the room. "Sean, no!" Her voice was nearly as piercing as the child's.

Through his barely open eyes, he saw she wore only a thin, loose nightdress. Her luxurious hair was unbound, tumbling down her back like some silken wave.

She grabbed Sean and pulled him off. Gray used the opportunity to breathe.

"Noooooo!" cried Sean, fighting her with flying fists and feet.

The child's struggles pushed the wide neckline of her gown off her shoulders. Gray watched as it slid down inch by tantalizing inch, revealing more and more of her full rounded breasts. Closing his mouth, which had dropped open at the sight, he reminded himself it was nothing he had not seen before.

He sat up and became suddenly aware of his own state

of undress, having tumbled into bed naked. He hurriedly covered himself toga-style with the bed linens.

"I do apologize, Gray." She tried to keep hold of the flailing Sean, pull up her gown, and back out of the room at the same time. "He escaped before I knew it."

"Noooo!" Sean raised his voice a brain-shattering octave. "Ride horfe!"

"Ahhh!" Gray grabbed again for his head. "Not the damned horfe again."

Well, horfe was almost a coherent word.

"He has been talking of nothing else for three days," she said, panting with the effort of keeping a grip on the whirligig who had been his tormentor. "Ever since he learned you took Rodney on a ride. We put him off because of the rain."

And because *Papa* was drunk as an emperor, no doubt, but Gray figured, somewhat gratefully, she'd not have described him this way to the boy.

She finally reached the door, gown nearly below the dusky rose nipples he'd seen through the thin fabric. She took one hand off Sean to reach for the doorknob, and the boy squirmed out of her grasp, galloping across the room back to Gray. Maggie ran after him.

This time Sean clamped his chubby arms around Gray's legs. As Maggie and Gray both tried to pry him loose, the bed linens fell away and Gray's line of vision looked straight down Maggie's nightdress. Their eyes met in mutual shock. Both let go of Sean and covered themselves.

"I'll take him riding," Gray said, feeling his face go red, double-checking to make sure his lap was covered.

Maggie held the neckline of her nightdress in her fist. "Are . . . are you able?"

He ignored his pounding head. "Am I fit, do you mean? Not at present, but give me an hour or so. Decker must have some remedy. Maybe some breakfast will do it."

"You are not obliged to indulge Sean."

Obliged? He was obliged in everything, was he not? Why not in indulging little Sean?

"I need to get outdoors. Do not fear. I'm not fit to ride at anything but a walk."

"Ride?" Sean perked up.

"Are you certain?" She tilted her head.

Sean looked from one to the other, his eyes wide. "Ride?" he asked, his voice pitifully infused with anticipated disappointment.

Gray's mouth twitched. He glanced at Maggie, who smiled back at him. It was a moment of connection between them, the sensation of time stopping.

He looked back at Sean, who regarded him with big, hopeful eyes. Gray could not resist another glance at Maggie. The time-stopping moment repeated itself.

"Ride, Maggie?" He mimicked Sean.

Her expression softened. "Oh, very well."

Sean started jumping up and down, still holding on to Gray's legs just in case. "Wodney too," he declared.

Gray looked to Maggie.

"He means he wants Rodney to come with you."

"Ah." He nodded in understanding and looked back at Sean. "Very well. Rodney, too, but be off and mind your mother first."

Sean's little face broke into a huge joyful grin. "Wod-

ney!" he cried at the top of his lungs. "Wodney! Ride!"
He ran out of the room yelling, "Wodney! Ride!"

Gray grabbed his head.

Maggie giggled and Gray discovered he liked the
sound. "Shall I send for Decker?" she asked.

He smiled at her, enjoying for this one moment the
sight of her, the feeling of connection with another person.

"I suspect he is right outside the room waiting to
enter."

She smiled back at him and the connection held a moment longer.

"Let me meet the boys in the kitchen in an hour. We
can beg breakfast from Cook before heading to the stables."

"It is kind of you, Gray," she said, turning and breaking the connection. She walked back to her room and
closed the door behind her.

The riders were long gone when Maggie met Lord
Summerton in the breakfast room. She could not help
wondering about them. Would they ride far? Would they
ride near the stream or toward the village? Would Gray
stick to the paths and road or take them over the hills?

She would be restless until they returned. She told herself the restlessness was due to worry about Sean.

After breakfast, she cajoled Lord Summerton into taking a turn around the garden with her, getting him in the
sunshine and fresh air and away from his study.

The earl could spend whole days in his study, looking
at the papers she and Murray had pulled out for him. Papers that appeared important, but would cause no prob-

lem if lost or misplaced. They used to leave books on his desk, on agriculture or horse breeding, but lately Lord Summerton's powers of concentration could barely sustain perusal of the latest newspaper from London. Since Gray had been out of the earl's sight for three days, Maggie was not certain if he remembered his son's presence. He certainly did not know of Gray's intention to remain at Summerton. It would be best for Gray not to mention this decision, but rather simply be present until the earl became accustomed to him, if he ever would.

Her heart skipped a beat at the thought of Gray. What did it mean for him to stay at Summerton? She'd spent the last three days in an agony of uncertainty. If he stayed at Summerton, would it mean she and Sean must leave? How could he bear to look at her each day, knowing what she had done to him? Of course he would wish her to leave.

She thought of the glimpse she'd had of him. Magnificently broad-shouldered, narrow-hipped, and as muscular as the Roman statues. The sight of him had reawakened desires she could not even damp down while they'd been circling each other like angry cats. She remembered the feel of his skin beneath her fingers, the exhilaration of his kiss.

Heat rushed through her, reaching that secret part of her as if he were touching her now, as if he were kissing her as he had in the parlor just three days ago. This excitement inside was meant for marriage. If they had been truly married she could feel the thrill of mating with him, could feel him fill the emptiness inside her, driving her to the very pinnacle of delight.

Maggie fanned herself with her hand, though the day

was fairly cool for midsummer. The earl plodded along next to her, apparently not noticing anything amiss.

She could not allow herself to be unsettled by such carnal thoughts, even if Gray had looked so unkempt, unshaved, and disheveled, like her first sight of him in the doorway of his rooms in London.

She must not think of that day any more than she should think of him unclothed. Thinking of that day brought back the despair and desolation of being friendless, penniless, and homeless. He would not totally abandon her and Sean, would he?

She forced herself to think of something else.

She thought of Sean. How happy he was to be riding a horse! Giddy and uncontrollable in his excitement. She did hope no harm came to him on this ride. He was so little and the horse was so tall. She shook her head. Gray would make sure he was safe, she was certain of it.

Lord Summerton stopped in midstride in the center of the path bordered by pink and white rhododendrons. He thumped his cane against the damp earth. "Enough of this frivolity. I need to get to work. There is much to do to run this estate, I'll have you know."

"You need exercise as well, my lord," Maggie told him. "And it is a lovely day to take a walk. See how pretty the flowers are."

"Hmmph," muttered Summerton. "She spent a bundle on these fool gardens. Waste of blunt. Better used for crops or livestock, something to make a profit."

The "she" was Gray's mother, Maggie knew. The earl never spoke kindly of his departed wife. It made Maggie sad for her.

"The gardens make Summerton beautiful."

He gave a snort in response.

She would not pursue this conversation and risk taxing his fragile temper. She sighed. "Very well, my lord. Shall we return to the house?"

She led him to a path that took longest to lead back to the house. When he was securely ensconced in his study, she did not tarry indoors. The day was too glorious. She grabbed a basket and walked back to the garden, strolling to the lavender bed that was thick with blooms.

Humming "Sally in Our Alley," she filled her basket with piles of lavender. The pleasant scent enveloped her and clung to her skin. She savored the sense of peacefulness it brought, fleeting though it might be. What more could she do than try to enjoy each day as it came? She'd done no less since arriving at Summerton. When the basket overflowed with the fragrant lavender, she put it on her arm and started back to the house, choosing to cross the park where the breeze was strongest and the sunlight brightest.

She heard a shout from behind her.

"Mama!"

Sean came running across the park, laughing as he went. Rodney followed close behind. Gray trailed after them at a distance, his pace a bit more sedate.

"Mama! Mama! Horfe jumped!" Sean cried as he collided with her skirts, causing a rain of lavender blossoms to fall from the basket.

Rodney caught up, laughing. "Not a big jump, Aunt Maggie, but he thought it quite daring."

Dear Rodney had read her worry. Maggie gave him a relieved smile. She put down the basket and stooped to Sean's level. "The horse jumped? What excitement!"

"Jumped high!" Sean cried, stretching his small arm up as high as he might.

"High," she repeated.

"Real high!" He jumped himself to show her.

"Not that high."

She looked up to see Gray towering over her. His neckcloth was a bit askew. He wore his coat with a casual ease and his eyes were shaded by his tall hat. She felt dizzy looking at him.

His expression was unclear. "A little jump," he explained to her. "Nothing to signify."

Maggie's feeling of ease fled, but it had nothing to do with Sean on a horse. "Rodney has assured me, sir," she said to him.

"Tell Miss Miles!" Sean cried, still at full volume.

"Yes, my darling." Maggie gave him another hug. "You must do so." She stood up and looked to Rodney. "Will you see him to Miss Miles?"

"Yes, Aunt Maggie," Rodney said agreeably. He took Sean's hand. "Come on, Sean. We'll tell Miss Miles and Mr. Hendrick, too. Is that not a capital idea?"

"Capital idea," repeated Sean as they walked to the door.

Maggie turned back to Gray. "I see he has had a high time. I do thank you for it."

Gray gave a small shrug, but his mouth turned up at the corner. "Unstoppably good."

She laughed. "Oh, dear. I gather the ride was longer than you might have wished."

He cocked his head, and she found her heart was beating quite rapidly. He leaned down and picked up the basket.

Unsettled, she reached to take it from his grasp. "I must put these in the still room."

"I'll carry them." His large, strong hands already gripped the basket's handle.

She resisted the impulse to touch them.

As they walked side by side, he was silent, and she could not reconcile the feelings of exhilaration at being in his presence with fright at what he might say to her when he did speak.

They made their way to the still room off the servants' wing. It was a large, tiled room with a long table and dozens of glass basins of all sizes and shapes on the shelves. On other shelves various flowers and fruits were laid for drying. The room held the scent of generations of fragrant oils, jams, and jellies.

Maggie placed the basket upon the table and set about removing the flowers, placing them next to each other in neat rows.

"Do not tell me you also distill spirits," Gray said.

She gave him a wary glance, bracing herself for another barrage of chastisement for all her work at Summerton. "No, I shall tell Mrs. Thomas I have gathered the lavender. She will attend to it."

He leaned against the wall. "I am pleased there is at least one thing you do not do."

He would mock her instead. "Yes, Captain."

She headed for the door, but he caught her arm. "Forgive me." He released her and folded his arms across his chest. "That was unnecessarily churlish. I ought to be grateful to you for your assistance to my family." He gave her a level gaze. "I cannot quite manage it, however."

Her sense of foreboding increased. She met his eye. "I do not require your gratitude." She proceeded to the door.

"Maggie?"

She stopped, but did not turn around.

"I am resolved to stay at Summerton." His voice was firm.

"I did not doubt it." The words she dreaded to hear were about to be spoken and suddenly she could not bear it. She could not bear that this man would send her away.

She reached for the doorknob.

"I can assure you there will not be a repeat of the last few days." His voice rose. "I am over that."

"You owe me no assurances." She turned the knob.

"Wait," he commanded.

Her shoulders sagged, but she stood tall again when she turned to face him, as if facing an executioner. She'd often thought of what that would be like.

His expression was stony. "You and I must come to some arrangement."

She lifted her chin. "Assure me the means to support my son and I will do whatever you require of me."

His brows rose. "Are we back there again? I thought we had settled all that." One corner of his mouth turned up. "What I require of you is to be my wife."

She gaped at him. "I do not precisely understand."

He gave a dry laugh. "Oh, never fear, this is not a proposal of marriage. I have no wish to be married to you."

Those words stung, which was foolish in the extreme. She had never truly fancied herself married to him. Not often, that is. "What is it, then?"

"A clarification. I do not perceive we have any choice but to continue your charade, even though I must remain here." He said this almost casually, as if it were a mere nothing. "It will be somewhat awkward, I realize, to maintain the pretense of being husband and wife when we must share the same house."

She was uncertain if she ought to feel jubilant or sick with anxiety. To be so near him, so prone to think of him in ways even proper wives would find scandalous. It would be awkward indeed.

He continued. "We have managed it thus far, however. I see no reason we cannot go on."

She raised her eyebrows. "You propose we live together here?"

The look he returned mirrored her uncertainty. "We must, Maggie. What choice do we have?"

What choice indeed. To wake in the morning hearing him move about the next room, to sit across from him at meals, encounter him on the estate, to go to bed every night knowing he was on the other side of her door. He, a husband who was not a husband. She, a wife who was not a wife.

She took a deep breath and again met his eyes.

And in them she perceived the same yearning that threatened to engulf and consume her.

Chapter TWELVE

Leonard Lansing blinked against the brisk sea breeze as he strolled along the Steyne in the company of Lord Camerville. Camerville, known as "Cammy" to his friends, fell short of being a dashing figure. A bit too stout, a bit too fleshy in the cheeks, but nonetheless Lansing congratulated himself on this new acquaintance, carefully cultivated through his meager respectable contacts at Brighton, the seaside town the prince regent had made all the rage. Lansing was certainly not welcome in Prinny's set, but Lord Camerville was not quite that high in the instep either. He was, however, a frivolous fellow quite willing to be flattered.

"Air is too nippy for sea bathing today." Lord Camerville raised his head, facing the sea breeze.

"Indeed," agreed Lansing.

"No chance of glimpsing the ladies," Cammy added.

Camerville was always on the ready for a pretty female. It was one of his all-abiding interests. His wife shared her husband's predilection to infidelity, and Lansing, in his desire to remain in both their good graces, had a tricky time resisting her rather blatant invitations.

"Been much too cold," Cammy went on. "Odd summer. Thinking of packing up and heading back to the country."

Lansing's ears pricked up. "Are you? Your lands are west of Faversham, are they not? Lovely country, I hear."

"Hmm. Lovely, yes. Damned dull, however." Camerville's attention shifted to a young woman whose skirt had been lifted by the wind, revealing slim legs and a delicate ankle.

He elbowed Lansing who returned the expected nod of appreciation. The young lady passed, and they strolled on.

"I believe I know one of your neighbors." Lansing kept his voice casual. "Served with him. Brave fellow. We were fast friends. Name's Grayson, Summerton's younger son."

Camerville stopped. "Do not say it! Went to school with his brother!"

"Ah, the deceased brother," said Lansing, adding an appropriately solemn expression.

"Damned good man, Palmely." Cammy leaned closer to his ear. "You should see the wife—I mean, widow. A diamond of the first water, that one."

Lansing pricked up his ears, suddenly very intrigued. "Is that so?"

Camerville got a dreamy look in his eye. "Nothing like her. Hair like spun gold. A figure like Venus . . ."

"I should like to meet such a paragon." A new idea began germinating in Lansing's head, one he was surprised he'd not thought of before.

Cammy clapped him on the back. "So would I! Haven't seen her in an age."

"She is not remarried?"

Camerville laughed. "Not a chance! The old earl got batty after Palmely died, they say. Became a recluse. All of 'em are rarely seen. But, you know, by now the widow could be fat as Mrs. Fitzherbert."

Lansing glanced around. It would not do for the wrong person to hear the prince regent's secret wife so maligned. The regent still had some affection for the woman, it was said. Certainly more than for his princess.

No one seemed to have heeded the comment, however, and Lansing felt free to return to his new interest, the widow Lady Palmely.

The earl had become a recluse, had he? Lansing mulled this tidbit over in his mind. Perhaps the old fellow would be as ripe for flattery as Camerville. Perhaps the earl could be induced to approve a match with his daughter-in-law.

Lansing turned back to his companion with a captivated look on his face, not daring to be quiet for too long or Camerville would change the topic of conversation. "You have me curious over the glorious Lady Palmely," he said smoothly. "I would wager a woman like that would retain her beauty."

"You'd wager on it?" Cammy's other weakness, wagering, was also well known to Lansing.

Lansing laughed. "Indeed I would! Say . . ." He calculated how much he could risk without sounding cheap. "Ten pounds?"

"Done!" Cammy grinned.

They walked on, shivering against the chill sea breeze.

"I say, Lansing," Cammy broke in, "how will we determine the winner? Nobody visits Summerton Hall except Sir Francis Betton. The man's property borders Summerton. It would cause talk if we just knocked on the door. I would not dare risk being turned away."

Knocking on the door was precisely what Lansing wished to do, but he, too, had no wish to be turned away. He thought a moment.

"I have it!" He gripped Camerville's arm. "It answers your need to retire to the country *and* your need for diversion."

"Do tell." Cammy gave him an eager look.

"Give a house party and invite both the widow and Sir Francis. I'll own she's probably pining for just such an entertainment."

"A house party. Capital idea!"

It *was* a capital idea, Lansing agreed silently. A lovely, wealthy, titled widow. Lansing laughed to himself. And what a marvelous trick on Gray! To be welcomed into the very home where Gray was banished.

"Capital idea!" Cammy repeated, clapping him on the back one more time.

Over the next few weeks, Gray often took the boys for a ride. When they could sneak out without Sean seeing, Gray took Rodney alone so the boy could learn of the land that would someday be his. The land brought the memories back to Gray. The flat stone by the stream where Vincent taught him to fish. The large open field where Vincent taught him to shoot. The cool shaded pond where Vincent taught him to swim. When Gray showed Rodney these places, he could almost feel his brother's hand upon his shoulder, could almost see Vincent's grateful smile.

The boy was like a hungry puppy, lapping up the attention and knowledge. Gray gave silent thanks to God that he had not returned too late for his nephew.

Summerton, however, had not suffered with his absence. Murray had been bred for the job of managing the estate and he'd done it well. He showed Gray the books, toured the fields with him, showed him the crops, shared his plans for the future. They lifted tankards of ale with the tenants, the grooms, the other laborers, and Gray listened to their concerns, their own hopes and dreams. Gray was grateful to them all. Their loyalty and dedication had more than made up for his neglect.

But Murray, the tenants, grooms, and others were not the only ones responsible for minimizing the effect of Gray's neglect. Maggie had filled any remaining void.

He could not go anywhere without seeing her or hearing of her. Whether it be visits to the tenants, the stables, or even the workers in the field. She had threaded Summerton through each finger so that she held it tightly in her grasp. She was more a part of Summerton than he ever could be, for some part of him would always pine for freedom. But the days were so filled with activity Gray rarely thought about freedom. Nights were a different matter.

At night he'd sometimes pace his bedchamber, feeling the four walls closing in on him like some deadly trap. He could often hear Maggie moving about her room as well. Sometimes he put his hand on the doorknob, wanting to talk to her. Ironically, she was the only one who could understand his situation, the only one who knew the total story. Then he'd remember she was the cause of his entrapment and he'd resume his pacing.

Other nights his hands were on her doorknob but not for conversation. Some nights his masculine needs would nearly drive him mad, because she was a wall away, beautiful and as beddable as any man could want. Those nights he'd ride to the village, telling himself he'd find another woman to slake his desire. But he never bothered to look. The woman he wanted to bed was Maggie.

His wife.

There had been more rain and the park was damp as Gray walked back from the stables after a morning ride with Rodney. The boy had run ahead, late for his lessons, but the head groom had stopped Gray to inform him that one of the horses had been injured. A cut on the leg. Nothing to signify, and all tended to.

As Gray reached the house, Maggie came out the door, with a basket in her hand and little Sean at her side. She was busy checking her basket and almost ran into Gray.

"Oh," she said in surprise. "I beg your pardon."

Gray stepped aside.

"I play, Papa!" Sean ran ahead to the park.

"What is all this?" Gray asked, pointing to the basket. He had not meant to make his voice sound so disapproving.

Maggie seemed to ignore his tone. Her eyes lit with excitement instead. "Mary Adams had her baby last night. Her son came with word a little while ago. I'm taking her some food and some baby things Olivia and I made." She pulled out a tiny cotton dress to show him.

"The ground is still wet," he said. "You'll be slogging through mud."

Sean's shoes were already muddied as he chased a small bird across the lawn.

She shrugged. "We shall manage." She walked past him, calling for Sean to come with her.

"One moment, Maggie," he said.

She stopped.

"I will drive you in the curricle."

She raised her eyes to his. When she did so, that sense of connection returned. It often did for him when their eyes met.

"I do not mind walking, Gray." The blue of her eyes sparkled like sapphires.

"I insist," he murmured, still caught in her gaze.

"As you wish," she responded, almost in a whisper.

They had not spent any time together, not without Olivia or his father or even Sir Francis being present. Gray found himself looking forward to the outing. He told himself it was due to Caleb's happy news. Sean would provide enough of a chaperone.

"Come back in the house. I'll send for the curricle." He looked toward Sean. "Sean," he shouted. "Come here!"

Sean turned and looked at him, but went on playing in the grass.

"Sean!" he shouted again. "Horse!"

Sean came running.

Gray and Maggie each kept up a running conversation with Sean during the short trip to the tenant's cottage. They did not talk to each other. It put Gray in mind of the first time he'd been alone in a girl's company. He'd not known what to say then, either. Sean rose to the occasion by having much to say about the "horfes" and the "curkle," so the time was spent pleasantly.

The roads were passable but not ideal and the mud that

might have caked Maggie's and Sean's boots instead gave the horses harder going.

When they reached the Adamses' cottage, Caleb's son ran to greet them and to hold the horses. Gray put Sean on his shoulders before he jumped down from the two-wheeled chaise. He flipped Sean to the ground, a dismount the boy loved. Gray turned to give Maggie his hand. As she started to step off, the horses shifted, jostling the curricle. He grabbed her by the waist and she fell against him. For a brief moment he held her in that sudden embrace, feeling all her softness and inhaling her lavender scent.

Then her feet found the earth, and Caleb limped out of the cottage. Young Bob tended to the horses and took charge of Sean, as he had done the last time they had visited.

Gray extended his hand to Caleb. "I understand congratulations are in order."

When Caleb let go of the handshake there was a gold guinea in his palm. The man stared at it.

"Something for the wee one," Gray said.

He glanced at Maggie. Approval shone in her eyes.

She turned to Caleb. "How is Mary? Is she well enough for callers?"

With pride, Caleb said, "She's right as rain. Wouldn't even stay abed. She'll be honored t'see you."

Caleb waited for them to enter the house first. A small fire was cheerfully burning in the parlor and Caleb's wife was hurriedly putting on a kettle to boil.

Maggie hurried to her. "Mary, do not trouble yourself. Ought you not to rest?"

Mary gave an awkward curtsy to Gray and smiled at

Maggie. "I am fit enough to serve you some tea, ma'am. The second was a breeze to the first."

Maggie put her arm around the woman and led her over to a rocking chair and handed her the basket. "We certainly shall not put you to the trouble. I have brought some food for you and some gifts for the baby."

As if receiving a cue on a stage, the baby began crying. The sound was jarringly familiar, Gray realized. He'd heard such cries when Sean took his first breath.

Mary tried to rise, but Maggie shooed her down. "May I pick him up? It is a boy, is it not?"

She stooped down to the wooden crib next to Mary's chair and picked up the infant who quieted suddenly. She cradled the baby in her arms.

"Oooooh." She beamed. "What a lovely boy."

"Come look at him, sir," Caleb said proudly.

Gray obliged out of politeness. He gazed down at the infant with his miniature features and shock of dark hair. The baby's arms and feet were waving about and his mouth was open. As Gray watched, the baby turned its head, rooting at Maggie's breast.

She laughed and their eyes caught.

Gray knew her thoughts as certainly as he was convinced she knew his. They both traveled back to that day a little over two years ago, in a small room not so unlike this one, where their eyes had met over another newborn.

The baby started to cry, having not found what he was seeking. Maggie smiled at Gray, a smile of remembrance. She did not speak, but there was no need of words.

She handed the baby to the mother. "We must go, Mary. We merely wished to deliver the basket. I will visit again another day. Send word to the house if there is anything you need, or anything we might do for you."

"Thank you, ma'am," Mary replied, clutching the newborn to her chest.

Another offer made as if she were lady of the manor, Gray thought, but he could not make himself care about it. The spell of the memory of Sean's birth remained with him, a day that had connected him to Maggie in more ways than a name on marriage papers.

"I'll see you out," Caleb said, and they finished their farewells.

Rounding up Sean, they were soon on the road again. This time their silence joined rather than separated them.

They had not gone far when Sean mumbled, "Mama." He crawled onto Maggie's lap and she cuddled him in her arms. A moment later he was asleep.

Gray peeked over at him. "Visiting makes him sleepy, I gather. He slept the last time, as I recall."

"He did indeed." She smiled.

Their eyes caught again and Gray felt her gaze warming him, in a carnal way as well as in the special sharing of a memory. What was he to do about such feelings with a wife who was not a wife?

He turned his attention back to his driving. "He seems often in your company." His voice came out brusquer than he'd intended. He glanced at her. "Do we not employ a governess?"

"I enjoy taking charge of him." She brushed the soft hair from the sleeping child's forehead, looking down at him with the same awed look she'd had that first day. It discomfited him more than his own carnal feelings did.

"Then why, pray, do we pay Miss Miles?" By God, he

sounded vexatious and prosy, as bad as his father. "Isn't the boy a bit young for a governess in any event? Would not a nurse do as well?" Could he not stop this absurd lecture?

She regarded him quizzically, as if he had just sprouted horns. Whatever had sprouted—or almost sprouted—had broken the connection between them.

Her countenance was stiff when she answered him, "Miss Miles was employed by the Camervilles before this, but Lady Camerville dismissed her."

He kept his eyes on the road ahead, telling himself he was not really the sort of person who pulled wings off of butterflies.

She continued. "Lord Camerville had shown too much interest in Miss Miles—"

His brows lifted in surprise. "Cammy? He was a schoolmate of Vincent's. Cammy was chasing maids in his school days."

Perhaps they could converse comfortably after all.

"Mr. Hendrick interceded on Miss Miles's behalf," Maggie explained. "So we hired her. You have noticed, of course, that he is sweet on her?"

He had not, but at this point was not surprised the flirtations of a boy's tutor were known to Maggie. It was merely another pie in which to dip her fingers.

He glanced at her and saw her softly rocking her sleeping son, rekindling the memories that connected him to her. He took a deep breath, determined not to foster this train of thought, but all he succeeded in doing was inhaling the scent of lavender.

"Hendrick is sweet on Miss Miles?" he finally managed. "We are matchmaking as well, madam?"

He had meant the comment as a jest, but she regarded him solemnly, as if he were demanding she explain herself.

"She would have been turned out without a reference. Olivia and I took pity on her."

"You do take care of everything and everyone, do you not?"

She turned away.

He had meant that as a compliment, but it had come out wrong, sounding petulant and unnecessarily critical, and so like his father.

"I shall endeavor to make more use of Miss Miles." Her voice was cold as frost.

Deuce. What she had done for Miss Miles was admirable. Why could he not have merely said so?

She fixed her attention on the distant landscape, pointedly not at him, and the distance between them grew.

He did not care, he told himself.

As they drew up to the house, one of the grooms ran out from the stables. Gray climbed down from the curricle.

"Come, Sean," Maggie said, gently waking the boy.

Sean mumbled something and burrowed farther into her.

"Hand him to me." As soon as he had Sean in his hands, the boy wrapped his arms around Gray's neck and laid his head on Gray's shoulder. Gray held him tight, remembering when Sean was an infant as small as Caleb's son, light as a feather.

Holding the child in one arm, he gave Maggie his hand. When they touched, they again looked into each other's eyes.

No matter how he protested, Gray thought, he was tied to this mother and child, and it was a bond that went much deeper than he had let himself suppose.

As soon as they crossed the threshold, Parker rushed up to him. "Master John, Lord and Lady Caufield have arrived. His lordship wishes to speak with you." The butler was obviously quite discomposed, to lapse into using Gray's Christian name.

"Trouble, Parker?" Gray asked. Why else this anxiety regarding a visit from his cousin? He handed Sean back to Maggie. "Is someone ill?"

"I have not his confidence." The butler's already wrinkled face gained additional creases. "You must come immediately."

Gray followed the butler to the parlor and entered to find Harry, Tess, Olivia, and Sir Francis. Olivia was urging tea and biscuits on everyone, but tension crackled throughout the room.

Harry popped to his feet. "Gray, you are here at last. I must speak with you."

Tess tossed him an agonized look. Olivia gave him a bewildered one. Sir Francis shrugged his shoulders.

"Of course, Harry. What is all this? What has happened?"

Harry gave a loud sigh. He rushed over and placed his hand on Gray's arm. "Your trunk was delivered to Caufield House."

"My trunk?" Gray blinked in bewilderment. This was the crisis? "I dispatched it to London."

Harry let go and began pacing. "First it was misdirected. Went God knows where. By the time it arrived in London, we were already in the country. Trimble sent it on to us."

"I apologize for the trouble of it. I shall collect it, of

course." Gray followed with his eyes, back and forth like watching a shuttlecock.

"No need. We have brought it to you."

Maggie quietly slipped into the room. Seeing her, Harry mumbled, "A pleasure, Maggie."

Tess jumped up from the settee and embraced her. "Oh, Maggie!" She dragged her to sit next to her, draping her arm around her.

"How nice of you to visit." Maggie looked mystified.

"Yes, well, it is nice, I suppose. Oh, I do hope you are well—" Tess said, drama in her voice.

Gray cut her off. "Harry, what the devil is this about?"

Harry barely slowed his pace. "I am talking about your papers!"

"My papers?"

"Your trunk was damaged, Gray," Tess cried. "Water leaked into the contents, so naturally we opened it to dry everything."

Oh, yes, naturally. What could be more natural than Harry and Tess snooping into his property?

"Naturally."

Tess blinked rapidly. "It was I who decided we must dry your papers. Do not hang that upon Harry."

"You looked at my papers?" What the devil had they found?

"We saw it, Gray," Harry intoned. "You may not deny it."

"Deny what?"

"Your marriage to a Spanish girl."

Gray felt the blood drain from his face. Of course. Along with other items of no importance, he'd packed the papers that had given permission for his marriage to Rosa.

All eyes were upon him. Olivia's and Sir Francis's confused. Tess's accusing. Maggie's? He could not tell.

He swept his arm over the room. "Harry, do tell us your conclusion of this inspection of my personal belongings."

Harry lifted his chin in his most self-righteous expression. "Two wives, Gray? That is bigamy, sir! You are lost to all propriety, to all honor—"

"No." Maggie tried to rise. Tess pulled her back down. "It is not true—"

Tess hugged her. "Dear one, there is no mistake."

Harry chimed in. "The papers are very clear. He married a woman in Spain, November, 1813."

Maggie wrenched herself from Tess's grip and stood. "There *is* a mistake, but it is not Gray's. You do not understand! He—"

"Silence, Maggie!" Gray's voice boomed, startling them, startling himself most of all.

Their eyes were riveted upon him, too ready to believe, to condemn. While they waited expectantly, Maggie's face contorted with pain.

Gray could not look at her. He swung around to his cousin. "You hasten to believe the worst of me, Harry?" He clenched his fist.

"The dates on the papers say it all, Cousin." Harry gave him a significant look. "The marriage took place when you returned to Spain after your leave in England that year. And by that time—if one counts the months—well—you—you would have already . . . um . . ."

Gray's eyes blazed. "I would have already been with Maggie. Is that what you mean?"

Harry gave him a priggish expression. "*Her* paper said—"

Gray's grip on fury was rapidly slipping.

"Gray, let me—" Maggie broke in.

"No!" he shot back. He glared at his cousin. "How dare you, Harry. You speak of honor. Was it honor that compelled you to disclose this in so public a manner? In front of Olivia and Sir Francis? In front of Maggie? You malign her name as well, do you not? And to her face. Why did you not seek a private conversation with me?"

Harry had the grace to look abashed.

Gray felt like a match set to powder. Harry had exposed the lowest point in his life: Rosa, his private shame.

He struggled to keep his voice cool. "True, I was married in Spain—"

Tess gasped.

"—but my wife was killed." He glared at Harry. "So you need not fear. I do not have two wives."

Maggie's hand flew to her mouth as Gray strode angrily from the room. She thought her heart would shatter from thumping so rapidly. For a moment she had thought her sins had been confounded. Never had she supposed there might be another woman who was his true wife. Worse, she was *relieved* the poor woman was dead.

She ought to have told them all the truth and cleared Gray's name once and for all. But he had forbidden her to speak.

Tess bounced out off of the chaise and gave her a big hug. Olivia looked as if she might cry.

"Oh, my dearest—" Tess exclaimed.

Unable to bear their sympathy when she was the cause

of all the trouble, Maggie pulled away and backed toward the door. "You are wrong. Gray is no bigamist."

They merely gazed upon her, dripping with concern for the wronged wife. She was not a wife, she wanted to protest! She opened her mouth, but closed it again. He had forbidden her.

She ran from the room. Parker was in the hall and had probably listened to the whole sordid interchange.

"Where did he go?" she asked.

"Above stairs," he replied.

She lifted her skirts and took the stairs two at a time. When she reached his door, she flung it open without knocking.

He stood with a vase of flowers in his hand poised as if to throw it against the wall. He swung around at her entrance.

"Leave me, Maggie," he warned. The vase was now aimed at her.

She ignored the vase as well as his demand and took two steps toward him. "I cannot allow you to do this!"

He gave her a dangerous look. "*You* cannot? You can stop me from shattering this vase against the wall?"

"You know what I mean," she snapped. "They think you are a bigamist."

He placed the vase down on the table and gave her a sardonic smile. "*Was* a bigamist," he corrected in a sarcastic tone. "They think I was a bigamist, and why shouldn't they? You have the papers stating I married you before Rosa."

She waved an exasperated hand. "I shall burn those dratted papers!"

"Noble of you, Maggie, but you already know Harry

and Tess can testify to seeing them. They are very willing to believe me capable of marrying two wives."

"But you are not such a man. I shall tell them the truth!" She turned and reached for the door.

He caught her by the arm and spun her around, grabbing her with both hands. "Tell *me* the truth, Maggie."

She looked into his eyes, seeing all the pain and rage she had caused him.

"What do you mean?" She gasped, knowing full well but prevaricating.

"The truth about you, about this whole charade." He shook her slightly. "If I am to be a bigamist for you, do I not deserve to know the truth?"

She continued to stare into his gray eyes, as hard as steel, as soft as smoke. What was she to tell him? That she was a murderer? A murderer of someone he must have known? Would he not expose her if he knew the truth?

She looked into his depths. Even if he did not expose her as a murderer, could he live with her day after day believing it was so? At this moment, she did not know which was the worse to endure. Her knees grew weak. Only his grip held her upright.

He laughed softly. "You will never confide in me, will you? You will keep your secrets."

She turned her head away, tears springing to her eyes, because he had freed her from telling him.

"I never meant to hurt you," she said earnestly. "We have both had enough of this. I will explain to them that I am not your wife. I will take Sean and leave."

Instead of releasing her, he wrapped her in his arms and held her close. She could feel the rise and fall of his breathing where her cheek rested against his chest.

"That is nonsense, Maggie. You are no more able to care for him than you were before." His voice was gentle. "The damage is done. Harry will not be persuaded out of his opinion. I suspect at this moment he and Tess are clucking over my scandalous behavior and exclaiming how fortunate it is that my Spanish wife is dead."

She buried her face deeper into his chest. "Never say it. You must despise me for falsely taking her place."

He eased her away from him and put his finger under her chin, lifting her face to his. "I do not despise you."

Her heart seemed to stop beating.

He took a deep breath. "You are not the only one with secrets, Maggie. I had hoped no one would discover my marriage to Rosa." His eyes filled with pain again. "I seduced her, you see. I was so full of drink during the event I do not even recall it, but she bore the consequences of that night. When I was told she carried my child, I married her. What else could I have done?" His eyes wrinkled. "She was not even eighteen years old."

This time she took him in her arms and felt him tremble against her.

"I told her to stay in her father's house. I had no wish to be with her, but she followed me to battle." His voice came out in rasps. "She was running toward me when the canister exploded."

"No!" Maggie cried.

"So you see," he went on, his voice achingly ironic, "bigamy is not the worst of sins."

She, the murderer, tilted her face to his. "No, it is not."

His eyes grew dark as he stared into hers. Her heart accelerated and her lips parted. He leaned down and covered them with his own.

His hands slid down her back and pressed her firmly against him. Her arms wrapped around his neck, and her mouth opened to allow the kiss to deepen. He lifted her, carrying her to the bed and seating her on it. Still standing, he pressed himself against her between her parted legs.

She wanted him. Wanted to join with him. To stir this swirl of emotions into one simple one, one that brought pleasure, not pain for both of them. No more thinking, no more memories, no recriminations. Merely holding him, touching him, allowing him to plunge into her, to drive everything else away and leave only the two of them loving each other as a man and wife might.

He lifted her skirt and she wrapped her legs around him, holding him tighter, pressing his groin against her.

"Gray," she pleaded.

She would free him of his clothes, feel his bare skin against hers. They would lie on the bed. They would love each other at last . . .

He pulled away.

She looked at him in confusion.

His face darkened. "I am not so reformed, am I, Maggie? I would seduce you as well."

Maggie's chest swelled with each gulp of air. She ached to touch him again, but his eyes turned wild and for a fleeting second she wondered if he would do something mad.

"I will not seduce you, Maggie." His voice was tightly controlled. "There is only so much my conscience can bear."

"But—" she said, but he held up a hand.

"Go, Maggie," he said quietly. "I beg you."

She slipped off the bed and ran out of the room.

Chapter THIRTEEN

Gray did not trust himself to move until hearing Maggie close the door behind her. He then flung himself in a chair and rubbed his face.

He could not blame drink for his behavior this day.

It had been supremely difficult to wrench himself away from her, to resist her willingness to bed him and drive away the high emotions of the moment. What had he been thinking?

He had not been thinking at all. That was the difficulty. He'd marched from the parlor before his anger got the better of him, and when Maggie entered his bedchamber only fraying threads of control remained.

He glanced at the vase of flowers and absently fingered one of the petals. At least she had stopped him from hurling it against the wall. The shattering of glass would have been quite satisfying, but it would only serve to create a mess for Decker or one of the maids. Maggie had not tried to stop him from seducing her, though, had she? Why had he stopped himself?

It had simply seemed dishonorable. Exploiting a

woman's willingness, as he had done so disastrously in Spain.

He twisted sideways in the chair. Maggie was no maiden, certainly Sean was evidence of that, and she had placed him in this coil. Did that give him the right to bed her? She was not his wife, damn it! Acting like a husband in bed would only further complicate matters between them.

He laughed aloud. And now, to top off everything, he'd also become a bigamist. Oh, no one within earshot would disclose his supposed moral decrepitude. Indeed, since Rosa had been blown to bits, they could cheerfully avoid ever addressing the subject again.

But every time one of them looked upon him, every time they conversed with him, a part of them would be thinking of him as a man so lost to honor that he would wed two wives.

Gray rose from the chair and prowled the room like a caged animal. He wished he *could* throw something. Rage at somebody. Maggie ought to be the target, but he had just seen in what direction his passions went with her.

He stared at her door. Was she in her bedchamber at this moment? Shaking his head, he began pacing again. If he did not escape this room he would certainly go mad.

Was he expected to return to the parlor? He could just see them all, Harry, Tess, Sir Francis, Olivia, heads together, speaking in hushed tones that would abruptly stop when he entered the room. Dinner would be another pleasant event. They would force amiable discourse, all the while stealing significant looks his way. Not only that, but he would probably have to face Maggie there, and her eyes upon him would be the most knowing of all.

No, riding straight into cannon fire sounded more tolerable.

Instead Gray rode to the village and sat in the tavern with men who talked of weather, crops, and the high price of corn. He stayed until darkness fell and he had to pick his way back to Summerton down a moonlit road. And though he did not sleep well, he rose early enough the next morning to avoid any entreaties by little boys who might wish to ride with him. He rode alone. By the time he returned to the stable, he felt almost himself again.

Still, he preferred to avoid another encounter with his cousin.

He asked the groom who took his horse, "Is Mr. Murray about?" Surely estate matters would provide an excuse for absenting himself still longer.

"Rode out with Wiggins, sir," the groom replied.

So much for that. Gray thanked the man and walked slowly across the park.

As he entered the house, he toyed with the idea of begging breakfast in the kitchen. He'd done so with Sean and Rodney and had often made it a practice as a boy, lapping up the affection and treats heaped upon him by Cook. The kitchen had always been an excellent place to hide.

He shook his head.

When had he turned into such a coward? Better to charge ahead at full speed. He straightened his spine.

First he would change out of his riding clothes, though. With any luck, everyone would have left the breakfast table by the time he got there.

But Harry stood waiting for him in the hallway. "Gray, I'd hoped to catch you . . ."

An ambush. He had not figured on that.

"May I speak privately with you for just a moment?"

A biting retort sprang to Gray's lips, something about it being a little late for privacy. He pushed the words aside, gesturing curtly toward the library.

They entered the room, Harry closing the door with the most serious of expressions on his face.

Harry's hand actually trembled as he leaned against the cherrywood table. "My dear cousin, I most sincerely beg your forgiveness. I do not fancy you will give it, but please accept my profound apology."

The hairs on the back of Gray's neck rose. Had Maggie disclosed her part in this after all? Damn his cowardice! He ought to have dealt with his cousin last night.

"Apology for what precisely?" he asked cautiously.

Harry's mouth suffered a spasm before he could speak. "For not addressing you in private. You had the right of it. It was so badly done of me."

Get on with it, man! Gray said to himself. He tried to be patient.

His cousin coughed and fiddled with the knot in his neckcloth and opened and closed his mouth several times before he spoke again. "You and I could have settled it. If I had known your Spanish wife to be dead—" Harry broke off, his chin shaking like it was made of jelly. "I . . . I might have spared your true wife any knowledge of how you deceived and disgraced her."

Gray almost laughed. As apologies went, this one left much to be desired. So he was still the dishonorable bigamist and Maggie, the *true* wife, his unwitting victim. What a riotous joke. Too bad the only person he could share it with was Maggie, and he doubted she would find the same humor in it.

Gray attempted to keep his face composed.

Harry swallowed several times. "I . . . I do not know why you did it, Gray, but I promise I will say no more about it to anyone. Tess and I will keep your secret. We will be the soul of discretion."

Gray did laugh then. Harry looked puzzled.

He tried to sober himself. "Did you tell Father?"

Harry's eyes widened and he vigorously shook his head. "No, no, I am not lost to all good sense. Hoped my uncle would never find out."

That was one small point in Harry's favor, Gray admitted to himself.

His cousin stared at him warily. "Is . . . is my apology accepted?"

Harry's soft cheeks and pale skin gave him a boyish, innocent appearance, although he was nearly as old as Vincent would have been had he lived. Harry had remained Gray's faithful ally throughout his flight from his father and during his army years. How much did it matter that he was prosy and self-righteous? Did Gray care that Harry thought him lost to all decency? That Harry would so readily believe he could wed two wives? By God, he'd not chosen to wed either one!

Gray held up his hand. "Say no more, Harry. The matter is forgotten."

Harry's countenance barely relaxed. "I never meant to insinuate myself in your business . . ."

Had you not? Gray thought, his anger rekindled. *You examined my papers readily enough.* He flexed one hand into a fist.

"It was all my doing. The responsibility is all mine."

Now that was a corker. Tess, Gray would wager, had a big part in the event. But one of the things Gray most liked about his cousin was his unwavering devotion to his equally bird-witted wife.

"Harry." Gray relaxed his hand and put it on his cousin's arm. "Enough. I realize you and Tess meant no harm."

But, deuce, they had created much havoc in his life. This whole matter might have been avoided had Harry done what Gray asked and given Maggie the money.

The money.

Gray leveled a glance at his cousin. "Harry, what happened to the money I provided for Maggie?"

Harry turned red. "Put it in the bank," he sputtered. "I always meant to give it back to you . . . with interest, of course. We . . . we thought it a better plan to bring her here, and I think you can agree now that our judgment had been correct."

A small knock sounded at the door. Before either man could respond, the door burst open, producing Tess in a flurry of skirts and tears.

She fell into Gray's arms. "Gray, it is all my fault. I only opened the papers to dry them and I couldn't help looking at them, could I? And they did not say she had *died*, you know, and I knew you married Maggie first because I read *her* papers— It was very bad of you to marry two wives, I am sure, but I do not pretend to understand the ways of men— In any event, Harry has explained to me we should not have looked at your papers, though how we could *dry* them and not *look* at them is beyond my powers of comprehension. But you must know it is my fault and my fault entirely—not Harry's—and it is I you should never forgive, though I shall be wretched if you do not!"

She spoke the whole in one breath and sobbed at the same time. It was quite remarkable.

"Tess." Gray's stomach hurt from the effort not to laugh. "It is over and little harm done."

"Except to Maggie." Her voice wobbled.

He took a deep breath. He must get used to being the villain in this farce, he supposed.

Tess's eyes filled with fat, glistening tears. "I promise I shall never look at papers that are not my own." She spoke with what was, even for her, exaggerated drama. "I shall never intrude into another person's affairs. From this moment, this very moment, I . . . I will mind my own business only."

Gray did laugh then and hugged her close. "Tess, be easy. Be easy."

She hiccoughed and sniffled, and he sacrificed a clean handkerchief into which she noisily blew her nose. Her husband opened his arms and she collapsed into them. He patted her back and looked as if he might succumb to a fit of crying as well.

"Cease this commotion at once," Gray insisted. "What is done is done. We shall simply forget all about it."

Both regarded him with mournful eyes.

He gave them a reassuring smile. "Have you breakfasted? Because I have not and I am famished."

Like puppets he'd seen once at the Mayday Fair as a boy, they shook their heads in unison.

Arm in arm, he walked with them to the breakfast room.

*   *   *

Harry and Tess, amid hugs, kisses, and more tears, departed later that morning. Gray sent them off, standing between Maggie and Olivia on the front steps while Tess waved from the carriage window.

Gray felt Maggie close to him as if they had been wrapped in the same clothes. When she'd entered the breakfast room with his father earlier, he'd barely nodded a greeting. Yet throughout the meal, he had felt no one else's presence, even though Tess filled the room with her lively conversation.

With Tess and Harry still calling out their farewells, the Caufield carriage began to roll, Sean and Rodney making a game of running after it. Gray felt rather than saw Maggie retreat into the house.

He turned to follow her, but Olivia drew him aside.

"I did not wish to say so in front of Maggie, but I most sincerely convey my condolences to you." She patted his arm in a sisterly fashion. "I . . . I am persuaded you must have married your Spanish lady out of love. I know you could not have done otherwise. You must have felt very desolate and alone in Spain after whatever transpired to estrange you and Maggie. I refuse to judge you harshly for your actions."

It appeared Harry and Tess were not the sole purveyors of melodrama. Gray tried not to cringe.

Olivia went on. "I have experienced love and grief as you have, so I completely understand. But I do wish you would give Maggie a chance. It is possible to love again, and she is such a fine person."

"Thank you, Olivia," he said stiffly.

They climbed the steps together.

She slowed a little. "I wish you would persuade Maggie to accept the invitation to the Camervilles' house party. It would be a treat for you both."

He stopped completely. "What invitation?"

She smiled warily. "Surely Maggie spoke to you of it? Lord and Lady Camerville are giving a house party in a week."

Cammy. Lecherous to lowly governesses. And, he figured, to lonely widows. But what of beautiful would-be wives? "Maggie declined the invitation?"

"Yes. She said she would not go." Olivia's forehead wrinkled. "The invitation came to me, but it quite properly included her. I am certain it was meant for all of us, but they could not have known you had returned to Summerton. So would you come and persuade Maggie to come, too? We need only stay a week."

By damn, it looked as if Olivia would water up. He'd had enough tears for one morning. He put an arm around her. "Do you wish to attend, Olivia?"

She nodded. "I have not been to such a party since . . . since Vincent was alive. Lady Camerville and I once knew each other, and there will be new company and games and entertainments."

Gray could imagine what sorts of entertainments Cammy might devise, but the man was not so lost to propriety as to engage in open debauchery. It was from clandestine debauchery Olivia would need protection.

"Sir Francis has an invitation," she went on. "He said he would drive me, but . . ."

But she could not very well attend in the sole company of a single gentleman and keep her reputation intact. Gray suspected Sir Francis was behind this invitation, wanting an opportunity to get Olivia away from Summerton. Not that Gray disapproved. Sir Francis was a good man and Gray had seen his eyes glow when they lighted upon Olivia.

Gray gave her a knowing smile.

Which she completely missed. "I don't know what I should do without Sir Francis. He has remained a faithful friend."

"Indeed." He gave her a fond squeeze, wondering if she were blind or simply thought him so. "Very faithful."

"So you will tell Maggie we will attend?" she asked hopefully.

Gray's forehead knitted. *Maggie.* The need to appear in public with her as husband and wife must eventually come, but so soon? "I cannot—"

She interrupted him. "I asked Harry and Tess, but they have not received an invitation."

And would probably not receive one. Cammy would have little use for a self-righteous prig totally devoted to his wife.

Olivia looked at him entreatingly.

How far did a brother's obligation stretch? To a country house party? Such an entertainment ought to have been commonplace for a woman of Olivia's age and position. She should have attended many such parties, instead of being secluded near to total isolation at Summerton.

But, then, he had not been present to give her escort.

He expelled a long breath. "I will speak to Maggie."

"Ohhh!" she cried, falling on his neck. "Thank you, Gray! We shall have the jolliest time!"

He had not precisely said yes, had he?

How the devil was he going to address this party invitation with Maggie? He had no idea how to even be comfortably in the same room with her.

Olivia released him and skipped up the steps. "I can hardly wait to tell Sir Francis! I do hope he will visit today."

Sir Francis's visits were as regular as the sunrise.

He watched her dance happily into the house. He followed less joyfully.

When he crossed the hall, Murray stood there, hat in his hand.

Another obligation, he suspected. "What is it, Ted?"

The man twisted his hat. "Your father summoned me. I thought you might bear me company."

"Of course." His insides turned to lead. After such a morning, he had no energy left to tackle his father. He avoided his father whenever possible, was rarely in his company without Maggie present, but he'd be damned if he'd ask Murray to wait until they could summon her. He ought to be able to handle his father without her.

Without complete confidence in that thought, however, he entered his father's study with Murray. The earl sat at his desk, which was piled with ledgers.

Murray cleared his throat. "You asked for me, my lord?"

The earl looked up, his baffled expression darkening when he spied Gray. "I did not ask for *him,* did I?" The old man waved a finger in Gray's direction.

"I thought I might assist you, Father," Gray said mildly.

"Hurrummph." The earl searched through the ledgers. "These are all old. I cannot find the current ledger. Someone has stolen it. We must alert the magistrate."

Murray gulped. "It is not missing, my lord. It is in my office."

"In your office?" Summerton's brows rose. "What the devil is it doing there?"

"So that I might make the entries, my lord."

The earl half rose from his chair, leaning on his cane. "You make entries? Since when do you make entries?"

"Since—" Murray began, but Gray put a restraining hand on his arm.

He stepped forward. "If I were you, sir, I would ask Murray to bring the ledger to you."

"You would?" Summerton sat back down.

"Indeed." Gray nodded. "In fact, I would insist upon it."

"Insist upon it?" Summerton's eyebrows rose.

"Yes."

"Hurrumph." He gave his son a sneer. "I suppose you think any manager I employed would steal me blind."

Gray shrugged.

"Well, I'll have you know, this fellow"—Lord Summerton wagged his finger at Murray—"is honest. I grew up with him. Selected him myself for this job."

Neither young man corrected the earl.

"You keep that ledger, my friend," the earl said to Murray. "You are doing a fine job. Don't know what I'd do without you."

"Very good, sir." Murray expelled a breath and darted a glance toward Gray.

"Yes, well, you may leave now. Got work to do," the old man mumbled.

Murray beat a hasty retreat.

Summerton looked up to see his son still standing there. "What the devil are you waiting for?"

A corner of Gray's mouth turned up, ever so slightly. His father's sharp words still stung, but not like before. More often they now made him sad. He would never discover which of all his boyhood crimes had netted him his father's enduring ire, would never have the chance to make amends.

"Your permission, sir," Gray said mildly. "I did not wish to leave you without it."

"I'll have none of your lip, boy. Begone with you." The older man waved him off.

Gray hesitated, but there was no more he could say. With a slight bow, he walked out of the room.

And ran straight into Maggie.

With Sean in her arms, she was hurrying toward the earl's study. Gray had to grab her shoulders to keep her from crashing into him.

"Oh," she cried. "I heard that you were in with Lord Summerton."

She looked delectably frazzled, but Gray pushed that thought away. "Did you suppose I could not be trusted in my father's presence without you?"

She colored. "It is merely that he can be so cruel."

And you must be there to protect me, he added silently.

He dropped his hands, realizing he had held her much longer than necessary for her to regain her balance.

"Papa!" Sean's chubby arms strained toward Gray.

He reached for the boy, to give his hands something else to do but touch her.

"Walk, Papa," Sean said firmly, pulling on the collar of his coat.

Not horfe? Gray turned to Maggie. "This is a twist. What does he mean?"

"We were setting off for a walk, but then I heard you were with Lord Summerton." She looked at him warily from beneath her lashes, but the effect was quite different than she might have supposed.

It put Gray in mind of the previous day's kiss, an ill-timed, inopportune thought.

"Do not let me alter your plans." His voice was husky.

As if she realized the direction of his thoughts, her eyelids fluttered. "Would you care to accompany us? You would be most welcome."

"Walk, Papa!" Sean demanded. "Now!" He squirmed to get down.

Gray released the child only to have his large hand captured in two small dimpled ones. Sean pulled him with all the strength a two-year-old could muster, which was quite surprisingly a lot.

"Seems I do not have a choice." He smiled, suddenly feeling almost lighthearted.

Chapter FOURTEEN

M aggie felt a thrill rush through her at seeing his smile, though she realized her delight was all out of proportion. They were merely going on a walk. Still her heart beat with mounting excitement as she collected her shawl and bonnet from the table in the hall. Her fingers trembled as she tied the ribbons of her bonnet under her chin.

She must learn to be in his company without feeling like a bride on her wedding night. She groaned to herself at this terrible analogy, but she could barely be in his company without such thoughts crossing her mind. Or influencing her behavior.

It had been shameless of her to throw herself at him the previous day when their emotions had been in such a turmoil. He had made it clear that her willingness to play his wife in bed was not to his taste at all. She could not blame him. Because of her he was trapped into another marriage he did not want and was branded a great sinner besides.

Still, she could not regret being in his company. The day was fine, brisk and clear and perfect for a long walk.

Rodney ran up to her. "Are we going for a walk after all?"

"If your mother and Mr. Hendrick have given you permission." Maggie smiled.

"They have." Rodney skipped along. "Are you coming, too, Uncle?"

"It seems so." Gray's hand remained thoroughly in Sean's possession, and the child tugged him along.

"Capital!" cried Rodney. "Can we walk down to the stream?"

"Stream!" parroted Sean.

Maggie disliked the stream. She disliked any bodies of water. She bit her lip.

Rodney grinned. "You could show Aunt Maggie and Sean where my father taught you to fish."

Gray looked to her for the decision.

"Oh, very well," she said, reluctant to disappoint the boy. "But you must be very careful and hold Sean's hand."

"I will!" shouted Rodney.

"Stream!" cried Sean.

The boys ran ahead, but as they were almost always in view and the stream some distance away, Maggie did not mind. The land they must cross to reach the stream was beautiful, if hilly. Where the boys scrambled easily, she took care not to trip. Gray often offered his arm to assist her, and when he did so, she could not fail to notice the firmness of the muscle beneath his coat sleeve or how much taller he was than she.

He lifted her over a stile, his hands firmly upon her waist. She still felt them long after he'd released her.

"I am glad of the opportunity to be alone with you."

His voice was as warm as the sun illuminating his handsome features.

Her heart accelerated for she was glad, too. Joyous, in fact.

"There is a matter I wish to discuss with you." Those handsome features took on a grave expression. "Olivia told me of the invitation to the Camerville house party."

This was not so bad a topic to discuss, she thought. Though what she could say about it she did not know.

He took her hand to assist her over a rocky spot. "I am persuaded we must attend."

"Of course." It was natural for him to want the diversion of company as much as Olivia did. She found no fault with it, except to wonder what other ladies might attend and how beautiful they might be.

He halted. "You agree? I confess I thought you would not so readily do so."

She turned to him. "I have no right to object to anything you wish to do." She took a breath. "I wish you a happy time."

She continued walking and he caught up to her. They took several paces in silence.

"You have no qualms about appearing as husband and wife?" he asked tightly.

This time Maggie halted. "Husband and wife? Surely you do not expect me to accompany you!"

He'd not worn a hat and the breeze lifted his hair. "It would appear odd otherwise. The invitation included you. How would it look if I went without you?"

She gave him an intent look. "Gray, I could not possibly attend such an affair. Appear in public as your wife? I do not think I am able to manage such a thing."

His brow furrowed. "We shall have to do so some-time."

"I cannot face it." She turned to look at the boys scampering down the hill and resumed walking.

He kept abreast of her. "If we do not attend, Olivia will stay home. You would disappoint her so easily?"

"Perhaps Sir Francis can escort her."

He took hold of her arm and helped her over another stile, using the moment to catch her eye. "Maggie, Olivia cannot travel to the Camerville estate in the company of a single gentleman."

She wished she could cover her ears against this reasonable statement. "But Sir Francis is perfectly respectable."

"That is not the point," he continued patiently. "Her reputation would suffer nonetheless."

She dared a glance at him. "I do not wish that to happen."

The boys shouted. Sean pointed excitedly and Rodney waved. The stream was at last in view.

"Do not run too far ahead," Maggie called to them.

"We won't!" Rodney shouted back.

She and Gray continued walking at their slower pace.

Gray finally spoke. "I am pleased Olivia wishes to attend this party. It has been too long for her. It is unnatural."

"I do agree, Gray." Maggie sighed. "She is ready to move out in the world. I have no desire to hold her back, but such an affair is no place for me."

"It is hardly presentation at Court." He gave her a half-joking smile. "It is a country party, and Camerville House cannot hold too many guests. I doubt there would be more than twenty."

She wrinkled her brow in dismay. Twenty guests seemed overwhelming to her. "I cannot."

"We ought to face this now. It is the course we have taken. We must appear sometimes as husband and wife." His voice was reasonable.

She peered directly into his eyes. "You must go wherever you please, Gray, but I am content to stay at Summerton. I have avoided making a spectacle of myself. That is why I do not attend the church services on Sunday, though Olivia has said the vicar remarks upon it. I do not believe I have been to the village more than half a dozen times."

He leveled a suspicious look. "You have led such a life? Are you in hiding, Maggie?"

She glanced away, afraid of what might show on her face. She was always fearful of being recognized. It was nonsensical. Gloucestershire was far away, after all. Until her flight to London, she had never been above twenty miles from Gloucester. Her school had been in a nearby parish, as had the residence of the lady to whom she had been a companion. No one ever looked closely at a lady's companion. No one except that one soldier and he could not come from the grave and identify her.

"I am not in hiding," she said, persuading herself it was only half a lie. "But I never wished to draw too much attention, since I was not truly your wife."

He gave an ironic laugh. "I suspect you have succeeded merely in increasing curiosity. Upon one of your rare appearances, I imagine people in the village opening their shutters and lining the streets to see you."

She felt a shiver go up her spine. When she had gone into the village, it did seem as if people stared at her.

The boys reached the shrubbery around the stream.

"Stream! Stream!" Sean shouted, jumping up and down. The water was visible through a patch of trees.

"May I show Sean the fishing place, Uncle?" Rodney called.

Maggie watched them anxiously. "Do not let them, Gray. They will get too close to the edge."

"There is no harm in it," Gray assured her. "We will catch up to them in two minutes. They will be safe until then."

"Rodney, do take Sean's hand! Do not let go of him!" she called. Her hands were trembling and her throat felt very tight.

"Mind you be careful," Gray shouted.

"We will!" Rodney responded.

Maggie quickened her step nonetheless. When they reached the shrubbery, she caught sight of Rodney's head.

"Uncle John!" Rodney cried and suddenly he jumped into the water.

She screamed. Where was Sean?

Gray raced to the stream's edge, throwing off his coat as he ran.

Where was Sean?

Maggie lifted her skirts, hurrying as fast as she could to reach the place where Rodney had disappeared. Ahead of her, Gray plunged into the water.

Her heart leapt into her throat. She could not see Rodney.

The stream was swollen and the water ran fast. It took Gray under.

"No!" she screamed.

God in heaven, not Gray, too. *Where was Sean?*

Gray's head broke through the water again. Maggie nearly wept in relief.

Rodney shouted, the sound coming from downstream. Twenty feet away Rodney clung by one hand to a thin overhanging branch of a fallen tree that jutted out over the stream. His other hand clutched the cloth of Sean's coat, holding Sean like a rag doll.

He was alive. Sean was alive!

"Hold on!" she called to Rodney. While Gray swam toward the boys, she scrambled through the brambles at the water's edge.

They tore at Maggie's skirt and scratched her legs, but she did not heed them. The sound of the rushing water nearly drowned out Rodney's cries. Gray shouted back to him, but she could not make out what he said. Sean was frighteningly silent.

A branch overhead whisked the bonnet from her head and dangled it behind her neck. She made it to the fallen tree, but they were out too far from the edge for her to reach them.

She searched the water for Gray and saw him go under once more. Oh, dear God! Was she to watch all three of them drown?

The branch Rodney clung to cracked, and Sean's head went under before Rodney could grab on to another and pull him out of the water again.

Maggie tried to climb on to the tree's trunk, but it was wet and her foot kept slipping.

Gray's head broke the surface of the water again. "Hang on!" he shouted loud enough for her to hear.

Rodney pulled Sean up higher.

The current was so swift. Maggie feared it would carry Gray away at any moment, and she would see his body float away like her false husband. She feared Rodney would be unable to hang on while the water tugged at him and at Sean. She would watch the water carry them away as well.

She straddled the tree trunk like a man on a horse and tried to crawl toward the boys, but Gray somehow reached them first.

Gray grabbed Sean out of Rodney's weakening fingers and grasped the branch with his free hand.

"Hang on to my back," he yelled to Rodney.

The boy climbed over him and locked his hands across Gray's throat. Gray held Sean in front, and the child clung to him like a monkey. They were still no closer to the shore. Maggie inched her way toward them.

Suddenly there was a crack and the branch broke.

"No!" Maggie screamed again as the current swept them away.

She slid off the tree and ran down the stream's bank, trying to keep sight of Gray in the water, both boys still clinging to him. Gray was struggling against the current, trying to swim closer to the shore, but the current pulled them farther and farther downstream.

Maggie managed to run ahead of them to a place where the land jutted out a bit. There was a thin tree growing right at the tip. Jumping as high as she could, she grabbed the trunk of it and bent it over the water. She was in the water herself, dangling from the bent tree.

Gray pushed himself close enough to grab the tree, and he used it to pull them to where the water was calmer and he could stand. He reached Maggie who was speechless with relief, but too frightened to let go.

He staggered out of the water onto the shore, both boys still clinging to him.

Maggie's fingers hurt and her wet clothes weighted her down even more, but she barely cared.

Sean was safe. And Rodney.

And Gray.

"Maggie!" Gray was suddenly next to her in the water, grasping her by the waist and carrying her to shore, to where the boys were. Rodney sat on the grass holding little Sean as he retched and vomited the water he'd swallowed. Both boys were pale and shivering.

"We must get them home. We must get them warm." Gray coughed up water from his lungs.

"Sean." Maggie rushed over to her son and swept him into her arms. She grabbed Rodney and hugged both boys tight. "My darling boys. My precious boys."

"We must hurry." Gray picked up Rodney, and Maggie held Sean. Wet, cold, and nearly exhausted, they carried the boys away from the water. Gray found his coat on the ground and tossed it to Maggie. "Wrap him in this."

She wrapped Sean as best she could as they climbed the hill.

Sean coughed continuously and Maggie feared for a lung infection. She pushed herself harder, trying to keep the pace Gray set for them.

"I can walk!" Rodney protested.

Gray put him down and took Sean from her arms.

When the bedraggled group finally came into sight of

Summerton Hall, workmen in the fields spied them and came running. Men grabbed the two boys.

"Get them to the house," Gray shouted.

Maggie stumbled, panting for breath. She saw Sean being swiftly carried to the house and to safety. She did not care if she could not walk another step.

Gray saw her stumble. Ignoring the weakness in his own limbs, he swept her into his arms and carried her down the hill and home to Summerton Hall.

People spilled from the house, alerted by the cries of the workmen who ran with the children. Gray's lungs felt near to bursting, but he could only think to get Maggie inside. To see her get warm. The men carrying the boys were some distance ahead, their burdens lighter and their muscles not trembling with fatigue.

The head groom ran up to him. "Let me take her from you." He stretched out his arms.

Gray glowered at the man and shook his head. He'd be damned if he let go of her until he knew she was safe.

"Rodney!" Olivia's voice pierced the air and she grabbed at her son, impeding the man's efforts to get him inside. Mr. Hendrick pulled her off. Miss Miles gave instructions to the man carrying Sean.

Gray carried Maggie into the house where the door was held open. Everyone seemed to be shouting. Above it all he could hear Olivia shrilly crying out Rodney's name.

Gray did not heed the mud caking his soaked boots as he climbed the stairway to Maggie's bedchamber. Miss Miles and one of the maids were already there, stripping Sean of his clothes and rubbing him with a towel. Gray put Maggie down, not sure if she could stand on her own.

She wrapped her arms around his neck, clinging close to him. He held her in return as tightly as he could.

"Thank you," she whispered to him. "Thank you for saving my son, for saving all of us."

He put his cheek on her wet hair. "I'm not sure it was me who did the saving."

They stood in the embrace, clinging to each other. Gray felt her shiver.

"You must get out of your wet clothes, Maggie," he said, releasing her.

She wrapped her arms around him again and kissed him full on the lips, though Miss Miles and the maid were present. Her skin was cold but her lips warm, and more than anything he wished to kiss her back. Were it not for her courage and determination, his life and the boys' lives would surely have been lost. He was full to bursting with pride in her, and he wanted desperately to beg her forgiveness for almost losing what was most precious to her.

She shivered again, and he woke to the need to get her warm and dry. He let go of her and turned to her maid. "We must get her warm. Help me remove her wet clothes." He fumbled with Maggie's laces, his fingers too numb to undo the wet knot.

"Let me, sir," the maid said.

Mrs. Thomas rushed in, her housekeeping duties abandoned for the moment. "What happened? The poor dear." She nearly pushed Gray aside to pull the sodden dress off Maggie.

"Fell in the stream," he managed, his energy flagging. "You must get her warm."

Maggie's attention had shifted to Sean, who now

whimpered while Miss Miles wrapped a blanket around him.

"Give him warm milk," she pleaded.

"And hot tea for Mrs. Grayson," Gray added. His teeth chattered and he began to shiver.

Decker appeared at his elbow. "Come, sir."

Decker led him into his own bedchamber. With the calmness and efficiency of a seasoned gentleman's gentleman, Decker peeled off Gray's wet waistcoat and shirt.

"By God, Decker," Gray rasped. "I thought the boys would drown."

"But they did not, sir," the valet murmured comfortingly, pausing long enough to hand Gray a glass of brandy, which he downed in two gulps.

Decker held out a velvet banian Gray recognized as having once belonged to his brother. He allowed himself to be wrapped in it, fancying it smelled of Vincent even after all these years.

I'm sorry, Vincent, he said to himself. *I almost let your son drown.* He should not have let the boys run ahead. He should have seen the danger.

Decker insisted he sit in the chair by the fire. Gray's limbs trembled while Decker pulled off his sodden boots.

"If you can salvage these boots, Decker, you'll soon be in demand in London."

"I fear that task might be beyond my powers," replied Decker, betraying a hint of a smile.

A maid appeared with a pot of tea and poured him a cup. Gray reached for the decanter of brandy and added a generous amount to the tea, gulping it down like a man dying of thirst. Soon the warmth reached his stomach and the pins and needles stopped piercing his feet.

"Help me dress, Decker."

"Dress, sir? I beg you to rest." The man dropped the sodden clothing he had been gathering in his arms.

"No. I've rested enough."

Decker regarded him somewhat disapprovingly, but provided a fresh set of clothes and helped Gray into them. The valet gathered the wet clothes in a bundle and bowed himself out of the room.

Gray opened the connecting door to Maggie's bedchamber. She sat in a rocking chair holding Sean, all wrapped in a blanket. Without asking for an invitation, he entered the room.

"How is he?"

She glanced up looking wan. She smiled at him. "He is sleeping, and his breathing is regular."

Gray found a chair and set it near her. "And you, Maggie?"

She searched his face and extended her hand to briefly touch his cheek. "I am shaken, Gray, but so thankful I can barely speak."

He turned away, ashamed. "I should not have allowed them to go to the stream alone."

"Yes," she agreed without a hint of censure in her voice. She gazed back at her son. "But this time the water did not take them."

It was an odd statement. "There will never be another time, Maggie. I shall make certain of it."

She gave a melancholic shrug of her shoulder. "There is no such certainty."

She looked like a schoolgirl with her damp hair tied back from her face, a soft dressing gown wrapped around her. He wanted to hold her as she held Sean. He wanted to clasp both of them to his chest and never let go of them.

A knock sounded at the door. Olivia entered. Gray rose to his feet.

"Maggie, dearest, I came to see how you and Sean are faring." Olivia's eyes were warm with concern. She gave Gray a small smile. "You, too, Gray."

Maggie smiled at Olivia. "I have nothing but a scratch or two, and besides being quite exhausted, Sean seems unhurt as well. Tell me, is Rodney all right?"

Gray gave Olivia his chair. "Oh, Rodney protests that he is unhurt, but I am so afraid he will become consumptive," she said as she leaned over to stroke Sean's dark curls.

"Does he cough?" Maggie asked.

"No," Olivia admitted, leaning back in the chair. "He seems perfectly fine. Mr. Hendrick bade me leave him, though it pained me to do so. He said I was keeping the boy from resting."

"He's a strong and very brave boy," Gray said. Recklessly brave, he thought, though it would not be wise to tell Olivia Rodney had jumped in the water on purpose.

"He saved Sean," Maggie added.

"Did he?" Olivia's eyes widened. "He said nothing of it. That is another worry. He usually chatters about everything, but he will say nothing about this."

Maggie sent Gray a worried glance.

"Would you like me to check on him?"

Olivia nearly came out of her chair. "Oh, please do, Gray."

He nodded and, with one more glance between him and Maggie, left the two ladies and the sleeping child.

He'd not visited the children's wing since returning to Summerton. He did not even know which of the rooms was his nephew's, so he opened doors at random. One revealed a room so neat and orderly it could only be Hendrick's. Behind another door he found a very startled Miss Miles, who told him Rodney and Hendrick were in the schoolroom. Gray knew which room was the schoolroom.

He gave a knock before entering. Mr. Hendrick sat at the tutor's desk, in the same location as it had been when Gray was a boy. Without a word, Hendrick cocked his head toward Rodney.

Rodney sat at the desk that had once been his father's. He had a slate and a bit of chalk and was busily writing. He did not heed his uncle's entrance.

Gray tossed Hendrick a questioning look. The tutor shook his head and gestured for Gray to go to Rodney. Gray crossed the room and put his tall frame in the small chair that had once been his. Mr. Hendrick slipped out of the room.

"What are you doing?" Gray asked mildly.

Rodney did not look up. "Sums." He wrote numbers on the slate and added or subtracted them. When the slate was full, he took a rag and wiped the numbers away, only to write new ones.

Gray had little experience addressing young boys. "Did Mr. Hendrick set you to this task?"

Rodney shook his head. "He said no lessons today." He scrawled five plus six equals eleven, six minus five equals one.

"Ah," Gray said, for lack of anything else to say. He shifted his body, trying to get more comfortable. "Well, he probably hoped to pass the afternoon with Miss Miles."

Rodney looked up then. "I have spoiled his plans," he said mournfully. He slammed down the slate and wrapped his arms across his chest.

"It is a good thing." Gray spoke softly. "For we do not pay him to court Miss Miles." He tried giving the boy a smile. "At least not at the expense of his duties."

Rodney stared down at his desk for a long time.

What the devil do I say? wondered Gray. He ran a hand through his hair and picked out a small twig.

"I should be flogged," Rodney finally said.

Gray looked at him in surprise. "Is that what Hendrick told you?"

"No," admitted Rodney. "He refused when I asked." He looked hopefully at Gray. "But perhaps you will give me a flogging?"

Good God. If anyone flogged this child, they would get a whole lot worse from Gray.

"Do not soldiers get a flogging if they do something very, very bad?" Rodney asked, his expression serious.

"Yes," Gray admitted. "But there is a trial. The charges are read, and the offender may refute them."

"No need for that," Rodney said firmly. "I'll not refute them."

Gray's heart was melting. "Might I be told what the charges are, before I go in search of the cat-o'-nine-tails?"

Rodney squared his shoulders and sat very straight on his stool. His big eyes, so like his father's, filled with tears.

"I let go of Sean's hand."

Gray felt as if someone had stabbed him directly in the heart.

Rodney, not moving a muscle, went on, "Aunt Maggie told me not to let go of him and I did and he ran to the edge and fell in."

Being well versed in guilt, Gray knew better than to brush it away. "Well, let us examine this more closely." He made his voice lower and quieter. "Did you deliberately let go of Sean's hand?"

"No," cried Rodney, the tears nearly erupting. "But I should have held him tighter."

Gray reached over and brushed the boy's hair off his face, but Rodney jerked away. "Did you ever see Sean pull away from your aunt Maggie?" he asked gently.

Rodney's eyes widened a bit, but he nodded.

"Is she not stronger than you?"

The boy pondered this. "But she is a girl."

Gray's mouth twitched. "I had noticed that. She is strong even so, can we agree? She bent the tree so we could catch on to it."

Rodney nodded again.

Gray reached over and lifted his nephew from the stool, setting him down in front of him so they were eye to eye.

"Let me tell you something, Rodney." He kept his voice steady, but with some effort. "I saw in your behavior nothing but bravery. I have served with many men and have fought in many battles, but rarely have I seen a man show so much pluck as you did when you jumped in the water after Sean."

Rodney tried to look away, but Gray caught his chin and made the boy face him again.

"You held on when it most counted. Sean would be dead if you had not. I am as proud of you as a man can be." His voice broke and he finished in a whisper. "Your father would have been proud of you, too."

Rodney fell against his uncle, who wrapped his arms around the boy, his own eyes moist. "I'll tell you what," he said. "Let us look in some of these cupboards. I'll wager I can show you some toys and books that were your father's."

Gray glanced toward the doorway and saw Hendrick standing there. The young man smiled.

Gray stood up, and with Rodney's hand in his, they walked over to the cupboards.

Chapter FIFTEEN

Sean slept nearly two hours, and Maggie held him the whole time, silently repeating thanks over and over. Thanks to Rodney for risking his young life. Thanks to Gray, who brought both boys safely to shore. Thanks to God, who again delivered Gray to her when she most needed him. And thanks to God that the stream had not carried Gray away from her.

If she closed her eyes, the scenes returned. Rodney jumping in the water. Gray going in after him and disappearing in the current. Sean gone. Rodney shouting, holding Sean for so long she had been certain he must let go. Gray rising from the water and bringing them all to safety.

So she kept her eyes open and gazed at the wonderful gift that was her son, the gift Gray had given her twice.

Sean woke and rubbed his eyes. "Where is Wodney?" He squirmed off Maggie's lap. "Where is Miss Miles?"

Maggie combed his hair, no longer damp, with her fingers. "Rodney should be with Mr. Hendrick." Sean knew he was not to disturb Rodney when he was with his tutor.

"I want Miss Miles. Tell Miss Miles I fell in water!"

Sean had apparently not noticed Miss Miles doting upon him the moment he was carried to this house.

He pulled at his mother's hand. "Find Miss Miles!"

"I cannot, Sean, I am not dressed." Maggie wore only the dressing gown her maid wrapped her in after removing her wet and torn clothing.

Sean was undaunted. Though in a nightshirt himself, he ran out the door, shouting, "Miss Miles! Miss Miles!"

She hurried after him, but when she opened the door, she saw Miss Miles in the hallway, lifting Sean up in her arms and carrying him off, probably to her room where she would undoubtedly have some sweets.

Maggie smiled, giving more thanks, this time for the quiet young woman who cared so much for her son.

She closed the door again and glanced around. Every object in the room looked dearly familiar, but somehow more vibrant in hue. She walked over to the little room where Sean slept. From the doorway, she gazed at Sean's small bed and at the little pair of shoes tucked in the room's corner. Sean was alive to wear those shoes. She had not lost him. Because of Gray, she had not lost her son. She swung around to the door connecting her room with Gray's. Her heart swelled in her chest at the thought of him.

She loved him.

This feeling was more than the yearnings of her body. She *loved* him. Maggie felt giddy. Joyous. Like she should dance up and down the room.

Kitt entered the room to help her dress for dinner. Maggie tried to maintain a sober appearance. This love for Gray must be kept secret, like all her other secrets. It would change nothing between them. It certainly did not mean his feelings for her had changed. Still, she needed to see him. To fill her eyes with his masculine perfection, to see his strength and his kindness.

"Oh, do hurry, Kitt," she exclaimed when the maid put too much fuss into arranging Maggie's hair.

When her toilette was finally complete, she rushed out of the room, almost colliding with Decker. "Do you know where Mr. Grayson is?" she asked breathlessly.

Decker always knew where Gray would be. It was his job to know, lest his services be needed. "Last I saw he was bound for the children's wing."

To Rodney. Maggie had almost forgotten. She hurried off in that direction.

The sounds of male laughter and banging furniture came from the schoolroom. Maggie cautiously peeked in. Like three little boys instead of one boy and two grown men, Gray and Hendrick and Rodney, battledores in their hands, knocked a shuttlecock about the room, bounding over furniture to hit it. Hendrick caught sight of her and immediately froze. It took Gray and Rodney a moment longer to see her in the doorway.

Her heart melted at the sight of Gray, hair disheveled, neckcloth totally askew, looking like a recalcitrant schoolboy. She *loved* him.

She pretended to be shocked. "What goes on here?"

Rodney was first to burst out laughing. "Lessons!" he finally managed, making the two men join in the laughter.

Maggie smiled. "So I see. I do apologize for interrupting, but might I borrow your uncle for a moment, Rodney?"

Hendrick and Gray sobered. Gray handed his battledore to Hendrick and crossed the room to her. "Is something amiss? Sean?"

"Everything is splendid." She suspected sunbeams must be radiating from her smile. "Sean is at this moment being fully indulged by Miss Miles. I merely wished to talk with you for a moment."

Gray glanced back to Rodney.

"Go, Uncle. Mr. Hendrick and I will straighten the room."

Maggie and Gray left the schoolroom and walked a few paces in the hallway before Maggie, feeling childish and giddy, grabbed his hand. "Come to the ballroom with me."

They hurried down the stairs to the ballroom, looking about them as if engaging in a mischief. Maggie could not even feel her feet touching the ground. She suddenly wished for music, to dance the scandalous waltz up and down the room with him. When they reached the room, she contented herself with throwing her arms around him, laughing.

He held her. "What is this?"

Her arms twined around his neck and she pulled his head down close to her lips so she could whisper in his ear. "I wanted to thank you in private."

Gray felt her curves mold to his body. He could still smell the river on her. He pressed her against him, wishing for a much more private place than the ballroom. His lips sought hers and she returned his kiss eagerly, as if they'd both been starving and the other was a waiting feast. His hands sought to explore her as he tasted her sweetness. But they were in the ballroom with its many windows and doors, where anyone might enter or walk by.

He made himself pull away, made himself become serious. "Maggie, your thanks are undeserved. It is I who should beg your forgiveness for endangering the children."

She waved her hand as if sweeping his words away. "You saved them, and the water did not take you under. That is all that signifies."

It felt as if she were speaking of something more than their episode at the stream. He remembered her earlier words. "Maggie, before you said, 'This time.' You said, 'This time the water did not take them.' What did you mean?"

She stiffened and withdrew.

"Tell me, Maggie. Who was taken from you?"

She gave him a panicked glance, growing smaller before his eyes, like a flower closing its petals.

"Tell me," he repeated.

She took a step back and shook her head. She sought his eyes, hers pleading. "Not now. Not when I am so—" She clamped her mouth shut.

Happy, he finished for her. She'd seemed so happy, so free of care, like a bird suddenly freed from its cage. He felt like a cad for spoiling the moment between them.

He opened his arms to her and she rushed into his embrace. "All right," he murmured, rubbing his cheek against her hair. "Today is not a day for revealing secrets."

He'd be patient, but not for long. He planned to discover what she guarded so closely inside her.

At the far end of the room a clock chimed. "Come."

He kissed the tip of her nose. "It is nearly the dinner hour. I must don my dinner clothes or face my father's sharp tongue."

He was rewarded by her glowing smile. Offering her his arm, they walked to the ballroom door. Before opening it, Maggie hugged him again.

Desire flared within him. He suspected he could open that door connecting their bedchambers this night and she would come to his bed, in gratitude, if nothing else. But when their bodies finally joined, he wanted nothing between them. No secrets. No barriers.

He would wait.

After another quick kiss Gray left her at the parlor door. Maggie watched him head for the stairway, off to dress. Her giddiness had mellowed, though his request to hear her secrets almost washed it away entirely. How wonderful of him to release her from that demand, but he was a wonderful man, was he not? She blushed, thinking of how she had flung herself at him, but she also felt the secure heat of anticipation warming her flesh. In time he would accept her invitation to make love to her. At the moment, she was content to merely love him.

She opened the parlor door. Olivia sat on the settee, sniffling and looking through her latest issue of *La Belle Assemblée*.

When Olivia looked up, tears were glistening in her eyes. "I did not think to see you this evening. I thought I was to be alone."

Maggie's brow wrinkled. She did not wish to worry over anyone this moment. She wished only to be joyous. "There is no need for me to be above stairs. But why are you crying, Olivia?"

"I shall compose myself in a moment." Olivia's chin trembled and she dabbed at her eyes with a lace-edged handkerchief. "I suppose it is merely the fright of this day's events still plaguing me. Do not credit it." She gave Maggie a brave look, one Maggie did not believe at all. "Is Sean still sleeping?"

"No." Maggie crossed the room, keeping a concerned eye on Olivia. She rearranged the vase of flowers on the table. "He woke with his usual energy, yelling for Miss Miles. I suspect she will get more than an earful of his adventure in the water and will not be able to make one bit of sense out of it."

Olivia attempted a teary smile. "I am glad he feels so well."

Parker came to the door. "Sir Francis, my lady."

Olivia sprang to her feet. "Oh, show him in."

Parker stepped aside. Sir Francis, who had been standing right behind him, rushed up to Olivia. "My dear lady, the news reached all the way to Rosehart. I took the liberty of returning. How is young Palmely?"

Olivia's face crumbled. Sir Francis took her hand, but Olivia leaned against him, so there was no choice but for him to close his arms around her.

"I have had such a fright, Francis." His ready comfort made mincemeat of her attempt at bravery. She wept against his lapel. "Rodney almost drowned! Gray and Sean, too!"

"There, there." Sir Francis patted her back, a look of bittersweet bliss on his face. "I am told they all are unhurt."

He finally noticed Maggie. "Oh! Bless me, I did not see you there, Mrs. Grayson." Red-faced, he released

Olivia, handing her his handkerchief. She wiped her eyes and blew her nose with it, even though her own was within reach.

He strode over and shook Maggie's hand. "How do you fare, ma'am? And your little boy?"

She smiled at him. "I assure you, we are unharmed." Her legs were crisscrossed with scratches from the underbrush and her hands raw from hanging on to the tree, but she did not credit that.

He's in love, too, Maggie thought happily, feeling suddenly as if she and Sir Francis were kindred spirits. She wanted Sir Francis to hold Olivia as Gray had held her, wanted him to feel that same sense of floating about the ceiling for the sheer joy of it.

Olivia recovered her manners. "Do sit down, please." She invited Sir Francis to share the settee with her. He took her hand again and she squeezed his. "Oh, Francis, my nerves are quite shattered."

He gave her an expression of genuine concern.

A tentative knock sounded at the door. Rodney stood in the doorway, Hendrick behind him.

"May I come in, Mama?" the boy said.

"Rodney!" Olivia sprang to her feet again and rushed over to her son, hugging him against her bosom. Sir Francis stood.

The boy pulled away. "Mr. Hendrick suggested I visit you before my dinner to show you I am all right."

"Dearest Rodney!" Olivia exclaimed, hugging him again. She turned to Sir Francis. "I have quite decided to forgo the house party next week. I cannot leave my son after that horrid accident!"

Sir Francis displayed the very briefest of disappointed looks before saying, "I quite agree."

Rodney's face fell, and as one round cheek was again squeezed flat against his mother, the corners of his mouth turned down. Olivia finally responded to the boy's efforts to push away, and he met her anxious countenance with a hastily transformed smile.

"Do not worry so, Olivia," Maggie said. "Rodney is undamaged by his ordeal."

Rodney gave her a grateful look. Sir Francis looked hopeful.

"Surely you do not think I might leave him?" Olivia whispered, aghast.

Hendrick stepped forward. "If I may presume, ma'am, it would be best at such a time if young Lord Palmely kept to his routine. In fact, we must keep him busier. With more lessons."

"Do you think so?" Olivia looked from one to the other.

Maggie regarded Rodney's tutor with amusement. The young man, who had so recently been bounding about the schoolroom after a shuttlecock, now sounded so serious, he could not be contradicted. Rodney seemed barely able to keep from bursting into laughter.

Olivia gave a deep sigh. "Oh, very well."

"May I be excused now?" asked Rodney, his lips twitching.

His mother smothered him to her breast once again and kissed him on the cheek besides. "Good night, my love." Rodney rolled his eyes. "Good night, Mother." He bowed very correctly to Maggie and Sir Francis, and left the room.

Maggie hurried out to the hall after him. "Rodney!"

Mr. Hendrick had his hand on the boy's shoulder. They turned, both grinning. Maggie crouched to look Rodney directly in the face. "I want to thank you, Rodney."

Rodney's smile fled, and he turned his face away. "I let go of Sean's hand, Aunt Maggie. It was all my fault."

"Oh, Rodney!" Her voice cracked and tears stung her eyes. She made him look at her again. "You risked your own life. I do not know how you could keep hold on to Sean for so long. I never saw anything so brave."

He gave her an almost prideful look. "That is what Uncle Gray said as well."

"So, again, I thank you." Before her tears embarrassed the boy, she stood and managed a smile. "I should have thanked you before, when I interrupted your . . . lessons."

Rodney grinned.

"We must go to dinner," Mr. Hendrick broke in.

Maggie nodded. "Of course."

With a wink, Hendrick allowed Rodney to lead the way. They passed Gray, who gave Rodney's shoulder a squeeze as he went by. For Maggie, Gray gave a smile that lit up her heart. He offered his arm and she took it gladly.

"You changed quickly."

He leaned down to her ear, his breath warm against her cheek. "I have an efficient valet."

They entered the parlor together, where Sir Francis and Olivia were busy conversing on the settee.

"So it is settled?" Sir Francis said. "You will attend the Camerville party?"

Olivia nodded enthusiastically. "As I told you this morning during our lovely ride, Maggie and Gray will ac-

company me, so there shall be no impediment at all."
Olivia noticed their entrance. "Is that not correct, Gray?"

Sir Francis rose to his feet and accepted Gray's handshake.

With a glance to Maggie, Gray turned to Olivia. "It is
not yet decided. Maggie and I need to discuss it."

"Maggie, please say yes," Olivia cried. "I do not know
when I shall have another invitation such as this."

Maggie was familiar enough with the ways of the
world to know if Olivia declined this invitation after hiding herself away for so long, there very likely would be
no others forthcoming.

"Leave it for the moment, Olivia," Gray said sharply.
"Maggie has had a difficult day."

Maggie's heart swelled. He was indeed wonderful.

Olivia's crestfallen face mirrored Sir Francis's.

Maggie regarded them all, love making her feel mag-
nanimous. "I will attend the party, Gray."

"Oh!" Olivia rushed over to give her a big hug.
"Thank you. Thank you. We shall have a splendid time,
you shall see!"

Sir Francis cleared his throat. "Now I must take my
leave. I merely came to express my concerns about your
shocking events this day."

"No," Olivia protested. "You must stay for dinner.
Lord Summerton will enjoy your company."

He glanced at Maggie and Gray, and back to Olivia.
"Intrude at such a time? And I am not dressed for it."

Olivia walked over and took his arm, leading him
away from the door. "You know we will not stand on ceremony for you."

"Very well." Sir Francis grinned with pleasure. "I most heartily accept."

Parker opened the door again, and Lord Summerton entered, shuffling with his cane. "That will be all, Parker." Lord Summerton waved the butler away. "Go find what is keeping dinner."

The earl often said these same words at this exact time. He leaned on his cane and looked about.

"Hmmph, it is you." He'd spied Gray.

Maggie rushed up to him. She would not allow the earl to abuse his son this evening. "Come and sit, my lord. Would you care for some port? The gentlemen were about to pour some."

"Well, I usually have a glass before dinner, you know that, Maggie girl." She escorted him to his favorite chair.

Gray had apparently taken her cue, because he'd removed the port and glasses from the cabinet and was in the process of pouring.

He carried the first glass to his father. "Here you are, Father."

His father was about to say thank you, but caught himself and scowled instead.

Gray gave Maggie an amused look that turned her all warm and glowing inside.

Gray remained near his father. "We have had some excitement here today. Has anyone told you of it?"

"Hmmph, no one keeps secrets from me, boy." His father glared at him.

Maggie bit her lip and silently pleaded. *Do not tell him. I will do it.* None of the servants would dare inform the earl of such an upsetting event. It would be even worse for his son to do it.

Gray kept his tone mild. "Then you have heard that Sean and Rodney fell in the stream, and that they were shaken, but unhurt."

She blinked in surprise. *Well done,* she thought, full of admiration. *You do not force him to admit to something he does not know. You preserved his pride.*

The old man's brows knit, but he did not respond. Instead he busied himself with his glass.

Oh, dear, thought Maggie. Perhaps not so well done. Lord Summerton looked as if he were becoming agitated. She cast about in her mind for some way to change the subject.

"You always warned of the dangers of the stream, Father," Gray continued very smoothly.

"Indeed I did." His father brightened. "I've seen men drown in that water. I recall one storm . . ."

Maggie suddenly felt nauseous. Gray had done a masterful job of distracting his father, but she was not so recovered by the experience at the stream as she'd thought. She wished she could cover her ears or run from the room. Anything but hear of people drowning.

Oblivious to her distress, the earl happily recounted every tragic mishap and gruesome scene involving the stream, but this time it was Gray who came to *her* rescue. He made one comment, and the earl began recounting more pleasant memories.

How had Gray known? Maggie glanced at him and briefly met his eye. It seemed an intimate look passing between them. She felt all warm and liquid inside.

Parker announced dinner just as the earl was recalling a boating party.

In the dining room Olivia and Sir Francis sat next to

each other at the table, leaving Gray to sit next to Maggie. Sir Francis made a quiet remark to Olivia and she giggled girlishly.

"What? What was that he said?" Lord Summerton asked in a sharp voice.

Olivia smiled. "Sir Francis and I were talking about the house party."

"House party? House party? I do not know of any house party," he snapped. "There will be no house party here."

Maggie broke in quickly. "Of course not, my lord. Olivia spoke of the Camervilles' house party. We are to go there in a week's time."

"Hmmph," muttered the earl. "I'll not step foot at Camerville's estate. Dislike the fellow."

She supposed he meant the old Lord Camerville. Maggie gave him a calm smile. "No one will expect you to attend."

The soup was served, with the earl's usual complaint of its temperature. He sipped noisily, finishing it all.

"House parties," he muttered, laying down his spoon. "Bunch of noisy people spilling food and drink everywhere. Breaking the furniture. Bed hopping and fornication!"

Bed hopping and fornication? Maggie and the others looked up at each other and then quickly looked away.

The turbot was served.

After consuming half of his portion, Lord Summerton pointed his fork at his son. "Your mother met *him* at one of those fool parties."

Maggie felt Gray stiffen, but he answered so casually,

one would have supposed he was bored. "Who was that, Father?"

"That reprobate. Stanfield was his name," his father replied.

The room became very quiet.

"Military fellow." He went on after chewing and swallowing. "Ha! Got killed in India. Some battle under that Wellesley chap."

The footmen served the meat course, and Lord Summerton busied himself cutting his mutton. Maggie prayed he would cease talking.

But he did not. "Damned fellow! I caught them in that garden of hers! Saw her with him! Kissing his face!" He popped another piece of meat into his mouth. "House parties!"

"Lord Summerton," Maggie began.

The earl waved his fork in Gray's direction. "No, sir, don't you try to convince me she didn't bed that damned military man! You remember him, boy? Sent him packing with the rest of her freeloading friends." He sawed off another piece of mutton. "Remember him? Stanfield was the name."

Gray went very still and did not immediately answer his father. When he did, his voice was as casual as if discussing the weather. "Not well, but I remember him."

"Damned military man," muttered the earl.

"I say, my lord," piped up Sir Francis. "It was some fine weather we had today, was it not? Sunny and warmer than usual. Good for the crops, would you not agree?"

The terrible moments had passed, and Sir Francis kept up an admirable amount of innocuous conversation to which the earl was able to respond. Olivia wore a constant blush. Gray was very quiet.

Gray ate the food without tasting it, trying to let his father's words wash over him without soaking in. It seemed an age before the last cloth was removed. Gray stood. "Please excuse me."

His father took no notice of him. Gray had no wish to look in Maggie's eyes. The earl was in good hands with Sir Francis. Gray was grateful to Sir Francis for putting a stop to this new way his father had devised to wound him. Gray needed to keep reminding himself that his father had no notion of what he'd done.

Gray slipped quietly from the dining room and went out to the garden. The waning twilight gave the flowers an eerie glow that suited his mood. He walked down the path to the oriental garden, with its tiny Chinese pagoda and curving walkways. He sat on the bench near the goldfish pond and watched the shining fish swim to and fro in the dark water.

He felt her approach more than heard it.

"Gray?" Maggie's voice was as soft as the evening breeze.

He looked up. She approached the bench and after some hesitation sat next to him. She did not speak, and for that he was grateful. He did not want anything to disrupt the memories his father had stirred.

After a time he said, "I remember Colonel Stanfield very well. Odd, but I do not believe I've thought once about him since leaving this house. He had kind eyes and was quite indulgent of a young army-mad boy who asked endless questions. He visited more than once over the years, I recall."

The breeze shook the leaves around them and rippled the surface of the fishpond. She listened quietly.

He went on. "I think I might have been nine years old, the time my father spoke about. He had been in a towering rage and sent everyone home. We never had another house party, and to my knowledge, Colonel Stanfield never visited again."

She reached over and very gently took his hand. He wrapped his fingers around hers.

"About two years after that, my mother received word he had died in India." Gray watched a goldfish disappear into the inky water. "She caught the influenza a few months later and never recovered."

He stroked the soft skin of her hand with his thumb. He fancied it was her grasp that kept him feeling so calm.

"When someone you love dies, it is difficult to go on," Maggie said at length. Somehow he felt like she'd shared a confidence, although it was the sort of statement anyone might have made, obligatory words of condolence.

"I like to feel my mother found some sort of happiness with her Colonel Stanfield. She deserved as much."

Gray surprised himself at how peaceful he felt, sitting here next to Maggie, recalling the painful memories of his father's cruelty to his mother. Had his father been a better man, his mother would not have had to look elsewhere for love. But the man the earl used to be no longer existed. Neither did the man who had so consistently berated his youngest son. The shell that remained could only be pitied.

Gray stood and pulled Maggie to her feet. Drawing her arm through his, he led her back toward the house. This had certainly been the very devil of a day.

When they reached the glass doors to the ballroom, he glanced back at his mother's garden, resplendently restored by Maggie. When they walked the length of the ballroom where his mother used to dance, he enjoyed the happy memory.

Perhaps the best one could do was accept love in whatever form it came.

They left the ballroom and walked toward the hall. He glanced down at her and she tilted her head to smile up at him. Their eyes met and he felt the jolt of raw desire. He could draw her closer, could taste those lips. Her smile faded and her eyes darkened, and he had that sensation again that they shared the same thought. He leaned down.

The parlor door opened and they jumped apart. Sir Francis and Olivia came out into the hall.

"I must take my leave, Gray," Sir Francis said. "Must get back before it is too dark."

Gray left Maggie and walked over to him. He shook Sir Francis's hand. "Thank you for coming, sir. You are very welcome here."

Olivia beamed and took Sir Francis's arm. "I'll walk you out."

Gray looked back to Maggie, the desire like a constant hum inside him. No doubt making love to her would strengthen the connection between them, a connection that continued to grow out of shared experiences and shared secrets.

But there was still too much she held back.

He walked to the parlor door and held it open for her. The fragrance of lavender brushed him as she passed. How nice it would be to mix that fragrance with the musky scent of two bodies touching and kissing and coupling.

He would wait, though. He would wait until certain she came to him totally, no secrets between them. Until certain she burned with the same desire as he, certain she wanted *him*, with all his present and past faults.

As he knew his mother had wanted her tall, kind soldier.

He would wait.

Chapter SIXTEEN

Leonard Lansing cursed the sudden rain shower as he hurried down the busy London street. He was none too pleased by this detour to the city, as it delayed his arrival at the Camerville estate. It could not be helped, however. His finances were strained, and therefore, he must visit his mother.

Dolly Lansing, or "Dorothea" as he preferred to call her, lived off St. James Street, in a pretty set of rooms somewhat more modest than the ones she'd inhabited in her younger, more profitable days. She had once been among the most expensive merchandise brokered by the procuress Mrs. Porter and had invested well enough to have purchased her son his lieutenancy and to live comfortably with her latest paramour, an aging and penniless actor. Lansing detested the man. He had no rank or consequence whatsoever.

Lansing did not object overmuch to visiting this street when it was for the usual reason men came to this part of town. He'd had his first taste of a lady's delights here, after all, as well as some excellent lessons in how to charm and seduce. But he hated to be reminded that he was born and reared in this neighborhood, a whore's bastard son.

The day would come, he vowed, when he could forget his origins and be where he rightfully belonged, but first he must call upon his mother.

A mere female servant, no butler, admitted him and showed him to his mother's parlor. He found her lounging on a long sofa, wearing a filmy gown that displayed her still voluptuous figure. The actor, luckily, was not present.

"Well, look who has come to see me." His mother tossed her not-quite-real red curls and raised a glass of Madeira to her lips.

"Good afternoon, Mother." Lansing took a chair near her and poured himself a glass. At least his mother had taught him about good wine, one of her continued extravagances. He sipped appreciatively. This Madeira was particularly fine.

"How much do you require this time?" she asked, stretching her tinted lips into a smile.

He pretended to be dense. "I beg your pardon?"

She laughed, a common sort of sound. "Oh, come now. You do not visit me unless you need money. How much? Have you been gambling again? I have told you to be very careful. Never lose more than you can afford—"

"Yes. Yes," he snapped. How he detested being lectured to by this creature, even though her frugal habits had come in handy at times such as these. "I was lately in Brighton and the stakes were high."

She wagged a finger at him. "Now, Lenny, how many times—"

He cut her off. "It's *Leonard*, Mother. How many times must I tell you?"

"Posh! You'll always be my little Lenny." She leaned over and patted him on the knee.

He crossed his legs and moved out of range.

She took a languid sip of her wine, but her eyes danced in amusement.

He swung one foot up and down. "I could use one hundred pounds."

Her brows rose, but her expression was mocking. "So much?"

"I have prospects," he said in a serious tone. "And I need to make a good show of it. New clothes and such. If my plan succeeds, I will be able to sell out and I'll request no more funds, I promise."

"Prospects?" Her eyes kindled with interest. "I daresay a young heiress is beyond your touch, so it must be a wealthy widow."

Lansing's mouth twitched. "Precisely."

And the wealthy widow he had in mind could not have been a more fitting choice.

Gray's week had been filled with estate matters, but he kept one day free to take Sean and Rodney back to the stream. The longer they stayed away, the more chance fear would develop. A return visit would be like remounting a horse immediately after falling off.

He proposed the idea to Maggie, who turned pale at the thought. Little Sean caught on quick enough, popping his thumb in his mouth and hanging on to his mother's skirts. Olivia burst into tears, but Rodney, standing straight as a soldier and setting his chin manfully, agreed firmly to the wisdom of Gray's plan.

In the end, they took a picnic basket, fishing poles, Mr. Hendrick, Miss Miles, and one of their strongest footmen, who was designated to rescue them should they fall into the water. Olivia also went along, certain her vigilance alone would save her son from another disaster.

The day turned out to be a success. At first Sean had been so terrified he would not let go of Maggie's neck, but Gray found a spot where the water formed a calm pool. Eventually he convinced Sean to stick his hand in the water. Before long Sean was throwing rocks and sticks to watch the water splash. When his mother was busy with the picnic, Rodney showed Mr. Hendrick the spot where he'd jumped in after Sean. He and his tutor walked the part of the stream where the events occurred and Rodney recounted every detail. Afterward, they cast fishing lines in the water near where Sean played, Gray close beside him.

Gray also kept an eye on Maggie, who often stared at the water. Whatever her thoughts, she kept them inside, with all the other secrets Gray resolved to discover.

As the sun sank lower in the sky, they returned to Summerton Hall relaxed and happy, though Maggie remained a bit withdrawn.

In the days since the incident at the stream, Gray did not seek out her company, but would often happen upon her by chance during the course of his day. Each time he felt like he'd received a surprise gift. Though they spoke of nothing consequential, their encounters were easeful, and Gray found he liked feeling that way.

Too soon the day came for the three-hour-long carriage ride to the Camerville estate. Olivia shed many tears saying good-bye to Rodney. Maggie was dry-eyed, though when she hugged Sean good-bye, Gray felt her pain deep in his belly. She had never been separated from the child.

They settled into the carriage and it began to roll. Olivia leaned out the window, calling farewells to her son until they were too far away for him to hear. Maggie sat at the other window on the same side of the carriage, so she could see Sean, held in Miss Miles's arms, his thumb in his mouth. He waved his little hand, and Maggie waved hers in a slow, sad movement. She continued to stare out the window long after the carriage turned the bend and Summerton Hall was no longer in sight.

Gray sat next to her, still fancying he could feel her sadness as if it were his own. When she finally leaned back, he put his arm around her, hoping to show her without words that he understood how difficult it was to leave her son.

Olivia sat in the more desirable forward-facing seat. She fidgeted and rearranged her skirts. She glanced at Maggie. "Oh, Maggie, you must come sit next to me where it is more comfortable."

"I am perfectly comfortable here," Maggie said, to Gray's great satisfaction. He liked having her by his side.

"I am so worried we shall look like dowds!" Olivia exclaimed.

"We shall look very well," Maggie assured her, though her voice had a distant quality. A part of her was still back with Sean, he fancied. "Have we not copied our dresses from the London fashion plates?"

"Yes." Olivia nodded. "But I wish we could have

shopped there and had a proper modiste make our clothes. I shall die if I look out of fashion."

All week Olivia had swung from excitement to anxiety about this infernal house party until Gray was sick of hearing it mentioned. One minute she could not wait another day before departing, the next she vowed she could not attend at all. Maggie simply reassured Olivia, but still indicated nothing of her own feelings.

As the carriage jostled them along, Olivia wailed, "I do not see how I can be parted from Rodney! I shall worry myself to the bone over him."

Maggie turned her face back to the window.

"Your absence will do the boy good," Gray said. "He'll be off to school one of these days. It is time he became accustomed to being without his mother."

"I cannot bear for him to go away to school," cried Olivia. "How can you suggest such a thing?"

That was an argument for another day, Gray decided. He turned to Maggie. "Sean will be all right as well," he said softly.

She returned a wobbly smile, but nothing more.

"I wonder if I should know any of the guests?" Olivia prattled on. "It has been so long since I have been to a party. I should know the Camervilles, of course. Gray, you should know people, should you not?"

He did not much care if he did or did not. He thought of this party more as something to endure, not enjoy.

"Perhaps," he replied to Olivia.

"Oh, Maggie, I do not think you shall know anyone. I do not suppose anyone from the west country will have been invited. Do not fear. I shall stay by your side." Olivia clasped her hand.

"Thank you," was all Maggie said.

West country? Gray almost asked Maggie what part of the west country, but he caught himself. Olivia would wonder why, as her husband, he did not know such a thing.

He tried to settle back in his seat and allow Olivia's nervous chatter to wash over him. He enjoyed having Maggie so close by his side. He supposed, at the country house party, husbands and wives would not be encouraged to remain so close. If he remembered Cammy correctly—and the story of Miss Miles's short employ there suggested he did—he ought to stay as close to Maggie and Olivia as possible. This party did not promise him much enjoyment. In fact, Gray noted with some surprise, he would much rather they all be home at Summerton with the earl.

Sitting within the warmth of Gray's arm, Maggie too dreamed of being back at Summerton, where she had been so safe these last two years. Olivia's nerves were nothing compared to her own. The closer the carriage brought them to the Camerville estate, the more intense were her waves of panic.

Suppose Olivia was wrong? Suppose someone did know her? The possibility was slim, to be sure, but it did exist. What if one of her schoolmates had married a man from Kent? What if they attended the party? She tried to recall if she'd read any such marriage announcement in the newspapers, but could not.

Being recognized was her biggest worry, but certainly not the only one. What would she talk of? What would she say if other guests asked her who her parents were, or where she was from? Or why their marriage had not been announced in the newspapers? She must invent replies.

She was no closer to composing answers to such questions when they turned onto the Camerville lands. Her pulse was beating wildly by the time they drove up to the front of a three-story red-brick country mansion, smaller than Summerton Hall and, Maggie decided, not nearly as beautiful.

Footmen ran from the house as they pulled up to the door. She and Olivia were assisted from the carriage.

Gray climbed out after them. "Our baggage and servants will be arriving directly," he told the footmen.

Kitt, Decker, and Olivia's maid were following in a separate coach. Bringing one's personal servants was an extravagance outside of Maggie's experience, but Olivia had insisted upon it. The footmen did not blink an eye, so it must be what was expected.

This was the sort of thing she did not know. If she made a similar slip, she would certainly direct attention her way. Above all, she did not want to stimulate anyone's curiosity.

"It is a lovely house, is it not?" Olivia exclaimed. "It has been an age since I visited here."

Since her husband had been alive, Maggie suspected. She tried to keep in mind how good for Olivia this outing could be.

"It is very nice," she replied.

One footman led them into the house while the other remained outside to give instructions to the coachman. Olivia grabbed Maggie's hand, squeezing nervously as they entered the house.

The entrance hall, smaller than Summerton's, was in

contrast to Summerton's classical white; ablaze with color, bright yellow and Chinese red. Maggie and Olivia had read about such modern colors in the *La Belle Assemblée*.

The Camerville butler greeted them and saw to it their hats and wraps were taken. He escorted them to the parlor and announced their arrival.

One lady, as blond as Olivia, but with more generous curves, sprang to her feet and rushed over to greet them.

"How do you do. So good of you to come." She turned to Olivia. "Why, Lady Palmely! You look not one day older than when we made our come-out! It is so bad of you. Do you remember? We had our first season together and luckily you snared your viscount early or there would have been no gentlemen to notice the rest of us."

Olivia extended her hand for her hostess to shake. "And I would have known you anywhere, Lady Camerville." She stepped aside. "Let me make known to you my brother-in-law and his wife, Captain and Mrs. Grayson."

Lady Camerville gave Gray a very direct look. "My, my, how fine you look, sir! I confess we were somewhat surprised to hear you were at Summerton after all."

"I hope my note did not distress you. The addition of an unexpected guest can be troublesome."

She shook his hand, looking at him as a cat might look at a dish of cream. "Not over much, sir, and very well worth it."

"My wife, ma'am." He forced her to direct her attention to Maggie.

Maggie saw the woman's brown eyes reluctantly leave Gray and begin to assess her. The lady offered her a limp handshake. "Yes, I do not believe anyone has had the opportunity to meet you."

"It was very good of you to include me," Maggie managed.

Lady Camerville fixed her interest back onto Gray. "Come meet the others." There were about eight people in the large room already. "We shall have more guests arriving, twenty in all."

"Twenty!" exclaimed Olivia, drawing back a little.

Lady Camerville led them over to the other guests. Maggie could not fail to notice the appreciative looks the ladies gave Gray. It made her want to snatch him away like a child's toy and declare, *"He's mine!"* though in truth he was free to make an assignation with any lady he chose.

Olivia was soon surrounded and happily conversing. Maggie remained at Gray's side.

"My husband is playing billiards with some other gentlemen, Captain," Lady Camerville said to Gray. "Would you care to join them?"

"I will stay here," he replied, to Maggie's relief.

They sat with another couple, who asked Gray polite questions about his father's health, the estate, and Gray's military career. Maggie remained as quiet as possible. She noticed that Lady Camerville's wandering gaze often lighted upon Gray, and felt wild with jealousy.

After a half hour or so, Sir Francis arrived. When he was announced, Olivia gave him a brilliant smile, but she did not leave the group with whom she was speaking. He wandered over to Gray and Maggie, his smile pasted on his face.

"I am glad to see you here," Maggie told him in all sincerity. "It is a comfort to me."

He glanced over to Olivia. "She looks to be enjoying herself." His sad voice betrayed his feelings.

Maggie did not know how to console him. He was not presently the most valued person in the room to Olivia. "Yes, it is what she hoped for."

Gray soon drew Sir Francis into the discussion. When the others were talking, Gray leaned over to Maggie. "Are you comfortable?"

No! she wanted to scream. *I am not. I want to go home to Summerton.* At least she could pretend Summerton was home, but here was only danger. And other ladies who found him attractive.

"Perfectly comfortable," she lied.

To her surprise and delight, he squeezed her hand.

There were more arrivals and more people to meet. Each time someone turned to face her, her heart pounded in fear of seeing a familiar face. So far she had not.

Soon it was time to dress for dinner. Lady Camerville, still casting occasional glances Gray's way, walked with the new arrivals above stairs, where maids waited on the landing to direct each new arrival to their rooms.

"Captain and Mrs. Grayson?" one of the maids asked.

"Yes," Gray replied.

"This way, please."

She led them down a hall, stopping in front of one door. "This will be your room," she said, opening the door.

"For which of us?" Maggie asked.

The maid looked confused. "Why, both of you, ma'am. I beg pardon, but her ladyship told me—"

Both of them. Her hand pressed against the sudden flutter in her abdomen.

"Thank you, miss." Gray's voice sounded stiff.

The maid curtsied and left them.

Maggie glanced at Gray. He entered, but she remained on the threshold. Kitt and Decker stood waiting.

"There is a dressing room for you, ma'am," Kitt said. "I have unpacked your trunk. Your dinner dress is ready."

She had no choice but to walk in. A large bed with white linen dominated her vision. Her glance darted to Gray. He was silent, but what could he say to her with the valet and maid present?

"Thank you, Kitt," she managed, trying to be grateful at least to have a private place to dress. Without looking at Gray, she followed Kitt into the dressing room.

Kitt, chattering with some excitement at being in a grand new house, helped Maggie into the blue muslin gown Olivia insisted complemented her eyes. Maggie heard none of it. When she emerged from the dressing room, Gray was in shirtsleeves and waistcoat, waiting for Decker to assist him on with his dinner coat. Her heart skipped several beats.

He turned away from her and her heart turned to lead. How unhappy he must be to be forced into such an intimate arrangement with her. The last time they had been so intimately alone together, he'd made it clear he had no fancy to bed her. She'd never lost that physical awareness of him, that sense of time stopping when he came near, but though she still ached for him far too often, he had never again approached her.

Maggie sat at the nearby dressing table and Kitt began to arrange her hair. In the mirror she could see Gray put his arms into the sleeves of his coat, and shrug his shoulders so the coat would fit over them as if molded to his back. Decker fussed with his neckcloth and dusted off imaginary lint.

"There you are, ma'am," Kitt said after placing a flower in among the curls she'd created to cascade from the crown of Maggie's head.

"Thank you." Maggie barely looked at herself. She stood and faced Gray.

"You both have done well," Gray addressed the valet and maid. "Take your leave. I am certain your dinner awaits you."

"Very good, sir." Decker bowed.

Perhaps he and Kitt would enjoy the novelty of being away from Summerton. Someone ought to. Decker closed the door behind them, and suddenly Maggie and Gray were alone. They stared at each other.

"I hope——" Maggie began.

"Maggie——" Gray said.

She gave a nervous laugh, then forced her pulse to slow its beat. "Do . . . do you want me to ask Olivia if I might share her room?"

He walked toward her, coming close enough for her to catch the scent of his soap. "Do you want to stay with Olivia?"

She shook her head, telling herself it would only cause talk. His eyes darkened, but did that mean he approved or disapproved of her choice?

He drew his finger across the bare skin of her neck. "You wear no jewelry."

His gentle touch caused her senses to hum. "I have none."

She longed for him to touch more of her. She suddenly wanted to feel his hand upon her breast, to feel it move down her abdomen, to her belly, to that part of her now aching for him.

His breath upon her face was cool. She closed her eyes, and her lips parted.

There was a knock at the door. "Maggie?"

It was Olivia.

Gray stepped away.

"Come in," Maggie called, but she still trembled inside.

Olivia flounced into the room. "Oh, you look beautiful, Maggie. How do I look? Will this dress do?"

She twirled around in her cream silk gown, a dress that perfectly complemented her complexion and golden hair.

"You look very well," Maggie said as her heart resumed its regular beat.

Olivia checked herself in the mirror anyway, and adjusted the string of pearls around her neck. "I did not want to go below by myself. Are you sure I look presentable?"

Gray spoke up. "You will cast the others in the shade."

Olivia smiled at that. "Then let us hurry. What if we are the last in the parlor?" She rushed to the door and stopped. "Or what if we are the first?"

A line creased Gray's brow. "Olivia, Maggie has forgotten to bring jewelry. Do you have at least a necklace she might borrow?"

Olivia skipped back to her, inspecting. "Yes, a sapphire pendant and earbobs. They will do quite nicely. Wait here and I shall fetch them." She rushed out the door.

Gray turned to Maggie. "We shall have to buy you jewelry." He glanced at her hand. "And a ring."

Maggie lifted her hand as if she'd never noticed her bare fingers before, fingers absent a marriage ring. "I do not expect you to buy . . ."

He held up a hand to silence her.

Olivia returned, not bothering to knock. She handed Maggie earbobs to put on and helped fasten the necklace. "I do not know why I did not think of this before. It is as if they were created for your dress." She looked over to Gray to see if he approved.

His eyes flicked over Maggie, and she had the sensation she could feel them on her flesh. "Yes," he said in a low voice. "That will do."

They left this room where Maggie and Gray would spend the night together, and descended the stairs to the parlor where they would await dinner. They were not, as Olivia feared, the first or last to enter. The room was at least half-filled with the expected number of guests. Lady Camerville stood near the door greeting each person as they came in. Next to her was a thick-waisted, fleshy gentleman Maggie presumed to be Lord Camerville.

Lord Camerville's eyes lit up as they neared. "Lady Palmely! My wife informed me you had come. Delighted to see you!" He regarded Olivia like a man might examine good horseflesh. "You are in excellent looks, my lady! I believe I have lost a wager."

Olivia giggled at this confusing statement, but her cheeks turned pink with the compliment. Camerville was so busy watching her, he did not immediately notice the brother of his old friend.

"Bless me!" the man exclaimed, finally seeing Gray. "Grayson! By God, look at you! Good of you to come."

"Lord Camerville." Gray shook his hand.

"Cammy, sir," he sputtered. "Cammy. It is what your brother—rest his soul—called me. Everybody does."

Maggie did not wish to intrude on this reunion, but *Cammy* caught sight of her before Gray could speak another word.

"What? Who is this?" Nearly pushing Gray aside, he grabbed her hand.

"My wife, sir." Gray's voice was tight. "Mrs. Grayson."

Instead of shaking it, Lord Camerville lifted her hand to his too-wet lips. "Enchanted!" He gave her a little bow.

Other people in the room looked over to see the recipient of their host's enthusiasm. Maggie's cheeks burned with the attention.

"Pleased to meet you," she murmured.

She felt all the eyes in the room upon her as Gray's hand firmly gripped her arm and extricated her from Camerville's grasp. Gray walked her over to where Olivia stood with Sir Francis.

"I hope I shall remember what fork to use," Olivia was saying.

Sir Francis patted her hand. "You will be faultless."

"Maggie." Olivia left Sir Francis's side for Maggie's. "I believe our dresses show off very well."

Maggie chanced a glance around the room. She and Olivia did indeed look presentable. When she had arrived at Summerton with only two very old and plain dresses, she'd allowed Olivia to indulge her in a new wardrobe, telling herself it encouraged Olivia out of her violets and grays. The truth was, Maggie loved the pretty clothes. She discovered she could barely wait to see the newest London fashion plates and decide which of them the village dressmaker should copy. Now she was glad she and Olivia had indulged themselves. To have dressed unfashionably would certainly have caused more stares.

Lady Camerville looked resplendent in a gown of deep crimson. Maggie's eyes narrowed when she noticed the lady casting lures at Gray.

Dinner was soon announced and the guests took their places to make the procession to the dining room. As the presumed wife of a younger son, Maggie's place at the table was not as high as Olivia's, but she was seated next to Sir Francis and another pleasant gentleman. Gray was nearby, in between two happy ladies. She tried not to keep her gaze upon him, though it wandered back to him often enough. Her fingers tightened on her fork when the ladies smiled at him and he smiled back. At least Maggie could be glad his place was not next to Lady Camerville, who, Maggie noticed, eyed Gray nearly as often as she.

The Camervilles served champagne with dinner, a wine Maggie had only read about in magazines. It was light, with bubbles that danced upon her tongue. Her glass was refilled several times as the dinner progressed. Her sharp jabs of jealousy became as blunted as worn-out blades. Conversation suddenly was easier. She even laughed once or twice.

After dinner when the ladies left the gentlemen to their port, Maggie moved as if she were floating over the floor. When she reached the parlor, she sat on one of the red-and-gold-striped settees, a seat tucked away but affording a good view of the room.

Lady Camerville slid in next to her. "You are a mystery to us all, Mrs. Grayson," she said with false gaiety. "No one knows a thing about you."

At least the champagne had also dulled Maggie's fears of such questions. "What is it you wish to know, my lady?"

Lady Camerville smiled. "Whatever you wish to tell."

Maggie suddenly felt very clever. She almost snickered as she hit upon the idea of telling the truth. At least part of the truth.

She took a breath. "I am no one at all. A mere schoolmaster's daughter. There is no reason at all why anyone should know me."

"How fortunate you were to marry an earl's son." Lady Camerville raised her voice as if to encourage more disclosure.

Maggie gave her a guileless smile. "Indeed," she agreed brightly, but added nothing.

"You are to be congratulated," Lady Camerville added, waiting.

Maggie merely nodded, making her head feel as if it were a leaf bobbing on the water. Her hostess left wearing a disappointed expression. Maggie smiled as she watched Lady Camerville stride away. A schoolmaster's daughter was so unimpressive, Maggie was certain she'd squelched any further curiosity about herself. She lifted her chin with new confidence.

After two long hours, the ladies fell into bored silences. The men finally joined them, and conversation soon became louder and more raucous. Maggie noted the exact instant Gray walked into the room, and it seemed to her he towered over the other men, though there were one or two as tall as he. He did not come to her side, but she was content to merely watch him, the changing expressions crossing his face, the masculine movement of his arms, the power in his step. He spent most of his time talking to the other gentlemen present, though Maggie noted with narrowing eyes each time one of the ladies approached him. When he glanced over at her, Maggie's heart seemed near to bursting with the sure knowledge that she would soon be alone with him.

Brandy was brought out for the gentlemen. When the ladies were served ratafia, Lady Camerville loudly turned it away, calling for more champagne.

Bravo! thought Maggie, suddenly liking Lady Camerville very well. When the footman passed her, she gladly accepted what was becoming her favorite beverage.

One of the ladies sat down at the pianoforte. Others, Olivia among them, took turns singing to her accompaniment. Maggie smiled to see Olivia so enjoying herself. She saw Sir Francis watching Olivia, too, but his smile was more melancholic.

Outside, day had turned to darkness. More champagne was served, and Maggie allowed her glass to be refilled, her mind wandering to the times Gray's lips had touched hers. As she took a sip, Lord Camerville plopped himself in the seat beside her.

He put his arm across the back of the settee and leaned in very close. "Are you enjoying yourself, my dear?"

His eyes looked glassy and his breath smelled of brandy, not the intoxicating scent when brandy was upon Gray's lips, but something rancid. It was impossible to scoot farther away.

"It seems a very nice party," she responded, her words coming out much slower than her usual speech. Camerville pressed even closer and she felt as if she had no room to breathe.

"We have a whole week to enjoy ourselves, my dear." His voice sounded raspy, like he ought to clear his throat. "And I do hope you and I will have a chance to become better acquainted."

Maggie's throat felt thick as if someone had stuffed it with cotton, blocking off all her air. She swallowed, but only succeeded in producing a niggling nausea. The possibility that she might vomit on Lord Camerville only made the nausea worse.

Gray appeared at her side like a handsome knight upon a snow-white steed. Her nausea fled. "My wife has had a very long day." He gave her an intense look and extended his hand. "Maggie, I will escort you above stairs."

She felt as if all the champagne bubbles in the world were sparkling inside her. She took his hand, so warm and strong, and let him assist her to her feet. Nearly giddy, she stumbled and his arm steadied her. It seemed as if all the candles in the room sparkled like the excitement mounting inside her as she crossed the room on Gray's arm.

They made their way to the door, but Lady Camerville caught Gray's other arm and fluttered her lashes at him. She leaned in to him, murmuring, "Captain, I look forward to your return when your wife is . . . settled."

Maggie heard no answer from Gray, but his voice might have been muffled by the sound of all the bubbles bursting inside her. All that was left inside her was a sob, trying to escape. She clamped her mouth shut and blinked away the tears that sprang into her eyes. Her handsome knight was not whisking her away to their own private castle, but rather forcing her into exile. Instead of guiding her carefully up the staircase one stair at a time, it would be more fitting for him to drag her to some cavernous dungeon, so dark and desolate it would match her spirits.

She would not go meekly. She raised her chin and tried to make her feet work on their own, but she needed his strong arms to keep her upright. It was far easier to melt against his warm body, to feel the smooth cloth of his coat against her skin and inhale the intoxicating scent that was uniquely him.

When they entered the bedchamber, Kitt jumped out of her chair where she sat with Decker.

"She needs to prepare for bed." Gray handed her off to the maid.

Kitt, clucking like a mother hen, helped her to the dressing room. Maggie allowed herself to be dragged along, but she took one last look at Gray over her shoulder. The sob grew inside her, pushing to escape her lips. When she emerged from the dressing room, he would be gone, and soon he would be in another woman's arms.

Maggie gasped for breath while Kitt unbuttoned her dress and pulled it over her head. The maid hurriedly unlaced Maggie's corset and helped her out of her shift. Perhaps it was the champagne that made her emotions feel as if they were loose beads falling from a broken necklace. Her tears stung her eyes and even the soothing tones of Kitt's voice couldn't still the jolts of pain attacking her heart.

He is free to do as he desires, Maggie repeated to herself, over and over, like the daggers stabbing her heart.

After helping Maggie into her nightdress, Kitt took her out of the dressing room to the dressing table. Maggie walked like a blind person, her eyes too blurred with tears to see. In the mirror, all she could see was a swirl of meaningless colors, and something white growing larger in the reflection. She blinked and her vision cleared.

Gray stood behind her in his shirtsleeves.

Removing the hairbrush from Kitt's hand, he spoke to the maid in a low voice that vibrated in Maggie's ears. "Leave us."

Chapter SEVENTEEN

Gray stood behind Maggie, his gaze catching hers in the mirror. The branch of candles on the dressing table cast her reflection in a luminescent glow that made her eyes sparkle like the sapphires she'd earlier worn around her neck. That neck was now bare but for the cascade of mahogany curls tumbling across her creamy shoulders. His fingers begged to slip through those silken tresses. Gray's hand gripped the smooth handle of her tortoiseshell hairbrush until his knuckles went white. In the mirror, Maggie's eyes darkened and her lips parted.

He barely stifled a groan. His hand was almost trembling with the desire coursing through him, as he lifted the brush and gently drew it through her hair. Inside he felt like tinder awaiting a spark to burst into flames.

In truth, he had burned for her the whole evening. No matter how carefully he'd avoided her, he felt the flames lick around him with her every move and gesture. When Camerville sat down beside her, when he touched her, Gray's vision turned red. He'd crossed the room like an animal prowling to protect what was his.

He glanced in the mirror as a dreamy smile came to

her lips. Dropping the hairbrush to the floor, Gray buried both hands in her thick tresses, using his fingers to smooth the tangles.

"Hmmmmmm," she murmured, closing her eyes. His hands slipped to her shoulders and her head lolled to the side.

The champagne had made her pliant under his touch, and his hands took advantage. Desire whipped through him like a firestorm, clouding his mind and intoxicating him every bit as much as champagne intoxicated her. If he did not break away from her soon, there would be no stopping him.

He ought to tuck her into bed and leave her. He ought to return to the dull company below stairs, a sure way to splash water on his fire. A woman like Lady Camerville, even so willing, merely turned him cold.

He burned for Maggie.

And he'd made himself ready for her, having had Decker help him remove his coat and waistcoat while Maggie readied for bed in her dressing room. Sans shoes and neckcloth and valet, he could not be more ready to seduce her.

"Gray?" Her voice was softened with champagne. He closed his eyes and clenched his teeth. Could he be so dishonorable as to take advantage of her now that the drink had removed her inhibitions? He'd promised himself that their first moment of lovemaking would be free of coercion, free of secrets. Was he so willing now to forgo that vow? Eyes still closed, Gray took long, deep breaths, hoping to regain the strength to think clearly.

She rose and swayed against him. His eyes flew open

and he grabbed her arm to steady her. His vision filled with her, so close, so soft in his arms.

She ran her hand down the front of his shirt and up again to settle against the bare skin exposed by the gap at the collar. "Are you not going back to the party?"

He shook his head, speech momentarily failing him.

Her expression turned childlike and vulnerable. "You do not wish to be with her?"

Her fingers fogged his thinking. Her words made little sense to him. "Who?"

"Lady Camerville. Our *host-ess.*" She had a bit of difficulty pronouncing *hostess,* but no difficulty reaching inside his shirt to let her fingers play with the dark hairs on his chest.

His hands grasped her waist and kneaded the soft flesh above her hips. He was barely able to keep from shoving her against his groin. "No," he managed, no longer certain what the question had been.

She gazed into his face, only inches from her. Her brows knit in puzzlement. "You do not wish to make love to her?"

To Lady Camerville? When his body ached for Maggie, when Maggie was so close her fragrance wafted around him and her skin felt like liquid silk?

"No." The word came out like a groan.

Fingers still playing on his bare skin, she searched his face, where he was certain every impulse in his body was etched. If he could have spoken, he would have said he wanted no other woman but Maggie.

She leaned even closer, sliding her hands up to caress the sensitive skin at the nape of his neck. "Oh, Gray." She gave a long sigh. "Does this mean you will share this bed with me?"

He knew it was the drink making her words come out like an invitation, an invitation he burned to accept. "What do you want, Maggie? Do you want me to share your bed?"

"I do." Her voice was suddenly as clear as the ring of crystal. Her eyes bore into him, smoldering with the same heat that burned inside him. "I want it very much. I want you to come to bed with me."

She tugged at his hand, pulling him toward the bed. Its covers were turned down, inviting them. She scrambled onto the bed and pulled him toward her.

He held back, salvaging one thread of his fraying self-control. "Maggie, you drank too much champagne. You do not realize what you are doing."

"But I do." She knelt on the bed and her eyes were nearly level with his. "I have not had so very much champagne, Gray. I know I have no right, and I know you did not want me before—"

"You think I did not want you?"

She nodded, her curls dancing around her face.

Gray stifled an almost maniacal laugh. The reality could not have been more opposite. She'd haunted his nights ever since first appearing at his door, and his body had burned for her since first tasting her lips.

She tilted her head, her expression again vulnerable. "I thought perhaps you could make love to me this one time and you could pretend to want me."

Gray put his hands on her shoulders, blood coursing through his veins. "I do not need to pretend to want you, Maggie, but you must be sure this is what you want."

"Yes," she breathed. "I am sure."

She wrapped her arms around his neck, bringing her lips to rest on his, lips that nourished a hunger in him so vast he felt like a starving man invited to a feast. Her fingers tangled in his hair and the thin thread of his resolve snapped.

He pressed her to him, wild with arousal and need. He tasted her with his tongue and stroked her with his hands while his loins throbbed for her.

Like clouds parting after a storm, freeing the sun to shine, he realized she *was* his wife, as truly as if they had been united in a marriage ceremony. He and Maggie were bonded together and had been from the moment of Sean's birth. Gray wanted to plant his seed inside her and claim her as his own.

He broke the kiss. "I want this, Maggie." His words came from the same depth as his hunger for her. "I want you."

He pulled her nightdress over her head and threw it aside, so he could feast on the sight of her. He devoured her, filling his vision with her full breasts, her slim waist, the dark thatch between her legs.

She put her hands under his shirt. He groaned as she slid her hands up his chest to remove his shirt. Slamming his body against her, he pressed bare flesh to bare flesh.

His fire seemed to catch hold in her. He was on the bed with her and her hands were all over him, pushing down his breeches, pulling them off. She nipped at his lips and dueled with his tongue, making small impatient sounds that threatened to whip him into a frenzy. She ground herself against his arousal and he almost drove himself inside her.

He would not be content with a frenzied coupling. No, he wished to give her more than a hurried delight. He eased her down against the cool linens. With a touch as light as gossamer, his fingers savored the creamy skin of her breasts, dancing lower and lower, only to climb again firmer and more insistent. He lowered his lips to taste of her rosebud pink nipples, ravenously hungry, yet taking his time to savor each taste.

She clutched at his back, her fingernails pressing into his flesh. He slipped his fingers into her, relishing how moist and ready she was for him.

Maggie writhed under his touch. "Please, Gray," she cried.

He knew she begged for release, but he wanted this first time of physical pleasures between them to match the intensity of his feelings for her.

"Please," she begged again.

With his own arousal aching and throbbing to grant her request, he still held back, finding new ways to touch her, to increase the promise of pleasure to come.

He touched her breast again, and she gave a primitive cry. Abruptly she rose above him, suddenly straddling him, touching him as he'd touched her. Any scrap of control within him burned to cinders. When he thought he could stand it no more, she positioned herself above him. He entered her.

All thought fled as the bellows of their rhythm fanned their flames even higher. Nothing existed for Gray except Maggie pushing their passion to a white-hot heat. Her strokes quickened, as did his, both so attuned to each other now that they moved as one, faster and faster.

Her release spasmed around him, and a second later he exploded inside her. The moment of their release seemed to make eternity stand still.

As their once-wild flames turned to embers that warmed Gray all over, Maggie slid off him. He held her close to his side, facing her so he could see how the guttering candlelight bathed her face in a magical glow.

"Thank you," she murmured in a voice so soft, he was uncertain if she spoke aloud or if he had simply heard her thoughts.

He lifted one corner of his mouth. "My pleasure."

She smiled, a warm, satisfied, sated smile. He pulled her even closer to him and wrapped his arms around her. She made a contented sound in the back of her throat.

Gray held her until her breathing assumed a slow, even cadence. As she slept, he kept hold of her, loathing to break the spell of their lovemaking. Eventually his eyes became heavy, and with her head cradled next to his chest, he succumbed to sleep.

Maggie roused to the strangeness of a dull headache, the arms of a naked man around her, and an acute case of shame.

Through the haze of half sleep, she recalled their lovemaking as if it had been a dream. How beautiful his masculine body had been, how skillful his hands, how intense her pleasure. She wanted to drift back to sleep, to never have to fully wake and realize she had seduced him. She had not consumed so much champagne that she did not remember every moment between them. She had asked him to make love to her. She had taken advantage of the intimacy of their situation to push him into giving her what she had so long desired.

She dared move enough to press her fingers to her aching temple. He rustled and resettled so she looked directly into his sleeping face. Maggie released a long sigh, examining the slight curl of his dark lashes, the faint lines creasing his forehead, the moistness of his bottom lip.

She wished he had come freely to her bed, instead of her forcing him into it, using feminine wiles she had not known she possessed. She wished he had been properly introduced to her, had chosen to court her, to marry her, and to make love to her. Never before this moment had she more regretted trapping him into a connection with her. If only she had met him in some respectable drawing room, to be properly introduced by respectable people, and properly married by a respectable country vicar.

But that was truly an impossible dream.

She could never make up for deceiving him, for making him her pretend husband. No amount of toil around Summerton would do it, no amount of care of Summerton's people. Her heart ached with loving him, the feeling grown more intense and painful since the gift of his body.

Maggie shook her head. Not a gift, but something else she'd stolen from him. She felt her throat tighten and her eyes sting. She wished she could give something back to him. She wished she could give him all that was good and happy in life.

A home. Family. Children.

Instead those were the things he had given her. She fought the tears of her regret.

He stirred and opened his eyes, gazing at her with an unreadable expression. A part of her went dead inside for what could never transpire between them. No real love, just a masquerade of it. Another part of her sprang to life, and she knew she would want to make love to him again. And again. And again. A pretend love between them was better than nothing at all, though she feared her desire to give him pleasure was a mere excuse for wanting the pleasure he could give her.

She closed the inches between them and put her lips against his. She ran her hands down the smooth muscles of his back and pressed herself against him, glad to feel the evidence of his arousal.

Was it so very bad to make him want her again? As his lips tasted the tender skin beneath her ears, her conscience flagged and the ache within her grew. His fingers soon sought that secret part of her as they had the night before, creating sensations she'd never experienced in hurried couplings with her false husband. How she wished that man had never existed and Gray had been the only man in her bed. She wanted no other man. Needed no other.

He stroked her and teased her and her excitement grew. She tried to match his every move, to give him as much pleasure as he gave her. More. She wanted to give him more. She wanted to give him everything.

She tried, tried when his body joined hers, tried when their mutual need built, tried when their release came, every bit as spectacular as the night before. Afterward, as he nestled her in his arms and planted soft kisses on her brows and cheek, she knew it would be impossible to ever give him as much as he had given her.

There was a soft rap on the door.

"The devil," Gray muttered, sitting up. "Who is it?"

The door opened a crack. "It is Decker, sir. Lord Camerville bade me fetch you for breakfast and some shooting."

"Of all the fool . . ." He glanced at Maggie. "I suppose I must."

"Go if you wish," she said.

He rubbed his face. "Give me a moment, Decker."

She thought Gray would hurry out of their bed, grateful to be released from the spell binding him. Instead, he gazed at her as if reluctant to leave her.

"You must go?" She wished valiantly not to once again impose her will upon him, but even she could hear in her voice a yearning for him to stay.

He raised her to him, clutching the back of her head as his lips hungrily devoured her. She savored once again the feel of his muscular body under her fingers, the heady intoxication of his lips.

"I suppose I must," he repeated in a groan. He broke the kiss, but came back to kiss her once more before he climbed out of the bed and searched among the scattered clothes for her nightdress. He handed it to her and caressed her hair gently. "Pretend to sleep."

Maggie put her nightdress over her head as he pulled on his drawers and hurriedly picked up his shirt and breeches. He started to close the curtains around the bed, but stopped and climbed back atop it, giving her another kiss so full of passion she was left aching for him all over again.

Then he climbed off the bed and closed the curtains before letting Decker in. Maggie listened to the two men speak quietly, unable to believe that a moment before she and Gray had been making love. Now ordinary life had resumed, a valet assisting his gentleman to dress. Because that gentleman was Gray, Maggie strained to hear every word of their ordinary conversation, until all too quickly, both men left the bedchamber.

As Maggie rolled over and burrowed beneath the

linens, she realized she and Gray had said nothing of what had occurred between them.

The beaters walked the fields ahead of the gentlemen, pounding the brush, scaring the grouse into the air. The gentlemen aimed the guns Lord Camerville had provided for their sport, and fired. More servants stood by to reload, saving the guests that tedious chore. Gray entered into the sport as best he could, given he had no wish to be traipsing through the countryside and no interest in shooting grouse.

He would rather be with Maggie. He rested the gun in the crook of his arm. He wondered if she was still abed, so warm and comfortable, so delightful to see upon awakening. So magnificent to make love to. Her dark tresses spread out upon the pillow, bed linens tangled around her—

"Gray!" Camerville shouted. "Take heed! You did not even fire!"

One of the beaters ran to retrieve the results of a successful shot.

Gray waved his hand to acknowledge Camerville's admonition and tried to pay better attention. Sir Francis was one of the party and he gave Gray a concerned look. The other four gentlemen handed over their guns for reloading, seeming to take little notice.

The fluttering of wings sounded again, followed by guns firing. Gray did not even raise his weapon.

"He's woolgathering," said one of the gentlemen.

"Thinking of that pretty wife of his, I'll wager," Cammy quipped.

All but Sir Francis laughed heartily. Gray frowned.

"I was reminded of the battle," he retorted, knowing he spoke nonsense. "The sounds of firing bring it back."

They knew which battle he meant. These gentlemen had been safe on estates like this one while thousands of men died at Waterloo. Or perhaps they had been frolicking in London or Brighton or Bath. They had only read about the carnage. One or two of them might have traveled to Belgium to view the aftermath of the battle, to walk those fields in search of souvenirs, like a button or a cannonball or the bone of a man's finger.

As Gray expected, his reference to Waterloo silenced them. They gazed at him with expressions so respectful, he thought they'd doff their hats.

The beaters found more birds and the shooting resumed. This time Gray fired with the rest of them.

It was midday before they headed back to the house with three brace of birds bagged for the host's table. Camerville fell in step next to Gray, who trailed the rest of the group.

"Have a surprise for you, Grayson," Cammy told him with a grin.

"For me?" That Camerville had given him that much thought was surprise enough.

"Friend of yours should be arriving soon. Expected him yesterday, but was delayed, you know."

"Who is it?"

Cammy laughed. "Won't be a surprise if I tell you, you know."

One of his army comrades, Gray hoped, though he could not immediately guess who might also be known to Camerville.

He slowed, making his way over some rocks. At another time he might welcome a visit with an old friend, but suddenly he was not so eager. He wanted nothing to keep him from Maggie, away from furthering their ties to each other in the bedroom until she might ultimately feel secure enough to trust him with her secrets. It was enough to deal with ridiculous distractions devised by Camerville.

"Say"—Cammy was oblivious to the distress he'd caused—"how is that pretty little governess of yours? Worked here first, y'know. Pretty little thing. A bit shy, but more's the challenge, I always say."

By God, he'd like to plant this twit a facer. "Miss Miles is in my father's employ and as such deserves to be spoken of with some respect."

They trod on several paces before Cammy spoke in a petulant voice, "I say, Gray, you are as stuffy as your brother was. Didn't think it possible, you a cavalry man and all."

If this man valued his unbroken nose, he had better not say one more word. Gray grimaced and walked on.

But Camerville was anything but wise. "I say, that wife of yours is quite a beauty. Where the devil did you find her? I daresay she's pretty enough to be a high-flyer."

Gray halted, letting the other gentlemen proceed out of earshot. He grabbed Camerville by the lapel of his coat and held his face inches away. "Heed your tongue, sir. You cross the lines of good conduct."

Cammy paled and silently nodded, making the flesh under his chin jiggle. Gray strode on.

"Stuffy," Camerville muttered from behind him.

Gray caught up with Sir Francis and walked along at his side.

"Something amiss?" Sir Francis asked.

"No," replied Gray, not quite calm. He'd come close to decking their host. "Not used to house parties, I expect."

Sir Francis gave him a sympathetic look. They walked along in silence for several strides until Sir Francis cleared his throat. "Do you think Lady Palmely is enjoying herself?"

Gray almost smiled. He obviously was not the only man present to have a woman on his mind. "She appeared to be doing so last night."

Sir Francis looked glum. "She blossoms in society, does she not? It . . . it is good to see." The man's bleak expression belied his words.

"There is no reason to heed me," Gray began carefully as they walked along. "You know too much of my history, but you ought to declare yourself to Olivia."

Sir Francis turned red. "Declare myself?"

"If you want her, you had better declare yourself directly, because some other fellow could come along and turn her eye."

The corners of Sir Francis's mouth turned down. "But perhaps some other fellow would give her more happiness."

Gray put his hand on the man's shoulder. "You would give up without a fight? I had not thought you so henhearted."

He'd meant only to jest Sir Francis out of the glums, but the words seemed to intensify his dejection.

They soon reached the house. "Think on it," Gray said as they parted.

Gray hurried to the bedchamber to change his clothes, hoping to find Maggie there, but the room was empty and restored to such good order there was nothing to suggest what kind of night they had spent together. Decker soon showed up to assist him.

"Do you know the day's activities?" Gray asked him, aiming for a casual tone in his voice. "What have the ladies been doing?" That is to say, where is Maggie and how might he get her alone for a spell?

"The ladies have all been in Lady Camerville's sitting room." Decker's expression retained its usual blandness, but Gray thought he spied a smile as the valet turned to fetch a clean shirt.

Soon Decker had him in fresh clothes appropriate for the afternoon. There had been times on campaign when Gray had worn the same clothes day and night for a week or more. It seemed a lifetime ago.

When Gray came back down the stairs, the Camerville butler waited at the foot. "Lord Camerville wishes you to know that luncheon is set out in the conservatory. He begs you join him."

The man directed Gray to proceed through the library to the glass doors of the conservatory. The profusion of windows captured all the sunlight, and the room was full of plants strategically placed to mimic the out-of-doors.

But Gray cared nothing for that. His eyes sought Maggie. He found her easily, looking like a flower among all the greenery. She sat with Olivia and Sir Francis at one of the tables, her eyes catching his as he crossed the threshold and walked to her.

Olivia caught sight of him. "Gray, you are back from your shooting party! Did you have a splendid time?"

"Splendid," he replied in an ironic tone, annoyed that anyone else was present besides Maggie.

"Of course you did!" Olivia turned back to Sir Francis, seated beside her.

Gray took the chair next to Maggie whose eyes were wide and uncertain. "And how do you fare, Maggie?" he asked in a low voice.

Her heart beating wildly, Maggie had difficulty looking at him. The sight of Gray had spurred both delight and embarrassment, and a very vivid memory of how he had appeared that morning in her bed. "I have had nothing to do all morning."

At first she had appreciated the luxury of remaining in bed with the scent of Gray still on the linens. She had fallen back to sleep, to a swirl of dreams of Gray. Kitt had finally entered the room, trying to be quiet, but Maggie woke and dressed for the most leisurely breakfast of her life. The ladies spoke of inconsequential matters, some of which she could participate in, like the latest fashions, and some she could not, like how splendid was the décor of the Brighton Pavilion. She had read about the Pavilion, of course, and suspected at least some of these ladies were quoting from the magazines and not the actual sight.

After breakfast they had retired to Lady Camerville's sitting room, a very pretty room with Chinese wallpaper and purple drapery, "in the style of the Pavilion," Lady Camerville said. There they had done absolutely nothing.

But none of that mattered now that Gray had returned. He took her hand in his large warm one, the same hand that had performed such magic in the bed they shared. He bent close to her ear. "A pity. We might have found some entertainment had we been together."

She felt her cheeks grow hot. "You were not offended?"

That worry had plagued her the whole indolent morning. Had he thought her too fast, too forward? Would he look upon her with disdain?

His eyes were warm with desire. He laughed softly. "I was not offended."

She breathed a sigh of relief and pleasure. They stared at each other and her heart did joyous flips.

"Take a turn in the garden with me," he whispered.

She nodded. They left the conservatory and found a maid to fetch her bonnet and shawl. Then they left their hosts and the other guests and hurried out to the garden, down one path then another until they found a place covered by a trellis of flowering clematis. Gray drew her into his arms and kissed her. Her hands plunged into his hair and desire flamed inside her once more. His lips performed wonderful sensations against her earlobe.

She could not help but smile. "I did not know if you liked it, Gray. I did not know if you liked making love to me."

"How could I not?" he replied, his voice husky. "You are my wife now."

She did not know if he meant his wife in truth or merely in bed, and was not sure she cared which, as long as he held her and kissed her like this.

He broke from her and cradled her chin in his hand, forcing her to look at him. "We cannot change the past, but that is no reason we cannot forge a future together."

She flung her arms around him. "I could wish for nothing more."

He kissed her again and held her close. The scent of honeysuckle played on the breeze and leaves rustled in the nearby trees. They could not remain here, nor could they leave the group and retire to their bedchamber. More than ever Maggie longed to be back at Summerton.

To her great regret, he released her. "We must wait until tonight, Maggie."

She looked up at him. "Very well."

He helped her straighten her dress and she, his coat. They walked leisurely back to the house. Silent, but peaceful and content.

He paused before they reached the door. "Maggie, there is something more I wish from you. Tell me the truth about yourself."

She felt the blood drain from her face. "Not here, Gray. Not now."

"Tonight, then, when we are alone?" he pressed.

She searched his face. After making love with him, she longed to remove this barrier between them, but she so feared he would despise her if he knew the truth. He might not believe her false husband's death had truly been an accident. He might feel duty-bound to turn her in to the magistrate.

"I will try," she said at last.

The answer seemed to satisfy him.

They entered the house, she feeling more solemn and subdued than a moment ago.

As they neared the library door, she held back. "Go on to the conservatory. I will be there in a moment. I . . . I wish to tidy myself a bit."

The truth was she needed a little time to herself before facing those people again and, more so, to set in her mind that tonight she would tell him her secrets. Tonight she would tell him and risk losing him. Perhaps risk everything.

"You can trust me," he murmured, his eyes dark and resolute.

She smiled, wanting so very much to believe she could trust him to love her in spite of all she'd done.

Gray gave her a quick kiss and walked back to rejoin the other guests. He suspected they were still at luncheon. The amount of food set up on a side table would more than tide them over until dinner, and he was suddenly ravenous.

He was crossing the library when Camerville ran up to him. "Here, here, sir. I have been looking for you! Come with me. I have the surprise I promised."

There was no choice but to follow Camerville through a throng of people to the conservatory. Gray could only see a glimpse of the surprise gentleman's back at first. The man was talking to Olivia, who had laughed and colored prettily at something he said.

"Here is Grayson," Cammy announced.

The man turned.

Lansing.

How the devil had Lansing connived to be invited to this party? It was bad enough to endure the company of people like Camerville and his wife, how was Gray to pass a week in Lansing's company as well?

Lansing looked equally as surprised to see Gray, and equally as displeased, but he quickly altered his expression and advanced on Gray with hand extended.

"Gray. So good to see you. I'd . . . I'd not expected you in this part of the country. This is excellent." He spoke as if he were indeed the friend Gray once supposed him to be.

Gray accepted the handshake with considerably less enthusiasm. "Lansing."

Camerville laughed. "A capital surprise, was it not? Neither one of you had a notion!" He clapped his hands and swept his arm over the guests gathered in the room. "Everyone! See what we have here! These two gentlemen served together in the same regiment. Had no idea the other would be coming!"

Camerville was rewarded by appropriately appreciative comments.

Olivia's eyes shone with enjoyment. "How nice for you both!"

Nice? Gray would have to pretend civility to a man he would cheerfully run through with a sword. He tried to disguise his feelings as others said "wonderful!" and "capital!"

Camerville jocularly repeated how he had contrived the dual surprise. He broke off. "I say, Gray, here comes your pretty wife."

Deuce! Lansing near Maggie? He'd not wish her in the same county with the man.

Cammy had already rushed over to her. Taking Maggie's arm, he said, "I have surprised your husband with a friend. Come. Come. Meet the fellow."

Maggie had as little choice as had Gray. While Cammy dragged her along with him, Lansing dipped his head to say something to Olivia.

"Come, come, Lansing," cried Camerville. "Come meet your friend's wife!"

Lansing looked up.

Gray took a step toward Maggie and caught her first glimpse of Lansing. Her eyes flashed with shock. She turned white, as if she'd seen a ghost.

This look was one of recognition. She *knew* him. She knew Lansing.

Lansing's charming smile was locked into place, but the recognition was on his face as well.

A curtain lifted in Gray's mind. He could suddenly see it. Maggie's west country had been Gloucestershire, where Lansing's militia had been posted. Lansing was the connection between Maggie and himself. Lansing. But, why? Why had they played this game with him?

Olivia had apparently noticed Maggie's pallor. "Maggie," she cried. "Are you ill?" She rushed over to her, causing some commotion. Other guests clustered around her. Olivia helped her to a seat and Sir Francis pressed a glass of lemonade to her lips. Another lady fanned her.

Gray backed away toward the conservatory door, the same door he and Maggie had so happily walked through such a short time before. The scene played out before him like the latest farce, but he found no humor in it. No one heeded him as he opened the door. The last person he saw was Lansing, whose stark expression mirrored Gray's darkening mood.

Gray returned to the garden, making his way down the same paths he and Maggie had strolled not a half hour before. He spied the trellis where he'd kissed her, and quickly changed direction.

Maggie and Lansing. Maggie and Lansing crafted the false marriage papers. Lansing fathered Sean.

Gray felt like vomiting. This was the secret Maggie had kept from him.

Lansing was the one.

Chapter EIGHTEEN

L ansing stood back as the object of his quest fussed over the woman who all but fainted at the sight of him. Cursed tart! It was not enough she had nearly killed him three years ago, pushing him in the river like she did, but now she would likely dash his opportunity with Lady Palmely!

He'd not dared to hope Lord Summerton's daughter-in-law would be so fair-haired, so delicate, the very vision of a lady. A magnificent decoration for any man's arm. Now he stood to lose her because some lady's companion he'd once bedded turned up as Gray's wife.

What irony! What a sick joke at his expense. To the devil with her!

Lady Palmely's attention was riveted upon this vaporous female. Maggie Delaney, pretty lady's companion, thinking herself so proper she required marrying. Underneath she was nothing but a Drury Lane doxy like his mother. How the devil had she found her way to Gray?

The gorgeous Olivia, Lady Palmely of Summerton

Hall, glanced about, not at him. "Sir Francis!" she called. "Come help me."

The dull-looking fellow was already standing at her side, clucking over Maggie. He gave Maggie his arm and escorted her out of the room. Lady Palmely went with him, asking him what they should do, begging him to tell her Maggie would be all right. She vanished from Lansing's sight without giving him a backward glance.

"Where is Grayson?" Camerville sputtered.

Gray.

He was the real spoiler. Always had been.

"Left the room," someone said. "His wife entered, and he left posthaste."

"There is some trouble in that quarter," another added.

Soon the whole room was buzzing with talk of the captain and his mysterious wife. The gossip had it that Gray, not Lansing, upset her so much she almost fainted. Fainted, indeed. No one would have even noticed her if Lady Palmely had not made a fuss.

At least he was not blamed for the dramatics. If he was very clever he might manage to carry out his plan after all.

He donned a very concerned expression and tapped Camerville on the shoulder. "Would you like me to find Gray and speak to him? Perhaps I can discover what is amiss."

Camerville nodded vigorously. "Can't have this. Ruins the party."

"I will do my best to put it to rights," he reassured the foolish fellow.

A quarter hour later Lansing located Gray near the lake that made such an elegant view from the house. One of the gardeners had seen him head in this direction and, sure enough, he was pacing moodily at the edge. Foolish Gray. Always did let emotions get the better of him.

Gray looked up at his approach. "Keep your distance, Lansing, if you know what is good for you."

Lansing obediently halted, immediately screwing his face into a picture of concern and distress. "How the devil did she find you, Gray? I cannot believe she has done so. Has she tricked you into marrying her?"

Gray gratified him by looking surprised at this barrage of questions, and Lansing credited himself for his ability to fool Gray whenever he wished.

He went on. "Did she tell you of meeting me? I suspect she must not have done so." Lansing put a trembling hand to his brow as if this whole situation had undone him.

Gray glared at him. "You came to say something, Lansing. Say it and begone."

Oh, he was going to play the wounded one, was he? Well, Lansing never backed down from getting what he wanted. He stepped toward Gray, making himself look puzzled. Gray stepped back.

Lansing gave a helpless gesture. "I can only tell you what I know of her." He bowed his head as if trying to sort his own thoughts. "I met her in Gloucestershire. But you might have guessed that. She was a lady's companion, a very ambitious one."

It was always good to use as many facts as possible when one told a lie. It guaranteed a ring of truth to the tale. "She was not content with her lot at all. She . . . she befriended me and, I confess, I did not resist her—it was a dead bore there, Gray—" He gazed out over the distance like he was remembering. "She was keen for bettering herself, and . . . and thought her way to do it was by—" He broke off again and laughed. "Well, with my birth, I was naught but someone to dally with. She dropped me fast enough."

Gray looked as if he might strike him. "Why am I involved?"

"That is what is giving me the devil of a headache," Lansing said, feigning ignorance. "I cannot fathom it at all."

Lansing did not miss Gray's skeptical look.

Lansing wrinkled his brow. "She'd seen you with me. Remember? You traveled with me to Gloucestershire." He tapped his lips with his fingers. "I did not credit it as important at the time, but she once asked me questions about you. We had to talk of something. It could not all be . . . you know."

Gray looked furious again. Could it be he had developed a *tendre* for a nobody lady's companion? How laughable.

Lansing gave him an intent look. "Did she come looking for you? Did she seduce you as well? I cannot believe you married her."

"I did not marry her," Gray shot back.

Oh? Lansing's brows shot up. The plot was thickening. What the devil did Gray mean?

Gray continued. "There are papers with my signature upon them saying I did marry her. Can you explain that?"

Of course he could explain it! He'd wanted to see what would happen if he were an earl's son, so he had pretended to be Gray. Still, the only way he could get her into bed with him was to marry her. Whose name was he supposed to have used?

Lansing pretended to look totally bewildered. "Your *signature*?"

While Gray glared at him, he posed as a man lost in thought. He started to speak, then shook his head. "No. She could not be so conniving."

Gray was hanging on his words, even though his face looked like thunder. Perhaps if he, Lansing, could be the one to save Gray from this treacherous female, he could get back in Gray's good graces. He could court Gray's sister-in-law and perhaps even have an ally in winning her hand.

But the prize was not yet totally within his grasp. He must take care not to misstep.

He waited for the silence to stretch a decent interval. "I kept a letter you once wrote me. It had your signature upon it. I thought I had merely lost it. Do you suppose she could have taken it?"

Gray's brows knit together ever so slightly. He was halfway hooked. But Gray swung away from him.

Time to back off. Let him stew in it. "I am sorry, Gray. I feel responsible somehow."

Gray turned back, that look of thunder still upon him. "What of the child?"

It was Lansing's turn to be dumbfounded. "What child?"

"She gave birth to a son, Lansing."

Lansing stiffened. He had no intention of being saddled with the responsibility of her brat. Any child he claimed must be born to an aristocratic mother. Like Lady Palmely.

Lansing slowly nodded. "It makes some sense now. She was so keen on bedding me, I'll wager—" He looked up. "Do you know what month the child was born?"

Gray glared. "I know precisely."

Lansing was not surprised Gray did not reveal the month. Gray might not be as clever as Lansing, but he was not a total fool. Lansing quickly calculated two or three months later than he'd actually been with Maggie.

"Well, I knew her at the beginning of 1814, just a few weeks that January. The militia left the area after that time." Lansing had really been convalescing from his near-drowning that month, having contracted a convenient case of amnesia, which stretched until the vicar's nubile daughter began to hatch a marriage plot. "Am I the father, do you think?" he added, just for effect.

Gray's expression became more austere. "You will have to ask her." He marched away.

When Gray had progressed a sufficient distance, Lansing indulged in a good laugh.

Maggie assured Olivia she did not need the physician and would do nicely if she could rest upon her bed, that Kitt could remain with her, and Olivia must return to the other guests.

Olivia felt her forehead, kissed her good-bye, and finally joined Sir Francis who waited for her right outside the bedchamber.

As soon as the door closed, Maggie sat up. "Kitt, peek out and see if they are gone."

Kitt hurried to the door and opened it a crack, then wide enough to poke her head out. "The hall is empty, ma'am."

"Good." She got off the bed. "Would you find Decker? I require his services."

Kitt looked puzzled, but she left to do as Maggie asked. Maggie walked over to the window and looked out, wondering where Gray had gone. She could only imagine what he must be thinking. He'd realized she recognized *that* man.

She did not even know what name to call him, this man who had returned from the dead, her false husband. Maggie had caught the shocked expression on Gray's face when she looked upon the man she'd so long thought dead. As she suspected, her false husband was someone Gray had known, though she was no closer to comprehending why the man would so falsely use Gray's name.

Maggie swung away from the window and paced the bedchamber, her arms clasped around her chest, as if she were trying to keep herself from shattering into pieces upon the carpet. She needed to find Gray. Nothing else was so important.

She crossed over to the door and peeked out, wondering what was taking Decker so long. After an agonizing ten minutes, Kitt finally brought him to her.

The valet hardly stepped into the room before Maggie accosted him. "Decker, do you know where Captain Grayson has gone?"

Decker's forehead wrinkled slightly, betraying worry, but he answered in a monotone. "Gone into the garden, I was told."

For once she was grateful of servants' gossip.

"Thank you." She grabbed her bonnet and placed it upon her head. "If you should see the captain before I return, please let him know I wish to speak to him." She wrapped her shawl around her shoulders and hurried out.

She had no idea where Lady and Lord Camerville were, nor the other guests, but she hoped she did not encounter any of them. Especially *him*. She dashed down a hallway that looked like it would be used by the servants, and finally found a door leading to the outside. It took her a few moments to get her bearings and to find her way to the garden, where she retraced the path she and Gray had taken such a short time ago. She wound up underneath the trellis where he had kissed her.

She persisted until she was persuaded she had covered every inch of the garden without success. She'd decided to head toward the stables next to see if any of the grooms had seen Gray ride out. Hurrying down a path leading out of the formal gardens to the park, she collided with . . . *him*, the man she had once called husband.

He grabbed her by the shoulders. She tried to pull away, but he held on tight.

"The very person I wished to see." His countenance was anything but welcoming. "Let us find a private place where we may talk." He gave her a sarcastic smile. "Not the lake. I do not trust you around water."

He pointed to a decorative Chinese temple peeking through a shade of trees. Gripping her arm, he nearly dragged her to it.

The temple was dark and cool and smelled damp. There was a bench, but she had no intention of sitting with him. He released her but blocked any escape.

Putting his hands on his hips, he looked as angry as he had that day she pushed him into the river. "What the devil are you doing here? How did you attach yourself to

Gray?" He bared his teeth. "I cannot believe this. I swear, if you have ruined things for me—"

"Ruined things for you!" Maggie cried. "I thought you were dead!"

"You tried hard enough to kill me," he huffed.

"An accident and you know it." Her eyes burned with rage. "You tricked me! And abandoned me! What did you think? You would leave me at that house thinking myself secretly married? The poor pitiable lady's companion, pining away for her absent husband?"

He laughed. "Yes! You have got it, Maggie. Clever girl. That is exactly what I expected. But the fault is all yours. You insisted upon marriage. I merely obliged you. You were happy enough after that sham ceremony I paid for!"

"You deceived me from the first, telling me you were Captain John Grayson. I do not even know your name."

He pursed his lips, like a petulant child. "Do you not realize it was a game, Maggie? A lark! That is all it was. You were so ready to believe my lies, were you not? To believe a man like me would want a lady's companion."

She swung her arm back and slapped him full on his cheek, the loud smack echoing off the temple's walls. He lifted his hand to hit her back, but stopped himself in time.

"You little bitch," he muttered, cradling his cheek. "If you have left a mark—"

"Stand aside." She tried to get past him.

He grabbed her again and shook her. "Now you listen to me! I will not have you ruin my plans!"

"*Your* plans?" she cried, trying to twist out of his

grasp. "What of my plans? What was I supposed to do with no money, no husband, and a baby on the way?"

He gave a snort. "Oh, yes. Your bastard. Gray informed me."

"You spoke to Gray?" She filled with sudden dread.

He released her. His eyes glittered dangerously and he gave a sardonic smile. "I told him how it was. How you were keen to marry into a wealthy family. How you threw yourself at me until you realized I was not highborn. How you kept asking questions about my friend John Grayson, the earl's son." He laughed with triumph. "I even told him that you stole a letter with his signature so you could forge his name. He thinks you set him up!"

Maggie felt a stab of pain so acute she had to wrap her arms around her waist. She could not breathe.

She lifted her head to glare at the man who so easily snatched happiness from her grasp. Once she had thought those features handsome. Once she'd thought she loved him. Now he made bile rise in her throat, and she could only regard him with raw hatred. For the first time she wished he *had* drowned in the river.

To her surprise a hint of wariness creased his brow. "What does he know?"

She straightened and wrapped her shawl around her shoulders and said nothing.

"What does he know?" repeated her false husband, taking a menacing step toward her.

She stepped back and held up her hand to halt him. "If you touch me once again, I shall scream." Her voice sounded as dead as she felt inside.

He started toward her again. "No one will hear you."

She lifted a brow. "Can you be so sure? Perhaps there

is a gardener nearby. Or one of the guests decided to take a stroll. Do you wish to risk it?"

He halted.

"Now," she said calmly, "I will leave." With her head erect, she strode past him. As soon as she knew he could not see her, she broke into a run.

Gray managed to stay away from the main house until the sun dropped so low in the sky that the dinner hour was certain to be at hand. His first impulse had been to drag Maggie and Olivia to the carriage for a breakneck ride back to Summerton, but he'd quickly seen the folly of such a flight. Not only would it have cut short Olivia's enjoyment of the house party, the gossip it would have generated would effectively prevent her receiving any future invitations. Gray would be damned if he let Lansing's arrival damage Olivia's emergence into the world. Besides, such a hasty retreat would not provide him with the answers he needed.

Gray had borrowed a mount from Camerville's stable and wandered the estate all the afternoon, hardly an effective way to get answers, but necessary to wrest some control over his raging emotions.

Gray did not believe Lansing's story that Maggie had been the treacherous architect of all the havoc in Gray's life. He knew Lansing too well to believe him such an innocent bystander. He also could not credit Maggie with a deliberate conspiracy with Lansing. Lansing would have led her into it. If Lansing had no qualms about bedding young virgins, he would be entirely capable of seducing Maggie, of lying to her, of using her to slake his own desires.

When Gray's thoughts veered in this direction, the image of Lansing tangled in linens with Maggie, touching her, making love to her, made Gray's vision turn red. Lansing had been the man who introduced Maggie to the pleasures of lovemaking, of that Gray was certain. *Lansing,* the man Gray despised more than any other, excepting himself for ever thinking Lansing a friend, for ever allowing himself to be led into dishonoring himself with Rosa. Thinking of Maggie with Lansing filled Gray with a crazed jealousy that flowed through every vein in his body.

Until he could get these emotions under control, he had little chance of discovering why any connection between Maggie and Lansing resulted in Maggie's appearing on Gray's doorstep with the tale of being married to a man with his name, or of her having papers with his signature forged. Lansing's tale about Maggie had succeeded in resurrecting Gray's doubts about her. No matter how she'd been duped by Lansing, she still appeared to have deliberately set a trap for Gray. Why? All hope of a future with her rested on the answer.

Gray entered the house and made his way to the bedchamber he would be required to share with Maggie this entire week. Only a few hours before, he'd been eager to return to this room with her. Now too much stood between them.

He walked in. Maggie was seated at the dressing table, her maid arranging her hair. She turned to him. Their eyes caught, but Gray looked away.

Decker stood off to the side. Gray went over to him. "My dinner clothes, Decker?"

There was a deadly tension in the room, like invisible

smoke choking all the breathable air. Even the valet and maid spoke as little as possible. Gray spoke not at all to Maggie, nor she to him. This evening he did not dismiss the servants so he could be alone with her, so he could touch her. This evening he merely completed his change of clothes.

When done, he spoke coldly to her. "Are you ready?"

"Yes, yes," she answered nervously as her maid straightened the skirt of her dress.

She wore blue again, this time the color of a spring sky. A white sheer overdress covered the blue, making it shimmer. Olivia's sapphires still adorned her neck and ears. With such an appearance she could easily dazzle any man's eye. He had no trouble believing Lansing had wanted her.

Gray knew his coldness was unfair. He could feel her upset as keenly as his own. He ought to have some pity for her, but he was incapable of excusing her this time. Nothing would do for him except to frankly address what stood between them, no matter what he feared he might hear from her. Now, however, was not the time.

Gray did not speak to her as they walked down to the parlor. Once there, he left Maggie and joined some of the gentlemen who were chatting in the corner. Lansing, he noticed, stood talking to Olivia. Gray's eyes narrowed. He must warn his sister-in-law about Lansing. At the moment, though, he could rest easy. Sir Francis stood stalwartly at her side.

Maggie remained where he'd left her, in the center of the room looking lost. She finally walked to a chair and sat. Gray saw some of the guests glancing toward her with curiosity. Let them. He would withstand any gossip by pretending nothing was amiss. If Maggie were wise, she would do the same.

Lansing, Gray noticed, paid her no attention at all.

Dinner passed well enough, although Maggie was seated on the other side of the table well within his view. He could not see Lansing, but endured the sound of the man's laughter as best he could. He also endured Lansing's presence after dinner, a more difficult matter. Camerville wanted them to entertain the other gentlemen with tales from the Peninsula. They managed to do so, without Gray ever speaking to Lansing directly.

The gentlemen finally joined the ladies, and Lady Camerville again insisted upon champagne. Gray watched Maggie, seated at the same settee as the night before, refuse a glass. He turned away, having no wish to recall how the drink had previously affected her.

Olivia walked up to him, Sir Francis momentarily detained in conversation. "Gray, Maggie is sitting all alone over there."

He avoided looking. "I am sure she will not want for company." Camerville would certainly seek her out. Let her deal with the octopus herself.

Olivia stared at him worriedly. "What is wrong, Gray? What happened?"

"It is none of your affair, Olivia," he said in a fierce whisper.

"But . . ." She bit her lip, but abandoned the topic.

She was about to walk away when he stopped her. "Olivia, Lansing appears to pay you much attention."

She smiled brightly. "Your friend? Yes, he is charming!"

"No, he is not charming," he said. "You would do well to steer clear of him."

She tossed him an offended look. "Perhaps who I spend time with is none of *your* affair." She stalked off.

All he needed was Olivia playing the coquette with Lansing. Before she knew it, the man would have *her* in his bed. Gray knew him too well. Sir Francis had better act with dispatch.

Lady Camerville swished over to him and took his arm. He'd ignored her lures the previous night when he'd had no thought but of being alone with Maggie. Tonight, knowing Maggie could see him, he would pretend at a little flirtation.

But he did not miss the exact moment Lord Camerville made his move. Gray felt himself involuntarily compelled toward Maggie when the man placed his hand upon her knee. Luckily, Sir Francis spared him the need to exert himself, coming quickly to Maggie's side and escorting her to where Olivia sat. Sir Francis kept watch on both the ladies the rest of the evening. Gray knew this, because his eyes could not help but seek out Maggie. Lansing made no effort to approach Olivia as long as Maggie was at her side.

Card tables were set up, and Lady Camerville begged Gray be her partner in a round of whist. Sir Francis joined with Olivia and found another gentleman to sit across from Maggie. The rest of the night was tolerable, although again Gray managed to be seated where he could not help but see Maggie. If that were not enough, Lansing's smooth voice grated in the background.

Eventually the room began to thin. As Olivia and Sir Francis rose from their seats, Gray walked over to Maggie and silently escorted her back to the bedchamber.

Gray turned to Decker, who was prepared to assist him

in readying for bed. "I will not require your services tonight," he said as casually as he could.

Maggie swung around to view Gray with surprise.

Decker's brows shot up but the young man immediately composed himself. "Very good, sir." He bowed and left the room.

Maggie gave Gray one more glance before she went into the dressing room with her maid.

Chapter NINETEEN

Maggie's heart thundered with impatience. Could Kitt not move any faster? How long did it take to undo buttons, even the tiny ones that ran up the back of her dress? Maggie could barely keep her foot from tapping, but she forced herself to remain still while Kitt removed her gown, corset, and shift and helped her don her nightdress. Finally they went back into the bedchamber.

Besides the glowing embers of the fireplace, only the branch of candles on the dressing table remained lit. Barely visible in the room's shadows stood Gray, a mere silhouette against the window.

Maggie's heart beat like a drum's wild tattoo as she quickly sat so Kitt could remove the pins from her hair. This night Gray made no move to dismiss the maid and comb out her tresses himself. He remained by the window, watching each stroke of the brush.

In the mirror, Maggie caught Kitt's worried countenance. When the maid finished putting Maggie's hair in one thick plait, she gave Maggie's hand a quick squeeze and left the room.

Maggie stood and faced Gray, still standing in near

darkness like some sinister stranger who suddenly has all the future wrapped in his fingers. He stared back at her for so long Maggie fancied she could hear the thundering of her pulse in her ears.

She took a deep breath. "You asked me to tell my secrets, Gray. Would you hear them now?"

He was more apparition than man when he answered, "Yes."

She wanted to beg him to come into the light, to sit with her where he would be close enough that she could see the expression on his face, and grasp his hand, holding fast lest he disappear in the mist like a phantom made only of air.

She remained where she was, straightening her spine, imagining she was a soldier bracing for battle. "I heard that gentleman referred to as Lansing this evening. Is that his name?"

He paused before answering. "Leonard Lansing."

"I did not know it before." She took another breath. "You do not know my true name. It is Margaret Delaney . . ."

She began by telling him of her parents, of her brother, of their deaths in the Severn River. She told of growing up in the boarding school, sent there by her aristocratic uncle who'd long before severed ties with her mother, an uncle who washed his hands of her as soon as she was old enough for employment. She described her life as a lady's companion, the loneliness of it, the tedium. She told of meeting a man who gave his name as John Grayson, the man she now knew was called Lansing.

Maggie tried to keep emotion from her voice, to speak clearly, to relate the events as accurately as she could.

Gray did not interrupt her. He asked no questions, made no comment. He remained, as still as a statue, in the darkness.

She continued, describing her foolish belief in this John Grayson's courtship and in the secret marriage she'd thought real. She told of how, after a few weeks, he failed to show up at their meeting place, of her panic at discovering she was with child, and of that final altercation when they struggled at the riverbank and he fell in. She described seeing his body whisked away by the current, disappearing under the water.

"—I believed I had killed him." Her voice cracked, and she paused to swallow. "I could think only to hide myself, for fear of being arrested and hanged. There was a baby inside me, my parents' grandchild. I could only think of the child."

The window's curtains fluttered in the breeze, but Gray did not move.

She went on, telling of losing her employment and taking her meager savings to London, where nobody knew her. She could find no work there. Her money had run out but then she'd read of Captain John Grayson in the newspaper. It was like winning a reprieve. He was alive and must take responsibility for her and for his child. She had found his address. But it had been Gray who opened his door to her, who saw her baby safely born.

"I was a murderer again, you see," she explained. "When Lord and Lady Caufield believed me to be your wife, I did not disabuse them, nor tell your father or Olivia or anyone else. I did it to keep Sean safe. I did it for Sean. Only for Sean."

Oh, she lied. She shook her head and peered across the

darkness to him, determined not to hold anything back. "Not only for Sean. I wanted to stay at Summerton. I had a home and a family again, and I did not want to lose those things. I did not want to be alone."

She waited for a question, a comment, a sign he had even heard her, but she knew her story was unbelievable. No woman would be so gullible. No luck strong enough to bring her to his door.

He said nothing.

She waited longer, her distress rising, engulfing her. She felt like he had slipped away from her as surely as the water had swept away her parents and her brother.

"I thank you for your candor," he finally said, but he sounded as disbelieving as she feared. He crossed the room heading toward the bedchamber's door.

She stepped in his path, grabbing his arms. "Do not leave, Gray. I have told you what you long wanted to know. Do not leave without a word."

She could finally see his face, but it looked like a storm about to unleash thunder and lightning. He pulled out of her grasp, taking a step back from her. "You have told me everything?"

She avoided the fire in his eyes. "No," she admitted. She'd left out her biggest secret.

Even though sure it would sound like a lie, she would say it. "There is one more thing." Her throat tightened with emotion, making her voice come out no more than a rasp. "I love you, Gray."

He flinched as if she'd struck him. His fingers curled into fists and she felt the thunder erupt in his silence. Finally, with seeming great effort he said, "Did you not say those words to Lansing?"

She'd lost all hope that he would enfold her in his arms and ensure her everything would be all right. A gust of wind came through the window, making the candle flames dance until they sputtered out, leaving little columns of smoke rising in the air. The only light remaining came from the fireplace, so dim it felt as if Gray were disappearing again.

"He was not Lansing to me," she finally responded. "What words I spoke were to an illusion. Nothing was real with him." She paused. "Not like with you."

Her energy was spent and she could not even understand how she remained on her feet.

His voice came back to her sounding as if from a great distance. "I cannot remain here tonight."

When he again walked toward the door she did not stop him. He put his hand on the knob and hesitated. Over his shoulder, he said, "I need time, Maggie."

As Maggie's spirits plummeted into a pool on the floor, he walked out of the room.

Gray hurried down the hallway and down the stairs, glad the hour was late enough that the house was quiet. He had no wish to speak to anyone. He entered the parlor, looking for a place to be alone. A loud snore startled him and he swung around to find Lord Camerville's large bulk half on, half off the settee. Gray hurried out.

He went to the library next. Finding it deserted, he finally collapsed in a wingback chair by a waning fire in the fireplace. He stared into the embers, watching until their glow faded and finally winked out in one funereal gasp. The room grew cold, and still he sat.

He wanted to believe Maggie's story. He wanted to run up the stairs to tell her so, to tell her he loved her, too. He wanted to make love to her, wanted to make her his proper wife.

But he could not.

Lansing had sown seeds of doubt, and try as he might, Gray could not erase them. He did not believe Lansing, by any means, but Maggie's story about the elaborate ruse of a wedding was equally as difficult to countenance. It was easier to believe someone crafted phony marriage papers than to believe any man, even Lansing, would go to such an elaborate and cruel length to get a woman in bed. Why would Lansing have done such a thing?

Even Maggie's profession of love for him, which pierced the very depths of Gray's soul, was not enough to dispel the biggest mystery, the one neither story addressed. Why the devil was *he* embroiled in it? Why use his name?

The first evidence of dawn peeked through the glass doors of the conservatory at the far end of the library. Gray stretched his legs, which had become stiff from the chill of the room and the long hours in the chair. He rose. He would have to return to the bedchamber, to be there when Decker arrived to dress him. He could not be seen wandering the house still in his evening clothes. He would have to bear the pain of seeing Maggie sleeping upon the bed, wanting to hold her, wishing to tell her all was at rights.

It was the uncertainty that stopped him. The uncertainty that would always be there with him, nagging at him, if he continued this ruse, if he made her his wife. He would rather give her up, send her away, settle her and Sean in some house of their own far away from him, rather than never know the true nature of her relationship with Lansing.

The truth lay with Lansing. Somehow before this week was out, Gray would wrench it out of him.

The next morning, Lansing lurked in the hallway near Lady Palmely's bedchamber. Most of the men, including Gray and that Sir Francis fellow, had gone out riding that morning, but he had begged off. This was his chance to get her alone, to begin his courtship. By the end of this week, he had every intention of making her so in love with him that she would agree to marry him.

If only he could rid himself of Gray and Maggie. He rubbed his cheek. Maggie's slap had left a faint mark, but nothing to be commented upon. When he was married to Lady Palmely, he had no doubt he could make sure Maggie and Gray were not welcome at Summerton Hall. If Gray had once been estranged from his father, Lansing had no doubt he could facilitate another estrangement. What a justice it would be to usurp Gray's place with his father!

Lansing heard a door open, but not Lady Palmely's door. Two of the other ladies walked by him. He smiled charmingly, showered compliments upon their appearance, and made a near-bawdy remark to make them giggle. Finally they were gone. Lady Palmely was his object, only she. Olivia, Lady Palmely.

He had best not encounter Maggie. She was an annoyance and an impediment. Still, it rankled that Gray had her in his bed. Lansing disliked Gray winning anything that rightfully belonged to him, even if he no longer wanted it.

Lansing turned and spied the ethereal Lady Palmely, the goddess of his hopes and dreams, walking gracefully toward him.

"Good morning, Lady Palmely," he said with just enough smile to entice, but not enough to frighten her off.

"Good morning, Lieutenant Lansing," she said brightly. She raised her chin as if greeting him were some act of defiance.

No matter. He liked the alliteration of his name on her tongue. One advantage of his military rank, lower than Gray's rank, was it saved him from being a mere *mister.*

He leaned toward her, just a little, and gave her a bashful expression. "I know it is forward of me to say so, but you look quite beautiful this morning."

She colored prettily, giving that chin lift again. "Why, thank you."

He sobered, as if he were placing his heart upon his sleeve. "Could I beg you to take a turn in the garden with me?"

"I should like it above all things," she replied with resolve.

He made sure his eyes shone with pleasure. "Not more than I."

He offered her his arm and led her to the garden. It would be ideal to take her to that Chinese temple where he'd taken Maggie. It was nice and private, but too far for this first excursion. Later, for certain.

As they walked, he dug deep into his ammunition of charm. He told his most entertaining stories. Gave his most sincere compliments. She laughed in all the right places, smiled when he willed it.

They came to a trellis festooned with flowers. He told

her she looked like a flower herself in her white morning dress. She blushed. This was splendid. She was beginning to admire him.

He gave a sigh and looked poetically into her eyes. "Tell me, my lady, before my hopes are dashed to cinders, is there any way I might beg permission to pay my addresses?"

The smile on her face vanished, and her eyes grew very, very large.

A blunder. Damnation! He took a step backward and made his voice as soft and as soothing as he could. "I beg pardon, my lady. I became quite carried away. I wish you no distress."

"I would like to return to the house," she said in a small voice.

He bowed. "I serve to please you."

They covered half the distance before she broke the silence. "They said you are a friend of Gray's. Are you?"

"It gives me great honor to consider myself his friend," he replied, wondering why the question was asked. Had Gray gotten to her?

"I see," she said.

What the devil did she see? Hell and damnation. Gray must have poisoned her mind to him. It was the only explanation. Gray caused this change in her attitude, and she would surely, like everyone else, listen to the son of an earl over the son of a doxy.

Maggie spent more excruciatingly idle hours in Lady Camerville's sitting room, with nothing more to do than think of Gray. She was determined to make him talk to her. He was the one keeping his thoughts inside this time.

He'd returned to the bedchamber early that morning. Maggie sat up when he entered the room, but he said nothing to her. He would not even look in her direction. Instead, he dressed himself in her dressing room. When Decker arrived, he said a brief word to him and they both walked out. Maggie had sat up in bed and hurled a candlestick at the closed door behind them.

Now she flipped through Lady Camerville's latest *Lady's Monthly Museum* without reading the words or seeing the plates, plotting when she might get Gray alone. Olivia wandered the room, stopping to look out the window near Maggie's chair.

"I wonder when the gentlemen will return," she asked absently.

So did Maggie. She planned to be in the bedchamber when Gray came to change his clothes, to ask him to say out loud what his feelings were. Never was she more convinced that total honesty was the only hope for them to salvage the promise their one night of lovemaking had given them.

Olivia paced some more and wound up back at the window.

One of the ladies said, "I will wager Lady Palmely pines for that dashing Lieutenant Lansing. We all saw how he could not take his eyes off you last evening, Olivia."

"Never fear, dear. He'll return soon enough," another added. The other ladies giggled.

Olivia spun around. "I do not pine for him, I assure you. Besides, he did not go riding."

Maggie looked up, surprised Olivia should know anything of Lansing's doings.

"Yes, we saw him this morning, did we not, Juliana?" one of the other ladies commented. Her friend agreed that they had.

Olivia gave Maggie a very guilty look before turning back to the window, raising more questions in Maggie's mind. She'd been so wrapped up in her own problems, she'd not noticed much about how Olivia had been faring.

Maggie rose from her seat and walked over to stand beside Olivia at the window. "You are restless." Maggie spoke quietly so the other ladies would not hear. "What has happened, Olivia?"

"Nothing." Olivia's retort was a bit too sharp.

Maggie opened her mouth to ask about Lansing, but Lady Camerville interrupted. "We will have no luncheon today, ladies." It was already past noon, and they had only left the breakfast room an hour ago. "We shall be quite rustic and dine early down by the lake. My dear Cammy and I have devised all sorts of entertainments! Archery and boating. Music and swordplay."

It sounded the sort of entertainment that would afford Gray more chance to avoid her, Maggie thought. She became even more determined to catch him after he returned from riding.

Maggie tried to speak with Olivia again while the ladies waited in idleness for the men to return, but Olivia made certain to attach herself to one group of ladies or another. Eventually word came that the gentlemen had returned. Olivia excused herself and nearly ran out. Maggie had only to rise from her chair and cross the room to catch up with her, but when she reached the hall, Olivia was nowhere to be seen. She hurried to Olivia's room and knocked upon the door. There was no answer. She turned to leave.

Lansing blocked her way. "Where is she?" he demanded.

"Who?" She stalled.

"Lady Palmely." His eyes looked dangerous.

"What do you want of her?" Maggie demanded.

He seized her by the arm and pulled her into a nearby alcove. "It is none of your concern. But I'll not have you or Gray speaking ill of me."

"I have nothing but ill to say of you, sir," she shot back.

He bent down into her face. "If you stand in my way with Lady Palmely, I will rid myself of you. You and Gray. Do you comprehend my meaning?"

For a moment she could not breathe, but she glared defiantly and tried to pull away. "Your threats mean nothing to me."

He squeezed her arm tighter, but the sounds of some other guests approaching made him let go. With a parting sneer, he marched away.

Maggie put a hand to her chest to calm her pounding heart. She ran to her bedchamber in search of Gray, only to find Decker brushing off his riding coat.

"I have missed him!" she cried.

He knew whom she meant. "He spoke of playing billiards."

She did not know where the billiards room was, but she hurried out again, ready to barge into it, if necessary. As she reached the bottom of the stairs, she realized she could not simply walk in on the men, not without explanations she did not wish to make. She decided to find Olivia before Lansing found her.

She started with the rooms where the guests congregated. The parlor. The library. The conservatory. Olivia was in none of them, and neither was Lansing. She asked one of the gentlemen in the conservatory if he had seen Olivia.

The man gave a vague wave of his hand. "I believe I saw Lady Palmely walking in the garden."

Maggie knew Olivia would not stroll through the garden by herself. A sick feeling settled in Maggie's stomach and she hurried outside without bothering to fetch her bonnet or shawl. Fearing Lansing would have taken Olivia to the garden's Chinese temple, Maggie ran down the path toward it. As she neared the temple's entrance, she heard the murmur of voices and Olivia's laugh.

She boldly stepped up to the entrance. "Olivia!"

From the corner of her eye, she saw a man and a woman jump apart. Olivia and . . . Sir Francis!

"Oh!" Maggie exclaimed, giddy with relief. "I beg your pardon." She turned to go.

"No, Maggie. Wait." Olivia caught her by the arm and led her back to where Sir Francis stood, his neckcloth rumpled and his grin stretched ear to ear.

"I must tell you!" Olivia laughed. "But it is a secret so I beg you not to speak of it." She cast an adoring glance at Sir Francis. "Sir Francis has asked me to marry him and I have accepted."

Maggie shrieked and gave Olivia a huge hug, laughing and crying, all the same, partly in relief that it had not been Lansing after all. Then she gave dear Sir Francis a hug. He dabbed at his eyes as well.

"How did this happen? I mean when?" Maggie sputtered.

"A moment ago," sighed Olivia.

Sir Francis wrapped his arm around his new fiancée. "I assure you I have loved her for many years."

"And I assure you both that nothing could make me happier! I have longed for this day!" Maggie hugged Olivia again.

"To think I almost behaved most foolishly." Olivia's brow wrinkled. "Do you think Gray will approve?"

"He will wish you both very happy."

Olivia hung on Sir Francis's arm, squeezing her cheek against it. "I never thought to be so happy a second time." She gave another worried look. "Oh, dear. Will Rodney like it, I wonder?"

"He will love it," Maggie assured her. "He is already greatly fond of Sir Francis."

"And I of him," said Sir Francis emphatically.

"Do we announce it here, do you think?" Olivia's brow wrinkled.

Maggie laughed. "I do not know how to advise you of that."

Sir Francis assumed a commanding expression. "We tell Gray. But before making the announcement public, we must inform the earl."

Olivia gazed at him with rapt admiration. "You are so right."

The three of them walked back to the house, Olivia nearly skipping along. Maggie was happy for her. She *was*. Even though her own happiness, a day ago so much like Olivia's, had plunged into jeopardy. She set her chin determinedly. Her love for Gray was worth battling for, and she would not allow Lansing to spoil their future together.

By the time they returned to the house, the estate was a bustle of activity in preparation for Lady Camerville's garden party. Servants were busy erecting tents and placing tables and chairs beneath them. An archery range was being set up, and a servant passed by carrying sets of foils. Maggie lost hope of catching Gray alone anytime soon. When she, Olivia, and Sir Francis entered the conservatory door, she spied Lansing standing nearby. Maggie could feel his eyes like daggers in her back long after they passed him.

Chapter TWENTY

Gray stood unseen among a throng of gentlemen whose company he did not desire. He watched Olivia and Sir Francis—and Maggie—walk by Lansing. He saw Lansing's eyes follow them.

Gray was biding his time, waiting for the proper moment to get Lansing alone again.

Gray went along with the planned events, as if the entertainments brought enjoyment. He conversed on such matters as the weather, the problems of unemployed soldiers, the escalating corn prices. He listened politely to town gossip, heard of the plays performed that past season, the attractions at Vauxhall Gardens. When the ladies left to change their dresses, the gentlemen went on to boast of their mistresses, arguing whose was the most expensive, whose the most talented.

Sir Francis came up to him. "May I have a moment of your time, Gray?" The man looked as if he were about to burst into song.

They stepped into a small corner of the library. "What is it?" Gray asked, though he was certain he'd already guessed.

Sir Francis attempted a sober look, failing entirely. "I wish to tell you that I have asked Lady Palmely for her hand in marriage, and she has accepted." His last words ended on a wide grin.

Gray clasped Sir Francis's hand, shaking firmly. "Well done, sir! My felicitations to you!"

They were interrupted from speaking further by the entrance into the library of the ladies, all wearing wide-brimmed hats to shelter their faces from the sun. Gray's eyes found Maggie before he remembered he was not ready to see her. She wore a pink gown as pale as a lady's blush. His senses stirred in spite of himself.

The party began their procession to the lake. Gray ought to have been Maggie's escort, but he hung back, not trusting himself to be so close to her. Sir Francis stepped in, escorting both Maggie and Olivia, one lady on each arm.

Down at the lake footmen stood ready to serve wine under tents. Musicians played pieces by Haydn. Lord and Lady Camerville shouted above the din to inform the guests of boats for rowing, of archery, quints, and fencing. Gradually the guests chose their occupations. Gray wandered around, keeping Lansing in sight. He also saw Camerville head directly for Maggie, who was momentarily standing alone.

"Come. Come, my dear!" Cammy said to her. "I will row you in a boat. Lovely idea, eh?"

Maggie looked horror-struck. Gray now understood her dread of the water, believing the part of her story about the drowning deaths of her parents and brother. His belief about her drowning Lansing was more uncertain. Gray hoped Sir Francis would intervene with Camerville, but he saw Sir Francis and Olivia walking arm-in-arm toward the archery range.

Gray took a breath and strode over. "Cammy, I will borrow this lady for a moment."

Cammy, with a frightened look on his face, threw up his hands and backed off. Gray walked Maggie to the tent where the wine was served and where several ladies were seated.

"Gray, I must speak with you!"

"Not now." He led her to a chair.

"Only a moment, I promise you."

He would not look at her. "Camerville will not approach you here." He turned to leave.

"But Lansing—" she cried.

He shot her a quelling glance and strode away to look for Lansing. He finally spied him alone in the area set aside for fencing. Lansing held a foil, testing its weight and strength.

Lansing looked over and saw Gray watching him. He held up the foil. "Indulge me," Lansing shouted, his voice not quite friendly. No one else had selected swordplay.

Gray walked over and chose one of the thin-bladed swords. The time had come to tease the truth from Lansing and Gray figured a blade, even one tipped with a protective button, could only assist.

He and Lansing stripped out of their coats and waistcoats. Gray balanced the sword in his hand and tested its action. He had often sparred with Lansing on the Peninsula when they had been friends practicing to battle Frenchmen bent on slashing at their necks.

Gray sliced the air with the foil as they walked to their places on the lawn. Compared to his cavalry saber, this sword was light in his hand. The action was familiar, though, and his arm retained the knowledge of how to use it.

A breeze fluttered the sleeves of his shirt. Gray glanced at the sun beginning its westerly descent. He turned so that it was at his back. Lansing nodded, acknowledging the tactic.

They stood *en garde,* knees relaxed, upper bodies erect. Carefully at first, they tested steel against steel.

The blades sang as they clashed, more musical than deadly, but it was early yet. They were reassessing each other. Evenly matched in the past, each knew the one who made the first mistake would lose the contest. Gray felt the pumping of his blood, as if he were again riding into battle.

Lansing thrust, the movement quick and surprising. The point stopped short of Gray's shoulder. Gray's skills were rustier than he'd thought.

"Becoming slack, man?" taunted Lansing, his grin holding none of the high spirits of their soldiering days.

Gray scowled. He defended, biding his time to attack. They thrust and parried, back and forth. Lansing lunged again, but parrying became easier now that Gray's muscles had warmed and his reflexes had returned. Lansing next scored a hit, pressing the buttoned sword tip onto Gray's chest, dramatically bending the blade. "Touché," he cried, returning to *en garde.* "What stakes shall we vie for, by the way?"

Gray breathed deeply, remembering he had more purpose here than a mere contest with swords. "How about the truth? The truth about Maggie."

Lansing's eyes flashed, but he quickly masked the emotion with a laugh. "Do you call me a liar?"

Gray seized the moment to make his first attack, which Lansing parried. The sound of the clash rang loud in Gray's ears.

"I propose other stakes," Lansing said as their swords clanged again. "If I win, you will support my suit with Lady Palmely."

Gray broke off. "Lady Palmely?"

Lansing nodded. "I am quite in love with her. I am determined to make her my wife."

"After only meeting her a day ago? Cut line, Lansing." Gray laughed. "Even so, you are too late."

Lansing looked puzzled. "What do you mean?"

"She is betrothed to Sir Francis."

Lansing's nostrils flared. "Now you lie!" He executed a barrage that Gray defended easily.

"They became betrothed this very day."

"After you set her against me!" Lansing slashed at Gray in a sloppy attack.

Gray easily deflected Lansing's blade. "After your treatment of Maggie, you expected otherwise?"

"Maggie," Lansing spat, striking again.

Gray ignored the sweat dampening his shirt and beading on his forehead as their contest heated up and they took turns driving forward and falling back, until Lansing lowered his sword.

"The truth, Lansing," Gray demanded.

Lansing raised his head, the smile on his face taking a sardonic turn. "The truth? The truth is, I have had quite enough of your self-righteousness, Gray. What right had you to spoil my opportunity of an advantageous marriage? You might be the son of an earl but that does not mean—"

Gray cut him off. "Your character is at fault, Lansing. Not my parentage."

Lansing's voice rose to a high-pitched whine. "That is what all aristocrats say, 'My parentage is of no consequence.' Try to get on in the world without it, *I* say."

They remained a few feet apart, the afternoon breeze flapping their white shirts, the blades of their foils sparkling in the sun. Gray watched his adversary begin to pace back and forth in front of him.

"*I* have not had the advantage of calling an earl my father. You think that is of no consequence?" Lansing swung his sword toward Gray. "Your precious Maggie would not have been dazzled by my name, but when I told her I was you—"

Gray stared at Lansing, feeling a weight lift from his shoulders as Lansing confirmed this part of Maggie's story. If Lansing had convinced Maggie he held Gray's name, the rest could easily follow. Gray ought to have believed her. His muscles felt leaden with guilt.

Lansing continued, still pacing back and forth. "What a lark that was! Seeing how far your name would take me. It took me far enough."

Gray's guilt quickly changed to an anger that boiled inside him. Suddenly it was more of a challenge to control his urge to run his sword through Lansing's gut.

Gray managed to speak. "Until she pushed you in the river."

Lansing slashed the air with his sword. "Yes, she thought to kill me, but I am not so easily disposed of, am I?" He flipped the sword around and pulled the button off its point. "Let us have a real contest, Gray. Let us see who can draw the most blood."

Gray was tempted to remove the button from his foil and gratify his urge to see Lansing's blood soaking the earth. His hand trembled, but he left his sword point protected.

Lansing stood *en garde* and Gray joined him.

Lansing struck with force, but Gray parried the blow in time. Steel clashed against steel, with ever-escalating fury. Lansing's anger made him strong and daring. The swords' engagement rang out like the clang of a ship's bell, loud and fierce, the rhythm of each contact like separate notes in a warrior's song. They clashed in earnest, two warriors in battle.

Back and forth they moved on the lawn, a zigzag dance of danger. First Gray beat Lansing into retreat, then Lansing rallied and Gray fell back. Gray's shirt clung to his skin with sweat, but he dared not tire.

Lansing struck a low blow and the point of his foil pierced Gray's thigh. Gray jumped back and the blade emerged bloody. The pain made him momentarily lightheaded, but he shook it off.

Steel clashed again. Lansing suddenly swept the point of his sword upward in an arc and Gray's blade twisted it off to the side. Lansing recovered with a quick move, tearing Gray's shirt. They broke apart again, both breathing hard, watching each other while they stole the moment to catch their breath. Gray's foil probed for weakness. His best chance was to twist the blade from Lansing's hand, but with a man of equal skill, the opportunity might not come. The sun was now at Lansing's back, and the light, low in the sky, pained Gray's eyes. His thigh ached and his leg weakened.

"Ooooh, look," one of the ladies tittered. "They are fighting with swords." Several other ladies hurried over.

The musicians playing in the tent nearly masked the conversation, but Maggie could no longer sit still. She rose to see what had captured the ladies' interest.

"It is that dashing Lieutenant Lansing! In his shirt-sleeves." One lady tittered. "I cannot quite see the other man."

"Your husband, Mrs. Grayson," cried another. "The two soldiers. How exciting."

Gray? And Lansing? Maggie pushed them apart to see better. In the distance their swords were flashing fast. The sun glinted off the blades and made their white shirts brilliant.

"No," she cried, desperately looking around for someone who could help. "No!"

She shoved her way through the ladies.

"It is only a game, Mrs. Grayson!" shouted a lady behind her.

She feared this was not a game at all, but only too real a fight. Some of the gentlemen had gathered at the edge of the park to watch the match. Maggie saw Camerville among them and rushed over to him. "We must stop this!"

Lord Camerville gave her a dismissive wave. "It is all part of the festivities, my dear lady." He patted her arm. "If it is too violent for your delicate eyes, allow me to—"

Wrenching away from him in disgust, Maggie lifted

her skirts and ran toward the swordsmen, her wide-brimmed hat flying from her head.

The sun was behind her, and Gray and Lansing did not heed her approach. She shouted for them to stop, but they made no sign of hearing her. She raced toward Lansing. If she could knock him off his feet, she would be able to warn Gray about him before it was too late.

"Stop!" she cried again, nearly upon them.

Gray saw her. "Maggie!"

Lansing whipped around just as she reached him, and his sword caught her upper arm. Its point ran straight through her flesh.

She cried out more in surprise than pain as he pulled the sword out again. Her blood spurted onto her dress, staining the pink fabric.

"No!" Gray dropped his sword and sprang toward her as she sank to her knees.

Maggie heard the shocked screams of the ladies, the outraged protests of the gentlemen. One lady wailed, "He's killed her!" A gentleman shouted, "Where is the sword's button?" Lansing stood nearby as if frozen in place as men came running toward them. Lansing's sword still dripped with her blood.

"Maggie!" Gray was on his knees next to her, pulling at the front of her dress where the blood made it stick to her skin. He touched the wound in her arm, and a stab of pain shot through her.

"It is only your arm!" He ripped the sleeve from his shirt and wrapped it tightly around her wound to stop the bleeding.

"I am all right." Maggie cradled his face in both her

hands, making him look at her. "I feared he would kill you."

Gray held her against him, so tightly she could barely breathe. "I thought he *had* killed you!"

Camerville broke through the throng gathering around them. "What sport is this I hear of? Taking off the button?"

"Grayson's sword has its button." Sir Francis picked up Gray's sword from the grass and raised it for all to see. Maggie shuddered. Gray had fought with uneven odds.

"My button fell off." Lansing finally spoke, his tone defensive. "I did not know."

Sir Francis pointed the sword at Gray's thigh, also bright with blood. "You drew Gray's blood and did not know there was no button on the tip?"

Disapproving murmurs rolled through the crowd.

Maggie pulled out of Gray's embrace. "Gray, you are injured!"

He laughed and quickly kissed her on the lips, not heeding their audience. "I do not credit it."

"Can you stand?" Forgetting her own pain, she tried to help him rise to his feet. Instead, he assisted her.

Two men had taken Lansing by each of his arms and were escorting him away.

Olivia came up to her. "Oh, Maggie! Maggie!"

Lady Camerville followed at her heels. "How could such a thing happen! I believe I shall faint." But she looked so robust no one took her seriously.

Handing the sword to a servant, Sir Francis took Olivia in hand. "She will be all right, my dearest."

"It is not such a very bad wound." Maggie gave Olivia

a wan smile, before turning to Gray with a wrinkled brow. "Are you able to walk back to the house?"

He laughed again, putting his arm around her back, careful to avoid touching her wound. "You see my scratch and forget you are hurt? Brave, foolish girl!"

She had not quite forgotten her injury. Her arm hurt so much she felt nauseous, but as long as Gray supported her as they walked back to the house, the pain simply did not matter.

Hours later they were finally alone, content to lie on the bed in each other's arms as moonlight streamed in the window and embers glowed in the fireplace.

Gray kissed Maggie's temple. "Does your arm pain you, love?"

Her eyes swept over him. He wore nothing but his drawers and the bandage on his leg. "Not so very much. Your leg?"

He gave a rumbling laugh. "Not so very much."

She released a contented sigh, so glad to be with only him after all the commotion the episode created. First Decker and Kitt had burst in on them, carting hot water, clean bandages, and poultices. Then Gray had been called away, to discuss with Camerville and Sir Francis how to deal with Lansing. Next, Olivia entered the room and refused to leave Maggie's side. A steady procession of the lady guests followed, all eager to give their solicitations and to gossip about the dramatic events. For all Maggie's desire to avoid attention, she had become the high point of the country party. By the time all had left her but Gray, she was so weary she could barely stand. He'd instantly insisted she go to bed. As soon as he lay down beside her, the weariness fled.

"Can we go home tomorrow, Gray?" Maggie longed for the quiet and comfort of Summerton Hall.

"I have already arranged it." The timbre of his voice sent a thrill throughout her body, awaking her senses.

"Is Lansing still here?" As soon as she spoke Lansing's name she regretted it. She wished never to hear his name again, nor see him or hear of him.

Gray rubbed his cheek against her hair. "Sir Francis and two of Camerville's footmen are this moment escorting him to the coast. They will see him on a ship to the Continent. He will not return."

She sat up in the bed, her heart pounding in sudden anxiety. "Can you be so sure? I want him nowhere near Sean!"

He reached over to ease her back down. "There is nothing for him to return to. He signed a letter resigning his commission, and the tale of his dishonorable behavior will fly through the *ton*."

She gave him a worried look, but again settled against him.

His arms encircled her. "Believe me, Maggie, I would have preferred to see him hanged, but a trial might have exposed his connection to you. It was too great a risk."

She buried her face in the pillow. "I have created so much trouble for you."

He made her face him. "It is nothing to what you have lived through. Forgive me for doubting you—"

"No," she broke in. "It is I who beg forgiveness. I have used you so ill. Why, your family believes you a bigamist because of me!"

They lay so close, eye to eye, that his breath warmed her nose. The corner of his mouth turned up in a half smile. "That is a little thing, known only to those who love me enough not to speak of it. It is something to be borne, like my father's infirmity. Let us not allow such matters to ruin our happiness." His eyes darkened. "I love you, Maggie. Will you do me the honor of marrying me? I want you for my wife."

Her heart swelled to near bursting. "Oh, Gray!"

She closed the scant inch of space between their lips. He tasted of brandy, like that first time he'd kissed her, when even in her dread of him, she'd felt the draw of his masculinity. He deepened the kiss, and pulled her against him. Through her thin nightdress, she felt the warmth of his bare chest, felt the power of his arousal.

His lips proceeded to taste of the tender skin of her neck and his hands pressed her harder against him.

She gave a small groan. "Gray, my arm truly does not pain me much. Is your leg—?"

"My leg is splendid."

To prove it to her, he quickly stripped himself of his drawers and knelt above her, pulling the nightdress over her head. With both her good arm and her injured one, she reached for him, eager for the lovemaking this night promised, and for all the lovemaking to come.

Epilogue

November, 1817

Maggie doubled over in pain. "Where is Gray?" she cried, her voice hoarse.

"We've sent for him." Olivia bit her lip. "Oh, dear, does it hurt so terribly?"

Maggie flashed her a venomous look. "Of course it hurts. You remember."

"That was nearly two months ago. All I can truly recall is holding my new baby daughter." Olivia smiled dreamily. "Oh, I do hope you have a daughter! Wouldn't that be lovely? Your daughter, mine, and Miss Miles's all growing up together."

"Mrs. Hendrick's, you mean," gasped Maggie as another contraction rippled through her.

The door opened. "Gray?" Maggie cried.

"No, it is Tess, my love." Lady Caufield rushed in. "Harry and I have arrived to help!"

Harry poked his head in. "Got here in time," he repeated, smiling and nodding his head.

"I just knew we should come today!" Tess turned to her husband. "Dearest, this is no place for a gentleman!"

He bowed and blew his wife a kiss. She turned to Maggie. "Oh, this is so exciting! Another baby so soon! I've hardly had a chance to make more clothes. I had to pull all my stitches out of the one little dress I was making. You ought to have seen it. It was the sweetest dress, but the needlework went awry—"

"I do not care about needlework!" Maggie shouted.

"Not care about needlework?" Tess said in a surprised voice. "But it was what made the dress."

Another contraction hit. "I do not care about dresses!"

"She is at that irritable stage," Olivia confided to Tess.

"I am not irritable!" Maggie screeched. "Where is Gray?"

The midwife pressed down on Maggie's belly. She was a capable woman, experienced in bringing about even the most difficult of births, but Maggie wanted nothing to do with her.

She wanted Gray.

Voices came from in the hallway, Harry's pompous tones the loudest. "Gentlemen are not allowed in there."

The door opened.

Maggie sat up. "Gray." She breathed a sigh of relief, but another pain came and she emitted a sharp cry. "At last."

"Why the devil was I not sent for sooner?" He rushed to her side, brushing her sweat-dampened hair from her eyes. "I should not have taken the boys riding."

"I sent for you as soon as I knew," she said through gritted teeth. She bit her lip and bore another contraction.

Even as the ripples of pain went through her, she

gazed at him in marvel. Gray. Her husband, the dearest father Sean could ever have.

After their wounds had healed, Maggie and Gray had traveled to London. With a special license, they'd been secretly married, truly husband and wife at last. Gray treated her to all the delights and entertainments London had to offer: the theater, the museums, Hyde Park. And the shops. How he had indulged her in the shops! She raised her left hand to gaze at the beautiful ring she wore on her third finger, all gold and sapphires. "Like your eyes," he'd said.

Another pain hit and she cried out again.

He moved the bed linens off her legs.

"You cannot do that, sir!" the midwife exclaimed. "It is not seemly."

"She's my wife," he retorted, as if that explained it.

The midwife pointed. "The baby is about to be born. You must leave here, sir. This is no place for you."

"No," Maggie cried, struggling to sit up.

Gray eased her down again. "I'll stay, mistress. I have some experience in these matters." He grinned at Maggie. "Lambing and calving and kittening, you know."

Maggie's laugh was choked off by another wave of pain. "He stays," she rasped.

Suddenly her hips rose off the bed and she cried out, a long agonized wail. Gray pushed the midwife out of the way.

"The baby's coming," he cried.

She felt the release, and heard Gray shout for joy, when he caught the baby in his hands.

"It's a girl, Maggie," he said, his voice cracking. "A beautiful girl."

The midwife managed to wipe off the baby around Gray's big hands. The newborn cried lustily. He handed her to Maggie.

He had been wonderfully correct. The baby was the most beautiful baby girl in the world.

Soon she was cleaned up, put in fresh bedclothes, and her baby was passed around for the others to admire. Tess cooed and ahhed and laughed in delight. Tears streamed down Olivia's face.

"I have been thinking of names," Tess declared as Olivia handed the baby back to Maggie. "And I have narrowed it down to Harriet, Jaquet, Vincentia, Hester, Mabel, Lucretia, Eliza, Katherine, Jane, Marianne . . . what are the others? . . . oh, Rosamund, Tabitha, Lettice . . . Did I say Harriet? That is the female form of Harry, you know."

"You did indeed mention it," admitted Gray, who planted a kiss on his wife's forehead and touched the downy head of his newborn daughter.

"We have selected a name, Tess." He gazed proudly at mother and daughter. "We shall call her Grace."

"Grace?" Olivia smiled. "Of course, after your mother!"

Gray nodded, gazing down at his wife and infant daughter. "After my mother."

Maggie thought her heart would burst with happiness. They were a family. She and Gray and Sean and Grace. And all those they loved were present in them. She reached for Gray's hand. He lifted it to plant a kiss on her fingers.

She returned the love in his eyes. "Do you remember?" she whispered. Her thoughts flew back to the other time he'd placed a newborn baby in her arms. How desperate and alone she had been, but this man changed everything. Because of him she had a home, a family, a son, and now a daughter.

His eyes shimmered with moisture. "Maggie," he murmured. One corner of his mouth lifted in the kind of half smile that always set her heart aflutter. "Will you next be asking for meat pasties and ale?"

About the Author

When Diane Perkins was a little girl she thought everyone had stories filling their heads. It never occurred to her to write down her stories, even though she loved reading, especially reading Historical Romance. Instead she spent a career as a county mental health therapist helping other people craft real happy endings. It took a lull in Diane's busy life for her to finally put fingers to the keyboard and bring her stories to life. Once started she never looked back, even going on to win the Romance Writers of America's prestigious Golden Heart Award, the Royal Ascot, and other romance writing prizes. She now writes Regency Historical Romance full-time. Happily married and the mother of a grown daughter and son, she and her husband live in Northern Virginia with three very ordinary house cats. Diane would love to hear from you. Contact her through her web site at www.dianeperkins.us

More

Diane Perkins!

Please turn this page

for a preview of

THE MARRIAGE BARGAIN

available soon

from Warner Books.

Chapter ONE

Spring, 1816

Mist still clung to the grass in a field on the outskirts of London, near the Uxbridge Road. Only the barest peek of dawn glimmered on the horizon. Spencer Keegan paced the length of the field and back, mist swirling around his feet like smoke above a cauldron.

"This is utter nonsense, Spence." His friend Blake's voice sounded crisp and clear in the damp air. It was also filled with exasperation.

Spence turned to him. "Nonsense it may be, sir, but the idiot accused me of cheating. What else was I to do but call him out?" He gave a wry grin. "You are my second. You were supposed to avoid settling the matter on the field of honor."

Blake shook his head. "Damnedest thing, Spence. There was no reasoning with these fellows."

As the heavy dew clinging to the blades of grass seeped into his boots, Spence crossed over to where Blake waited with their other friend Wolfe. Who else but these two men would have stood by him through this foolishness? At this ungodly hour as well.

Spence looked at them, Blake rocking on his heels, hands in his coat pockets, Wolfe pacing back and forth at the edge of the road, checking every two seconds to see if a coach was coming. Spence saw not the tall, imposing ex-soldiers they were, but the young, skinny lads he'd befriended at Eton. He grinned again, this time at the memory of standing shoulder-to-shoulder with these two against larger, older bullies. And of sitting in the dark, risking discovery from the matron for not being abed, naming themselves *The Ternion*, one plus one plus one, stronger together than apart. Even Napoleon, the biggest bully of them all, had been unable to vanquish them.

Wolfe, still searching the fog-filled road, walked up to where Spence and Blake stood. Spence glanced from one to the other. Theobold Blakewell, Viscount Blakewell, with his impeccable breeding and handsome good looks that never failed to make the ladies swoon. Gideon Wolfe, as dark as Blake was fair, the son of an East India Company nabob and a half-Indian mother, always ready to fight anyone who dared take issue with that fact. And finally Spence himself, the reluctant Earl of Kellworth, resisting the use of his title ever since the reckless accident that caused his brother's death eight years before.

Spence laughed out loud. The *Ternion* stood shoulder to shoulder this day because of one foolish young cub who dared accuse Spence of cheating at cards. That night, the whole of White's game room had pleaded with young Lord Esmund to render an apology to Spence. Blake and Wolfe had demanded it. But Esmund, looking as frightened as a cornered fox, with hair every bit as red, had shaken his head like a willful child, refusing to retract his ill-conceived words. And Spence, feeling a leaden dismay, had been left with no other choice but to call Esmund out to this duel at dawn.

Wolfe turned to Spence with a furrowed brow. "The youngling cannot have any skill with the pistol."

Spence, on the other hand, had had almost a decade of war during in which to hone his skill, but that need not be said.

"As we all well know," agreed Spence.

Blake slapped Spence on the shoulder. "You might actually hit the fellow and kill him, you know. Then what? We all dash off to the Continent before you are hung for murder?" Blake gave him a teasing expression. "I have had my fill of France, Spence, old fellow. I pray you will delope."

"Shoot into the air?" Spence pretended to bristle. "I cannot so dishonor myself. I shall simply have to miss my target."

For all his levity, Spence's gut twisted painfully at the unlikely prospect that he might draw the blood of that foolish pup. Spence had spilled the life's blood of many an enemy, but this mere boy was not that. Esmund was nothing to him. Still, he did not desire the burden of ending a young life merely for the preservation of his good name.

Besides, he no more relished fleeing to the Continent than Blake did. Why, the *Ternion* had just begun to sample London's delights. There were sport, gambling, drink, and women aplenty left to enjoy.

Spence set his chin in resolve. He would simply use his skill to make it appear as if he aimed directly at Esmund's vitals. With any luck, the pistol ball would not go wayward and accidentally kill the fellow.

"You *could* kill him, Spence." Wolfe's voice was as serious as Blake's had been jesting.

Spence almost smiled. How like Wolfe to read his thoughts and perceive his worry.

"I shall try my best to miss him." Spence patted his friend's arm.

The *Ternion* were still young and unfettered, Spence thought. At least Blake and Wolfe were unfettered, and Spence had arranged his responsibilities in a way that very nearly demanded no attention at all. It was only a matter of time before they must change. Eventually Blake and Wolfe would marry and set up their nurseries.

Oftentimes Spence considered telling Blake and Wolfe about his own wife, residing safely at Kellworth Hall, but his friends had never understood his decisions about his inheritance, his title or his property. His friends would never understand the bargain he and Emma had made.

"I have examined the pistols." Blake's voice cut through the sad turn of Spence's thoughts like his boots had split the mist. "An extremely fine set. Made by Manton."

Blake, as any good second ought, had negotiated all aspects of the duel, especially the pistols. He lifted a finger and shook it at Spence. "What foxes me is where a nodcock like Esmund would acquire such a pair."

Spence goodnaturedly pushed Blake's arm aside. "Devil if I know."

"I insisted upon firing them both," Blake went on. Blake had been meticulous about the duel, as meticulous as he was about the tailoring of his coat or the cleanliness of his linen. Blake tugged at the snow white cuffs of his shirt. "Seems to me both pistols pulled to the left."

Perhaps Blake was succumbing to a fit of nerves, Spence thought, because this must have been the fifth time he'd mentioned the pistols pulling to the left. Spence bit down the impulse to tease his friend about turning soft after only a month of civilian life.

As in all else, the *Ternion* had together sold their commissions, all agreeing they'd enough of war after Waterloo, when their regiment, the 28th Regiment of Foot, bore the onslaught of wave after wave of French cavalry.

Wolfe gazed toward the road for the hundredth time. "Where do you suppose Esmund found a surgeon willing to risk attendance at a duel?"

Blake shrugged. "His brother located the man." He gave a soft laugh. "Can you imagine what sort of surgeon would take the risk? I pray he is not needed."

So did Spence, who wheeled around and trod into the field again, busying himself in judging distances, searching for a tree branch or rooftop or something in the distance that would make a good place to aim.

The mist thinned as the sky grew lighter, but the morning's unseasonable chill gave Spence a shiver. The plain brown coat Blake and Wolfe insisted he wear had no buttons. "Nothing to give Esmund a place to aim," Blake had told him. "Stand sideways," he'd also instructed. "But turn your head toward him." Spence had listened, nodding agreeably, going along with the instructions as if he did not already know this trick to make himself as small a target as possible.

"I hear a carriage." Wolfe stepped into the road to check.

The dark chaise clattered into view, rumbling to a stop not far from where Wolfe stood. Two men stepped out. Lord Esmund was hatless, and his shock of red hair glowed in the early morning light. Spence studied him. The fool was in debt to his ears from gambling, and naught but a boy—eight years younger than Spence himself, and as unfledged as a bird just pecking out of its shell. He played at a man's game, however, and Spence figured Esmund was too green to even know it.

Blake and a young man who, judging from his bright shock of hair must, be Esmund's brother Lord John, bent their heads together in conference. A third man stumbled out of the carriage, a bulbous creature with an unkempt coat and a weave to his step.

Wolfe strolled up to Spence. "The surgeon looks as if he's been dipping deep into his medicine."

"His brandy, more like," laughed Spence.

"Precisely." Wolfe looked grim.

Spence and Wolfe tried to hear the discussion between the two seconds.

"I'll be glad when this is over and we might get some breakfast," Spence whispered.

"It still makes no sense why that boy carried things this far." Wolfe frowned.

"Spence?" Blake called to him as casually as if asking him to gaze upon some interesting shard of antiquity.

He walked over.

Blake's handsome features looked chiseled in stone, as Blake always looked before battle. "The pistols are loaded."

Spence nodded as Wolfe joined them, a deep line between his eyebrows. "I dislike this whole matter, Spence. It smells rank."

Wolfe always smelled trouble, but at the moment Spence did not care what drove Esmund to make his false accusation. He merely wanted to get the business over with, so the three of them could set off toward that fine inn they'd passed on the way.

He glanced at his offender, who shook like a wagon rolling down a stony road. God help the lad. Esmund would be lucky not to shoot himself in the foot.

Spence gave Wolfe a wry smile. "Do you seriously think that fellow capable of some intrigue?" He cocked his head toward Esmund. "In any event, there's nothing to be done but see it through."

Lord John handed Esmund the pistol. To the young man's credit, he seemed to garner some backbone. His trembling ceased.

With his customary cocky smile, Blake handed Spence the other pistol. It was a fine weapon with a walnut stock, textured to keep from slipping in a sweating palm. Its barrel was heavy and nearly as thick at the muzzle as at the breech. Sighting would be more accurate. If this pistol contained some of Manton's secret rifling, it would be more accurate still. All in all it was a fine weapon.

Blake and Lord John consulted their watches. "Stations, gentlemen," Blake announced.

Spence and Esmund each counted out twelve paces and turned, arms at their sides, pistols pointed to the ground. The scent of new grass and honeysuckle filled Spence's nostrils. In the distance a cock crowed. The breeze was light but bracing on his cheek. It was like any fine day in the country.

"As agreed, you will fire simultaneously at my signal," Blake used his best Captain's voice. Its volume threatened to summon the magistrate from the next county.

Spence drew in a breath, held it, and watched Blake from the corner of his eye.

"Attend!" Blake called, his white handkerchief raised high above his head. "Present!"

Spence's heart accelerated. He raised his arm, glancing from the church spire just visible over Esmund's shoulder back to Blake.

Blake's fingers opened and the handkerchief fluttered from them like a butterfly in flight. Spence fired.

Through the smoke from his pistol, Spence spied Esmund, frozen in place. Unbloodied, thank God. The barrel of Esmund's pistol swayed up and down, back and forth.

Spence faced him, unflinching. He'd stood fast countless times as French soldiers charged straight for him. Their sabers and pistol balls had not killed him then, and Esmund's swaying hand was more likely to shoot one of the birds soaring overhead.

Suddenly Esmund's face contorted and he emitted a sound more like a sob than a battle cry.

Fire and smoke flashed from the barrel, and the crack of the pistol broke through the air. Spence heard the pistol ball zing toward him. He smiled and thought of how cool the ale would feel on his throat.

The ball hit Spence with a dull thud. Its force knocked him backward as it passed through his coat, through his shirt, and, with a sharp, piercing pain, into the flesh of his chest.

He realized with a shock that he was hit and was

falling backward. This was not the way the *Ternion* should end.

Then, as if time stood still, Spence thought of his wife, the only secret he'd kept from Blake and Wolfe. He remembered her fresh unspoiled beauty, her vulnerability, her gratitude when he'd made her his wife—in name only. He opened his mouth to beg Blake and Wolfe to protect to her, because now he could not. The only sound that came out was a moan.

Emma, he thought, as his head seemed to explode against something hard on the ground. *Forgive me.*

THE EDITOR'S DIARY

Dear Reader,

Some loves are meant to be: Romeo and Juliet, Bogie and Bacall, Beauty and the Beast. But there are always little hiccups along the way to the most destined of love affairs. Just watch what happens in the two Warner Forever titles this November.

Romantic Times calls **Amanda Scott** a "most gifted story-teller" and *Rendezvous* raves her "characters jump off the page into your heart." Well, all ye lads and lassies, pre-pare to be dazzled by the first in a new pair of novels, **HIGHLAND PRINCESS**. Lady Mairi, the stunning daughter of the Lord of the Isles, has never had a man come close to claiming her heart—especially the prince she is expected to wed—until she meets Lachlan "the Wily" Maclean. The latest addition to her father's court and a skilled warrior with a vast network of spies, he knows every secret, and soon, Mairi becomes his heart's desire. Though she scorns him, everyone can see the desire in her eyes and hear the hunger in her voice. But as their passion draws them closer together, it also inflames the jealousy of an enemy determined to claim the kingdom—and Mairi—for his very own.

Journeying from the lush hills and the intrigue of medi-eval Scotland to the masterful guises and disguises of Regency England, we present **THE IMPROPER WIFE**, a heart-wrenching and haunting new novel by **Diane Perkins**. Maggie Delaney can't believe her misfortune.

Swept off her feet and hastily married, she's horrified to learn the husband she thought she knew has lied about his identity, leaving her stranded, penniless, and with an infant son. But she has found the man who can rightly claim her husband's false name and with him, hope for survival. For the real Captain John Grayson is a soldier, a hero with an honorable reputation and limitless coffers who would never turn a woman and her infant away. Her plan: to become his "wife" in truth. After all, his family has fallen in love with her and her son and is eager to embrace them both. But can she convince Gray that she is his wife, both in name and deed alike?

To find out more about Warner Forever, these November titles, and the author, visit us at www.warnerforever.com.

With warmest wishes,

Karen Kosztolnyik, Senior Editor

P.S. The holidays are right around the corner so throw another yule log on the fire, grab some eggnog, and relax with these two books: **Mary McBride** pens a lighthearted story of two childhood sweethearts whose relationship ended in disaster, the strange thefts that bring them together and the undeniable sparks that still fly in **SAY IT AGAIN, SAM**; and **Marliss Melton** delivers a thrilling new romantic suspense about a woman grieving for her Navy SEAL husband who has been presumed dead . . . only to discover he's alive with absolutely no memory of their life together in **FORGET ME NOT**.